EXTRAORDINARY ENGINES

THE DEFINITIVE STEAMPUNK ANTHOLOGY

Edited by Nick Gevers

OTHER BOOKS BY NICK GEVERS

Infinity Plus: The Anthology (editor)

EXTRAORDINARY ENGINES

THE DEFINITIVE STEAMPUNK ANTHOLOGY

Edited by Nick Gevers

New stories by
Kage Baker
Keith Brooke
Jeffrey Ford
Jay Lake
Margo Lanagan
James Lovegrove
Ian R. MacLeod
James Morrow
Robert Reed
Adam Roberts
Jeff VanderMeer
Marly Youmans

SOLARIS

First published 2008 by Solaris
an imprint of BL Publishing
Games Workshop Ltd
Willow Road
Nottingham
NG7 2WS
UK

www.solarisbooks.com

ISBN-13: 978 1 84416 634 3
ISBN-10: 1 84416 634 1

10 9 8 7 6 5 4 3 2 1

A CIP catalogue record for this book is available from the British Library.

Designed & typeset by BL Publishing
Printed and bound in the UK.

TABLE OF CONTENTS

INTRODUCTION

STEAMPUNK IS A particularly engaging, entertaining, as well as thematically resonant, subgenre of science fiction, fantasy, and horror. Looking affectionately back to the scientific romances that got SF rolling back in the late nineteenth and early twentieth centuries, today's steampunk stories express nostalgia (sometimes quite ironic nostalgia) for the days of H.G. Wells and Jules Verne, for the technologies they described and imagined: Airships! Land leviathans! Brass automatons! Cannon shells fired to the Moon! Great ornate submarines! Time machines! Such glorious devices, which expressed both a wide-eyed anticipation of the wonders science could bestow on the world and a sinking fear that the industrial age had the potential to destroy us all, or plunge us into dystopian lives as Eloi and Morlocks. The period 1837-1914, the Victorian and Edwardian eras, was full of such simultaneous expectancy and apprehension, witnessing as it did the rise of steam power and electricity, railways and telegraphy, ironclad ships and the first primitive aircraft; as lives and living standards improved, as mental and physical horizons widened, there were also the nightmares of colonialism and factory sweatshops and warfare become mechanised, soon to climax in the unprecedented carnage of World War One. A universe opening up, yet disclosing infinite prospects of peril: this is the landscape explored in the twelve stories collected in *Extraordinary Engines*.

THE PERIOD LITERATURE that steampunk references is of course very rich in itself, a formidable ancestry to live up to. Key texts include, as mentioned, the adventure tales of Jules Verne, such as *20,000 Leagues Under the Sea* and *Journey to the Centre of the Earth*; and the penetrating SF novellas of Wells's early days, notably *The Time Machine*, *The War of the Worlds*, *The Island of Doctor Moreau*, and *The First Men in the Moon*. Add the Gothic inspiration of Mary Shelley's *Frankenstein, Or, The Modern Prometheus*, the splendidly morbid stories of Edgar Allan Poe, *Dr. Jekyll and Mr. Hyde* by Robert Louis Stevenson, and *Dracula* by Bram Stoker; and the Professor Challenger cycle by Arthur Conan Doyle, not to mention his seminal detective series featuring Sherlock Holmes, which so dramatized gaslit London and its criminal fraternities; and the penny dreadful and dime novels that echoed these canonical works; and any number of influential books by Jack London and M.P. Shiel and Arthur Machen and... well, the catalogue goes on. In the background looms Charles Dickens and his vast urban mythology. The Victorian age was the epoch in which mass education assumed momentum, and the talented writers of the time poured their dreams and anxieties into vast quantities of popular fiction, attracting millions of newly literate readers; steampunk echoes that huge cultural leap, recapturing the preoccupations of a hundred years ago with appropriate vividness and verve, recasting fantasies of steam and steel for the fast developing present. In the process, our contemporary concerns, information technology, lifestyle libertarianism, energy shortages, the bending of gender, terrorism, and much besides, merge with the apparatus of the scientific romance to create a hybrid literature of huge fascination. Here are a few key examples from the last few decades:

MICHAEL MOORCOCK PIONEERED the steampunk form with two major trilogies in the Seventies: *The Dancers at the End of Time* and *A Nomad of the Time Streams*. Brian Aldiss paralleled these with *Frankenstein Unbound*. Howard Waldrop and Steven Utley added superb shorter works like "Custer's Last Jump" and "Black as the Pit, From Pole to Pole". But it was in the Eighties that the subgenre truly shot to prominence. Three disciples of Philip K. Dick got the ball rolling, K.W. Jeter with *Infernal Devices*, Tim Powers with *The Anubis Gates* and *The Stress of Her Regard*, and James Blaylock with *Homunculus* and *Lord Kelvin's Machine*. Brian Stableford took the movement in an intellectual direction with *The Werewolves of London* as the Nineties began, and Bruce Sterling and William Gibson influenced many with *The Difference Engine*. Since then there has been a torrent of fine work. Paul Di Filippo indulged great postmodern wit in *The Steampunk Trilogy*; Philip Pullman portrayed a steampunk Oxford in *The Golden Compass*; Colin Greenland depicted sailing ships in space in *Harm's Way*; Ian R. MacLeod wrote grave moral tales in *The Light Ages* and *The House of Storms*; Jeffrey E. Barlough recreated Dickensian society in his alternate histories of the Sundering; Gordon Dahlquist gave steampunk an erotic turn in *The Glass Books of the Dream Eaters* and *The Dark Volume*; Jay Lake erected a wall around the world in the ingenious *Mainspring*. Consider contemporary series by Jonathan Barnes, and Naomi Novik. Or *Swiftly* by Adam Roberts. Or Stephen Hunt, with his *The Court of the Air* and *The Kingdom Beyond the Waves*. Even giants of the mainstream have heeded the possibilities of steampunk, as witnessed by Thomas Pynchon's enormous masterpiece *Against the Day*.

IN 2008, STEAMPUNK is flourishing, and two anthologies pay it tribute: *Steampunk* (Tachyon

Publications), edited by Ann and Jeff VanderMeer, an excellent reprint retrospective; and the book you hold in your hands, *Extraordinary Engines*, in which the best short fiction writers of today explore steampunk in wonderful, innovative ways. Here it all is: sabotage of the Atlantic Cable... Prizefights between giant steam robots... Abe Lincoln as android... A strange electric milieu... Sexual jealousy and automata on the colonial frontier... Miracle substances that replace oil... An exile and the airships that pursue him... And much, much more.

—Nick Gevers
Cape Town, May 2008.

ACKNOWLEDGEMENTS

MY PROFOUND THANKS to Christian Dunn and George Mann at Solaris for all their help on this project, and their confidence in its success. My gratitude to all the contributing authors also, for sterling work under a sometimes stringent deadline. And I dedicate this book to Peter Crowther, boss, mentor, and colleague, in token of his general inspiration as well as his invaluable assistance on the paperwork.

STEAMPUNCH

James Lovegrove

The first of our British writers, James Lovegrove writes fine satirical SF, full of formal jokes and witty perspectives on the present. His novels include The Hope, Days, The Foreigners, Gig, Worldstorm, *and* Provender Gleed; *his short fiction is assembled in* Imagined Slights, *with a second collection forthcoming from PS Publishing. In "Steampunch" he takes us straight to the core of steampunk—big machines, Victorian political hypocrisy, and a penal colony far beyond Botany Bay...*

HOI! HOI, YOU! Yes, you, kid. Over here. I want a word.

No, don't look like that. I'm not some poncey mandrake, though there's a fair few of them around here, I warn you. I won't be trying to stick my Nebuchadnezzar up your jacksie. Strictly a Lady Laycock fellow, me, always have been. Just want to give you some advice, that's all. I've seen hundreds of your sort, fresh off the ship, all scared and boggle-eyed, standing trembling on the dock without the first clue what to do with themselves. I've been here nigh on twenty years now and I know the ropes, so I like to share some of my wisdom with the newcomers, give 'em a bit of a helping hand if I can. This is a hard, harsh place you've been transported to. You're here for life. Might as well try and get off on the right footing, eh?

So you'll listen then? Good lad. Sensible. I'm a trustworthy man, after all. As trustworthy as you could hope to find round these parts. You can tell by my face. Look past the reddened skin. That's just the dust, what has become sort of *ingrained* after all this time. It's the mark of an old lag. The red deserts with their whirlwinds and their storms stain us. As a rule of thumb, the rustier-looking you are the longer you've been here. Kind of a native coloring, you might say. But ignore that. Look at my eyes. Honest pair of lamps they are. I'd even go so far as to call them the eyes of an innocent man. Which is something, I admit, you're going to hear an awful lot. Everybody you meet here will tell you they're innocent. "The beak did me down. The rozzers stitched me up. The jury were a bunch of mugs. I didn't deserve this ticket-of-leave." Bollocks. They're rotten to the core the lot of 'em. Me, though, I really didn't do anything wrong, at least not as such. I was the victim of a witch-hunt, and there's a story behind that that'd break your heart, but I shan't lumber you with it.

Tell me, what did *you* do to get sent to a penal colony at so tender an age? No, wait, don't say a word. Let me guess. I've become a bit of a dab hand at sorting crook from crook. Now, you don't have the build for a bludger or a demander. You don't have the narrow cunning features of a fawney dropper or a sharp. You look the type who's had a few setbacks, fallen on lean times, and had to turn to crime in order to make ends meet. A dipper, right? Right. Thought so. Maltooling on the omnibus. Flimping in crowds. An eye for a mark, a hand that got skilled at fanning a toff's clothes for a fob watch or a silk smatter or a lill stuffed with sterling. Bit of palming at the shops too, I shouldn't wonder. And then one day you slipped up, were a little too slow, a tad too clumsy, got caught in the act, your pigeon raised a hue and cry, along came a copper—always a copper around when you don't want one—he felt your collar, took you down to the station where you got a right old dewskitch from the boys in blue, then it was up before the bench and in no time at all someone'd taken a razor to your head and given you a terrier crop and you were wearing the broad arrows and on the next ship out.

That was it, wasn't it? More or less? Yeah, not fair. You were only trying to survive. If you'd had a choice you'd never have turned to pickpocketry. It's a cruel world. And *this* is a cruel world as well, believe you me. You'll need your wits about you, even down in the rookeries which is where most of us live and which is supposed to be the safest spot going. You'll have to learn who to be friends with and who to avoid.

Like, for example, him over there, scowling at the new intake. See him? Bloke with the slicked-down jug loops and the weak chin and pasty complexion? Stays indoors, that's how he keeps so pale. Never strays from the rookeries, never even thought of heading for one of the outlying settlements. Never faced a dust storm in his life. Doesn't look too dangerous, does he? Don't you believe it. Whitechapel Jack's the name. Could hold a candle to the devil, that one. Killed five dollymops. Five that we know of. It's probably more, maybe as many as eleven. He should've swung for it but some damnfool of a judge thought he'd be better off living out his days out here so's he could learn to feel guilty about what he did. But he won't, he's not the type. There's something... missing inside that man. A hole where his heart ought to be. Don't ever cross him. He'll have your lights out with his chiv soon as look at you. He wants you to give him an excuse to do so, so don't.

And him, that hook-nosed Shylock with the bushy Newgate knockers either side of his fizzog and the smile like a sickle. The one with that cluster of prettyboys around him. He's not only a mandrake with a thing for young flesh, he's a kidsman. That's his gang there, nary one of 'em a day over twenty. He can get you anything you desire. Has the black market sewn up. Nice as nice can be, he comes across as, but steer clear of him if you can and never, ever, whatever you do, fall into his debt. Those lads are his punishers, and I've seen what they can do to a defaulter with those spiked cudgels they carry. Not a pretty sight.

And then there's——

Me? Why d'you want to know about me?

All right then. Since you asked. Most polite of you. I'm Chas Starkey. Everyone, even my pals, just calls me Starkey. Don't suppose the name rings a bell? No, no reason why it should. You're too young to remember anyway. The age of the Steel Scrappers ended well before you were born. But you've surely heard of Steampunch, haven't you?

Of course you have. Everyone's heard of Steampunch. The "Tin Titan." The "Brass Bruiser." King of the Iron Arena.

Well, I was his trainer. Swear to God I was. I mean, I was a lot more than that. I was his mechanic, his joint oiler, his furnace stoker, his panel beater, his fixer and riveter and what all else besides. But when you come down to it, what I did most for him, and what I did best, was train him. It was thanks to me more than anyone else that Steampunch became what he was—undisputed, undefeated champion in the twelve-tons-plus weight class, and a mechano-boxing legend.

You'll never have seen a mechano-boxing bout, not since they were outlawed. You've maybe watched one on an old kiné reel documentary but that's a pale shadow of the reality. I tell you, you've missed something. There's nothing like it. Picture the scene. A crowd of nearly a thousand, men and women alike, old and young, poshos and paupers, swells and muck snipes, rubbing shoulders together like there's no difference between them, all of 'em ranged around the ring in raked seats, waving betting slips and fistfuls of finnies and hollering to the rafters. The ring itself, a hundred foot on each side, sand on the floor to soak up spilled oil and stop fires spreading, four huge cast iron posts marking the corners. And in the middle of it, lamping merry hell out of each other, two giant automatons. Ten foot tall, fifteen foot tall, some of them even larger, their arms pistoning away, pounding with fists like cannonballs. The noise! The clang of each blow louder than a bong from Big Ben. The shrill hiss of steam from vents. The rumble of boilers on full heat. Every footfall a thunderclap. The crowd roaring and howling. My ears are still ringing from it even to this day. And the smell. You won't get that from the kinéma either. Sparks, fire, smoke, grease, oil. Metal. Damaged metal has a smell, you know, like lightning on a stormy day, like blood in your mouth when you bite your tongue. And sweat from the throng. The animal stink of a thousand overexcited bodies.

Far as I'm concerned mechano-boxing was the crowning achievement of the industrial era. Oh, I know there's the super-foundries, the etherships, the vacuu-rail, the space mortars, the overcities, the self-steering hansoms, all that stuff. Forget about it. You want the distilled essence of mankind's brains and ingenuity? You want a perfect fusion of modern science and ancient art form? Mechano-boxing. Look no further.

I started out as a boxer myself in my youth. Won a few purses in the bareknuckle lists. Took my fair share of knockouts as well. But I knew even as a young shaver, not much older than yourself, that I was never going to be one of the greats. So I got out of the Fancy—that's our name for the brethren of the boxing ring—while I could, before the old gray matter got too badly mashed and I ended up all drooling and slow-tongued and glockey. I'd always had a knack with machinery, got it from my dad who was a production-line fitter. Ran in the blood. And just about then, when I quit the Fancy, was when the first mechano-boxers appeared on the scene, so the timing was right. Seemed logical I should take a sidestep into that field, combine my two skills, especially seeing as mechano-boxing was fast becoming all the rage and the ordinary sort of boxing wasn't capturing the public imagination like it used to.

The early days, the automatons were pretty crude. I used to think of them as steam locomotives turned inside out. They didn't really have faces or personalities, they were just these sort of metal effigies that'd move stumpily and slowly and often as not break down in the middle of a contest. Still, there was something about them. The sheer power on display. When those piston rods shot forward with enough force to kill an elephant or demolish a small building—when those huge lumbering mannequins moved toward each other and clinched and closed with no aim other than to smash each other to smithereens—it was a thrill, and no mistake. A hairs standing up on the back of your neck experience.

It caught on, and soon business was booming, the money was pouring in, bookies were clamouring for more bouts, promoters were investing heavily in developing new and better and above all more lifelike automatons. I'd been working for a while with a bloke by the name of Blarney Mick, Irish of course and a slang cove of the old school, fairground background, decent enough sort but a huckster through and through. He'd got into mechano-boxing right at the start, when it'd just been a sideshow attraction, back-tent stuff in travelling carnivals. Between us we ran a couple of fighters, neither of them what you'd call cream of the crop but worthy sluggers in their way. Mick, though, he was in the pay of some pretty shady dealers, Fenians with shallow morals but deep pockets. When they realized how good the earnings could be they shoved more posh our way than I'd ever seen in my life and told us to get on with constructing the mightiest and most indestructible mechano-boxer the world would ever know.

Took us best part of a year, using a team of eight engineers drawn from the railway and shipbuilding trades, along with some help from a physicist, Professor Challoner, a man who'd never normally have gone near so low an enterprise but he needed employment because he'd lost his seat at Oxford on account of some scandal involving a parlor maid and a riding switch. What he didn't know about pressure and alloys and heat coefficients wasn't worth knowing, and if there were times when he was too far inside a bottle to do more than blather and rave, he more than made up for it during his lucid moments. And who could blame a scholarly gent like that for sinking into lushery? That kind of fall from grace is hard to bear. When you move in refined circles you're entitled to your sins like the rest of us but for gawd's sake, rule number one, the *only* rule: don't get caught.

Anyway, end of that year, there he was, Steampunch. Built and finished. And what a magnificent beast he was and all. His great brass head had a... a proudness and a nobility to it, like one of those antique Roman busts. His torso, with its reinforced ribs and its interleaving layers of armour plate, looked sturdy enough to stop a dreadnought. His arms and legs—well, he moved with such grace, such springiness, you'd never know just how much bulk he was carrying. He was precision-built and clockwork-tight, and within his chest burned a furnace that would've shamed a volcano and the pounds per square inch inside his pipework would've blown the mercury out of any barometer.

His first fight was against Chromebolt, who at that time was the reigning heavyweight champion. Steampunch was very much the young contender, the challenger, the upstart underdog. The smart money was against him. The odds on his winning were as long as a giraffe's knee-britches. He was an unknown quantity, and Blarney Mick was desperately talking him up but the more Mick pattered the less he was believed. Everyone thought he was a leg, puckering and gammoning away like that, and only a complete gulpy would have put a ha'penny on Steampunch lasting a single round.

That all changed when Steampunch took Chromebolt down with three straight shots, each more devastating than the last. The fight was over almost as soon as it'd begun. No one in the audience could believe it. There was absolute silence in the arena, a thousand jaws hanging wide open, the only sound in the whole place coming from Chromebolt as oil spurted from his hydraulics and spattered on the floor and chunks of broken platework fell off with a clunk and this long, low groan of his dying furnace. From fully functioning automaton to scrap metal in a shade under six seconds.

And then, from a thousand throats at once, came a cheer. A scream, really. Sheer amazed delight. All at once the nation had a new mechano-boxing hero. Overnight Steampunch went from a nobody to the name on everybody's lips. He was on the back pages of all the papers the next day. The front pages of many of 'em too. The *Times* called his victory "the greatest reversal of expectations this nascent branch of the pugilistic craft has yet beheld", and I'm not sure what half of that means but it sounds about right.

It didn't come as such a surprise to any of *us*, Steampunch's makers. We'd had a pretty clear idea what our man was capable of. But I'll admit, even I was taken aback by just how swiftly he took down Chromebolt, how decisively. I'd known he had the power. I hadn't realized just how much heart he had as well.

Now, I'm not boring you, am I? You're not thinking, "This old Starkey, he doesn't half yatter on"? Because that looked like a yawn you were stifling there. But then it was a long journey, wasn't it? Arduous. I wouldn't blame you for being exhausted. All those weeks confined at close quarters, skimming across the trackless expanse, surviving on meagre rations, suffocating on the stink and breath of your fellow transportees... No fun. I remember it all too well.

Then I'll carry on, as you insist. Where was I? Oh yes. Well, after Chromebolt, they were queuing up to take on Steampunch. Other promoters couldn't wait to let their mechano-boxers have a crack at him. There was Steely Tinderbox, short of stature but a lively opponent all the same. There was Thundersmith, a.k.a. the Rotherham Rocket. There was The Ironclad, who had these two vast funnels sticking out of his back. There was Diamond Face, whose mush was actually made of toughened glass rather than diamond, meaning he was vulnerable there—he literally had a glass jaw. There was Rory the Ramrod, from north of the border, also known as the Tartan Spartan. There was Kid Colossus and Ferro and the Battling Bronze Behemoth and many, many more. All these pretenders to the crown, and Steampunch faced them all down and knocked them flat.

Not all his fights were as easy as Chromebolt. Oh no, he received plenty of scrapes and dings and dents along the way. He took his lumps, and got dumped on his nancy more than once. But he'd always get up again and keep going. Whatever his opponents dished out, he soaked it up and fought on till he won. One time, up against Galvanissimus I think it was, he had his entire left arm taken off clean at the shoulder. Now, that might have stopped any other mechano-boxer, what with the loss of oil and the bearings being thrown and all that, not to mention Steampunch being a southpaw. But did he falter? Did he hell! He went on and gave Galvanissimus such a drubbing, they never found all the missing pieces.

Ah, it was a glorious few years. Steampunch's career went from strength to strength. The money was rolling in. Blarney Mick was happy, his Fenian bosses were happy, and best of all the punters couldn't get enough of their automaton hero. He'd be showered with sprats and joeys whenever he strode into the ring—copper coins a token of respect, valuable metal to acknowledge valuable metal—and they'd bounce off his steel hide like ringing rain. And he took to saluting the crowd after he'd trounced whoever, just a little touch of finger to forehead but it sent 'em wild.

I taught him to do that. I taught him all his tricks. It was from me he got his fighting style. And yes, I know, mostly it was just a case of arranging cogs and flywheels to follow certain set patterns, and putting flaws in the chains and gearing to create unexpected combinations and manoeuvres, and ironing out any weaknesses I might spot by rebuilding or welding or polishing smooth. It wasn't *training* as such. But training's what I call it and there's simply no other word for it. God's honest truth, Steampunch was an intelligent being. He was. Yes, yes, he was just a thing made of iron and steel and rods and sprockets, with a boiler inside and hundreds of valves and mile upon mile of duct and pipe. But he understood what he was. I swear it. He was aware of himself. And he had spirit and, like I said, heart. He was the gamest sparrer I ever saw, in human boxing and mechano-boxing alike. He was—make no mistake about this—no mere machine. Or if he was, then you and me are machines too, and the only difference is we're made of flesh.

So all was going swimmingly. Life was good. Can't complain. The future seemed bright.

Then it all went wrong.

Two things happened. One of them was a tragic accident. The other was John Sholto Douglas.

Not familiar with the name? Try the ninth Marquis of Queensberry.

Yes, him. None other. Right nasty piece of work he was too. Sometimes you can be high-born, have all the privileges life can offer, want for nothing, and still be low-down dirty scum. An ancestor of his, the third Marquis, killed, roasted and ate a kitchen boy. At the age of ten! Did you know that? Insanity early on in the family, and six generations of breeding and nurture didn't manage to weed it out of the bloodline. Not completely.

Now the ninth Marquis, or Mr. Douglas as I prefer because he's no nobleman to me, was never a big fan of mechano-boxing. As a founder of the Amateur Athletics Club he was all for physical prowess, men making the best of themselves, and don't get me wrong, I'm not against that, of course I'm not, and mechano-boxing was never intended to replace the noble practice of one person bashing the stuffing out of another. But Mr. Douglas, he'd got the notion that all of his beloved sports were in decline, that the machines were taking over and soon it'd be automatons running steeplechases and rowing on the Thames and suchlike, and us humans would end up nothing but a bunch of soft, docile jellies. He saw mechano-boxing as the thin end of that particular wedge, and as a representative Scottish peer in the House of Lords he'd stand up almost on a daily basis to rant against the Steel Scrappers and demand that laws should be passed banning the

Iron Arena, and he'd call anyone involved in the game—such as me—a traitor and a menace to society and a threat to the future of the human race even. He was an atheist, quite open about it, so perhaps he couldn't understand that mechano-boxing must be part of God's plan for His children, otherwise why would the Lord have given us the wherewithal to invent it?

At any rate Mr. Douglas was for a time a lone voice in the wilderness. I'd see him on the news now and then, going on in those pinched-posh tones of his about how the country was going to the dogs and mechano-boxing was leading the way, and you could tell he didn't have the will of the people on his side because everyone in the kinéma would start booing and jeering and throwing stuff at the screen whenever he was on, and demanding that the projectionist change the reel. I'd be booing and jeering as loud as anyone in the auditorium, and I'd be no less delighted than anyone when footage of Steampunch would come up straight afterwards, as it often did—Steampunch winning his latest bout, Steampunch tapping forefinger to forehead, the arena lights maybe catching one metal eye to give it a bit of a glint, a wink of brightness. Britain loved Steampunch, yes it did. Music hall songs were written about him. "Steampunch, Stee-ee-eampunch, you're the one we count on when it comes to the crunch." Ever heard that one? Catchy little ditty. Time was you could hardly walk past a gattering without it wafting out at you from the snug, either some chap at the piano singing it or else the selecto-calliope churning out Ellen Terry's version or Marie Lloyd's, thick with shellac-disc crackles. Then there were the tales about him in the penny-dreadfuls, "Steampunch Saves the Day," "Steampunch and the Mystery of the Missing Chapel Organ," that type of thing. He'd be fighting crime, doing detective work, even though he was an automaton who couldn't speak and the concept was totally absurd and didn't make any sense, but the readers didn't seem to mind and any editions of *Boys Standard* and *Planet Britain* with a Steampunch story in would sell out faster than hairbrush handles at a convent. We copyrighted his name and likeness and took a cut of the royalties, so we were laughing. Everybody was happy... except our pal Mr. Douglas.

He was canny, though, Mr. D was. Kept his campaign bubbling along and bided his time, waiting for the mood to change, the prevailing wind to turn his way. Somehow he knew his chance would come. Boxer like him, he understood that one of the ways to win a fight is to stay low-key, dance and defend but hold back from hitting till you spot a weakness in your opponent, a moment when his guard drops, then strike instantly, swiftly, mercilessly.

The moment came, and it was that tragic accident I mentioned. Now, I wasn't there, I never saw for myself what happened, but I've listened to first-hand reports, dozens of 'em, and as I understand it nobody was really to blame. It was just one of those things. Unless you credit the rumour that it was a set-up and Mr. Douglas himself was responsible behind the scenes, which I don't. Opportunist, him, certainly, but not a string puller. Not his style. A hyena, not a lion.

Ferro was taking on Prometheus II at Crystal Palace, which had just been finished—I mean the *new* Crystal Palace, the one perched on top of London overcity like a gemstone set in a silver brooch. It was an exhibition match, the outcome wasn't supposed to affect the rankings in any way, which is ironic because it did, more so than anyone could've foreseen. The crowd was probably slightly larger than usual on account of this being the first bout to take place in a new, purpose-built arena in the capital's latest, greatest landmark, fully half a mile above the earth's surface. And Prometheus II himself was new to the game, this was really a trial run for him, and his promoter had barked on for days beforehand about the extraordinary new technology employed in creating him, the Babbage calculators and the Lovelace analytical engines that would give him almost human-level craft and skill. Novelty all round.

Couple of minutes into the fight, Prometheus II snapped. Went crazy. Had a complete nickey fit, veered away from Ferro and hurtled off into the crowd and started beating up humans instead.

He killed nineteen, all told. Left another three permanently crippled, and several more with lifetime injuries. Not to mention the dozens who got crushed and trampled in the stampede to get out of the arena. He dashed brains out, and punched people in half, and tore off limbs, and nobody could've stopped him, not even Ferro, who just stood in the ring still ducking and weaving and throwing uppercuts into thin air, like he was designed to. God knows how many more spectators would have died, it could have been a massacre instead of just a slaughter, if Prometheus II hadn't abruptly halted his murder spree and turned on himself. He slammed his own fists against his chest, hammering holes in his armour plate then pounding the moving parts beneath till his boiler blew and he keeled over in a heap, gushing flames and embers and scalding-hot water everywhere.

I insist that nobody was to blame. Oh, maybe you could argue that his makers should have constructed him with greater care, perhaps put him through a few more test fights before launching him on his public debut, made sure he wouldn't blow a gasket like that. But when a seal bursts on the vacuu-rail and a train hits an air pocket and crashes into the tunnel wall, or when an ethership comes down from azimuth at too steep an angle and burns up, or when a space mortar misfires and sends its projectile thumping straight into the moon, it isn't necessarily human error. Often as not it's an accident. It's awful and sad and horrible but machinery going wrong is a simple fact of life. No device is perfect. People die every day connecting their home kinés to the electrical outlet wrongly. The robot hansoms are forever mowing down pedestrians in the street. And we don't say, "Let's ban kinés or hansoms outright," do we? We don't say, "Let's turn our backs entirely on all the benefits of the modern age, all the marvels we've wrought, simply because they occasionally cause a death or two." Such is the price of science, of progress. There's never any gain without pain.

But not according to John Sholto Douglas. Straight after the Crystal Palace disaster he leapt up to say that mechano-boxing was a public health hazard, a danger to all. He claimed he'd suspected there'd be a catastrophe of some sort sooner or later. It was only a matter of time. The sport should be outlawed forthwith and every last Steel Scrapper smelted down and beaten into ploughshares. Those were his exact words: beaten into ploughshares. Lifted from the Old Testament, of course. Book of Isaiah. "They shall beat their swords into ploughshares." The atheist quoting the Bible. Which ought to give you some idea of the brazen hypocrisy of the man.

What's that? Yes, I know that saying. "The Devil can cite scripture for his purpose." Spot-on, my son.

Now, this time Mr. Douglas had people's attention. He also had the ear of the prime minister, whose cousin was among the nineteen dead from Prometheus II's rampage. In the blink of an eye white papers were being drawn up, emergency legislation rushed through parliament, unanimous votes, the whole kit and caboodle, and all of a sudden mechano-boxing found itself on the wrong side of the law. In particular Mr. Douglas came down hard on Steampunch. He'd learned about Blarney Mick's Fenian connections and he wasn't slow in using that as a brush to tar us with. "Enemies of Her Majesty," he said, "have funded this mechanical so-called hero. Sworn foes of the Crown have forged a monstrosity that makes a mockery of all that is good and British and true. Steampunch is nothing more than an insidious plot to mislead and undermine the sentiment of our nation." I know the speech by heart. I bought a copy of the edition of Hansard it appeared in, just so I could see it with my own eyes, and even printed in black and white the words were as green as bile.

And their effect was like poison. The following morning a mob gathered outside the warehouse on Cheapside where we kept Steampunch. People hurled stones at the windows and yelled insults, "Bog trotters out!" and the like. I'd guess many of 'em were the same folk who not so long ago would've been cheering Steampunch along as he laid into his latest opponent and would've coughed up lolly to buy the magazines and the songsheets. They felt betrayed, cheated. And perhaps, just perhaps, I don't blame them. Before Crystal Palace it might not have mattered to them who his backers were, if they'd known. Now it did, because all mechano-boxers were potential mass murderers it seemed. And a mechano-boxer with links to proven mass murderers? Well, that was too much to bear.

It was terrifying to be trapped inside the warehouse while stones crashed and broken glass rained down. I heard someone shouting about torching the place, burning it to the ground, but thankfully that didn't happen. In the end the bluebottles arrived, broke up the mob, sent 'em on their way. Then the inspector in charge asked to be let in, and he delivered the bad news. By the powers vested in him et cetera et cetera, he instructed us to dismantle Steampunch forthwith or else take "the machine" to a breaker's yard to be dismantled. We had three days in which to comply. Failing that, Steampunch would be seized and the cops would do the job themselves.

Once the peelers had left, Mick and I argued long and hard about what to do. Basically neither of us was ready to let our boy be taken apart and turned into slag. But what choice did we have?

"We go on the run," Mick said finally.

I looked round at the twelve or so tons of hulking metal sitting on the warehouse floor, partly covered by a tarpaulin.

"We go on the run," I said, "with *that*?"

Mick reckoned it could be done, it would be difficult but not impossible. All we had to do was get Steampunch down to the docks, load him onto a boat, sail for Dublin. There Mick had friends who'd hide him away and keep him safe. Keep *us* safe, in fact, since there'd be no returning to England afterwards. We'd be wanted criminals for the rest of our lives. The trip to Ireland was one-way only. Much like the trip to here.

I didn't want to say yes, but I felt as protective of Steampunch as a father is of his child, so in the end yes had to be my answer. While Mick went off to make the arrangements, I got Steampunch ready. I lubricated him and gave him a good all-over polish, just like I used to before a fight. I'd got into the habit of talking to him too, softly, a little bit of geeing-up while I went about my work. Now I told him everything was going to be fine, we were up against some stiff competition but it was nothing we couldn't handle, we were on the ropes but we'd keep battling on. He listened. I know he did. His head rolled slightly to one side with a creak while I was priming and stoking his boiler. He was giving me his ear.

Mick came back late that night. Some urgent telegraphing and some costly bribery had got us the use of a small freighter, the *Melmoth*, berthed at Tilbury, but we had to leave straight away. We stole out of the warehouse. I say "stole" but there's only so stealthy you can be with a mechano-boxer in tow, heaving and clanking along behind you. The city was dark, the moon obscured by the overcity, and a right old London Particular had set in, so that even the gas lamps' light was dimmed. It was hard to see where we were going but that meant *we* were hard to see, so that was to our advantage. But still, Steampunch's tread on the cobblestones was like cannon fire, the sound channelled and amplified by the streets.

The echo of each of his footfalls never seemed to fade. And I had plenty of time during that long, that endlessly long walk to Tilbury, to think about what had happened, all the success, all the adulation, how it had just evaporated, and what I was giving up, the life I knew, the places I knew. Luckily I'd never married, never settled down with a haybag and raised brats. I'd confined myself to judies and actresses, buying with cash what a husband buys with suffering and loss of freedom. I didn't have any real attachments to break. Mick and Steampunch were my family.

We made it to the docks safe and sound. No one spotted us, no one raised the alarm. Once I'd got a whiff of the river reek—silt and fish guts—I was sure we were home free.

Then, just as we'd got one of the wharf cranes working and were about to start winching Steampunch aboard the freighter, out from the fog stepped a score of coppers, armed with shotguns.

Turns out the captain of the *Melmoth*, though he'd accepted a hefty sum of money off Mick, had decided to double his wages by tipping off the police. I've no idea how many thick 'uns he earned for chaunting on us. I only hope he choked on every single note, the bastard.

Mick and I had no choice but to surrender. The jig was up. We stepped off the boat, all prepared to come quietly. Then a voice rang out from the fog, one I knew only from the kinés but couldn't have mistaken.

"Abscond would you?" said the Marquis of Queensberry, emerging from the gloom of the pea-souper into the dockside lamplight. "Scurry back to your paymasters in Erin? I think not. I asked to be alerted if any of you lot tried to evade the law or go underground. Surprise surprise, who should be the very first felons I encounter but the Steampunch gang? I'm going to take great personal pride in overseeing your arrest and prosecution. Moreover, I'm going to make sure I'm the one who pushes the button that starts the steam press that turns your glorified wind-up toy into iron filings."

There he was, all wrapped up in a raglan overcoat, his bushy black eyebrows like a pair of caterpillars nestled below the brim of his beaverskin high hat—the man himself, the bane of our lives, the arrogant aristo who'd ruined everything. And I'm not ashamed to say I gave him a piece of my mind. I couldn't help it. I called him all the choice names I know, and I know a lot. I loosed off at him, for all the good I knew it'd do me. Naturally he just sneered. What did a commoner's insults mean to a blueblood like him?

But then—and this is the eerie part—all the hatred I was feeling toward Mr. Douglas, all the venom I was spewing at him, it was as if it sparked off something inside Steampunch. As if the sound of my anger triggered some deep, unknown part of his mechanism. Either that or a cog slipped somewhere, a drive-chain came loose, it was just a coincidence, a fault occurring at exactly the same moment as I was giving His Worship an earwigging.

Steampunch jerked into life. He rose up and lumbered along the wharf toward Mr. Douglas, fists raised, and the look on the bloke's face, you should have seen it! I've never seen anyone that frightened. I bet he cacked his longjohns right where he stood. This mechano-boxer heading straight for him, completely spontaneous-like and of its own accord, and by then we all knew only too well what one of 'em could do to the human anatomy… The Marquis was rooted to the spot, Steampunch bearing down on him, and he knew he'd be mincemeat once that giant automaton got within hitting range.

That's when the coppers opened fire. They managed to overcome their shock and lift their shotguns and start blasting at Steampunch. They'd come loaded with army-issue twelve-bore shrapnel rounds, the kind that can knock holes through a tank. They'd taken that precaution because, after Prometheus II, it was a precaution well worth taking.

I'm glad, in a way, that they did what they did. Much as I despise Mr. Douglas, I wouldn't have wanted his death on my conscience. I'm a Christian, a believer, and even if it was Steampunch not me who'd dealt the fatal blow, I'd have had to bear some of the responsibility, and I don't want to spend eternity in Hell. Two decades in this godforsaken place has been bad enough.

I'm hoping to find much better lodgings when death finally transports me out of here.

The shrapnel rounds tore into Steampunch, a blizzard of metal shards coming at him from all directions. The coppers were relentless. They worked their pump actions and fired and fired, not taking any chances. Steampunch reeled. He staggered. He tried to carry on but the impacts kept throwing him this way and that, he couldn't get to where he wanted to go, and besides his target was well away by then, Mr. Douglas having scarpered pell-mell, showing us a clean pair of heels as he fled into the fog.

A great steel arm flailed helplessly in the air. Steampunch collapsed, one leg blown off at the knee. His brass head turned. He was looking around. Looking for me and Mick. Fresh ragged holes kept appearing in his platework. Fragments of him flew off. The sound of the gunshots became one long ear-shattering roar. Cordite fumes mingled with the fog...

I'm sorry. Something in my eye. Speck of dust. Hold on a mo.

Right. Anyway. In the end Steampunch went down. This was one fight he hadn't a prayer of winning. He was outnumbered, hopelessly outmatched. I saw his face as he sprawled on the ground, leaking from a dozen different places. I held his brass gaze. It was all I could do. I tried to tell him by my expression that it was all right, he was going to a better place, he was too good for this world if this was the way they treated him.

I think—I hope—he understood.

And then he was gone. His furnace went out. His boiler was destroyed beyond redemption. He lay still on the wharf, shredded, and I just watched, sobbing like a babe, as the last billows of steam and smoke poured out of him, vanishing into the fog. When the rozzers placed handcuffs on my wrists, I didn't even notice.

I shan't bore you with the details of the trial. You know what the inside of a court of law is like, the dust and the wigs and the Latin jargon no one understands, probably not even the barristers who use it so liberally. Mr. Douglas himself appeared on the witness stand to testify against us, and would you believe it, seems he and the judge were old chums. Went to school together at the Royal Naval College. So that put the seal on it. Mick and I were doomed. Not that we hadn't been doomed from the outset. The only uncertainty we faced was whether we'd be hanged or just transported.

Mick got the rope. The luck of the Irish—in England. I was due to dangle too but the beak very kindly commuted the sentence, being as I'd had the good fortune to be born British. Week later I was on my way here.

Ah now, hang on, the ship's about to disembark. Fingers in ears, I'd recommend. Wait for it. Wait. The mortar's going up, the charge is being shunted into position, they're finding the angle...

POOM!

Loud, eh? And there she goes, sailing skyward. So fast you can barely follow. Going... going...

gone. That's it. Out of sight. Next one's not due for another couple of months.

No, no, don't cry, lad. It'll be all right. Believe me, you'll adjust. Might take a while, but time'll come when you'll scarce be able to remember what it was like to live anywhere but here. The cold thin air. The faint sun. The wretched dust. You'll get used to it. Soon enough it'll all seem normal and reasonable and even bearable.

Come on, let's get you down to the rookeries and fix you up with a bunk and a bedroll and a bite of food. Then we'll look at getting you a placement on one of the work details. They've started building a road to Olympus Mons. See that pimple over there on the horizon? That's only the most enormous mountain ever. Dwarfs any other peak you can name. The plan is to erect shelters on the slopes and start prospecting for ore below. Roadwork's a good job to get in on. We'll see if we can sign you up. Soon you'll be red-skinned with the best of us. Treat it as a badge of belonging.

Welcome to Mars, young man.

STATIC

Marly Youmans

The author of novels Little Jordan, Catherwood, The Wolf Pit, The Curse of the Raven Mocker, *and* Ingledove, *as well as the forthcoming* Valorson *(PS Publishing), Marly Youmans writes subtle, stylish stories—like this one, a vision of a neo-Victorian world irradiated with electricity...*

ESTELLA HIGHTOWER KNEW instantly that something had gone wrong because the flutes had stopped. It was quiet and cold, and when she pushed back the coverlet a star of static leaped into her hair. The ranks of pipes by the door wore caps low over their silver faces. She wrapped herself in a cloak and stood on the upper landing a moment, listening.

Static snapped in the folds of velvet as she slid down the handrail to the front hall, her feet slapping against the floor just when the thunder rumbled, ending with a whipcrack of lightning. As she skimmed from room to room—age to age—Estella saw that all the flutes were dead, even the newest ones from the Syrinx Company, chased with images of dancers and garlands. A house had stood on the spot for almost a thousand years, so there were pipes from many eras, the oldest ones in the shape of priests devoted to the cycle of Cloud, Rain-and-Snow, and Vapor.

She fled past the parlor doors to the narrow rear staircase. One level below, she tiptoed by the kitchen and found the steps that gyred into the dark. She had to cling to the wall, not wanting to go clattering down to the lowest cellar more quickly than she liked. Her breath made puffs that froze and tinkled onto flagstones that had been worn almost to bowls; here and there the earth broke through. She stamped her feet, now soled in ice.

An immense berg of sapphire shed a faint blue glow, lit from above by an oil lamp.

"Joe! Joe Tinker! Where are you, Joe?"

She found him sleeping on rags and so cold that she could hardly wake him. Static glittered in the shreds of cloth.

"Joe, Joe," she called; "Wake up and light the boiler fire!"

"Let me be, miss." He rolled away from her. "Let me forget this here trouble and commotion."

"There's not a bit of commotion," she said, "not one blessed bit. But Ma Furey will make some commotion on your backside if the boiler's not working straightway, Joe Tinker! And what did you do with the wool bed rug I found in the attic?"

He sat up in his nest. "I sold it, miss, for a jacket and trousers because the chilblains bothered me so bad. And for blood sausages and pie with tripe and gravy when Ma Furey beat me with her blackthorn stick and sent me to bed without supper. I run off to the station and ate with the rail men. Some day I'll be a coal-shoveling man on an engine."

A tear froze on his face and made a pathetic chink when it struck pavement.

"Hush, Joe," Estella whispered, looking behind her at the shadows. "Daphne Basket says my great-aunt's a witch, and that the pipes whistle secrets."

"They're asleep."

"Yes." Having groped in her pocket for lucifer matches, she now hesitated about handing them over.

"Be careful, Joe. The static's very bad. Who knows how long the steam has been out?"

"Burned off my eyebrows once. Didn't make no difference to me." Nodding his thanks, Joe Tinker lit a match. It flared and made a fierce rumpling noise when the fire took hold.

"Oh, good, excellent. I was afraid the boiler had failed."

The boy gave a lopsided smile. "We could've lit her with your hair, miss, it's that flamey."

"I'd love to give my hair to light the boiler," she said, the weight of the braid pressing against her spine.

"Ma Furey queens us all, don't she?"

"It's all right." Estella combed the spikes of hair from his forehead with her fingers.

His was a good face, she thought, one that was meant to be glad, but Joe Tinker was nothing but an orphan chained to sweeping the ice, chipping shards, and feeding the fire. At ten he was thin and malnourished, and all his play had been moments stolen from the boiler. Every house had such a child or else some worn spinster or bachelor who would serve the purpose, shivering in the cellarage with a chisel and hammer for company.

The boy caught her wrist, his black eyes shining in the light from the ice. She bent close to the snub nose and the misbehaving hair and the dead-white thumbprint on one cheek that meant the frost had marked him.

"Joe Tinker, you'll be scooping coal, if that's what you want to do. I promise it! And I'll find you another bed. My great-aunt should've given you a new suit of clothes. The law says sweeps must have an outfit, smallclothes, and a visit to the cobbler twice a year. Is the jacket warm and snug?"

"The trousers, too," he said; "they're a treat."

The boy snatched up a pick and broke shards from the block of ice.

"Old Blue here, she's having her some babies," he said, tossing ice into the chute that fed the boiler.

"That's right, Joe; do your best, and maybe Ma Furey will never notice that the pipes fell asleep."

And with that bit of parting hope, Estella crept up the twist of stair toward daylight.

In the front hall two women could be heard arguing.

"I'll blister him. I'll bite the scalawag. I'll set savage pups on him—"

"You don't have dogs, Mary Furey, and what's more, I wouldn't let you do such a cruel thing to a motherless, fatherless child. The Securities would come and plunk you in a dungeon." The voice of Mrs. Daphne Basket rose an octave. "It's nothing to do with Joe Tinker. I've sent for the boiler man. Something amiss with the line, I expect."

Estella listened, her hand smothering a trill of laughter.

Though Daphne was unlovely with her too-rigid carriage and long face with its frizzled awning of curls, she had taught the girl to read and write and calculate, amused her whenever she was locked into the tower, and helped her to survive the demands of Ma Furey. Spunk and defiance had kept Estella out of the static storms many times when the old woman wanted to send her on errands in the meadows where lightning played and occasionally skewered a wanderer. Daphne had told her stories about her parents, passing on tales of Hightowers and Ravelers and all her kin. Mary Furey would have been happy to raise the orphan child in ignorance—particularly of the fact that *The Towers* was Estella's to govern once she came of age.

"When I can boot the witch out the door, and wallop her if she comes sniveling back," she had said once, eliciting a warning "Hush!" from her governess.

Now Daphne Basket glanced over at Estella and gave a slight shake of the head.

Great-aunt Furey was a demon at intercepting signals. She whirled, eyes glaring; the pointy tip of her nose twitched.

"The pipes will be on soon. Joe Tinker fixed the boiler." Estella crossed her fingers under the cloak. A spark bit at the spot where skin rubbed against skin. A lie to Mary Furey didn't count, or so she had reasoned, back when she realized that the old woman would steal her inheritance if she could do so in safety.

"Ptoo!" Ma Furey spat, and a stream of tobacco spanged into a spittoon. "Dead ringer," she noted. "We'll see about his ice majesty later. I've just come from a trip to town on business with our lawyers. Get Eliza to poke up a blaze in my sitting room, do you hear? After that, miss, gather greens out of the lower garden—"

"Lightning has been striking in the fields all morning," Daphne said. "It's terribly dry, and the sirens have gone off several times. I'm sure you wouldn't send the child to her doom, particularly after discussing the family estate with her attorney. Just the sort of mischief that would make a man like Peeblestock suspicious."

Ma Furey scraped out a laugh, and drew herself to full height. As her backbone had contracted into the letter C years before, the attempt was not particularly impressive.

"You have given yourself too much authority in your roles as nanny and governess and companion to this unruly girl. Miss Basket, do not trespass—"

"I'll go," Estella said. "It's all right, I'm good at dodging the bolts," she added, moving close to Daphne Basket. She hardly noticed the sparks that frisked between them. "Don't make her angry," she whispered.

The great-aunt slumped onto a bench. "Perhaps it's about time to dispense of your heretofore invaluable services, Daphne Basket. Perhaps you are growing too costly for me to pamper in this over-sized mansion."

"No." Estella grasped her friend's arm.

"That feckless boy ought to be whipped," she went on. "What nonsense, an idiot like that being competent to fix a boiler. I know your schemes to swallow up the truth. Fetch me a basket of tender new greens, Estella Blanche. And you, nanny soon-to-depart, count yourself lucky that I don't deliver you to the Statics for discipline on this very day. Tomorrow morning we will discuss your exodus from my house."

After delivering herself of this mouthful, the old woman wilted. Though a woman of frequent fire, Ma Furey was nonetheless prone to fits of trembling from the cold, feared death by hypothermia, and believed strongly in layering. Undergarments that hadn't been removed in many winters, as frail and full of holes as a spider's web, clung to her skinny body. Around these tatty nets had grown a cocoon of shifts veering between silk and wool, all part of her grand unified theory of attire. At bedtime, without the outermost husks of day, these layers made her resemble an immense shriveled peony. Come morning, her dress was invariably black, followed by a mercerized jacket, and over these a mackinaw steeped in paraffin to repel snow and rain. Outfitted in these, along with what she called "a sufficiency" of bonnets and sometimes a wool blanket, she appeared robust and not like the crabbed stick that she was.

"Ouch!" A crackle under the heap of skirts meant static had just jabbed at flesh.

A rill of giggles sprang from Estella's mouth.

In answer, a black corrective shoe stomped against the floorboards.

"Send Eliza! More coals for the fire." Mary Furey marched toward the door that led to the former sitting room of Rose Raveler Hightower, Estella's mother.

"Horrible old witch," Daphne Basket said, just before the door slammed.

"Hush," the girl whispered.

But it was too late.

"After you fetch my greens," the old woman shrieked, "come to me, and I will comb the elf-knots from your hair."

The two in the hall exchanged a look.

Mrs. Basket made a strangling motion with one hand; with the other, she shook a fist in the direction of the sitting room.

Estella muffled a laugh with her cloak.

"I'll pick the greens for you," Daphne Basket said in a low voice. "It's dangerous out there today. Only a witch would go rambling about the streets with not so much as a lightning-rod umbrella."

"I don't care. I can out-run and out-jump the lightning, and you can't. You'd be out there too long."

The two friends embraced, and the younger laid her head on the older one's shoulder.

The truth was that Estella did not mind harvesting greens from the gardens near the fields. The race through cold to rip the plants from the ground was almost her only freedom, and though once she had been so close to a bolt that the hair around her face shot outward like a corona, she was too young to believe that lightning would strike her dead.

Out there she felt strength, as if the branched nerves inside her were a tree that flashed and burned.

Shut up in the tower room, she had learned every expanse of meadow, every inch of street. She knew the look of each servant on the whole of Starfell Avenue, every parent and child, every dog and cat. Any blush of romance she had felt came from watching young men alighting from carriages, or coming and going by steam tram.

Her current interest was a member of the Society of Statics. She knew because he wore the guild's silver sunburst on his greatcoat. Her mother's opera glasses, by means of which she had made many imaginary friends, lurked behind the curtains. They had revealed the shining detail and so showed her that he possessed the second sight.

She held the sight too, but it was of no use. She had never seen anything that would help and only sorrow had come to her that way. The great-aunt would not permit anyone to speak of the sight. Estella was sure that Mary Furey meant to keep her youth bottled, until it lost effervescence and the sight slipped into flatness and depression, as happened to those who made no use of the gift.

Yes, Ma Furey wanted her, and not for any fair purpose. Hours they wasted with a cat's cradle of twisted silk and wool, playing impossible games: sending stars of static along the threads, catching and prisoning a star at the center. Was she the light at the heart of the cradle, and the game a spell woven by a woman whose thumbs prickled with power? Sometimes it seemed so.

At other times Miss Mary Furey seemed a mere insect, capable of no more than fleabites of annoyance. Was it so strange that a great-aunt liked untangling the waves of a niece's hair, letting the stars stream from the comb?

No, even that felt perverse.

Who else but a witch would keep static alive in a bottle like a jailed fairy or treasure the red nests of hair that she pulled stealthily from the brush and combined with a green parrot's feather, a bit of static, and cobalt blue powders?

Perhaps she was no witch but simply a fearful old woman who had not meant to become a jailor.

Estella wanted to ride a clacking train to the capital and meet with the guild members, whom she imagined as a kind of exalted family. As a Static she could move freely, rifling through secrets. Instead, her life was a secret, its petals closed over a golden eye. One had to be known and nominated, but nobody ever saw her.

Once she had seen the young Static leave the house in disguise. He glimpsed her in the tower and stared, secure in his false beard and moustache. But she had watched him too often to be fooled. She thrust open the window to toss him a white rose that Daphne had picked in the glasshouse. Though the flower froze before ringing against the cobblestones, he tucked the stem into his buttonhole, pushing the black beard aside to do so. She daydreamed of a crime that would bring him to The Towers: a subtle one that would hurt nobody.

"No use to wish," she had murmured.

Now she dressed quickly, putting on a muslin dress sprigged with leaves. It was Empire style, new several generations back, but Ma Furey would have nothing to do with dressmakers and fashion. Nothing was thrown away at The Towers, so time accumulated its sediments inside hatboxes and wardrobes. Over her gown she wore the velvet cloak, made over from a man's garment discovered in a chest.

She said the morning prayers under her breath. "Bless me, O Cloud. Bless me, O treasuries of Rain and Snow. Bless me, One who ascends as Vapor and returns..."

At the kitchen door she judged the sky. The weather had been difficult lately, with thunderstorms not just in the late afternoon but at any hour. Wind turned the nap of the winter grain one way, then another. The greenhouse plants were drooping behind glass, although pipes were beginning to cloud the walls with moisture. Vegetables and flowers were so quickly blighted by cold that the first heat from the boiler was always theirs. Joe Tinker was in for a harridan's scolding and perhaps would be traded to another family. If so, she would miss his antics and tales of the street. She imagined that such a change could only be good for him, given his current mistress.

"So wretchedly cold," she said, ignoring the nip of static on her arm.

"Careful," Daphne Basket said, coming to the door; "Such a fool's errand, endangering a child to feed a crone's maw."

Sparks like thistledown snapped in the air.

"I'm shooting for cheerful defiance. Those things are nothing but lightning bugs," Estella said.

"Don't take any risks."

"Off goes the fool," she called, racing away from the house.

The long cable of her braid stirred like the torso of a dragon, arching and falling heavily, while the wings of the cloak struggled to leap into sky. All things stood apart and distinct in the static. Beyond the paling a bolt slammed into the winter grain, and a smell of ozone and burnt grass suffused the landscape. The immense steam-organ pipes of the public works sang out and pushed up clouds of vapor like a million white peonies shattered on a blue china tray. When an engine chugged by with its steam shooting straight up in the dry air, Estella ran faster, feeling a ravishing sense of power: if only she could beat the train to the farthest edge of fields, past the ranks of flutes, where mountains were a promise of adventure!

At the lower vegetable bed she ripped out plants by the roots, thrusting them into the basket. Lightning jabbed the earth so close by that she saw the faint bands inside what old people called *ladders-for-demons*. The blood in her veins glittered as if flecked with ice. As if hypnotized, her gaze fixed on a crystallized insect. Then she heard Daphne shouting her name. The rut of path seemed longer going back, and the muddy ground tripped up her feet.

"She wants you. She wants you." Daphne Basket danced in tiptoe agitation at the kitchen door.

"Now? What does she want?"

"The combing."

Safe inside, Estella flung herself onto a chair by the door. Greens scattered from the basket rocking at her feet.

"Did I ever tell you that I hate that dreadful old tartar?"

"Don't talk so." Daphne Basket nodded at Marguerite, bent over the sink.

Estella had a liking for the cook, who had never been adverse to treats after hours. She was not the least bit like a marguerite flower, having a rump like a horse's and a thin mane pinned into a knot on top of her head. Her features looked as though malleable clay had been bunched into the center of her face by a potter whose dream of beauty meant heavy-lidded eyes, squashed nose, and pursy mouth. Despite a past history that included afternoon damson tarts and midnight Welsh rarebit and much use of the long-handled corn popper, Marguerite tended to be secretive and unreliable, cramped under the scaly thumb of her mistress.

"Are the pipes going yet? She likes it dreadfully hot up there. I'd rather have cold."

"Ma Furey's in a mort of temper after visiting with attorneys," the cook said, coming over to scoop up the greens, a bloody cleaver in one hand. "And then her coming home to find the house so chilly and dead-like. No sooner did I see her than she found fault with the gravy in my rabbit pies. And she's gone and set Eliza to work, so the room'll be as hot as herself likes. The poor noodle has fetched pans of coal and hot bricks and antique church braziers that nobody's used in years. When I carried up tea, the missus was screeching that the winter ache had wormed into her bones. Gave me a fright with her scratchety cries."

"Marguerite," Estella said, "why—thank you for telling me."

"Be careful." Daphne Basket was staring at the cook.

One hand on a newel post worn to silk by generations of servants, the girl hesitated and then called back to Marguerite: "Your rabbit pies are famous. Joe Tinker told me that the deputy mayor's wife declared that you made the finest meat pie in the county and deserved a blue ribbon."

"That's kind of you, Miss Estella." The cook might have blushed, though her cheeks were already so red and polished that it was hard to know.

"Just truth."

"Too much salt in the gravy! I'd like to soak her head in the rain butt."

Perhaps now Marguerite would be on their side and not so quick to tell tales. Still, one couldn't count on it since fresh quarrels ignited in a wink.

"Best to get the thing done, I suppose." Estella gathered up her skirts and dashed up the stairs.

Inside the sitting room Mary Furey hunched in her rocking chair, still wearing mackinaw and jacket. Portable braziers had been set haphazardly along the walls, and the chamber seemed a furnace. Static fussed in the air, sparking on the mantelpiece and flecking the drapes with light.

The girl approached the humped-over bundle of clothes, hunkered so snug by the fire.

"What a bonfire! You could burn the place to ashes," she said. "You've no right to endanger The Towers when the pipes are out and the air's so dry."

As usual, Mary Furey took no notice of references to the proper ownership of the house, though the hairbrush trembled in her hand.

"Sit down."

Estella drew the low stool as far from the fireplace as possible. The combing was always the same, beginning with a ceremonial unbraiding that left tresses in waves on the floor. After the tug-of-war between bristles and hair was finished, the old woman would pull the red nests from the brushes and stow them in silk bags.

The pipes had not yet begun to let moist air into the room; static crept between the muslin of Estella's gown and the shift beneath. Drops of perspiration trickled down her back.

"Hold still."

She didn't answer.

"Sullen thing."

"Fine," Estella said. "Crotchety witch," she added under her breath.

"I've a mind to jerk at your hair, even if you are my great-niece. I'll lash your impertinence to a bedrail with your own braids and leave you to starve. I've done it before! Wait for you to howl for bread and water." Laughter bubbled from the hole of her mouth. As she leaned back in the rocker, the layers of silk and wool rustled and set off shooting stars.

"Go ahead, ma'am. You would relish it."

"I would indeed." She spattered the logs with a squirt of tobacco.

"Am I really your niece?" A splinter of anger ran through Estella. "You don't look one blessed thing like me, or like the portraits of my mother. She had red hair and green eyes, a proper oval face, and pale skin. I look like her, but you're not like that, all gnarled and withery. You're nothing but an old tree root."

A laugh like the *skreek!* of a door startled the girl. She wondered how Ma Furey could be tickled by anything she had to say.

"You wretched imp! I'm surprised at you, dishing out such insults. Once upon a time I was a paragon of lady-loveliness," the old woman said. "When I was even younger, the boys thought me an incomparable maiden, fresh as a flower."

"The fairest of them all, I suppose."

"Something like that."

"I should like to have seen such a spectacle."

Mary Furey paused, her fingers twitching. "Damn the pudding-headed boy! How could a steambrat dare to let the pipes go out? This horrible air makes me feel like I'm breathing fizz. Jittery, that's what I am."

"It's because you made Eliza slave to build a bonfire and the room's so awfully dry. You've made it worse." The girl leaned forward, away from the odors of unwashed flesh, cheap dusting powder, and hair oil, and tried to picture the face of the young man with the sign of the Society on his lapel. Her eyes crossed as a dandelion head of static bloomed at the tip of her nose.

"I'm not comfortable," Great-aunt Furey fussed, plucking at the buttons on her mackinaw. "Strange to say, but I feel a little too warm. Hot, even. I'm much too—"

"You poor crooked root. I'd like to open the windows, it's so dry. Maybe it's better outside," Estella murmured, bending to cradle her head on her knees. "Hair is hot, and I've got more of it than a horse-knacker's mattress."

A squawk made her jerk upright and turn to see Ma Furey flapping her skirts. Static burst from layers of wool and silk. A red strand crinkled and rained in bits onto the floor.

"You've scorched my hair!"

The old woman groaned as smoke spiraled up from her hips and curled around mackinaw and bonnet.

Estella bolted to her feet as though bitten, dragging the torrent of red out of the skinny arms. Ma Furey tipped to one side, and the tinder in her lower regions flared up. She jigged like a figure carried in effigy, the paraffin-soaked mackinaw bursting—*whoomph!*—into a shroud of flame. Estella's cry mingled with a rumpling noise as fabric ignited and steam pipes shrilled with a blast of heat and long-delayed moisture. Mary Furey crumpled, engulfed in a stench of burning wool and hair. Seizing a poker, the girl thrust at the shaking heap, but there seemed to be nothing to rescue. Features distorted in pain proved to be bulges in a drawstring sack. A reticule exploded into a green fireball. Estella stepped away, feet sliding on a tide of unloosed hair. Black and rainbowy and with the viscosity of mercury, a puddle bubbled below the remains of the rocker.

Her screams became audible to the rest of the house when the skirl of pipes settled into a breathy pulse.

Daphne Basket reached her before anyone else, rushing past Marguerite and sweeping aside broom-thin Eliza. Joe Tinker tiptoed into the room, peered over the upholstered chairs, and listened for a time before creeping away. The attic tenant didn't show up, although he would have been useful as a witness.

Someone must have sent a street sweeper to summon the Securities, because two of them let their presence be known by a whistle and thumps at the main entrance.

Estella was shrieking in the middle of the room, arms out, and her raveled hair tickled the ankles of the other women.

"Of all the blazing static." Daphne Basket peered out the window. One of the Securities was rocking on his heels as he surveyed the front of the house, while the other battered the door with his truncheon. One was fat, one thin, but both affected walrus moustaches and appeared to be cartoon images of Securities.

"This is your doing, Marguerite; you show them in!"

The cook nodded, perhaps in confession, and continued to blubber, honking her grief into a tiny handkerchief.

In the puddle lay a cinder of skull matted with oily hair.

"Tubular! By static," Daphne Basket swore. "You great baby, was Ma Furey ever kind to you? Did she give you an ounce of care? What did she say about your dratted coney pies? And you have to fetch these terror-mongers who are always tossing the wrong people into jail. Quit sniveling. Buck up and let them in, you fool of a cook!"

Pretty soon the Securities were jostling at the doorway. Finally the thin one popped through, shedding a shower of sparks. The other nudged him to one side and stood with hands on hips while Marguerite and Daphne Basket launched into explanations of what was a mystery to each. Despite the best work of the pipes, static bloomed on the wool coats of the Securities and fizzled on the gesturing fingers of the women. Estella began to alternate screams with hiccups and laughter.

When the thin Security slapped her across the face, a hush took hold of the chamber.

The shape of fingers blossomed on Estella's cheek.

A figure stepped into the room, trailed by the ice sweep, and addressed the assembled company.

"It's not written in the Code of Securities that an officer shall strike young ladies, even those afflicted with shock. You two may accompany this woman in cook's apron to the kitchen, and let her fix you a hot drink and something from the larder. Then she may come back and wait in the next room, in case I need her assistance. This boy tells me there has been an unexpected death in the house."

Tears brought on by the slap were in Estella's eyes, though she laughed softly. The sweeps knew everything about the neighborhood, and Joe Tinker had gone for the Static man, who would save her from the Securities.

"Yes, sir," the plump Security man was saying. He didn't seem displeased at the idea of being sent to the kitchen. He sounded quite ordinary now, and not like the force of terror that could banish them to jail. *Why, they're afraid of him,* the girl thought with a touch of wonder, *though I'm not.*

"Perhaps someone could go for the young lady's *sal volatile*?" the voice went on.

Daphne Basket was answering; all would be well.

Jet stars like reverse flecks of static spattered the air. The young man from the Society of Statics took hold of her wrist, as if he would count the rushing of her blood beneath his fingers. Then black confetti blotted out her sight, and she plunged into a well of static.

Then there was a series of light and dark bursts. She was seated, watching the static arc streaking across the twilight sky, her hand…

The queer joyfulness mixed with grief that always came with the sight flooded in and buoyed her up toward the lamplit room where *zt zt zt* tiny stars of static fizzed in her hair. She lay on the settee, her mane blending with the wine-colored plush and spilling onto the floor, so that she appeared to curl inside an immense red nest.

Her gaze flicked to the starburst of the Society of Statics, pinned to a collar. The young man removed his coat and rolled up his shirt sleeves.

His arms were muscled like the arms of the stained glass angel in the front parlor. No Security had ever glimpsed an angel, received a message, or caught a single word spoken by the bright ones. Even when they stumbled into a bit of drama, the Securities remained heroes to nobody and had to hire storytellers to spread their fame. But the tales didn't manage to make them beloved. Everybody was afraid of them because of their confidence, and because they always did what they were told, no matter how wrong-headed it was. Their suspicion of anything otherworldly made it rather wonderful that they still trusted in the Statics. Perhaps they had once belonged to brother guilds, before the Securities lost the capacity to laugh.

"I saw something," she whispered.

"Did you, love?" Daphne Basket squeezed her fingers. "She has the sight, sir," she told the Static man.

He tilted his head as though listening for a far-off music and held quite still for a moment before speaking: "I was told that only men had such gifts."

"The poor child used to have nightmares about lightning and a white horse. Then her mother was struck by a bolt and killed, though it was cloudless and static readings were low. Not until later did I find out that Rose hadn't been riding her bay but a white mare belonging to the stables." She tucked a tendril of red behind the girl's ear. "After that she had no more nightmares—not the kind at night, anyway."

"The sight can be difficult."

"Indeed, it has been a plague to her, seeing glimpses of time to come and unable to tell any but me or little Joe Tinker." Mrs. Basket unfolded an ivory fan that had been left on the pianoforte and swept it back and forth above her charge's face. "It enraged our Miss Furey to hear of such things."

"Tell me," he said gently, bending over the girl. "Will you trust me? My name is Charles Rowan. We have been neighbors for many years, though we've never spoken. What came to you?"

She closed her eyes. *Rowan. Charles Rowan.* Hadn't she seen him grow up, along with every other child on the street? For the past ten years, she had watched their comings and goings from the tower. Now that he was here, the imagined man had turned to vapor. The straight nose, the blond hair with its silken sideburns and the darker brows, and the arch of real lips had driven him away.

What had she seen?

"I was on board a train. I haven't been on one since I was six or seven. My great-aunt forbade my leaving the house."

"Was there anything else?"

"The steam whistle. Someone else with me. A hand—a man's hand—was holding mine. Stars in the dusk. And static." She pointed to her collarbone. "Here, on the collar to my jacket. Green velvet."

"Static. The pin, you mean?"

She nodded, feeling the sureness well up: she would leave The Towers. The years of quiet rebellion against Ma Furey lay behind her, and a better time was ahead. She would be someone of use. And she would have what other women had. She knew that love was sometimes a dubious good; she had seen the squabbles, the sullen faces, the breaches that ended with one walking away from a door on the street and never, never returning. But she wanted family all the same and would take her chances in the world.

A thought came to her. "Have you seen me before? Not in the tower. Somewhere else, in the sight?"

"Perhaps. I think so."

The three of them were quiet, listening to the *xpt xpt* of the static.

"It's lucky that I was at home. I've brought my instruments," Charles said at last, "but I'll need more paper. Later I may want the sweep for errands. Perhaps you could have someone bring us tea, Mrs. Basket. You may leave your charge here to rest until she feels better."

With a nod, the older woman passed from the room.

He opened the bag, laid a few tools on a table—mostly tweezers and scrapers—and then knelt to examine the smear of grease and the cinder with its attachment of hair. Taking up a pair of tongs, he turned the remains before slipping them inside an envelope of waxed paper.

"Ice sweeps are great gossips. Yours says that the old lady crisped in an instant."

"Joe Tinker is quite right."

"Did you like "our Miss Furey," as your governess—I take it she is a governess—called her?" Charles Rowan's back was to her as he methodically scraped the floor and filled his packets, but he turned to survey Estella when she answered.

"Daphne Basket has been many things to me, a nanny and a governess and a maid, but most of all she was the companion who saved me from going mad when my great-aunt locked me in the tower. And no, I did not like her. I often hated my great-aunt because she took my freedom and my house, and what pleased her did not amuse me. But I would never harm her. Isn't there enough death in the world?"

"Quite enough," he said.

The girl's glance had fallen on the bag and its array of tools. "Those scissors: are they sharp?"

"My scissors? I have severed a two-inch hemp rope with them."

"Before anyone comes back, could you—"

She sat up, one hand on the scrolled arm of the settee.

"What?"

"Cut off my hair."

A packet of dust dropped from his fingers onto a marble-topped table. He picked up the little envelope again, turning it absently between his fingers.

"In shop windows, I've seen photographs of fashionable women with their hair down. Only one or two had as much as you do. Perhaps you don't know, being shut up, but it's considered a rare and valuable thing."

"Please." Estella put her hands to her head. "My great-aunt—they say she was a witch—forced me to grow it long. Once she tied me to the bedpost with my own hair. I hate it. The loose mass burns on my back, or else the braid twists and smacks me like something alive."

"Yet it's lovely," Charles Rowan said. "I don't like to be the one—"

"She combed my hair every day. That's why it was undone when you arrived. Even now, I can feel her gnarled fingers catching in a tangle. It will grow and be cut again and again, until some day none of it will have been touched by her. That's what I want. If I had my father's cavalry sword in my hand, I would slash my hair even if I bled for it. I never knew Mary Furey existed until my parents died. It was an ill day when she rapped on my door." As Estella turned toward him, the four slapped petals on her cheek shone out.

He caught up the scissors.

"I'm afraid you'll have to stand," he said.

She rose and stood with her feet set apart, steadying herself, and indicated the desired length with a finger held just below her shoulders.

"There's a reason the word is *locks* of hair," she said. "I was a prisoner inside myself."

The blades flicked away a strand. This first stroke past, he began to clip quickly and steadily. Segments of hair dropped and then clung to her gown.

Sparks flew between them, the stars of static smarting against skin. By the windows the flutes were singing, shooting vapor into the room.

Coolness bathed Estella as weight was lifted from her head. A tiny piston pounded in her neck when his hands grazed her dress. Closing her eyes, she reveled in the sensation of weightlessness.

A single spark arced from the scissors to her collarbone. The last clip made her open her eyes and look about the room. Reflected in a mirror, her throat gleamed by lamplight. Newly cut threads floated on the staticky air and sought Charles Rowan's shirtfront and face as if to tether him.

"It's not as even as I had hoped. I've never cut a woman's hair before."

She looked at him, half-gleeful, half-desiring to follow her hair and pull him near.

"I glimpsed something once," he said, "but didn't know what it meant: an image of wading through burning filaments."

"Gracious clouds and showers! What business is this?"

Daphne Basket had returned with Joe Tinker, who hoisted a tray loaded with teapot and cups and sugar and delicate pastries. The bun of coarse hair had slipped askew—she must have hurried to the corner bakery.

"Here, let me help." Charles took the tray from the ice sweep and set it on an ottoman.

"Your face, Daphne! What a preposterous look you had." Half-hidden by a veil of newly freed hair, the young mistress of The Towers laughed.

"I had no idea a Static could possibly consider the hair of Estella Blanche Hightower to be one of his duties."

"You are brave enough to say that much, but not quite brave enough to scold him outright," Estella said. "But it's not his fault. I have powers of persuasion."

"Miss Hightower was quite insistent on her freedom," Charles Rowan said, his glance moving slowly from one to the other.

"I have no doubt! We'll have to save the cuttings. Long hair is worth a good deal of money, and we may need to sell it before the estate is settled, or else have nothing to eat." Daphne Basket hurried to save the treasure from being trodden underfoot. "Wigmakers could make any number of fine wigs from this much hair, and I dare say that watch chains might command a price."

She gathered the locks and loose threads while Charles sat down and began peering through a microscope at samples he had taken from the smudge of grease, the floorboards, and the cinder of skull. Once the shearings were secured by a ribbon, Daphne hastily pinned Estella's remaining hair into a knot. Suddenly she looked like a proper young lady of some years prior—or perhaps like a girl dressed in her grandmother's gown for a game of charades.

"I suppose it was for the best. You look lovely with your hair up," Daphne whispered in her ear, "and that old muslin is pretty."

"Soon I'll be impossibly, breathlessly up-to-date," Estella said, "and amaze the neighborhood with my style. I want a green velvet jacket."

"Won't you need to wear mourning?" Daphne frowned as she began to pour the tea.

"I won't. And I won't change my mind."

Estella and Joe Tinker handed around tea and pastries, the ice sweep positively melting with pleasure at being allowed to eat a raspberry tart from a china plate with rosy garlands.

"Thank you." Charles managed to balance a tea cup on his knee, hold a pastry, and scrutinize the tar-like substance through the lens of his microscope.

While he looked at one slide after another, he kept up a running flow of conversation with the sweep. Twice he had him bring in Marguerite to discuss Mary Furey's diet—a rather greasy one—and once he had him fetch Eliza to ask the questions over again, as well as to discuss the types of oil used in the lamps: whale, mostly. Several times he interrupted his work to dash out on expeditions to remote corners of the house. Somehow he found out about the tenant, Mr. Edward Hustables Mainwarren, and that he kept a shop in Water St. where he sold daguerrotypes on Mondays and Thursdays until teatime.

Rubbing his hands together as though they felt dirty, he asked Joe Tinker to fly for a bowl of water and soap, which he brought "lightning-quick, sir" and earned a penny for his trouble.

"And now, Miss Hightower," Charles said, "I have been neglecting you and your companion. Perhaps Miss Basket will scurry about and tell the Securities that they can toddle on home, and inform the cook that she may go about her business. Supper, I suppose that would be. And perhaps the kitchen maid could throw a few chunks of ice into the boiler for Joe Tinker. As for Joe himself, if he will stay right here and keep a sharp watch on the scene of the crime, as we may call it until we know exactly what words to call it, I would be most grateful."

"Thank you, sir, although I don't think there is a crime," Joe said.

"I have my orders and ways of doing things that I must follow, just as you must keep the flutes in tune."

The boy ducked his head at this reminder of his failure to feed the boiler.

Daphne had paused at the door and now asked, "What about Miss Hightower?"

"I'd like to pay a formal call on Mr. Mainwarren. If she would be so good as to accompany me, I would take it kindly. Since Joe has no doubt informed him of events, I imagine he's expecting us."

Estella sprang up and held out her hand to Charles Rowan with an air of freedom that led Daphne Basket to reprove her. But the girl's high spirits were irrepressible.

"Follow me," she said gaily, leading him from the room.

She whisked up the stairs, rapping on the door with a quick rat-a-tat-tat. "Here is my dear Roses in his den under the eaves. Once I climbed out his parlor window and onto the roof to see the lightning rods.

"Let's not wait for him to answer." She darted inside, followed by the Static.

"Roses," she told him, "otherwise known as Mr. Edward Hustables Mainwarren and Hustables or Neddie to his friends, is a very fine daguerrotypist and a grand poet who is writing a long epic called *The Multiverse*. And it certainly is, having 144 parts, complete with rhymes and outlandish meters and tornatas and tornados and I don't know what else. Sometimes he calls it *The Myriad*. It tells all about the different-but-similar worlds that he believes populate the universe, or universes, or something like that. He knows things that the rest of us do not."

She led him into the main parlor, where the poet-photographer had been napping on a sofa but was now sitting up and sliding his feet into a pair of needlepoint slippers.

"Roses, I present Mr. Charles Rowan of the Society of Statics, arrived to save me from any unjust accusation and unpleasant bumblings of the Securities."

Estella perched on the sofa and put her arm on her friend's shoulder to stop him from rising.

"You mustn't get up. He is young and fit and capable of grasping your hand without you struggling with a cane. Aren't you, Mr. Rowan?"

At that, Charles came forward and shook hands. The two exchanged a few pleasantries before the old man turned to the girl.

"I'm so sorry for—"

Estella cut him off. "You musn't try to console me, Roses, because I don't need the consoling, as you well know. It was horrible, the way she—but I'm not sorry that she's gone. In fact, I keep forgetting she's dead, because all this freedom keeps washing away the whole idea of mortality. Instead of consolation, I need a repression of gaiety."

"You are right not to grieve too much, child, but it doesn't do to be too free with the Society of Statics, does it? One must have tact and not let go of every thought that flies into the mind." He swept his white hair back from his face. It was a handsome square face, despite a nose that was bulbous and red and pebbled with tiny growths. "I am happy to meet you, Mr. Rowan, and I should be very glad to think that you would help my Estella. She is kind and long-suffering, two qualities that ought to win friends but often don't."

"And I am quite willing to think well of Miss Hightower," the Static man said. "Indeed," he added, "I can see that one must fight against the tendency. Though she can sit quietly on a chair when it is needed, she has a store of good cheer and gusto, despite her imprisonment in this house."

"You cannot praise her enough for me. She is a wonder, a zephyr of springtime, and a joy," the old man said, patting her hand. "We never know how sweet youth is until it sails away. But this one is full of life and precious, precious—"

"You are precious, Roses," Estella said. "Mr. Rowan would like to ask you some questions, I suppose, and to see your work. He can't leave without a glimpse. Everyone wants that, don't they?"

"My pictures, you mean," Roses said. "That's what everybody means. But the poem is more important. The greater art."

"Perhaps he will come back to listen some time. We could have an evening with poetry reading and music and a viewing of your photographs, you know. Now we can do what we like." She reached for the bamboo stick that lay on the floor near his feet.

"I would love to hear a recitation of your poetry at some less disastrous time." The Static gave a short bow.

"He rises in my estimation," Roses said, turning to Estella.

"Mine, too."

The old man smiled in answer to her giddy laughter. Clambering onto his feet, he waved the cane toward an alcove of the room where pictures were hung. Estella ran forward and began to light the lamps for him.

"Static is a mystery to us all," Roses said. "My life's work is what we don't see."

Becoming visible as the lamps brightened, swirls and mysterious figures glowed on dark backgrounds. Charles moved from image to image—a pale crowned figure, an ethereal woman, a pair of wings, a shape like entwined leopards dreamed from snow, a figure caught inside a bolt of flame. Many of them were impossible to make out, being shapes vaguely resembling spirals or ladders or flowing cloaks. Among these were scattered several portraits of Estella, with fairy glints of static in her hair. The Statics man examined them closely.

"I've never seen anything like this," he said. "Your daguerrotypes should be better known. This is important work."

"He wants to photograph God," Estella said, linking arms with Roses.

"Terrible impertinence of me," the old man murmured. "I do hope it will be forgiven."

"Did you make a picture today? I'm curious." Charles took a pair of spectacles out of his pocket and put them on, leaning over a table to examine a stream of static more closely.

"Yes. It's in my workroom. I believe the image may be an angel, holding something. Perhaps a banner. But taken at dawn, long before the demise of Mary Furey."

"The Angel of Death," Estella suggested. "Maybe he was coming for her."

"Who can tell? I've never tried to make my pictures explain what they mean. They are what they are. I've never seen any of these things with my own eyes. They emerge from the static. Most of the time, there's nothing on the plate. Then I go photograph rich society ladies and gentlemen, so that they can support my habits and curiosity."

"And they do. People crave a Mainwarren portrait," Estella said.

"I would like to see an angel with my own eyes," Roses said, his voice plaintive.

"Perhaps later on. It's not as nice as you imagine."

"Have you seen one, child? And never mentioned such a thing to me?"

"Hush," she said. "You didn't ask. My father fell down in the garden and died. I was only nine, but I remember the angel. Wings covered up its face, and there were more wings, like petals: like a peony, only frightening, or a burning cumulus cloud. Maybe I fainted. I recall tumbling into the gold depths of a flower, though that memory can't be right."

"Star of my heart," the old man whispered.

Charles had pulled up a chair and was taking notes on a pad, his gaze ranging from picture to picture.

"Perhaps you could come talk to the Society," he said, "and bring a selection of your daguerrotypes."

"I would like that if I were not so infernally old," Roses said.

"Perhaps Miss Hightower can accompany you. I believe that the Society will be interested in her abilities."

The old man tapped his cane against the floor. "That's a capital idea, isn't it? I'd forgotten that she can leave the house now, with the Furioso no more. Can't she? Leave the house, I mean? And come with me?"

"Yes, if I don't have to go to jail for the willful destruction by fire of my crabbed ancient auntie."

"Bosh and static," Roses said. "Your auntie was a regular witch, and witches pop and sizzle, don't they?"

"Perhaps that's what I should say in my report." Mr. Rowan gave them a faint smile.

"Say that there's no one quite like Estella, that she is blameless. Madame my landlady was a Fury in the classical mold. She was fond of tearing people to pieces for her amusement. If not for the child, I would have left this house long ago. Mary Furey's heart was cut from shadow."

"Roses gives me more credit than I deserve," Estella said.

After declining an offer of tea, the visitors left Edward Hustables Mainwarren in sole possession of his attic and retreated to the sitting-room. Attorney Peeblestock and his clerk, Timothy

Buttles, arrived and were sequestered for some time with the Statics man. Next the attorney closeted himself with Estella, though everyone already knew that The Towers belonged to her. Still, there was a question of a new guardian because she had not yet reached the age of majority—unless she married, which would change things considerably. Estella reminded the attorney that she couldn't possibly marry because until today she had not spoken to a man other than himself, the clerk, and her beloved Roses in almost ten years. Attorney Peeblestock pointed out that she was the only person to benefit from the death of her great-aunt and asked whether she had thought of that niggling matter. Wasn't she the prime suspect in such a case? Indeed, the old woman had tried to harry a portion of her great-niece's inheritance out of him only that morning, a bothersome fact that he did not want to confess to the investigator.

"I tell you that you are Mr. Rowan's main concern, and you just gleam with pleasure, as though it were a game." Attorney Peeblestock waggled an extraordinarily long finger at her.

The lawyer despaired of making her understand the situation, advised her to think carefully about her guardianship and consult him on the morrow, kissed her forehead—a musty, papery sort of kiss that must have been prisoned in a law book for many years before it was used—and took his leave, Timothy Buttles in tow. The Peeblestock steam car had been whistling at the door for an hour, while small children gathered to admire its arabesque lightning rods and chains. Joe Tinker stood foremost among them, having been given three pennies by the attorney with the binding oral agreement that he was to protect the blue enamel from all comers. He strutted up and down the walk, shouting orders.

Prime suspect. The words echoed in Estella's thoughts.

Charles was seated beside a table, reading his notes.

If it is not an accident, she thought. *Surely it was an accident! Yet what if someone had done this thing to the terrible old woman.*

"You don't think that somebody," she began.

When he looked at her over the tops of his glasses, she discovered that his eyes were hazel.

She plucked at a thread on the frayed gown. "Who?"

He had gone back to writing on the edge of his notes.

"I don't believe it," she said softly. "Daphne is good. The others had no motive at all. And Roses lives in another world."

His pen stopped.

"If you want to do something useful, why don't you find Joe?"

When she returned with the ice sweep, Charles Rowan was using the microscope once more.

"Found anything, mister?"

"Interesting things, Joe Tinker, but nothing conclusive." He smiled at the boy, and then cleaned the metal-rimmed glasses on a handkerchief and put them on again.

"I thought you would just see it. Dream, maybe. That's what the sweeps say about the Statics men."

"Often I have a glimpse but don't quite trust it. Maybe something's not quite clear, or maybe it's something that I'd like to see—to have my way. Then I have to rely on analysis, you see? On my brain."

"Don't seeings come from brains?"

"In part. I don't quite know the answer to that one. How about if I ask you some questions? You won't like all of them, but just answer them anyway. Questions have to be asked."

They came quickly.

"Was there anything strange about Miss Hightower this morning, or about Mary Furey?"

This Joe found to be a ridiculous question. Any day when an old lady burned to a frizzle was bound to throw people off-kilter.

"Did you ever hear raised voices?"

"All the time, guv."

"Does Miss Basket commonly go about in that shawl?"

"What shawl?"

"Do you ever help Mr. Mainwarren with his workroom or the closet where chemicals are kept? Did you smell anything odd in the sitting room?" The Static seemed detached, as if not entirely interested in the replies to any of these questions.

"Why did the boiler go off?" He had taken a quick look at the furnace and found it in excellent shape.

"Was he unusually sleepy this morning? Did he have anything to drink the night before, and who had given it to him?"

Estella sat listening on the settee. She was surprised that he hadn't sent her away. Was this part of his method? Did he want her to be afraid? She was a bit frightened, wondering whether he imagined that she could be a murderer. She had thought he would know, as she knew what she needed to know from looking into his face.

Daphne Basket came in with a fresh pot of tea.

"You have a streak of wax on your paisley shawl," Charles told her.

"Oh," she said, twisting to look. "Isn't that too bad? Candles are a dirty business."

"Who bought the old lady her clothes?"

"I did whenever she ordered me to. But she didn't buy much. Very set on a new mackinaw each fall, she was. But it's my considered belief that most of her clothes were never removed. Never! The mistress might add a layer of wool over silk, or silk over wool. She couldn't bear anything but warmth, and kept us all too hot for any comfort."

"You got along?"

"We were as different as iron and steam. In many ways, we were enemies." She worked the wax on the shawl between her fingers, breaking it up into fine pieces. "Awful old crone, sending a girl out in storms to pick greens in the lower garden and hoping she would be killed. Ma Furey prevented Estella from going into the street to find friends near her own age. The child was penned in her room for days at a time. Poor thing, sometimes she burned like a star trapped in a box."

Charles twiddled the pencil between his fingers. "Eliza said something about her mistress being 'electric.' I thought it a curious description."

"Eliza's a sharper knife than I thought. Because that's true. Mary Furey snapped with electricity. She had pent-up rage against anyone young."

"I gather that she was obsessed with the static. Why? Pity there's no use for it," he said.

"Oh, but she had use, old Ma Furey the Traveler. You know what that means, the Traveler? The family has a tinge of gypsy blood. In her, it came out strongly. I don't have anything against gypsies, but she made me uneasy from the start. She crackled when she walked. I've seen her wearing static stars like rings and speaking the syllables of static on her dry leaf of a tongue. Who else was hit five times by lightning and lived to tell of shapes climbing the rungs of fire?"

"Five times! I've heard of such things, and that people who are prone to being lightning-struck have to take shelter in rooms without windows."

"It's as sure as static. Though I just imagine that the figures she saw were not on the side of daylight. Lucifer riding the lightning was more her style."

The thought came to Estella that Daphne Basket might be as bad as Ma Furey about holding her too tight, even though she had loved her governess and never Ma Furey. Hadn't she been abetting the witch these past few years? The two of them were afraid of any man who came strutting down the street with a cocked set to his hat. Abruptly Estella decided to ask Attorney Peeblestock to act as her guardian.

Daphne could not keep her from her freedom! She lacked the ferocity of the old woman.

Ma Furey had been a Traveler.

But she, Estella, was the Raveler.

If the world had to be raveled in order to be made over to her heart's desire, she would do it. If not one stone of The Towers could be left on another in order for Estella to live a different and larger life, she would disassemble the house with her bare hands, though she loved the place—even the tower room where she had stayed awake many nights, watching the static sizzle in the sky.

Her thoughts had gone far inward. She was startled to realize that Daphne Basket and Joe had left and were now returning to the room with clothes in their arms—all that was left in Ma Furey's wardrobe.

Charles Rowan shut the cut-off valve to the pipes and opened the window. Dry air pushed into the chamber, crackling in the folds of the curtains and setting stars on the heavy cords and tassels that held them. Alternating layers of silk and wool, he stacked the garments on an upholstered rocker, putting Ma Furey's second-best mackinaw with the paraffin against moisture on the very top. The old woman had always hated the rain and snow, Estella remembered, feeling something almost like sorrow. Wasn't every death the end of some precious twig on the tree of life or some possibility of straightening what had gone bent? Ma Furey was a crooked branch.

Estella poured another cup of tea, sipping as she let in the something-like-grief and watched Charles Rowan gently rub the layers of wool and silk together in the starry air until the cloth cracked with static and a small plume of smoke licked at the paraffin on the mackinaw.

Quickly he scattered the garments and turned the silver flutes back on. They sang, full-throated and pulsing with steam.

He told Joe Tinker to hurry and feed the boiler with ice. Daphne Basket was sent for a bowl of water and an atomiser.

Now he paced the disordered room, his glance going to the velvety smudge on the floor, his scattered papers, and last of all to Estella.

"You believed us," she said.

He stopped and stared at her, unspeaking.

"But there's something uneasy in your face," she went on.

She wondered if the sight could not join but only come between them because it flashed into the mind without pity or innocence. Even a man from the Society of Statics might fear it in a woman as he would fear guilt and betrayal.

Perhaps he was not the one she had seen, the love who would grip her fingers on the clackety train that sang under the stars and the static.

Estella drew close to him.

"I am as innocent as it is possible to be and yet be human and possess the sight."

Charles Rowan took her proffered hand.

"Roses says the worlds are fallen, all those that open like a fan endlessly pleated. Maybe in a world at an angle from our own, somebody like me has killed a mad old witch. Or a woman like Daphne has plotted with silk and wool and paraffin. Maybe a Roses has taken a picture of an angel with its wings, all of it from the soles of the feet to the fire around the hair. In some world there may be no static or less than here."

She rushed on, wanting to put an end to his silence and confess everything there could be to confess.

"We never hurt Ma Furey, though she was evil or perhaps only played at evil until we believed. But she did keep me a prisoner and try to catch my dreams, so I sat at the window and imagined another life." Again he didn't speak. She said softly, "Perhaps I am still sitting there, and my dream has soaked up air and color until it seems real."

"No, this is quite real," he said, catching at her hand.

She guessed at some uncertainty in him—the mingled doubt and trust in his own sight that all of them must have, those who were born with it and those few rare ones who received it as a gift after being struck by lightning. Mary Furey had wanted it, but the sight never came.

Though Estella could go anywhere now, she and Charles Rowan wandered downstairs and into the garden where the winter greens grew. To go out the door when she wished: how simple it seemed! Out there were friends she did not yet know and things to do that mattered. The big landscape pipes were beginning to whistle the hour, sending up puffs of cloud. An aura of foretelling was so strong on Estella that the years at her back and the future tangled together until she hardly knew whether the moment was past or passing or a dream of time-to-come, except for the white fire in her bones that said the moment was *now now now*. Lightning sprang from the sky and lit the distant crowns of the mountains. She gave a shivering laugh.

Charles seized hold of her fingers. "Must be forty miles away or more."

The wind lifted a skein of red hair and blew it against her face, bringing tears to her eyes.

"What will you write in your report?"

"Spontaneous combustion due to various factors, some caused by the deceased and others beyond her control but not due to any malicious act."

Estella closed her eyes and glimpsed secrets of times to come. "The air tastes like freedom," she murmured. Stars prickled on her lips as the flutes shrilled and clouds like fresh white peonies blossomed overhead.

SPEED, SPEED THE CABLE

Kage Baker

Resident in California, Kage Baker is the author of the very popular Company *series of time-travel novels, in which the twenty-third century Zeus Corporation quietly ransacks the past of its treasures using an army of immortal once-human cyborgs. The books in the sequence are* In the Garden of Iden, Sky Coyote, Mendoza in Hollywood, The Graveyard Game, The Life of the World To Come, The Children of the Company, The Machine's Child, *and* The Sons of Heaven; *companion collections are* Black Projects, White Knights *and* Gods and Pawns. *One of the Company's key operatives in the Nineteenth Century is Edward Alton Bell-Fairfax, who in this story must safeguard the laying of the trans-Atlantic cable...*

"MY FRIENDS, IT is nothing more nor less than the Tower of Babel come again." The speaker, a benign-looking gentleman with white side-whiskers, watched as his audience took in the statement. "Consider. Vile Man, in his pride, once more seeks to demolish the natural boundaries placed for his benefit by the Almighty. He does not now say, 'I shall build great foundations and ascend through the stars, that the Lord may see I am exceeding great.' No, he says rather: 'Time and Space I shall make as nothing, that my voice may be heard when and where I will!'

"My friends, you know that punishment must be handed down from on high for such sinful ambition. Yet I wonder whether any of you have truly considered the extent of our misfortune, were this Atlantic Cable laid at last!"

Among those listening was a man in his mid-thirties, pleasantly nondescript in appearance. His name was Kendal. The patient observer might study him at length, failing to find anything memorable in his features, save for one singular detail: Kendal's left ear differed slightly in color from his right.

Kendal shifted in his chair, wondering who had written Mr. Hargrove's speech. He'd heard it all before, when the Preventers had first recruited him, but Mr. Hargrove spoke with much more elegance now: how the dear old familiar world of our infancy vanished a little more each year, with each unthinking embrace of the Machine in the service of Industry for the pursuit of Wealth. The dark satanic mills were invoked, the horrors of railway accidents and the carnage of steam boiler explosions. Each was a little foretaste of Hell, a warning from Heaven; and yet, that warning went unheeded!

Kendal suppressed the urge to yawn. He knew that half the men in the room with him were wealthy, sons of men who'd amassed fortunes by embracing the Machine. Their clothing had been woven on steam-driven looms; some of them had come here by rail. Kendal was a poor man's son, but he sat there with the rest of them, nodding solemnly as Hargrove spoke, now and again joining in when one or another of them cried, "Hear! Hear!" with evangelical fervor.

One man cried out that anything that brought them closer to the Americans—vulgar, ignorant, *expectorating* Americans—was a dreadful idea. Another shouted that worse was to come, if the Atlantic Telegraph Company had its way. What of national security? What should happen, if spies were able to transmit vital information to enemy forces instantaneously? What of the captains and crews of packet ships, who might be expected to lose revenues if the Atlantic cable were laid?

An elderly man stood and declared that he had made a study of galvanometers, and knew for a fact that a cable of such length, passing through such a quantity of seawater, would most certainly deliver a monstrous charge from the larger continent to the smaller and incinerate the whole of Britain in the very moment the first transmission was sent.

Whereupon someone pointed out that only Ireland was likely to be incinerated, since the eastern end of the great cable was to be fixed in County Kerry.

"Even so," said the elderly person, with a sniff.

"My friends!" Mr. Hargrove raised his hands. "We are all agreed in what is essential: that this infernal device *must* be prevented. We want only the financial means to guarantee our victory."

Kendal rose to his feet. Removing his hat, he said: "Gentlemen, while I must commend Mr. Dowd for his heroic actions on the eleventh of August last—" a ripple of applause ran through the room as the saboteur smiled and half-rose to acknowledge his compliment "—I feel obliged to point out that next time, it will require more than simply jamming the release brake to sever the cable. My informants have given me to understand that the paying-out machinery has been completely redesigned at the behest of Mr. Bright. It is now self-regulating. What are we to do?"

"Fear not!" Mr. Hargrove beamed at him. "It is true we have suffered setbacks, but so have our opponents. Mr. Cyrus Field may pop up as often as a Jack-in-the-box, bearing fistfuls of cash with which to advance his infernal design, yet we too have friends among the influential and powerful. For all that, gentlemen, we do require your support as well. Please give as generously as you may when the basket comes before you."

A pair of gentlemen solemn as church elders rose and flanked the audience, sending two baskets up and down the rows of seats. This signaled an informal end to the gathering. Kendal duly dropped in a five-pound-note, but remained seated until the room had nearly emptied. When Kendal rose at last, making his way to the front of the room, the astute observer would have noticed something more: for he walked with a slight limp.

"Mr. Perceval!" Mr. Hargrove extended his hand. "How delighted I am to see you again! We had hoped some would remain steadfast, and answer the call once more."

"I confess I was astonished to receive your letter, sir," Kendal replied. "When I heard about the fire in Bridge Street, I assumed the whole enterprise had been given over."

Mr. Hargrove shook his head. "We thought so, too; yet a new friend has stepped forward to lend us his considerable powers of assistance. You'd recognize his name, sir, if I told you what it was, indeed you would. I have never been so confident of success as I am now!"

"Thank God," said Kendal. "I had some hopes of scotching the damned cable on my own, you see. Even made some inquiries about getting into the Gutta Percha factory to spoil it at the source. It won't do; they're a great deal more particular about whom they hire, now."

"Ah, we know," said Mr. Hargrove ruefully. "No matter; we've quite an ingenious ruse to get around that. Our new friend pointed out that the later we wait to strike, the more of his resources the enemy will waste. Sooner or later we must ruin him completely, if we cut him off from his investors."

"Why, what's the ruse?"

Mr. Hargrove looked around, then leaned close to Kendal, lowering his voice. "A simple and effective one. Not only have we got a man aboard the *Agamemnon,* our new friend has supplied us with the funds for a diving-suit, if you please! When the cable ship comes into Galway Bay, our men will be at hand, disguised as Irishmen, in a fishing vessel. They will sail close and pretend to cheer on the *Agamemnon*, but will note carefully where the cable falls. Then one will slip overboard, descend to the cable, and cut it. Simplicity itself!"

"Yet ingenious indeed!" Kendal pumped Mr. Hargrove's hand. "And will it be Mr. Dowd aboard the *Agamemnon* again?"

"No, alas. He departed under a cloud of suspicion last time. It'll be Mr. Cheltenham."

"Ah! But he's a stout fellow too. You will succeed, sir; I feel it in my heart."

They exchanged cordial farewells.

Kendal emerged from a side entrance, climbing stairs to reach the street, entering the Strand quite unseen at that hour of the night. He had not gone above five paces when a hulking shadow detached itself from the greater darkness within a colonnade, following him.

No human ear could have heard as it came up behind Kendal, for it made no sound; yet Kendal turned his head, acknowledging its presence with a nod. The next pool of lamplight revealed the two men walking side by side. Kendal's companion was remarkably tall, with a long broken nose and pale eyes. But for these distinctions he had been as anonymous as Kendal, one more gentleman in evening dress returning from some amusement.

They had reached Whitehall before the tall man spoke, barely moving his lips. "Much good?"

"Oh yes," Kendal whispered. The other nodded, saying nothing more for the duration of their journey, which ended in Craig's Court at their club.

Redking's occupied premises not nearly so imposing as those of the Athenaeum, nor as cheerful as Boodles', having as it did an undistinguished brick frontage. The two gentlemen climbed its steps, nodded to the porter who admitted them, and handed their hats to the waiter who met them within.

"Mr. Greene requests your presence at once, sirs," said the waiter. Kendal cast a longing glance at the dining room, where clinking cutlery suggested some fortunate party was enjoying a late supper. Nevertheless he turned and, with his companion, descended a flight of stairs.

A right turn and then a left took them past a number of undistinguished-looking doors to one bearing a blank brass plate. Kendal heard the drone of a voice within, and recognized the speaker as Mr. Hargrove. Kendal's companion knocked on the door.

"Come in," said a different voice, as Mr. Hargrove's flow of speech went on without interruption.

At a desk within a sparsely furnished study sat a single individual, glaring at the apparatus occupying one corner of the room. It resembled a glass-fronted cabinet, in which could be glimpsed a rotating cylinder. From the cabinet's top protruded a brass trumpet similar to those used by persons hard of hearing. However, it was presently sending out sound, rather than receiving it.

"*...Mr. Cyrus Field may pop up as often as a Jack-in-the-box, bearing fistfuls of cash with which to advance his infernal design, yet we too have our friends among the influential and powerful...*"

"Now, whom do you suppose he means?" said Mr. Greene, turning his glare on Kendal and his companion.

"He never said, sir," said Kendal. They listened to the rest of the conversation. When the voices receded into silence and nothing more was heard but Kendal's recorded footsteps, Greene rose and took the cylinder from the cabinet.

"Not impossible, I shouldn't think," said Greene. "But it should have been unnecessary. That was *your* business, Bell-Fairfax."

Kendal's companion bowed his head in acknowledgment, but said nothing. "He did burn down their headquarters, sir," Kendal protested. "We had every reason to believe we'd rooted them out."

"Clearly they were not sufficiently discouraged." Greene looked meaningfully at Bell-Fairfax. "I expect more drastic measures are called for now."

"Yes, sir," said Bell-Fairfax, in a quiet voice.

"We don't have unlimited resources, man. Have you any idea what it cost to produce enough gyttite for the job? Or what we had to bribe the factory, to have it wound into the cable? Or how much we stand to gain, if the cable is laid? They cannot sabotage our efforts again!"

"No, sir."

Greene returned to his chair, scowling. "So they have a diving suit, have they...? Damn. This wants some planning. The *Agamemnon* sails on the 17th, with its portion of the cable. They're anticipated at Knightstown the 5th, ergo..." He fell silent. Kendal and Bell-Fairfax waited patiently, until Greene seemed to remember they were there.

"Go on, go to your beds. I'll have orders for you later. Must think this through."

"Yes, sir," said Kendal. As they were leaving, Greene called after them:

"Probably have Bulger work with you on this one."

Kendal rolled his eyes, but said only, "Yes, sir." Bell-Fairfax snorted.

Neither man having dined that evening, they spoke to the club's cook before he went off duty and were shortly sitting down to cold chicken and a bottle of hock.

"Thanks for your indulgence," said Kendal. His hands were trembling as he picked up his knife and fork. Hunger weakened him oddly, had done so since the war. He was a former marine, having served aboard the *Arrogant* when Bomarsund was taken. There he lost an ear and his right foot to a bursting Russian shell, and was shipped home, half-deaf and lame, to starve.

One day, as he lay dizzy and sick in an alley, he'd been approached by a kindly-looking man who'd offered him food and a doctor's care, if he'd join something called the Gentlemen's Speculative Society. Kendal would have done anything the man asked, for a chance of healing his suppurating wounds; and so he allowed himself to be carted off to a clean hospital bed, expecting to be visited by some sort of absurd debaters' club.

Instead he had seen doctors, a great many of them, and undergone delightfully painless surgeries that had given him a remarkably lifelike prosthetic foot and reconstructed ear.

To say his hearing had been restored would be an understatement; Kendal had lain there fascinated, listening to conversations of tradesmen three streets away from the hospital. He had listened all the more attentively, therefore, when his benefactor returned.

The Gentlemen's Speculative Society was (as Kendal had been told) merely the modern name for an ancient association of philanthropists who attempted to improve the lot of mankind through scientific invention. The Society owed allegiance to no kings, bent its head to no gods. Many famous men had been members down through the ages since its founding, creating ingenious devices for its agents to use in the great struggle. Universal enlightenment, an end to War, and Paradise on earth were its goals.

Kendal had taken his vows eagerly. The Society had granted him lodging at Redking's Club, its London home; they fed him and clothed him. He was now in every respect their man. If his portion of the great struggle seemed to consist solely of spying for them, transmitting private conversations through the mechanism implanted in his skull, Kendal had only to remember starvation and deafness to restore his sense of gratitude.

He knew nothing of Bell-Fairfax's story, other than that he too was a former Navy man. The two men spoke little as they dined, Bell-Fairfax limiting his remarks to an enthusiastic comment on the wine. The waiter had cleared the cloth and they were rising to go to their respective rooms when Bell-Fairfax said, "Was there anything else said that might have identified this 'new friend' of the Preventers? Any intimation of his name?"

"I did get the impression he's providing them with advice, as well as money. Hargrove used to maunder on at those meetings; usual old Luddite cant. Tonight he made his points much more effectively, as you heard."

"He's hired a writer, I suppose. Pity." Bell-Fairfax shook his head.

"I'll tell you what's a pity, is having to work with Pinny Bulger again," said Kendal crossly. Bell-Fairfax suppressed a smile.

PINWALE BULGER WAS a sailor and professional grotesque. He had taken a faceful of shot at the Battle of Navarino, which had, as he was fond of telling anyone who'd buy him a drink, "spoiled his looks a bit" in that it had destroyed his right eye, cheekbone and ear. Having been discharged, he wandered Portsmouth with a bag over his head, charging a penny for a look at his injuries and tuppence to put the bag back on again.

This paid so well that the representative from the Gentlemen's Speculative Society was hard pressed to persuade Mr. Bulger to submit himself for surgical improvement, though Bulger was willing enough to become an agent when the Society's principles had been explained to him.

Nor need he have worried about losing his livelihood; for the doctors' best efforts, while restoring his hearing and rebuilding his face, had been unable to make him look any less appalling. His prosthetic eye in particular, though affording him vision superior to the undamaged left one, tended to roll and stare unnervingly, and there was an audible shutter click when he took photographs with it.

To conceal this he had developed a repertoire of tics, tongue-clacking and muttering to himself, which also helped disguise his transmissions to the Society when he sent them through the apparatus built into his ear. Muttering to himself had become something of a habit, unfortunately.

"Do-de-do-de-dooo. Hello!" He waved cheerily to an ashen-faced pair of young gentlemen emerging from the Queenstown telegraph office. "Mr. Field and Mr. Bright, ain't it?"

They glanced at him and stopped, startled. "How did you know our names?" asked Field, the American.

"Why, ain't everyone heard of the great cable?" Bulger grinned at them. "I was wondering if you had a berth on that *Agamemnon* for an able-bodied seaman."

Bright, the Englishman, looked him up and down in disbelief. With a brief humorless laugh he replied, "If she puts to sea again. Just at present that is very much undecided, my good man."

"We'll persuade them, never you fear," Field told Bright. His confident expression faded as he regarded Bulger. "Ah... tell you what, sir: I'll bet they'd be grateful on board for someone to help them clean up. The *Agamemnon's* just been through some real bad weather. Now, if you'll excuse us, we have business elsewhere. Why don't you go apply to the captain?"

"Aye aye, yankee doodle," said Bulger with an affable leer, and went tottering away to the *Agamemnon's* berth. Field and Bright watched him go, shuddered, and hurried off to catch a fast boat to London, where they had the formidable task of persuading the Atlantic Cable Company's board of directors not to abandon the entire project after two costly false starts.

Bulger, for his part, went aboard and found the *Agamemnon's* first mate only too glad to hire on someone to help clear several tons of coal out of the saloon, where it had accumulated during the most recent attempt to lay cable during a catastrophic storm. Whistling merrily, Bulger stowed his duffel, grabbed a shovel and was soon hard at work.

"NELL GWYNN USED these tunnels to visit Charles II, you know," remarked Greene, as he led them downward.

"Really." Kendal put a hand to his ear to muffle the echoes of the porter, who went before them with their trunks on a handcar. Bell-Fairfax was obliged to carry his hat and bend nearly double to follow them. They had been descending steadily for the better part of a minute, under vaulted brick arches.

"Oh, yes. Found a few interesting things when we excavated the club's cellars! We cleaned the tunnels out and extended them a bit... Quite useful, and never more so than now. Ah! Here we are, gentlemen."

Kendal heard Bell-Fairfax sigh with relief as they emerged into a vaulted chamber, brightly lit. It looked rather like a railway station, full of bustling men; but they were mechanics, rather than travelers, and the immense thing mounted on a track at one end of the chamber was not a locomotive engine but... Kendal peered at it. A wooden fish? A life-size model of a whale, perhaps, crafted in oak and copper and brass?

Plainly the thing was meant to swim, for its track led down into the mouth of a tunnel, from which came the unmistakable reek of the Thames. "The *Ballena*," said Greene with satisfaction. "Cost us a pretty penny, I can tell you, but she's quite the finest of her kind. Considerable improvement over Bauer's vessels, and rather safer. Ah! And here's the Spaniard. Señor Monturiol! Tell him his passengers have arrived."

This last remark was addressed not to the man himself but to his clerk, who translated the remark. Señor Monturiol, a slightly built gentleman with sea-blue eyes, stepped forward and bowed. He said something to the clerk.

"Señor Monturiol wishes to assure you that the *Ballena* is ready to depart."

"Very good!" said Greene. "Convey that I wish to introduce Mr. Kendal, our communications specialist." Kendal bowed, extending his hand, and Monturiol clasped it briefly as the clerk chattered away.

"And this is our diver, Commander Bell-Fairfax," added Greene. Monturiol looked up at Bell-Fairfax, visibly startled by his height, but he bowed and said something courteous. Bell-Fairfax responded in Spanish, shaking his hand.

"Señor Monturiol is a recent recruit for our continental branch," said Greene. "A self-taught genius. He had the idea, we had the money, and the *Ballena's* the result."

Monturiol said something in fervent tones, at some length. "The señor wishes to express his joy upon discovering a fraternity of brothers who use wealth, not for their own gain or to advance military objectives, but for the benefit of all mankind. He is honored and gratified to have joined your ranks, and to have the opportunity to develop his idea in your service," said the clerk.

"*Very* good," said Greene. "May we go aboard?"

THEY CLIMBED A scaffold to step onto the upper deck, gripping brass handrails. The *Ballena* was the color of a violin, golden oak under thick spar varnish, polished to a glassy shine. Her two fore portholes, set with rock crystal panes, increased her resemblance to a living creature of the sea rather than a vessel. Monturiol led them to a hatch in a snub tower protruding from the top, and, opening it out, indicated that they ought to descend into its interior.

Kendal and Bell-Fairfax climbed down sailorlike, followed awkwardly by Greene, Señor Monturiol and the clerk. Kendal found himself on a narrow walkway that extended the length of the vessel, though his view aft was blocked by a great many brass tanks and apparatus he could not identify. Uniformed engineers paused in their preparations there to stand to attention and salute.

The whole was lit by a pair of glass tubes, filled with some sort of blue-glowing fluid, that snaked along the interior hull at roughly eye-level, held in place by copper brackets quaintly shaped to resemble starfish.

Directly to their left there looked to be a lower hatch, to which Monturiol pointed and said something, then gestured forward. "The airlock for the diver," translated the clerk. "If you gentlemen will proceed to the saloon, you will find it much less crowded."

"By all means," said Bell-Fairfax, who was having to crouch once more. They sidled into the area corresponding to a ship's forecastle and there congregated in a tight knot, as the porter carried in the trunks.

"The saloon. Here are hooks for your hammocks," the clerk translated for Monturiol. "Lockers for your trunks are under the benches. A sanitary convenience is in this cabinet."

"It seems smaller inside than it appeared from the outside," said Kendal. Bell-Fairfax translated his remark, and Monturiol's reply:

"That is because we are double-hulled, for safety."

"You needn't fear suffocation either," said Greene, waving an arm at the machinery aft. "She's got an anaerobic engine—produces oxygen, if you please! As well as driving an auxiliary steam engine to propel her. No need for sailors sweating away in close confines at a tedious cranking mechanism. Oxyhydric lamp running off a hydrogen tank, so as to light her way through the depths. She'll descend a hundred and fifty fathoms with ease, and make twenty knots regardless of the weather. Positively swanned her way through her sea-trials!"

The porter had finished stowing the trunks by this time. With his departure hands were shaken all around; Greene and the clerk departed. Monturiol's valet, Arnau, closed and sealed the hatch. From that moment they were isolated from the world, and could not hear the order for launch; they only felt the jolt as all hands without lent their weight to pushing the *Ballena* down the ramp.

Kendal scrambled to the starboard porthole. He looked down on bowed heads and straining backs for a moment. A lurch, and then the brick walls of the tunnel went sliding past, only to vanish in universal darkness as the *Ballena* entered the water. Her engines churned to life, with a vibration that entered Kendal's spread palms where they pressed her inner hull. He felt a thrill of mingled terror and glee.

Kendal turned from the window. Monturiol and Arnau had gone aft, Monturiol to the helm amidships and Arnau to assist the engineers. Orders were shouted in Spanish; suddenly the black beyond the portholes lit to a dim green. Bathed in the blue light from the illumination tubes, Bell-Fairfax had sat down and was straightening his back at last.

"For God and St. George," he remarked to Kendal, with a wry smile.

* * *

THEY SURFACED WHEN they were well out into the Thames. Monturiol demonstrated the periscope that allowed them to peer above the surface, thereby avoiding collisions with ships. The young moon had long since set, but the periscope had been fitted with a lens that penetrated shadow, lighting the night with an eerie green glow. At half speed, they traveled downriver cautiously.

By dawn they had rounded Margate and caught the gleam of the North Foreland light, winking pale across the water under the brightening sky. The *Ballena* moved out beyond the sands until she swam free in the open ocean. Monturiol gave the order to take her up to top speed then, and she cut through the blue world like a Minié ball from the barrel of a rifle, making for Ireland.

MR. FIELD AND Mr. Bright having faced the investors, and Mr. Field having worked his eloquent miracle of persuasion, they returned to Queenstown and boarded their respective vessels with permission to make one more attempt to lay the cable. Mr. Field steamed away to the mid-Atlantic rendezvous point aboard the *Niagara* on 17 July as agreed, while Mr. Bright went aboard the *Agamemnon,* whose captain insisted on leaving under sail alone and never even made it out of Church Bay until the 18th.

Mr. Bulger had ingratiated himself into a berth by then, since there was still no end of clean-up and repair to be done. It would be a stretch of the truth to say the rest of the crew became used to him, but, preoccupied as they were with catching up with the *Niagara*, they learned to ignore the sight of Bulger shuffling to and fro with a broom, a mop or a bucket of paint.

He had noted one other crew member who sat apart from the other sailors in the mess and was given menial tasks suitable for a landsman. They were on the same watch; accordingly Bulger wobbled up to him and sat, at the evening meal on the fourth day out.

"How-de-do!" He grinned companionably. "I'm Pinny Bulger. What's your name, matey?"

The other looked across at him and blanched. "A-Anthony Cheltenham."

"Is it! Well, ain't that nice. Want some of this here plum duff?"

"No, thank you."

"Sure?" Bulger spooned up a mouthful and made ecstatic noises, rocking himself to and fro. "Oh, it's fearful good! Well, more for me. This your first cruise, is it? Come to sea for your health, eh?"

"I did, yes."

"That's just what I done, when I was a lad," said Bulger. "Made me the man you see today. This is a fine cruise we're having, ain't it?"

"I suppose so."

"And just think what it's in aid of! We'll get into the history books, sure. I been down helping 'em unstick glued-up cable in the cable-holds, so it'll run smooth. That's a sight to see, all them miles of cable coiled up down there!"

"Eleven hundred miles, as I understand," said Cheltenham, looking at him more attentively. "Tell me, do you need any assistance?"

Bulger's right eye rolled madly for a moment, until he brought it to focus on Cheltenham. He thrust his head forward and took a photograph of Cheltenham, chattering his teeth on his spoon to obscure the sound of the lens shutter. "Why d'you ask?"

"I would dearly love to get a look at the cable, you see."

"Why'nt you just take a peep at what's on the forward deck, then? The guards would let you have a nice close squint at it, I'm sure."

"Oh, I've seen that, certainly, but... I should like to see all of it."

"I reckon you would!" Bulger gave a cackling laugh, and elbowed him. "Something to tell the grandkids about, eh?"

"Indeed." Cheltenham managed a friendly smile. "And I'd be happy to accompany you when next you—"

Kendal to Bulger, Kendal to Bulger, are you receiving? Repeat, Bulger, are you receiving? called the silent voice in Bulger's inner ear.

"Aye, aye, receiving! Just a-sitting here having a chat with my shipmate Mr. Cheltenham," said Bulger.

"I beg your pardon?" Cheltenham stared at him.

"I hears voices in my head. Don't mind me, matey; just a little piece of scattershot from

Navarino, what got left in my brains. Always makes me need to go to the water closet, though. Here!" Bulger thrust his helping of duff toward Cheltenham, as he stood up. "You finish it, matey."

He hurried off, crouched over with his hand to his hear, muttering to himself as he went.

Kendal to Bulger! Did you say you'd found Cheltenham?

"Right enough, I did, and him all eager to get down to the cable holds where there ain't no guards to watch him. Hey diddle dido, my son John!" Bulger added, for the benefit of a sailor who passed him. "I reckon you're in range, now?"

We are directly below the Agamemnon. *What's happened? You ought to have been at the rendezvous point by this time!*

"Well, that ain't my doing; Captain Preedy's trying to save coal and ain't firing up the boilers. Ring-a-ding deedle, you ladies of Spain!" Bulger reached the fore cable hoist and scrambled up to the recently rebuilt head, where he dropped his drawers and sat cautiously. "There! Now we got some privacy. But it's the Cheltenham lubber right enough, and up to no good. Any chance Commander Bell-Fairfax can come topside and wring his neck?"

No. Repeat, no. You'll have to deal with him yourself. Take any measures necessary.

"Aye aye, then. Orders is orders. Singing way-hey-hee-hi-ho!" shouted Bulger, as a foretopman slid down a stay within hearing range. "The way we're proceeding, I don't reckon we'll meet up with the *Niagara* before the 29th. You lot got enough air and food and such down there?"

Yes. We are all well.

"Jolly good! Wish I could see aboard. Must be funny, looking out and watching the fishes swim by at eye level. As I was a-walking down Paradise Street—"

KENDAL SIGNED OFF, rubbing his ear with a sigh of irritation, and turned his attention to the porthole once more. He was soothed and endlessly entertained by the blue world, with its steady progression of vistas of kelp forests, open sandy wastes and the occasional sunken wreck. Now and again they came upon fish who darted ahead a while, as though fearful of the chase, before falling back and being overtaken. Once they passed a great gray shark, with its dead black passionless stare, cruising slowly in the opposite direction. Even the occasional silver bubbles, rising from the *Ballena's* passage, were diverting to watch.

Monturiol and Bell-Fairfax had been absorbed in a game of chess, as one of the engineers manned the helm, but gradually set the game aside for conversation. Monturiol was a passionate speaker, undoubtedly eloquent in his own language. Kendal knew enough Spanish to pick out words like *Exploration, Revolution,*

Rationalism, and *Utopian.* Monturiol's blue eyes shone with belief as he spoke.

For his part, Bell-Fairfax answered with nearly evangelical zeal as regarded the Society's objectives. There was a gleam in his pale eyes and a ring to his voice now as he orated on the Society's behalf. The voice got inside one's head, somehow, irresistibly. It made Kendal rather uncomfortable.

"Sandwiches, Señor?" The valet was at his elbow, proffering a tray. Kendal accepted a sandwich and a glass of sauternes. The others broke off their discussion.

"What says our humorous jack tar?" Bell-Fairfax inquired, unfolding his pocket handkerchief to serve as a napkin. Kendal related the substance of their conversation, which Bell-Fairfax then translated for Monturiol's benefit. Monturiol looked horrified and said something emphatic.

"Haven't we enough supplies to get us through after all?" Kendal asked. "I should have thought Greene had planned for delays!"

Bell-Fairfax replied to Monturiol in a conciliatory tone, then answered Kendal: "No. We've enough. He became rather exercised at the prospect of putting me aboard the *Agamemnon,* however."

"You assured him it wouldn't be necessary?" Kendal held out his glass to be refilled.

"Quite." Bell-Fairfax had a sip of wine. "I expect Bulger will be equal to the task."

He set his glass aside and returned his attention to the chessboard. The blue light reflected coldly in his pale eyes.

Bulger lay in his hammock, snoring to feign sleep. He had, that very morning, taken Cheltenham down to the cable-holds, and shown him the three lower decks, each with its vast coil of cable wrapped about a hollow center cone. He had been on his guard then, watching Cheltenham closely to see what he might do. Cheltenham had merely looked around, however, apparently satisfied to note how one got in and out.

But now Bulger heard the rustle of Cheltenham's clothing as he sat up, the barely audible creak as he climbed from his hammock. Bulger opened his prosthetic eye and watched, piercing the darkness as Cheltenham drew something from his sea-chest. Thrusting the object into his pocket, Cheltenham took something else from the sea-chest. A match flared briefly, a moment's glow was quickly concealed; he had lit a shuttered lantern. Cheltenham took it with him as he climbed the companionway, his naked feet making no sound.

Bulger rolled out of his hammock. Reaching into his bolster he drew forth a clasp-knife. Opening it out, he slipped it between his teeth and followed Cheltenham unseen.

He emerged into the galley just in time to see Cheltenham's feet disappearing at the top of the next companionway. He pursued closely and ducked down on the topmost step, for from this vantage point he could see Cheltenham on deck, crouching in the shadows between the capstan and the pen that held the topmost store of cable. The cable was braced there in an immense spool, one end threaded carefully through a loosely fitting hatch cover to the compartments below.

Bulger watched a long moment, as Cheltenham waited for the attention of the deck watch to stray elsewhere. Ten minutes passed before the watchman gave a furtive look around and hurried forward to the head.

Cheltenham scrambled aft to the cable hatch and had it aside in a second, sliding through, dragging it shut above him. Bulger, glancing over his shoulder at the watchman, followed Cheltenham swiftly and silently.

He dropped into darkness, his knife drawn, expecting to grapple with Cheltenham at once. Yet he was alone; he felt nothing but the gutta-percha covering of the coiled cable under his bare toes. He heard the echoing breaths that told him Cheltenham had already gone farther down, into one of the lower holds. Bulger grimaced and rapped his right temple two or three times. The deep-night-vision filter in his prosthetic eye dropped into place at last.

Bulger went at once to the hollow cone around which the cable had been wrapped, that gave access to the next tier below. He put the knife back between his teeth and slid straight through to the orlop-deck. Cheltenham crouched there, atop the mass of coiled cable, in the narrow space below the underside of the deck above. He opened one shutter of his lamp, throwing a narrow beam of light on the cable.

Bulger heard him fumbling in his pocket, as his breaths came shallow and his heartbeat thundered. Cheltenham pulled out a pair of blacksmith's tongs at last, with a sigh of relief. He pulled up a length of cable and applied the tongs to it, pinching to crimp and fracture the cable while leaving no obvious cut in its gutta-percha covering.

Clearly his plan was to so damage the cable that it would easily break when fed through the paying-out apparatus. One break wouldn't set the enterprise back much, but Cheltenham had privacy and hours to work on the whole mass of the cable...

Bulger crawled toward Cheltenham, grinning around the knife. "He'oh!" he said, as the beam from the lantern fell upon his fearful countenance.

Cheltenham saw him and jumped up, screaming. Which is to say, he tried to jump and tried to scream; both were cut short, the one by violent contact with the underside of the deck above and the other by immediate unconsciousness.

Bulger took the knife out of his mouth. "Stroke of luck for me," he told the unconscious saboteur. "Saves me getting blood all over the cable, don't it?"

He hauled Cheltenham up through the tiers, climbing with apelike strength, only pausing at the hatch to assure himself that the watchman was still enthroned forward.

That worthy heard a splash, but as it was accompanied by no shouts he ignored it. When he returned to his post a moment later, he saw Bulger leaning on the rail, peacefully rolling a cigarette.

"Pleasant night, ain't it?" said Bulger.

"BULGER INFORMS ME he has dealt with the saboteur on board," said Kendal, as Arnau brought them tea next morning.

"Capital," said Bell-Fairfax. He was shaving, having propped a pocket mirror on a bulkhead shelf. He glanced over at Monturiol, who was amidships at the periscope. "I shouldn't discuss it with our host, were I you. What else did he say?"

"That they saw the lights of the wire squadron at eight bells in the middle watch, and expect to close with the *Niagara* this morning."

"Very good," said Bell-Fairfax, just as Monturiol said something in an excited tone of voice. Laying aside his razor, Bell-Fairfax joined him amidships. They conversed in Spanish and Monturiol stepped back from the periscope a moment, in order to let Bell-Fairfax look through its lens. Stooping, he did so.

"And there they are, *Niagara* and all," Bell-Fairfax announced. "We're standing off as they rendezvous."

"At last," said Kendal. He accepted one of the ship's biscuits Arnau offered him. "I don't believe I could ever tire of the view, but the close quarters have become a little oppressive. Must be rather worse for you."

"One endures what one must," said Bell-Fairfax, returning to his shaving mirror.

"And in the best of causes, after all. Think what the world will be like, when everyone's connected by cable! Instantaneous transmission of knowledge. Wars ending sooner, if the news of treaties can be sent out the day they're signed."

"It's my hope wars won't start at all," said Bell-Fairfax. "It will be a great deal harder for nations to lie to one another, when their citizens may telegraph the truth to anyone anywhere else in the world."

"Though I suppose we'll use it to make money," Kendal said, gazing out at the depths, which were steadily brightening as the dawn progressed. "Stock fixing, for example. Assuming the gyttite works."

"It works." Bell-Fairfax set down his razor and reached for a towel. "You weren't involved in that business, but I was; and I can tell you that gyttite conducts at virtually the speed of light. One strand hidden in the cable ensures that *we* receive any transmitted information hours before anyone else. The Society profits, the great work goes forward, and mankind continues its advance to the earthly paradise."

"So it does," Kendal agreed hastily.

"Nor is the Society the only beneficiary for the common welfare," Bell-Fairfax continued, tying his tie. "Consider that scholars and scientists on opposite sides of the world will be able to exchange ideas as easily as though they were walking next door to a neighbor's. How much more swiftly must civilization progress, in the time to come!"

"They'll still require translators," said Kendal.

"Not at all," said Bell-Fairfax confidently. "Most professional men speak Latin."

THE BALLENA MOVED in once the cable ships had made fast to each other, hovering at four fathoms in the *Agamemnon's* shadow. The *Niagara* passed one end of her freight of cable to the *Agamemnon*, and the *Agamemnon's* electricians set about splicing it to their end.

"I'm watching 'em," muttered Bulger. "A fine sight it is."

Is the cable connected?

"Almost," said Bulger. "Whang dang dill-oh! It's been spliced together in this big wooden splint. Now they're a-putting the sinkweight on her. Derry diddle dido! And now they're a-lifting her to put her over the side! Huzzay! Oh, bugger."

"What is it?" Kendal demanded, as something hit the water with a splash and shot straight down past the *Ballena*.

The sinkweight broke loose. Derry diddle dee! Powerful lot of cursing going on. Mr. Bright's just a-standing there chewing his fingernails. Somebody's saying it's because they didn't weld no lucky sixpences into the splice.

"Have they lost the cable again?" Kendal felt his heart constrict.

No. They're a-hauling it back aboard, splint and all. Haul on the bowlin, Nancy is me darlin'! Here's a lad with another weight. That'll do the job. Haul on the bowlin, all the way to Liverpool—there! She's fixed up proper. There she goes! Look out down below!

"It's the cable!" cried Kendal. Bell-Fairfax and Monturiol rushed to his side in time to see the cradle that held the main splice dropping through the water, pulled inexorably by its weight of thirty-two-pound shot. The double line of cable sank. Here came a tiny silvery flash dropping with it, close to the portholes.

"Good God," said Bell-Fairfax. "It's a sixpence."

Monturiol shouted in triumph. He embraced them both in turn; Kendal and Bell-Fairfax shook hands, grinning.

Heyho dumpty oh! Mind you, there ain't much cheering going on up here. I reckon they seen this go wrong so often they're afraid to jinx it. Down-a-down-a-down she goes, where she stops—oh. She stops at 216 fathoms. They're doing something, I can't see... lot of shouting back and forth between us and the Yanks... Oh! They was testing the signal. It's coming through. Stand by below there, they're firing up the engines to go about—

Those aboard the *Ballena* could feel the turbulence as the two great ships prepared to steam away from each other. Monturiol ran to the helm and took the *Ballena* to a safe distance as they maneuvered. The *Niagara* set off for Newfoundland, the *Agamemnon* for Ireland, both paying out cable as they went. Four fathoms under the *Agamemnon's* bow coursed the *Ballena,* like a dog trotting before its master.

THERE WAS NOTHING to do now but pace the *Agamemnon* eight hundred nautical miles, until Galway Bay where the next attempt by the Preventers was expected. The crew of the *Ballena* relaxed. Monturiol, who had been at the helm for twenty straight hours, slung up his hammock and climbed in for some well-deserved rest, leaving Arnau at the helm. The engineering crew divided their watch; two slept in their hammocks aft while two observed the dials and gauges, and occasionally made small adjustments to the mechanisms. Bell-Fairfax immersed himself in a copy of Shakespeare's *The Tempest*. Kendal returned to his serene contemplation of the depths.

He had lost track of the passing hours when Kendal beheld small silver fish—sardines, he supposed—shooting toward the *Ballena* from the waters ahead. A moment later something immense and dark loomed into view. Kendal glimpsed an eye. Before he could open his mouth to exclaim, the *Ballena* had been struck with an audible crash and scrape that rocked the vessel.

Kendal was thrown to his knees, Bell-Fairfax flung backward against a bulkhead, and Monturiol startled awake as his hammock pitched wildly. Shouts sounded aft. The *Ballena* heeled over, from the impact they thought. All hands braced themselves and waited for her to right. Instead, she tilted at a sharp angle and rose through the water.

Kendal glimpsed sunlight and sky through the portholes. "They'll see us!" he cried. Arnau meanwhile was struggling at the helm, but the *Ballena* in her present state was proving almost impossible to steer, veering back toward the *Agamemnon*. Bell-Fairfax climbed to his feet and went aft to seize the wheel, lending his strength to Arnau's. Monturiol, frantically attempting to get out of his hammock, fell from it at last. On his hands and knees he scrambled to the starboard porthole and peered out. One of the crew, bending over a gauge, shouted to him in Spanish. He shouted a reply.

"What are they saying?" cried Kendal.

"Three of the exterior ballast weights have gone," Bell-Fairfax answered.

What's going on below, there? They can see you!

"I know! We're in trouble!"

"What?"

"I'm talking to Bulger!"

Bulger, leaning on the rail with the other sailors, watched in horror as the *Ballena* shot along the side of the *Agamemnon*, coming perilously close to the steadily dropping cable. "Damn, that's a big whale! What a great awful whale that is, to be sure!" he announced.

"Surely that's no whale," said Mr. Bright, craning his head to watch as the *Ballena*, with a flash of her rudder, dove again and vanished, just nudging the cable in passing.

"Aye, sir, that's a, er, brown whale! I served aboard whalers forty years, man and boy, and I seen 'em many's a time!"

On board the *Ballena,* meanwhile, Monturiol had got to a chain drive and hauled on it. A metal weight came shuttling forward along a track under the walkway; at once the *Ballena* righted herself. Monturiol threw a lever that filled a ballast tank, and she descended. Arnau stood back, gasping with exertion, as Bell-Fairfax swung the wheel around and put her on course again. Monturiol closed off the valve. He rose to his feet, saying something in a satisfied tone.

"What was that?"

"He said he built this fish to save lives, not to take them," Bell-Fairfax translated. Monturiol smiled wearily and went back to his hammock.

THEREAFTER THEY SPED on through an effortless week, weathering gales that caused the *Agamemnon* above them to labor hard on her way. Once or twice there were difficulties with the cable, but the *Agamemnon's* electricians resolved them easily. Just before dawn on 5th August, Kendal woke with Bulger's voice in his head.

There's Skellig Light. That's Valentia Island, by God. We made it!

Kendal sat up in his hammock. Beyond the portholes he saw only night sea, still thinly illuminated by the *Ballena's* lamp. Bell-Fairfax had risen and pulled on a suit of woolen underwear; he knelt now beside the trunk that held his diving apparatus. Monturiol, at the helm, smiled. "Do you see any sign of the saboteurs?" said Kendal.

"I beg your pardon? Oh," said Bell-Fairfax.

No sign of 'em yet... only, there's small craft over to port. Let me get my long-distance lens up... A dull thudding sound transmitted to Kendal. *Ah! She's a little steam launch. Looks like a crew of three. She's making for us.*

"Keep watching her, then." Kendal climbed from his hammock and assisted Bell-Fairfax into the immense canvas diving suit. There were innumerable straps to fasten and weights to attach. Bell-Fairfax's face was white and set; Kendal wondered if he was afraid. By the time Kendal had lifted the bronze helmet into place and fastened the screws that fixed it to the suit's breastplate, morning blue was visible through the portholes.

We're dead on for the strait between Valentia and Beginish islands. And here's the launch, coming up hard to port!

How many? Bell-Fairfax spoke through the transmitter in his helmet.

Who's that? Oh. Morning, Commander sir! All I'm seeing now is two... there was three before. They got a tarpaulin spread aft and I reckon he's lying under it. T'other two are all got up as Irishmen. Red fright wigs and such. Pretending to be fishermen, likely. They're grinning and waving, cheering us on. They're marking pretty careful where the cable's falling, though.

Bell-Fairfax opened the plate on the front of his helmet and spoke to Monturiol, who nodded and sent the periscope up. He peered into it and evidently spotted the steam launch at once. Calling Arnau to the helm, he came forward to the deck hatch, where he turned a crank. The domed lid of the hatch opened back, like an eyelid over an empty socket, disclosing a round chamber underneath. He stood and gestured to Bell-Fairfax.

Bell-Fairfax removed a long narrow box from the trunk, something like a map-case. Monturiol looked curiously at it as Bell-Fairfax lowered himself into the diving chamber, but he asked no questions; merely knelt to make the several connections for the tether and air lines.

We're past 'em now, and they've come right up in our wake and dropped a buoy! Sly-like, pretending to be casting nets. Ah! Here's the third bastard after all, sitting up. He's in diving gear. He's got something in his hand. Looks like a pair of hedge-clippers. There he goes, over the side!

Monturiol cranked the hatch back into place. It sealed with an audible hiss. He turned another crank, and the hiss was replaced by a bubbling splash. Bell-Fairfax's lines paid out as he descended. He dropped perhaps five fathoms before they stopped.

"Bell-Fairfax, are you all right?"

Yes. There was a peculiar metallic quality to Bell-Fairfax's voice, as it came over the wall-mounted receiver. *I can see the saboteur. Señor?* He said something in Spanish, and Arnau took the *Ballena* forward slowly. Kendal went to the porthole and saw, just ahead, the line descending from the buoy the saboteurs had laid. Looking up he saw the bottom of the little launch, gently rocking, silhouetted under a bright morning sky, and what must be their diver's lines going down into the depths.

We're dropping anchor now. Look at them crowds, all turned out to welcome us! It's up to you lot now. Best of luck, commander.

Thank you.

Kendal clenched his fists, knowing what must happen next, trying not to imagine it in any detail. When the sudden bubbles came belching up—and some of them seemed to bear a scarlet tinge, that brightened as they broke the surface—he let out his breath and sagged backward. He told himself it was the saboteur's own fault; he told himself that Progress required certain sacrifices.

Bell-Fairfax's voice came crackling over the receiver once more, giving what sounded like an order in Spanish. Arnau obeyed, unthinking, though Monturiol cried "Que? No, no!"

His countermand came too late. The *Ballena* had gone shooting up to the surface, ramming the saboteurs' launch and capsizing it. Kendal, regaining his feet, looked out the porthole and straight into the face of one of the saboteurs, whose eyes were wide with astonishment as he struggled in the depths. Kendal had only a moment to register the absurdity of the man's costume—music-hall Irish, green knee breeches and buckled shoes, and on the surface a pair of red fright wigs floating—before a spear came flashing up from below and pierced the man through.

Monturiol shouted something in tones both horrified and accusatory. There, another cloud of scarlet came drifting by, just visible through the other porthole. Bell-Fairfax, standing on the bottom, had aimed upward and shot both saboteurs as though they were a pair of grouse.

Trailing bubbles through red swirling water, the saboteurs sank from sight. Monturiol cranked away at the winch angrily, as though to haul Bell-Fairfax up before he could do the dead men any further injury. There was a faint thump on the *Ballena's* lower hull, and a moment later Bell-Fairfax sat on the deck beside the diver's hatch, laying his chambered spear gun aside. Kendal worked the screws and got the helmet off.

At once Monturiol unleashed a furious torrent of denunciation. Bell-Fairfax merely sat there, breathing deeply, no expression on his pale weary face. At last he raised his hand.

"Señor, lo hecho, hecho esta," he said dully. "Esta es guerra."

* * *

THE FIRST PUBLIC message was sent from the London company directors to their American cousins, lauding God and observing that Europe and America were now connected by telegraphic communication. It took all of fifteen minutes to transmit. The next message was sent from Queen Victoria to President Buchanan, was rather more effusive, and took sixteen hours to transmit and receive.

On 14 August, a Cunard vessel collided with another passenger ship off Cape Race. The friends and relations of those aboard were unspeakably relieved to learn, in a fraction of the time the news would have traveled without the transatlantic cable, that all lives had been saved.

On the 31st August, the commanding officers of two Canadian garrisons learned, via cable, that the Sepoy Rebellion had been crushed and neither the presences of the 62nd nor 39th Regiments were required in India after all. Her Majesty saved approximately a hundred and fifty thousand pounds in troop transport costs.

An anonymous Yankee wrote a fervent hymn of praise, one of whose verses ran:

Speed, speed the cable: let it run
A loving girdle round the earth,
Till all the nations 'neath the sun
Shall be as brothers of one hearth.

"PITY ABOUT SEÑOR Monturiol," said Kendal. They were sitting over a decanter of port at

Redking's. Bell-Fairfax, who was lighting a cigar, shrugged.

"Yes, shame. Dr. Nennys tried to dissuade him from resigning, but to no avail."

"You won't be required to—?"

"Hm? No, no, he took the vow of silence. And, you know, he approves of our goals overall; he's simply unable to reconcile himself with our methods. I admire a man with a conscience."

"I hope we're keeping the *Ballena*." Kendal swirled his port in its glass.

"We are. We paid for it. I understand he's got another one half-built in Barcelona. He won't have our money any longer, but so it goes. How have the Preventers taken defeat?"

"Cheltenham and the others have been declared martyrs, naturally. Oh, and I found out the name of their new patron, by the way. He wrote them a fine fiery speech, exhorting them not to give up."

"Rather irresponsible of him." Edward sighed, exhaling smoke through his nostrils. "I suppose the usual arrangements will be necessary?"

"Well, that's the thing, you see—" Kendal broke off, startled, for Greene had appeared in the doorway like an apparition of doom. He strode to them, clenching a yellow dispatch-sheet in his fist.

"The damned cable's dead," he said. Kendal leapt to his feet.

"Sir, on my honor, the Preventers couldn't—"

"They didn't. Some idiot of an electrician tried to boost the signal and sent two thousand volts through the cable. Burned out everything. Even our gyttite strand."

Bell-Fairfax closed his eyes and swore quietly. "Well, we'll try again," Kendal stammered.

"Not for some time. Our usual informants advised us this morning that there won't be another attempt until 1865. The Americans are going into a civil war, apparently. Freeing their blacks."

"Really?" Bell-Fairfax opened his eyes. "That's something, anyway."

"It's more complicated than you'd suppose," said Greene bitterly. "Everything is. You may be sure your Preventers will take this as a sign from God, Kendal. Pay a call on their new money man and put the wind up him, do you understand? Take Bell-Fairfax with you."

THE GENTLEMAN WAS angry. His domestic situation was inescapable misery, and the only manner in which he might let off intolerable pressure was by walking as far and as fast as he might. It was past midnight, but London was unseasonably warm for November, and he was on his fifth circumnavigation of Gordon Square when they caught up with him.

He never heard the other gentlemen coming up behind; they seemed to materialize, one on either side of him. He glanced at the man to his left, then at the one to his right; he had to tilt his head back. He made an incredulous sound.

"Good evening, sir," said Bell-Fairfax, as they walked along. "May we have a few private words?"

"As many as you like," the man snapped.

"May I say, first, how much we admire your work? Your efforts on behalf of the poor are laudable. Justice, charity, compassion, reform, have all found a powerful champion in your pen, sir."

"True," said Kendal.

"Therefore it pains us to discover you have lent your considerable talents to the destruction of a device certain to improve the lot of mankind."

"I beg your pardon?" said the man, and then gave Bell-Fairfax a sharp look. "Ah. I see. Well! Let me ask you this, gentlemen: have you ever labored with your hands?"

"We have, sir."

"And were you paid for your labors?"

"Yes, sir."

"The fellow who earns his bread making chairs, do you believe *he* ought to be paid when citizens furnish their homes with his work?"

"Unquestionably, sir."

"The cobbler ought to be paid for every pair of boots that leave *his* shop, then?" The man's eyes flashed with anger. He seemed relieved to have someone with whom to argue. "Therefore—ought not the writer receive payment for the entertainment he provides?"

"And you do, sir."

"Not in America," said the man. "No. In the Home of Liberty, any publisher is at liberty to pick my pocket, sir, without respect of copyright. I'm told my novels are popular, read by thousands who enjoy them in American editions for which I have received not one farthing in royalties. I complained to the American authorities, if they can be described as such; I was insulted, and my character defamed in their press, for my pains!

"And are our own politicians interested in my welfare? No. Literature does nothing to get them into Parliament, and therefore they choose to do nothing on the literary man's behalf.

"My ideas change the world for the better—you yourself said so. Why then am I, their author, not accorded the legal protection an artisan enjoys? And what of American writers? How can they persuade American publishers to buy their efforts at fair prices, when the stolen works of British writers are available free of charge?

"And now the industrialists seek to break down the barriers of time and distance between nations. I tell you that there is no invention so nobly conceived, that some base rascal will not find a way to corrupt it to his own ends! When a man's property may be transmitted instantaneously to a foreign shore, what laws will protect him?"

"With respect, sir," said Bell-Fairfax patiently, "it would take longer to telegraph the text of one of your novels than it would for a copy to be sent across by packet ship."

"Today," said the man. "But tell me, in good conscience, that it will not be so in twenty years. The telegraph is profitable, it is convenient; the brightest minds of the age will turn their attention to improving its speed and reliability, with no thought of the consequences. And in any case, that is not the point! The work of hands is protected by law; why not then the work of the mind?"

"Sir, you are in some distress, but we must ask you to consider the greater good," said Bell-Fairfax. "The world will progress more surely from barbarism to civilized behavior, if all men may exchange news freely. Copyright laws will adapt, in time. Balance that in the scales, against your lost profit, and bow to the inevitable."

He stopped on the pavement, staring down into the man's eyes as he spoke. The man pulled his gaze away with effort, shivering.

"You're devilishly persuasive, sir," he said sullenly.

"It is our earnest hope that you *can* be persuaded with words, sir," said Bell-Fairfax. "We should be sorry to have to employ any other means."

His pale gaze traveled past the man, into the courtyard before which they had stopped. "This is your home, is it, sir? Yes, I thought so. The one on the end. You live here with your children.

"I do hope you'll reconsider your opinion in this matter. Good evening, Mr. Dickens."

ELEMENTALS

Ian R. MacLeod

The author of poetic, brilliantly characterized novels such as The Summer Isles, The Great Wheel, *and* Song of Time *(the last just out from PS Publishing), Ian R. MacLeod is probably best known for his short stories—collected in* Voyages by Starlight, Breathmoss, *and* Past Magic*—and for his two big, magnificent steampunk fantasies:* The Light Ages *and* The House of Storms. *Those books introduced the concept of Aether, an alternative and corrupting energy source; in the unrelated but similarly resonant story that follows, MacLeod ponders the spirits that stand subliminally behind our actions...*

I CAN'T REMEMBER exactly when it was that my friend James Woolfendon first propounded his theory of elementals. James had an active mind, and an easy way of expressing it. You could always tell when he was there at the club from the crowd which had gathered around him, and from the ring of his high and excitable voice. If it wasn't one theory or idea, it was another. Hypnotism, magnetism, the hollowness of the earth, new varieties of engine governor, the imminence of man-powered flight, and methods of educating orphans—they all came and went. In fact, with James they often swirled together. One day, for example, orphans might be hypnotized. On the next, fallen women placed on the island of Atlantis (once its discovery had been made, which James was sure was imminent). Or perhaps, to save those women from falling, they might be taught to fly instead. So James's theory of elementals, bizarre though it may strike you now, seemed less surprising to us back then.

James embraced what we thought of as the modern in the late days of the last century as happily as anybody. More, in fact. Nothing escaped the searchlight of his enthusiasm. He made studies of the corpses of criminals in Pentonville Morgue. He climbed the Great Fire Monument to take samples of the city air. He designed new treadmills and restraints for the correction of criminal tendencies. He measured the limbs of foetuses. His townhouse in a square off Grafton Street was filled to the brim with so many wonders that people joked that he must employ a permanent roster of removal men to take things out of the back to make room for the things which were coming in the front.

Not that James lived in chaos. Far from it. If there was one thing which characterized James Woolfendon, at the least the James of then, it was tidy precision and impeccable punctuality. Turn up late for one of the afternoon lectures he gave on his theories and discoveries in a small theater he favored off the Strand, and you were likely to receive a withering look and an equally withering put-down. James had no time, as he said often enough, for vagueness or fiddle faddle. If he had a weakness, it was that he had no weakness.

As I've already said, I have no precise recollection of this first mention of his theory of elementals. Mostly likely, it would have swirled up with many other thoughts and suppositions. Equally likely, it would have been at our club, and probably at that time in the evening when things had started to become enjoyably blurred. Most of the usual crowd would have been there, young gentlemen whose fathers or grandfathers had done well out of the coal beneath their estate, or the gypsum quarry they had inherited from a spinster aunt, or a fortunate freehold of land needed for a main railway station, or, like myself, had done well out of the South American trade. But if we were considering anything at all in those gay times, it would have been whether to call for another cigar from the humidor, or perhaps summon a cab to sample the feminine delights to be found in the meaner streets between Drury Lane and Covent Garden.

Elementals, the way James would have put it, were no new discovery. In fact, they were oldest of all possible phenomena. The Sumerians and Egyptians had recorded their existence—had worshipped them and called them gods, just as the savage Hottentot and wild Blackamoor still did. Elementals, James would have exclaimed over our slurring laughter, were genuine physical entities. Not that they were made of a type of matter which was yet generally understood. But he had proof of their existence. Proof—and this is one phrase which I'm sure I do remember—which could bite your finger, or burn your hand.

Relaxed as I and many of my friends would have been, the idea of elementals would have drifted by easily enough. And from there, and however we filled the rest of that particular night, there was less of James Woolfendon to be seen in the next few months. There were no more lectures for us to enjoy at that little theater. There were few, if any, appearances at the club. The man, we decided, when we talked of him at all, must be abominably busy. Perhaps, we joked, the next we would see James Woolfendon, he would be perched sporting a pair of wings on top of Saint Paul's, or navigating the Thames by submarine boat. Inasmuch as we'd ever remembered this theory of elementals at all, we'd soon forgotten about it.

It was a particularly hot summer's afternoon. I remember that exactly. An afternoon so hot that one spent one's time wishing one could climb out of one's own skin and lie somewhere hidden and cool. I was walking back through the flat heat toward my bachelor apartment from a fine lunch with the vague plan of clearing an incipient headache, when I found that my route had led me along Grafton Street. Even then, I didn't immediately think of James, but, passing the entrance to his square, seeing those tall white houses, I had the idea that I could call in to trouble his servants for some quinine and ice. As to James himself, I suppose I half-entertained the idea that he had gone travelling. He'd visited enough strange places in his time. So the idea that he might be at home on that doldrum afternoon, and actively engaged in some project, wasn't uppermost in my mind.

The house was a smart four-storey establishment of the sort which are impossible to obtain nowadays unless you belong to the super-rich set. I'd never paid it much thought, but what I noticed on that sweltering afternoon were signs of surprising neglect. Bits of gutter hung awry. The white plaster was peeling from its walls. The windows were dirty. The curtains were poorly drawn. It didn't strike me as odd at that precise moment that a place might deteriorate so rapidly. But odd it certainly was. And the pavement in front of the place was oddly lumpy, and wires of the sort which were soon to become common throughout the city looped toward the house from an ugly succession of tarred poles. The withering look which a lady of the square gave me as she emerged from her own doorway a few houses on said it all. I was already a little concerned about my friend James Woolfendon when I stepped up to press the bell button. My shock was even greater when it was James himself who opened the door.

"Oh, oh—it's you!" He seemed delighted to see me, even though he was dressed practically as a workman in rolled up sleeves, moleskin trousers and a stained leather apron. His skin was somehow both flushed and pale. If I'd have passed him in the street, I'd have given him a wide berth, and maybe tossed him a few pennies.

"On this hot day, I..." I looked around, and then back at James, rather lost for words "... just happened to be in the neighborhood..."

"Well *here* you are." He nodded, then barked a laugh as if the phrase was the funniest thing he'd heard all day. "Perhaps I can show you what I've been working on?"

The house was dim and it was hotter than Hades. It was hard to make anything out at first. But the smell—the smell was extraordinary. Or rather, smells. Every breath, every movement I made, seemed to bring some odd new savour to my nostrils. The smells weren't exactly bad, most of them, anyway, but neither were they the sort of smells you expected to find in a gentleman's city residence, even if that resident was James Woolfendon. There was coal gas, for a start. And hot metal. And a whole variety of dark and singed smells of a kind which I associated dimly with transformers and telegraphs. And there was a wet smell as well—that sense you get when you stand beside any large body of water. And, as an occasional unpleasant counterpoint, there was an unmistakable whiff of the sewer.

"Come, come," before I could make a quick exit, he'd scooped an arm around my shoulder. "I believe I mentioned this work to you when I last saw you. But things have progressed. Nothing will be the same, not once I have published."

At least there was more light in some of the rooms he led me into, but it gave through dusty windows and rotting lintels onto ever greater chaos. Some sort of explosion seemed to have occurred in his library—such were the numbers of papers and books which lay scattered on every surface and across the floor. Some, I thought, actually seemed to be clinging to the ceiling, fluttering there as if struggling to escape like trapped moths. The next, a bathroom, was so filled with pipes that getting into it would have required the skills of a contortionist. There were endless sounds of hissing, creaking, bubbling, groaning. The whole house was like the pump or engine room of some factory. And there were no servants. No wonder that neighboring lady had given me such a look. It was as if the services which might have lit, powered and watered, and indeed, flushed, most of this city had all been drawn into this one spot.

"How much power do you need?" I shouted to James. "The bills must be huge."

"Huge at the moment," he said, laughing again. "But not for long. Soon, all of this will be self-sustaining. And not long after, every house in this city will be the same." He laughed even louder when he saw my expression. "This is just a work in progress! Everything will be far more compact once I have filed the patents and worked out a more precise method of controlling elementals."

It was his first mention of the word that day, and I still had no real idea what he meant. James took out a spanner from his torn trouser pocket and began to tap and twist and tighten a variety of outlets and inlets. Between dodging thin jets of water, and odd slips and splashes, he told me more about his theory. As much, in many ways, as I would ever know.

"It must be acknowledged that our pre-Christian ancestors worshipped, and feared, a whole variety of lesser powers." He waved his spanner. "You can imagine the sort of thing. Spirits of the wood. Spirits of the fire. Spirits of the beasts we hunted, or who hunted us. Spirits, indeed, of what were then thought of as the four elements. Even when our forefathers started ploughing fields and building homes, and churches, we still maintained many of our old beliefs."

I nodded. That much seemed self-evident. Although, as a cultured and well-educated man, I was less than happy with his use of the word *we*.

"Now..." he waved his spanner. "...you're going to tell me that these are enlightened times. You're going to say that such beliefs have faded, and that no sane or sensible fellow now believes in such things."

"You put my case for me."

"And, indeed, you are right. Especially in this last century. Forests have been felled. Farmsteads abandoned. Even in the matters of the land, science has replaced the old beliefs. And the power of those spirits which stemmed from those beliefs has also faded. But where have they all gone, eh? What do you think's happened to them?"

I laughed. I felt I had to. "If I didn't know you better, James, I'd think you were talking of fairies."

"It's not a term I use, for the reasons of which your expression speaks eloquently. I much prefer elementals." His face was entirely composed.

"Elementals..." I nodded. Part of me was wondering why I had allowed myself to be drawn even this far into the thoughts of someone who was clearly losing touch with reason, although I was also consoling myself that, at the very least, I had an amusing story to be told tonight at the club. But I also had a genuine fondness for James, and he was always a persuasive talker, and perhaps a small part of me already believed.

"If you hear of superstitions now, they're much more likely to be some presence in some sooty workshop or alley in the East End, or a ghostly tram glimpsed at midnight, or a shop bell which sounds when the shop is closed. It makes perfect sense. After all, think of how many of us there are crammed so close together into this metropolis. Think of all the dreams and hopes and delusions and prayers... !

"I've wandered endless streets and back alleys, explored the far corners of factories. Long exposures of photographic plate will sometimes capture a movement, but merely as a faint blur. I've recorded drops in temperature, but only by a half of a degree. I've registered small changes in the potential of charged electric wires. I've tried dustings of flour or iron filings, on which the elementals leave vague disturbances, and of course all the more common methods by which one might trap a thing of more ordinary substance, all of which failed. But then I had a thought. After all, I'd already theorized that elementals arouse spontaneously out of the life and industry of the city—so why not simply create one myself...?"

He trailed off for a moment. He seemed to have achieved whatever it was he'd been trying to do with the leaking pipe, whilst I had so many objections to what he was saying that, when I opened my mouth, all that came out was a gasp.

"I can see," he said, "that you still need proof. And that's understandable—and commendable. Come this way, my friend..." He beckoned toward a low doorway. "...let me show you."

The space beyond led steeply down a dark set of stairs. The heat increased as we descended. I had almost forgotten that my stomach was queasy and my head ached in my amazement since entering the house. But the feeling rushed back to me now.

The space into which James had led me must once have been a large cellar, but this one seemed abnormally large even for so fine a house. Perhaps it had been extended. Or perhaps, the ridiculous thought struck me, his house had been built above some sort of natural grotto. Whatever its origins, it now resembled a cross between a workshop, a factory and a cave. All the buzzings, thumpings and gushings which filled the rooms above met their junction here, where they thudded to some final rhythm like some huge mechanical heart. Iron walkways had been built across some of the deeper spaces, I might almost say chasms, where the thicker pipes crossed and coiled. But there were pipes everywhere. And wires, and pumps, and coiled devices I vaguely associated with the gimmicks I'd seen performed on stage to demonstrate the effects of electricity, and clattering relays which made me think of telegraphs, and hissing mantels of gas flame. I banged my head on conduits, my vision swam, as James led me through and around into a somewhat clearer central space, in the center of which stood a tall gray object. It was rectangular, about three times as high as it was wide, and constructed of wire mesh shaped around a bolted metal frame. If it reminded me of anything at all, it was of a crude birdcage or upright rabbit hutch.

"What on earth's that?" I thought to ask.

"A Faraday cage, named after the great man himself. They've been used for many decades to isolate a subject from exterior influences and fields."

"And what subject would that be?" I peered forward, still half-expecting some bird or animal to be scurrying within.

"Can't you see?" James gave another laugh. It was the sort of sound which you might hear some dying soprano give in the final act of an opera, it was so high and long and fluting. "Don't you *believe*?"

I looked more closely, as one might at a disappointing zoo exhibit. And as I looked, James Woolfendon ducked and prowled amid the hot and hissing interstices which surrounded us, still gleefully talking. And as he talked, I became less and less convinced that the space within the

Faraday cage was totally empty. Churning within the center of it was a *something*. My skin pricked. The hairs on my neck started to rise.

"Ah—you see it now, don't you? More clearly. That seems to be some part of the process of how elementals work. It was just a small thing to me at first. A mere churning ball of energies. Columbus must have felt much the same when he first sighted land."

The thing was so vague that it was hard to discern as a shape at all—more of an idea than a vision, a sooty smudge, a heat shimmer, a blur cast across the eyes in a glimpsed after-image, and I thought at first that it had a bluish tinge. I saw it as a slide of falling darkness defined by dancing sparks.

"You created this, James?"

"If created is the word. And I don't think it is."

The light was coiling more clearly now. But it was no longer blue—or if it was blue, it was the same bluish tinge which you often see close to sunset hovering above this city—a blue which is also edged with gray, and with flecks of sooty black, and with swirls of bilious green, and with edges of fiery yellow. It made you think, as well, of other things. The elemental was a murmur of telegraphs—a clatter of squiggly numbers and half-murmured letters. And it was the roar of furnaces, and the clamour of trams, and the cry of newspaper vendors, and the grind of railway points, and the odour, which caught now in the back of my throat, of a thousand gushing sewers, and a million pouring chimneys. And James, darting and prancing about me like an elemental himself, was still talking.

"Yes, yes! *There* it is. Almost as strong as I've ever seen it. You see now—you see what has happened? Trapped under the streets, crudely contained in wires and cables, within the mechanisms of factories, are endless elements, powers, energies. Imagine, the servant who turns on the gas, or the lover who waits for a telegram... Imagine each time we fill a cup, or pull a plug in a sink... These are rituals, endlessly repeated by millions. These are the presences we believe in so strongly that we generally take them entirely for granted. But we *depend* on them, we *believe* in them, as much as a forester once believed in the powers of the seasons. And with at least as good reason. The elementals are there. They are *here*. They exist. And they can become self-sustaining.

"Of course, the term elementals could in itself be seen as misleading. What I've created here is a vortex of *all* the energies of the city, not just one. I tried at first using gas light, or tap water, or pressurised steam, or surges of electricity alone. Not one of those experiments worked. In fact, I've come to believe that the ancients were wrong when they associated elementals with particular powers, be they fire, water or earth. For elementals are essentially emanations not of one power, but of all of them. See, how it pulses and changes, moment by moment? One minute, you think of a flame, the next of glinting water. But I do feel that the ancients had a method in their beliefs. For what good is untamed power alone? It must be channelled, contained. That, I feel, is why the elementals of old were associated with a particular spring, wood, or field. The reason was purely practical. That way, the water was persuaded to run pure, the fire to burn more strongly, the crops to grow without disease..."

James was in full flight now—whirring and laughing around me. Talking of elementals for trams and elementals for train timetables. Of shop window elementals, and elementals for money. The hot, confined space within the Faraday cage seemed to grow stranger and darker. Now, the shape was becoming clearer to me. So clear, in fact, that I wondered how my previous vision had been so vague. The elemental was a tall thing, roughly human in shape and size, although the sense of swirling movement remained. It was cloaked in light of flickering shades. It had arms, a gaze—a face. Eyes like an ever-changing flame. The thing now struck me as beautiful as it floated there, its falling hair a glitter of light. It smiled and reached forward to me. The hand was thin and pale—it was the most graceful thing I'd ever seen. And, as would any man alive, I reached toward the cage to take hold of it. I would have given anything to touch, to see, to believe.

Then James was helping me up. "Almost fainted there, my friend. I've found it's best avoided, touching the cage. But what did you *see*?"

In my dazed weakness, I found the journey back through the cellar and up into the house even more difficult than the descent had been. Still, it was a relief to be back in the hallway, and an even greater one to lurch out through the front door and escape this pounding, gurgling, stinking place.

Then the good residents of that select square just off Grafton Street had another cause to feel offended as I hunched over the gutters to be copiously sick.

THUS IT TURNED out that the story I'd hoped to tell to my friends at the club wasn't one that could sensibly be told. Was James mad? Had I really seen what I thought I'd seen? Had I, too, been infected by his madness? There were too many questions left unanswered, not least my own somewhat nervous thoughts every time I asked my butler to turn on a light for me, or to run a bath. This city, so populous and busy, seemed strangely changed to me throughout the rest of that summer. The trams rattled by like fairy carriages. The smoke above the chimneys formed angels.

Although I kept quiet, and made no further efforts to visit that square off Grafton Street, I felt an odd sense of pride, you might even say vindication, when it was announced that James Woolfendon would, at long last, being giving another of his famous lectures in that little theater just off Drury Lane. No one else seemed to have any idea what it was about, but there was a consensus that it was of an import which would push Newton, Archimedes and Galileo to the sidelines of scientific thought. And it *was* science—that was what I found reassuring, even though it was nothing more than James had repeatedly said himself.

After several postponements, the lecture finally took place on a Wednesday afternoon in late October. I say afternoon, but the day had been so dark that the carriages swept by with their lamps blazing, but still were only vague presences in the fog. You could get lost on your own street. The city was a changed maze, filled with unrecognisable shapes and half-heard sounds. If there was ever a day for believing in elementals, this was it.

I arrived at the theater early and stood at the side of the aisles to watch as the great and good of curious city society entered coughing and red-eyed. There were writers and professors, journalists and inventors, there were the highly knowledgeable and the merely curious. In those days, the distinctions were not so very great.

The theater that day had absorbed much of the fog itself, along with breath and pipesmoke and all the mixed emanations of humanity. The apparatus which cluttered the stage was already the subject of much surprised comment as people settled into their seats. But it made a kind of sense to me. Theaters, after all, have always drawn considerable amounts of the city's resources, and these had now been formed into a cat's cradle of wires, pipes and pulleys around a tall, sheeted rectangular object at center stage. The surrounding mechanism already thrummed and pulsed. It dripped and gave off odd smells, sharp judders, even small gouts of flame, which caused some members of the audience to gasp or express concerns about its safety.

Prompt as ever, although looking even more ragged and weary, James emerged to loud and expectant cheers.

Pacing the stage, occasionally stumbling over the obstacle course which he had created on it, he talked without script or lectern in that high, passionate voice. More than ever, I was reminded of some diva in an opera. All he needed was a cloak and a mask—and then an orchestra. There were shuffles, nudges and glances. After all, this was a theater. Even when the subject was scientific, people came to such places to be amused. That sheeted shape, meanwhile, stood at center stage like a mute sentinel. Let them doubt, I thought, as James talked in much the same way he had to me that summer of powers and presences and the lost beliefs. Let them snigger. They will soon be amazed.

"I ask you to picture for one moment the household of the future, when the size of these Faraday cages—" he gestured behind "—can be reduced. Once elementals are stabilised, there will no longer be any need for all the external wiring and piping which so clogs up our city. Not only that, but I believe that elementals can be made to multiply and divide. What I bring you, gentlemen, is a new world of infinite energy!"

After that, and much turning of taps and knobs which caused the whole stage to rattle and throb even more loudly than it was already, and then a flourish which was only slightly reduced by the number of pipes which got in his way, James dragged the covering sheet off the Faraday cage. There were gasps. It was a moment which I, for one, had been waiting most of an hour for, not to mention all the time since I'd called in at James's house that summer. People might mutter and sneer—my own dreams might have become clotted with fevers—but here was incontrovertible evidence that elementals were real, and that James Woolfendon was not insane.

The gasps continued. There were cheers and jeers. The harsh lights poured down on a cheaply made metal box of chicken wire surrounded by a crippled snake's nest of pipes.

Apart from a few hanging specks of theater dust, the Faraday cage was empty.

In many senses, James's notoriety after that failed lecture was at least as great as it would have been if his revelation of elementals had turned out to be a success. People, after all, had come to be entertained, and that they had been royally. The initial confusion of that first moment, which was followed by James's own dumbfounded inspection of the Faraday cage, and a rising tide of laughter which seemed to sweep out from the theater and then across all of the city on thick spumes of fog, gave him a far greater fame than his widely verified researches into other less spectacular areas had ever done. He was a feature of penny dreadfuls. He became a subject of an extra verse in popular songs. Anyone with a far-fetched idea was, for a brief time until some other figure to be pilloried came along, likely to be chided for being a James Woolfendon.

As for James himself, as far as I knew, he retreated back to his house, and to his studies, and the sort of obscurity which only comes after a certain kind of short-lived fame. I, meanwhile, listened to all the jokes with ashamed good-humour. I was, of course, quietly grateful that I had never seen fit to mention to my friends what I was still certain I had witnessed on that summer's afternoon. I had no desire to be tarred with the same contempt which had been aimed at James. But it sat oddly with me. Did elementals exist, or did they not? And when, as that particularly foul winter persisted, and fellows would stumble into the club flapping the odorous fog from their cloaks and loudly proclaiming that they had been assaulted by several particularly mischievous elementals on their journey, I would join in with their laughter, but feel a twinge of guilt.

Although my life went on in its normal desultory fashion that winter, my thoughts often returned to James Woolfendon and his bizarre theory. I almost wrote to him. I nearly had one of my servants call with my card. Whilst out walking, my steps would sometimes tend toward Grafton Street, but they never quite got me there. Much though I might have thought of contacting James Woolfendon, a combination of fear and lassitude held me back.

It was an evening late into long winter when everyone else had forgotten about James Woolfendon when, of all things, he finally came to me. I was at my club. You can probably picture the scene. The seven courses of dinner had been predictably fine, and the claret with which we had washed it down had been of a good vintage. I, meanwhile, might have been gazing at the new electric bulbs which had been affixed to the chandeliers, perhaps noticing with my sated gaze how each of the tiny filaments seemed to dance and flicker into tantalising shapes, and how, when a log shifted, the flames of the fire within the vast fireplace would almost form a face. How, indeed, the very air itself and the vapours which came from the dark well of my glass of port all seemed to move and entwine as if nearly alive. But then a card was presented beside me on a silver tray, and I, sleepily half-bored, turned and inspected it. I imagined it to be nothing more than an invitation to some soirée. But the handwriting was far too jagged, the message too abrupt.

I must see you now. JW.

The porter indicated in whispers that the author of the note was waiting in one of the club's private suites.

I don't know how I quite expected to find James. When he presented himself as he often did in my dreams, it was as an undefined shape caught in a theater's floodlights beneath a floating, mask-like face. So it was a relief to find him solid and living, for all that the details of his aspect were undoubtedly odd. In the opulent brightness of that private suite, surrounded by French china, Dutch paintings, Kidderminster carpets and Venetian glass, he looked not so much out of place as somehow *imposed* onto the opulent chair on which he was squirming like a ragged scrapbook cutting. His presence, for all that it was unmistakably vital, seemed to have been pushed through from some other place.

"My friend..." I held out my hand and he half-raised himself to take it. It was a shock to touch him. His skin was both hot and cold, and yet it was neither. The room itself, along with my own sense of being in it, gave a pulse and drew away. "...I'm glad to find you back amongst..." I stopped. It hardly seemed appropriate to say *the land of the living* when he plainly wasn't dead.

The sense of urgency and excitement which had always been part of him, and which had been so obvious last summer and at the theater had, if anything, increased.

"I'm so sorry that things didn't go well for you that afternoon at the theater," I muttered. "Still, these things happen, and Newton and Galileo... well, I'm sure they both had their problems. Ideas are slippery things, aren't they? They come and go like..." I was conscious that I was babbling. "... well, like elementals."

He clapped his hands as he sat down to squirm in his chair. "You've hit the nail on the head."

"Have I?" I felt uneasy. For all that he was an old friend, I had no particular desire to hear someone like James Woolfendon telling me that I was right.

"I realized the truth almost as soon as the lecture had finished. You see, I was just standing on that bare stage and staring at that empty Faraday Cage, when the elemental began to reappear." He laughed. The sound was high as a gull's. "Soon, it was as strong as ever—and I realized the simple truth. It was the very thing I'd been telling you last summer! The power of the elemental's being is governed by the level of belief which surrounds it. Look..."

He burrowed in his pockets, then unfolded what I thought at first was an old handkerchief, but turned out to be a grubby sheet of paper.

"The equation for an elemental's existence is as simple as are all the great calculations—those which govern the turn of the planets and the geometries of this very room. It's purely a matter of putting the square of the level of belief over distance."

I—who had always avoided math lessons at school in favor of extra time at the cricket nets—was hardly equipped to judge the calculation. It did strike me, though, that a supposed means of improving the supply of power and sanitation which relied so strongly on pure belief seemed dubious, even if mathematically expressed. I think I may even have voiced such a thought, but there again James was ahead of me, and telling me that that was exactly *the point*.

"What is required," he went on, "is a process of *solidification*—a means of re-framing the calculation so that b over s squared is always more than one. It's a simple matter of giving the elemental a physical being..."

And so it went. I believe I may have ordered a drink to settle myself. I was braced for some odd request, or even odder revelation, but never in a million years would I have anticipated what came next.

"I'd like you to take me out, my dear friend—out to one of those parts of the city, beyond, I believe, the markets, of which you and the other club fellows are always telling such uproarious tales."

"You're talking about finding *a girl*?" I could scarcely believe that I was having to ask James such a question, but I also felt quietly relieved. In my dazed state, I imagined that this request had come about from the sort of abrupt change of subject of which James was always capable. At least, I thought as I called for my coat, he's putting aside all this dangerous nonsense about elementals and is attempting to discover the traditional pursuits of a gentleman.

THE GUTTERS RIVERED. The overflowing shone. It was pouring rain.

The cab which the porter had organised turned out to be one of the then new-fangled motorized things. It sat outside the club's entrance fussing and clattering and spewing smoke. It would hardly have been my transport of choice, but this was no night to argue. After I'd shouted my instructions to the cabbie through the slide window which admitted to the front, we moved off.

After the great establishments, the banks and the newspapers, the main offices of big businesses, the other clubs, the buildings lowered. Then the streets narrowed. The cab rocked and clattered. It was too late, or too early, for the markets to be open, and the theaters had long closed. The girls who went about their business here—the better, healthier ones, anyway—would have either found themselves a client, or gone home, or would never have come out on a night such as this. There was no illumination here beyond the needling lights of the cab, not gas or candleflame, and I was no longer entirely sure of where the cabbie had taken us, but it was the sort of place which would have seemed dank and dark, even in dry daylight.

"I really don't think," I shouted to James, "that we're going to have any luck this evening. Perhaps if we tried again some other night. Either that, or I believe Madame Suzie's—"

His hand grabbed mine. "There's someone! Look..."

I peered out of the streaming window, not sure at first if he was right, and then not particularly wanting him to be. A thing of rags even more sodden than the dreadful night itself was lying before us in the streaming street. I still wasn't sure whether it was alive, or that it was even human.

"I think she'll do," he said. "In fact, she's perfect."

Perfect for what? But I was certain, as James and I helped the girl—for the thing did seem to be female, and perhaps even young—up from the mud and into the vehicle that my friend's intentions had never been the simple amatory ones I'd so stupidly imagined. The creature just slumped there as the cab moved off, and foul pools of water sloughed off her. She was scarcely there. Her face was a thing of hollows: the mouth, the eyes, the nose. The stink of illness was incredible. She was plainly dying—and a risk of contagion—and I contented myself (although contented is hardly the word) with covering my mouth with a handkerchief, and reasoning that, whatever it was that James had planned for this wretch, the city itself had plans far worse.

The night, our journey, must have proceeded. I certainly awoke next morning in my own bed in my own apartment with the not unfamiliar sensation of not being entirely sure how I had got there. My butler was little help. Neither was my usual restorative breakfast, or the irritation of several letters from tradesmen about unpaid bills. All I was left with was an impression of returning to the better streets of this city burdened with the gray, wet creature we had found. Then, we had surely arrived at James's house. But the stairway into the cellar down which we struggled seemed endless, and my confusion and weakness were great, but the cab driver was with us, and he was huffingly strong. Or perhaps there was some new mechanical device of James's own invention, for I thought I glimpsed a slide of steel and pistons within his cloak and leggings, a sparking grit of oil where there should have been eyes and teeth. Then we were down once again amid a mass of pump engines and pipes which looked capable of powering, lighting and cleansing half of the city. And set in the middle was the Faraday cage, and within that cage, toward which we dragged and carried the girl, was a swirl of darkness.

And then we somehow had the girl propped in it, or rather she was standing now as if borne up by some impossible breeze. Her filthy hair flailed about her. Her drenched robes floated and tore. And James was leaping from pipe to pipe, switch to switch, valve to valve. He was opening every sluice and circuit. It seemed as if the whole cellar, the entire city, came flooding around us. And he was shouting, shrieking about how this could only have happened because of me—because his precious equations required someone who *believed*...

From there, everything faded into a tumbling roar. Somehow, I must have left James's house. Somehow, I must have got myself home. It would all have made so much better sense, I decided as I fiddled queasily with my breakfast and pushed aside the bills, if I had been seriously drunk.

I HEARD NOTHING from James Woolfendon after that strange night, although as spring progressed into summer I found to my surprise that the name of a cousin of his called Chloe Sivorgny—recently arrived from the country and making a name for herself amid the so-called new smart set—was being mentioned at our club.

But who *was* this Chloe Sivorgny? From the occasional glimpses I had of her face in the society photos as I flicked through the Times on my way toward the racing results, and one brief sighting as she emerged amid much hoo-ha and fawning from a carriage outside the Clavendon Hotel, I detected a resemblance to the creature we had rescued from the gutters on that rainy night several months before, for all that the two beings could scarcely have been set further apart in station and apparent wealth. How had James managed such a trick? Was this just a feat of clever dressing, training in deportment and style? A dying gutter-snipe turned into the talk of the season by the action of some strange machine...? Once again, I found that I had the makings of a story too impossible to tell.

I wish I could entertain you now with all the tales about Chloe Sivorgny which were circulating then. About her grace, her wit, her beauty, her deportment—but I was cross with these fawning nincompoops. And I was confused. And I had my own life to lead, or at least to continue drifting pleasantly through—or at least so I told myself. And I didn't want to believe, to be part of James Woolfendon's bizarre equation. And I was essentially incurious by nature, and I had other matters to deal with in my life, which soon became all-consuming.

My father telegrammed to call me back to the family estate. Travelling beyond the city had become an unfamiliar experience for me. I remembered the adventures of my Grand Tour, the lost sense of risk, excitement and discovery—that feeling that the whole world is yours, and simply waiting for you to perform the huge favor of discovering it. But, as I struggled to find the correct platform at Kings Cross, and then the right carriage, the whole experience seemed changed and alien. Even when I'd settled into my seat, I could scarcely believe from the accents, clothes and manners of the people who surrounded me that they, too, were travelling first class. Staring out of the window at the fading city as the train pulled out, I caught the reflection of someone staring back at me through the glass. I started with a yelp, and the other people looked at me. But it was only my own, sadly aged, face.

What had James said about elementals fleeing the countryside for the city? The landscape certainly seemed under-inhabited, a scatter of empty farmhouses, abandoned mills and fallen stone walls. Our estate was in the same sad way. Once, it had been a monument to the South American trade—or at least the money which came from it. Fountains had fountained. Lawns were laid like cool summer sheets. Lakes had glittered like watery jewels. But much of it had been shut down or turned over to grazing and the rest looked as if it had given up the effort.

So did my father. He sat slumped wheezing in an armchair in his dark study, surrounded by an oddly appalling stink. The fire in the grate which his few remaining servants attended was like him; half dead, and muttering and spitting. The desk in the corner, which I had once thought of as a fine thing, a hugely prowed vessel veneered with walnut and ebony which he'd steered through the seas of commerce, was equally diminished. Drifts of papers, telegrams and share statements were piled upon it in sedimentary layers.

"Ah—it's you," he spluttered, although I got no impression that he realized he had summoned me.

"It's a long journey," I told him, "from the city."

"The city?" He still looked puzzled. Then he nodded, his loose jowls quivering. But it wasn't a nod of assent. The tiny sparks of life which still remained in his blurred and rheumy eyes flared. "It's the city that's dragged us to this state. Don't tell *me* about your city..."

He went on like this for some time. What he said is scarcely worthy of recording. You've probably heard it expressed far more eloquently. I had, certainly. At the club, especially, as people disgustedly threw aside the share reports in their newspapers and complained of how the banks had let them down. Or the government. Or the French, or the Belgians. Or your typical working man, who was fundamentally lazy. All I was thinking as I heard this diatribe was that I had delayed far too long in taking a proper interest in the family investments, and that I would see my solicitors as soon as I got back to this city which my father still wheezingly berated, and have the necessary powers of attorney drawn up to enable me to take control of the family affairs, or at least to appoint some competent underling to do so.

"Do you know what our family business really entails?" my father asked me.

I shrugged. "As I always tell people, our interests reside mainly in South America."

"But have you *seen*?"

"I study the share reports," I lied. "But no, I suppose I haven't seen in any literal sense. I mean, these dealings in the sales of materials and produce originate far from our shores. And the Americas are a long way off—savage lands, so I imagine. What is there to see?"

"I think it's time you did..." My father nodded and blinked. I'd never seen someone look so exhausted, or so gray. But at the same time he still held some little power over me, at least until my solicitors made it otherwise, and I was suddenly struck by the terrible idea that he was proposing that I might actually visit South America. The dim room seemed to palpitate. I felt dizzy, and weak.

"It's here somewhere..." My father's hands flickered and his bare scalp shone as he rooted half-blindly amid the litter which surrounded him. Instead of producing the steam ticket for passage aboard some ghastly merchant vessel which I'd been dreading, he lifted up a small box. Even in this filthy room, the thing seemed cheaply made, but he offered it up to me in his trembling hands with all the reverence of a priest raising a chalice.

"Go on. Open it up."

I did so. Expecting—I don't know, some lost family treasure, deeds or jewels or letters of intent. But instead there was just this gray powder, and with it came a terrible stink. It was the smell, I realized now, which had been hanging at the edge of things since I'd entered the room. In fact, since I'd entered the house. It was the sort of smell that, once you've smelled it, never really goes away.

"Go on. Breathe it. Look at it. Touch it. *That's* where all your precious wealth comes from. All the life you've lived, the schools you've been to, the clothes you've worn, the food you've eaten—and all the women, I don't doubt, with whom you've laid. Or it did."

"I don't understand."

"It's guano. Comes from South America by the boatload and we've traded in it for generations. The world's best fertilizer. Things will grow in it to feed all the gaping hungry mouths in your beloved city in a way in which they will grow in nothing else. Dried bat shit—the shit of a particular bat which lives by the million in certain huge caves in Peru. I believe it's quite a sight to see them. The walls and roofs are crawlingly alive. They darken the sky when they come out to their prey each evening. The locals say they bring their own night. And they shit prodigiously, and they've shat for centuries, and the stuff lies across the floors of the caves in mountainous heaps. It's alive, as well, with billions of insects. Fall into it, and you dissolve, you die..."

Even without this unwanted description, the stuff was disgusting. Enough to put you off food, once you knew what it grew on. Enough to put you off business, as well.

"Perhaps you can see, my son, why we've chosen to distance ourselves from our trade. Yet, for all the talk of futures, options and indices, it all comes back to the same thing. Or it did."

I longed to close the box, but somehow couldn't. The guano breathed out at me.

"The guano trade is failing. Shit as they will, the bats cannot produce the stuff as quickly as we need it." My father coughed. The fire crackled.

"What are you telling me?"

"I'm telling you that it's all gone. That it's too late."

Dark things seemed to crawl across the ceiling as the room swayed biliously around me. I shook my head. "It's never too late."

MY FATHER DIED not long after that last interview. Long enough, though, for me to find time to contact my solicitors, and for them to reply that they had received several summons and notices of possession with which, seeing as the old man was clearly no longer competent, I should also be served. Men in bowler hats and cheap cellulose-collared shirts—the sorts of creatures who would once have been sent away with a threat of the police—arrived at the steps of my club. Now, they were meekly admitted. There followed scenes of a kind with which we members were unfortunately starting to become familiar. Things were thrown. Objects broken. Various deities—imaginary or real; I was no longer sure that there was much of a distinction—were cursed.

Without the aid of my solicitors and accountants, and with the resignation of my butler, along with the withdrawal of credit by several shops and suppliers, I was forced to attempt to make arrangements for the old man's funeral almost entirely on my own. Then I had to arrange for his body to be disposed of, seeing as our family chapel had collapsed beyond repair. Despite the early promises of economy which I was given, the then-new process of cremation was costly. All to be given a box of cheaply made wood, filled with a disgusting gray powdery stuff. I cannot say that my father's remains really smelled like the sample of guano which he had shown me, for the smell—rich, ammoniac, inescapable as a rotting facecloth stuffed into your sleeping mouth—seemed to have infused my life already. It was everywhere long before what was left of my father blew over me and lodged itself in every crevice of my flesh and ears and eyes when I attempted to toss his remains into the river from a city bridge.

SUMMER FADED AMID the usual gouts of rain. My apartment wasn't the place it had been; the place seemed dark and under-inhabited. Even my neighbors complained that the rooms stank. My club was no refuge. Like its members, it had gone down in the world. The gypsum business had fallen on the rocks of some obscure new process for the making of cement, the coal deposits beneath the old grand estates were almost exhausted, and the workings had caused the once spectacularly beautiful homes to fall toward ruin, whilst the railway companies had successfully challenged old deeds for various parcels of land. So I was confronted each evening with vistas of rotting velvet and damp stains where the club's roof had leaked in the autumn deluge, with servants confused to the border of senility and with dusty spaces where once-valuable paintings had been sold for far less than they were worth. And all of it had happened so quickly—in fact, impossibly so. I studied my old friends in the dwindling gas light of torn mantles and the flames of cheap, sulphurous coal. Old suits leaked trails of gritty dust, crumbling limbs staggered on walking sticks, faces corroded by gout, too much good living or the clap stared glumly into other faces much like their own. My own skin had grayed even more, and had an odd powdery texture, and—I supposed from the way some people recoiled from me—an even odder smell.

Was I the only one who saw all of this? Was I the only one who understood? The power of this city was a swirling thing, bluely dark and sparklingly capricious. I saw it under railway bridges and in the shadows of the new electric lights which now lined the embankment. I heard its shimmer in the clatter of telegraph relays and the hum of transformers and the tingle of the new telephones. And it was there in people's eyes and in their clothes—the new sort, anyway, the sort who arrived in their new motor vehicles outside bars and clubs which seemed, like them, to have sprung up from nowhere, but yet to have been there forever. Wealth, even of the newest kind, has a sort of permanence. Poverty and ill fortune is temporary as frost.

I wandered the changed streets toward the bizarre new outroots of the city. I saw the fairy towers of the new pumping houses which bore fresh water from some remote man-made lake, the metal forests of the pylons, the spires of the new chemical factories, the steel castles of the gas silos, the ceramic dragons of the sewerage works. And all of it was strange to me, and yet all of it made a kind of sense. I cursed James for his talk of elementals, and I cursed myself all the more for believing in it.

I was no longer the man I was. I had become one of those types of creatures you see often enough in this city, muttering to themselves, bearing some or other kind of stink and wearing ragged once-good clothing, although you make a wide berth as they pass you by. One day, you have a decent living, a fine enough place to live in, prospects so solid they sometimes almost seem a burden. The next, your debtors are foreclosing, your club has been closed to be redeveloped and your apartment has had its locks changed. And you find, when you stumble back out into the street, that Christmas has passed without you noticing, and it's snowing.

White stuff. Falling everywhere. Lying lace on the railings. Stinging like ash on your face. You stumble onwards, and the other people, if people is what they are, pass you by as vague presences, swirls of city dark. But then I glimpsed something—I cannot say it was more solid, but to me it seemed more real. Human in shape, or at least approximately human, and wild and ragged, but seemingly *pushed through* from some deeper space toward which I, too, felt myself falling. Even before I glimpsed the ruined mask of the face which had once belonged to James Woolfendon, I felt a sort of affinity with whatever he'd become. I called out after him or it. I ran. I followed.

So, in pursuit of shadows, I found my steps leading once more toward Grafton Street and then the square off it. Sleek new cars were drawn up in fussing lines outside the finest and whitest of many fine white houses. I had to blink and peer at the place through the wafting blizzard to convince myself that it really was James's old townhouse, and not some illusion of the falling snow. But it was, and some party or gathering was proceeding there—the sort of thing which I would probably have avoided in the old times, but which now seemed filled with an almost unattainable pomp and glamour. I heard laughter and music as I moved closer to the steps like the surge of the greatest of all symphonies. I saw lights blazing at all the windows like those which call dying sailors to their rest. And I felt a near-impossible warmth. I limped toward it all, stumbling up the steps.

There was no sign of James, but there were footmen at the door. Their job was to collect hats and fur coats, shake off umbrellas, and offer the first of many warming cups of punch. No doubt, they were also supposed to keep out undesirables of the type I surely was. But their gaze—as I lunged past a German countess and her paramour who were exclaiming over the sheer *fuss* and *bother* of their journey—seemed to pass through me. And then I was inside.

The reception rooms of my friend's old house were filled with loud voices and even louder clothes. Everything, under the searing blaze of the electric chandeliers which hung like glass suns from the gilded ceiling, seemed newly made—and freshly cut, washed and dyed. Especially the people themselves. And it was so *hot*, as well, although the firegrates were filled with nothing but enormous flame-like arrangements of flowers. Newfangled radiators squatted like ornate iron sea monsters in every corner. I was dripping, I was sweating, I was breathing like some ragged animal, and I surely stank, but no one seemed to even notice my presence. People were talking in the usual clusters which form at these gatherings. The men were grinning widely and the women were tossing their heads back as they laughed. They were all taking drinks and canapés from the passing servants, who seemed oblivious to me as well. In many ways, the whole scene was recognisable, but I no longer fitted. I was the lost piece of some other jigsaw. I was no longer part of it. I wasn't really *there*.

I stumbled back out into the hallway. The door into the library—now, that did seem like a remnant of the old house. I pushed inside through the hotly glittering air. Books no fluttered from the ceiling as they had when I had glimpsed the place on that hot summer's afternoon when I had called in on James. In fact, the whole scene was immensely orderly, and beautifully lit by many electric lanterns and the sheer whiteness of the day which washed in from the garden. There was still no sign of James, but a woman was sitting at the wide desk. She was writing, and surrounded by gifts, wrapping paper, cards.

She looked up, directly at me. She took me in her gaze. It was a pleasant surprise to be seen at last. Then she put down her pen and stood up to move with impeccable grace around the desk across the fine Persian carpet. I knew that this was the famous Chloe Sivorgny. She was so beautiful that I let out an unintended groan. The idea of any resemblance to that creature which James and I had rescued was instantly ridiculous. But I did recognise her nevertheless: she was the vision I'd glimpsed within the Faraday cage on that first afternoon made flesh. Although flesh was scarcely the word.

"And who are you...? No." She paused. A smile played upon her lips. You could tell that she did everything in this same teasing manner. That life for her was all a dance, a play, a game. "You're one of James' old friends."

"What have you done to him—to this place? I'm sure I saw him outside. You know this is his house, don't you. You and your friends have no right to be here."

"I'm sure James is about somewhere. He generally is, although this kind of occasion has never been his metier, as you as a friend will surely realize. As to the house..." she smiled again. "Things change within families and life moves on as I'm sure you're aware. This house belongs to my side of the family now."

Even though my gaze was swimming and my head ached at the wrongness and strangeness of all that I had witnessed, I almost found myself smiling as well. It was almost impossible not to be drawn into this woman's sense that everything was a harmless game. "I know..." I managed to make myself mutter, "I *know* how you were made. You came from the gutters. You came out of the rain."

"You really think so?" She moved toward the tiers of books which rose on either side of the library in leather and gold. Unhesitatingly, she selected a particular volume. There was no doubt, when it fell open, that the page was the one she intended. As she bore it close to me, I found myself wanting to kneel, and holding my breath.

"You will see here that the Sivorgnys go back as a landed family to a deed of grant for services in the crusades. And here..." Her finger traveled down the columns of spinning words. "... you will notice that an ancestor of mine married a certain lady Woolfendon soon after the Reformation. And the association has continued since." She chuckled. The sound was like cool water over mossy rocks. "So you could argue, if you wished, that we Sivorgnys are in fact the senior, more elevated side of our esteemed family. As for our current status, and although I hardly feel comfortable in talking about something so crude as wealth, you see across the page..." The flickering pages made a soft breeze. "...that we owned a large amount of property in a certain village in a valley in Wales. That valley was flooded to provide the water which is needed to quench the ever-rising thirst of this city. From that," with a delicious shrug, she closed the book, "I admit that we have done well."

I gazed at her. The clothes she was wearing were so finely chosen, so appropriate to what she was, that you hardly noticed them as clothes at all. She was all of a piece. It was the same with her face, her manner, her riverine scent, her flowing hair. I was reminded of the statues I'd seen in fountains in Italy, in the way the silk in which she was dressed flowed across her body. But the effect was sheerer and far darker. It was shot through with flares of light.

"You're not human," I heard myself mutter, more in awe than in accusation. "You're an elemental—a thing made of the hopes and dreams of this city."

"Am I?" She had to laugh at that, and I found that I, too, had to suppress a smile. It would hardly be more ridiculous to accuse the finest Derby-winning filly of not being a horse. "Elemental..." Still, she turned the word over as she replaced the book on the shelf and ran her fingers along to another level, and took out a thinner, far dustier and meaner volume. It split open with a wizened cackle. "Is this what you mean?"

There were dark woodcuts and barely legible words on cheaply printed pages inky with damp and neglect. Images of goblin-like creatures squatting over wells, of lumpen things half earth and half flesh wrestling with the moon or the sun. Things of flame and things of scudding air. Sylphs, nymphs, salamanders, gnomes. It was plain to me as I looked down into it that the contents of this book didn't belong in the modern world.

"Do you really believe in such things?"

Looking at her, looking into those blue eyes, I knew that the idea was ridiculous. But still—but still part of me couldn't shed everything which James had once told me, and which I'd felt in my own heart, and witnessed with my own eyes.

"Yes," I muttered. "Yes, I do. But what I didn't realize before—the thing which James never explained to me—is that we're all elementals. Made not just from the stuff of flesh, but also from electricity, water, money, stocks, trading options, land grants, sheer and simple greed... I've seen it happen all my life. The way old friends and acquaintances fall on bad times—how you don't notice them at parties and gatherings any longer, even if they're there. How the chairs where they used to sit at the club lie vacant for a while, and then just seem to fade. And then come the new people, the fresh ones who've made some lucky marriage or inheritance—even those who've fallen into wealth and fame through their own genuine efforts. How they have that new gloss, that special glow... But it's down to what we believe. It's all down to the powers and energies which flow beneath and above us across this city."

Chloe Sivorgny gazed back at me, unblinking and proud. And for a moment, I thought I detected the smallest change about her. A surge of something, a weakening, a rush of chill air. For the pulse of one impossible moment, she almost seemed to fade. But then she shook her head, and I saw that she was taller than I was, and infinitely younger, and more beautiful—and infinitely stronger as well.

"You have," she said, with the smile still on that face of hers as if it had never faded, "the most extraordinary ideas."

Then I heard something crackle. Looking down, I saw that the tattered book which had once recorded those ancient scenes was collapsing in her hands. Not falling apart, but folding in on itself like some impossible parlor puzzle until there was nothing left. Not even a dark smudge. Not even dust.

The library seemed to flee from me, the spines of the books slipping by like the rails on a track until I was standing outside in some empty hallway, unnoticed by the milling crowds who seemed to lie in every other direction but the one in which I found myself. I might have left then. But the house seemed to have changed and grown so vastly that I stumbled along stairways and corridors, uselessly lost.

And then I saw something. It was a shape framed in a tall mirror at the end of a long space of crimson carpeted hall. No wonder, I thought, seeing myself reflected there, that I'd been ignored. I was scarcely there, and scarcely recognisable as human, if that was what I was still. I and my reflection aped each other's movements as we stumbled toward each other. Then, as I reached it, I saw that what I'd imagined to be the frame of a pane of polished glass was a doorway, and that the figure which was emerging from it, weakened though it was, was subtly different from my own.

"Is that you...?" I think James and I both spoke at the same time, and that our fingers reached to touch each other at the same moment. Both met barely nothing, and we jumped back like startled animals. In some other time and place, it would have been enough to make you laugh.

"It *is*, isn't it?"

"My old friend."

We were too faint, too tired, to embrace.

"Everything you said was right," I told him. "Though that's hardly a consolation, is it?"

"No..." if James had still had a proper head, he would probably have shaken it. As it was, he was just a shadowplay of smoke. "You were the only person who ever believed."

"What happens to us now?"

"We continue to fade as we are already fading. Me with my discredited theories, your with your lost South American trade. With it fades what we were, what we did, what we owned. It's not such a bad way to go, is it? And it still fits entirely with my theory. If elementals arise from the energies of life and power which surrounds them, so must they also decay."

Decay was an uncomfortable word. Looking down at myself with what now passed for my sight, I could see the process all too clearly. After all, what had my family been founded upon, of what were we made, if not seething piles of bat shit? And that was me now, a centuries long-rain of shit and piss, a fog of odours and insects and dead things piled in the subterranean dark of some other continent. I would have screamed if I had the strength left in me. But instead, I had what might have been my last thought, my last idea.

"But this is still the house in which you did your experiments—it still has that cellar with the Faraday cage?"

It was less of a doorway now than the entrance to an abandoned cupboard, and the sounds of the party were a million miles away as we squeezed what little was left of ourselves past lumps of old furniture and ruined scullery equipment. Even the steps down, which had never been grand, had deteriorated into a slide of rubble of the sort you might expect to find in some ancient pyramid.

The cellar, or cavern, was still there. But it was a dangerous place, filled with the stink of sewergas and rumblings of suppressed flame. The miles of pipe and wiring had turned in on themselves into a pulse of bared fists knotted around the central Faraday cage amid the damp and cobwebs. Inside it, although almost undiscernibly faint, was a swirl—a presence—the raw stuff of which all elementals are made.

I gestured toward James in a spill of darkening wings. It seemed only right that he should go first.

"No, it must be you," I heard something mutter. "You are the one who believes."

The cage was a dusty, rusty thing. It wheezed like an old gate as I squeezed my thinning being within it. And the elemental aura was feeble. I could barely feel it even though I knew it must be flickering somewhere within me. But beyond the cage, amid all these coiled presences of the city, something moved with a dervish purpose, leaping from spigot to transformer like a wind-blown flame, and the semi-slumbering mechanisms in the cellar shuddered and drew themselves up as new power surged into them—and into me.

I wish I could say that the process was extraordinary, but it wasn't. It felt like nothing more than awakening, like stretching yourself and getting up from your own bed. And it felt like quenching a mild thirst and warming your hands before a fire after a brisk walk. It felt like the most natural thing in the world. I was simply *there.* I was *me.* Now I understood why Chloe Sivorgny had found me so amusing. I amused myself, to think that I could enter her fine library as a thing of stinks and shadows to berate her for not being humanly real. As I stepped from the Faraday cage, I laughed out loud.

"Look at you—it must be working..."

Seemingly only shadows, I glanced around for the source of the voice. "It isn't working," I declared. "It's *worked.*"

"But you understand what to do for me?"

I did. Of course I did. I nodded. I smiled. I looked down at myself. A mirror, perhaps, would have been helpful, but I already knew how fine I looked, and how well this whole city would take to me. I knew it with the kind of certainty which only comes with the utmost self-confidence, that fine certainty of knowing that things are exactly as they should be. The world no longer owed me anything, for whatever I took would already be mine.

Something scuttled toward the Faraday cage. The door wheezed open. Then it closed.

"...now..."

The presence, whatever James was or would become, was growing stronger within it already. Just as I had done, it was gaining substance and power. No longer a ragged mist, but the dawning of a man of the kind this new age would be certain to welcome. A man of exciting prospects. Of new ideas. And one of the ideas was this cellar itself—or at least the mechanism which was contained within it. I could see it strengthening as James Woolfendon himself became more of what he longed to be. No longer a leaky contraption of old pipes and lost workings, but a sleek device, an outpouring of new energies. It thrummed and sheened. And the Faraday cage itself was no longer some rusted bird cage, but a finely shaped device, a beautiful sarcophagus which would house not death but endless life.

In one way, I realized, James had been wrong. He'd talked of some prosaic device to improve the supplies of gas and water in this city when what he'd really been creating was a means of making improved human beings. He was becoming one himself now. Or almost. I could see the fine figure he would soon cut. And I could hear his voice, calmer now, but still beguilingly fluting, and knew that not just I but everyone in this city would listen and believe. And from there, the whole concept of elementals would become the discovery which would reshape everything, and I would soon be surrounded by people who moved as I moved, and felt as I felt. It would be heaven on earth, forever remade. An endless, endless, parade of elementals in their fine houses and gaudy clothes. Elementals who would vie with me for power and influence. Elementals who would compete, and would always succeed.

The way the machine worked was a matter of sheer simplicity to me. Turning it down, stemming the flow of its energies, was easy. But as I did so, there was at first a strange resistance. It wasn't that the wheels, handles and switches had stiffened in being opened, worn and old though they had previously been, but that they wanted, they willed, the creation of the elemental machine which James had formed from them—just as did the thing of shadows which flailed and screamed within the Faraday cage. But soon it was finished, as it had to be. It was as simple as turning off a tap.

The wires loosened. The pipes ceased their thrumming. I was surrounded by nothing more than the same remains of old endeavour and industry which you will happen upon if you dig up any city street. I wished again for that mirror, but decided I did not need it. I brushed a little dust and picked away a small cobweb from the nap of my fine suit. As I prepared to head back up the remains of the stairway to meet the happy throng who I was sure would now welcome me, I already felt renewed, complete.

This, as well, completes my story of James Woolfendon and his theory of elementals—bizarre though I am sure it seems. As you can imagine, my own life has continued well enough. I am married now. I found an heiress to one of the patents of the new steel Bessemer process, and we are lucky enough to be happy in each other's company, as well as being a fine match in our connections and trades. We even have children, and they are bright and alive things as only children can be. As for the return of my own personal wealth and success after the brief period of doubt and decline which I have narrated, and although I find it crass to speak of such things directly, it began easily enough from among the first acquaintances I made at Chloe Sivorgny's winter party. There was a man there, a keen young man of the sort which you will often encounter if you keep the right kind of eye out for them, and he had an idea, a theory, an actual patented invention, which he was sure would bring nothing but wealth and success if only he could find the necessary backing. A backing which I, who understands better than anyone that money accrues around self-belief in the same way in which a pearl forms itself around a speck of grit in the depths of the ocean, was happy to supply. So now, I no longer say that I make my living in the South American trade. What I do instead, or at least employ others to do for me, is finance the new chemical processes by which the nitrogen which the farmers still crave is now provided. The guano trade is so long gone that it is barely remembered at all, but I take some pride in the fact that I am still making my fortunes, just as my dear father did, out of helping crops to grow.

There are many people of new wealth now. People who have made new kinds of living in this new century. People such as my wife who derive their fortunes from the processing of new kinds of metal which I believe are especially good for the machining of guns, and others who make barbed wire, or build battleships in endless competition with the Germans, or who experiment at government subsidy in the manufacture of new types of poison gas. Indeed, this is a fine time to live, and I am blessed to have such lovely children, three boys and a girl, and I rejoice that they may live amid the fruiting of so many new possibilities.

And as to the rest, as to James Woolfendon and his odd theory, that is so far gone, such ancient history, that I wonder how I ever believed. Or at least, I do most of the time. And if sometimes, when I wander the electrically lit embankment after a fine evening at the Palladian building of my new club, and see some odd shadow swirling in a place which the fall of light in this dazzling city does not seem to match, I shake my head and move on. If I believe in elementals at all now, it is the remnants of a belief which I hope the record of these pages will erase, and which I now pass on to you.

MACHINE MAID

Margo Lanagan

Margo Lanagan is probably Australia's finest author of speculative short fiction, as attested by her superb story collections Black Juice, White Time, *and* Red Spikes. *Her latest novel is* Tender Morsels. *In the following tale, she takes us to the Outback in its gritty frontier days, examining the plight of a rancher's wife and her last resort, a servile automaton...*

WE CAME TO Cuttajunga through the goldfields; Mr. Goverman was most eager to show me the sites of his successes.

They were impressive only in being so very unprepossessing. How could such dusty earth, such quantities of it piled up discarded by the road and all up and down the disembowelled hills, have yielded anything of value? How did this devastated place have any connection with the metal of crowns and rings and chains of office, and with the palaces and halls where such things were worn and wielded, on the far side of the globe?

Well, it must, I said to myself, as I stood obediently at the roadside, feeling the dust stain my hems and spoil the shine of my Pattison's shoes. See how much attention is being paid it, by this over-layer of dusty men shoveling, crawling, winching up buckets or baskets of broken rock, or simply standing, at rest from their labours as they watch one of their number return, proof in his carriage and the cut of his coat that they are not toiling here for nothing. There must be something of value here.

"This hill is fairly well dug out," said Mr. Goverman, "And there was only ever wash-gold from ancient watercourses here in any case. 'Tis good for nobody but Chinamen now." And indeed I saw several of the creatures, in their smockish clothing and their umbrella-ish hats, each with his long pigtail, earnestly working at a pile of tailings in the gully that ran by the road.

The town was hardly worthy of the name, it was such a collection of sordid drinking-palaces, fragile houses and luckless miners lounging about the lanes. Bowling alleys there were, and a theater, and stew-houses offering meals for so little, one wondered how the keepers turned a profit. And all blazed and fluttered and showed its patches and cracks in the unrelenting sunlight.

The only woman I saw leaned above the street on a balcony railing that looked set to give way beneath her generous arms. She was dressed with profound tastelessness and she smoked a pipe, as a gypsy or a man would, surveying the street below and having no care that it saw her so clearly. I guessed her to be Mrs. Bawden, there being a painted canvas sign strung between the veranda posts beneath her feet: "MRS. HUBERT BAWDEN/Companions Live and Electric". Her gaze went over us as my husband drew my attention to how far one could see across the wretched diggings from this elevation. I felt as if the creature had raked me into disarray with her nails. *She* would know exactly the humiliations Mr. Goverman had visited on me in the night; she would be smiling to herself at my prim and upright demeanour now, at the thought of what had been pushed at these firm-closed lips while the animal that was my husband pleaded and panted above.

On we went, thank goodness, and soon we were viewing a panorama similar to that of the dug-out hill, only the work here involved larger machinery than the human body. Parties of men trooped in and out of several caverns dug into the hillside, pushing roughly made trucks along rails between the mines and the precarious, thundering houses where the stamping-machines punished the gold from the obdurate quartz. My husband had launched into a disquisition on the geological feature that resulted in this hill's having borne him so much fruit, and if truth be told it gave me some pleasure to imagine the forces he described at their work in their unpeopled age, heaving and pressing, breaking and slicing and finally resting, their uppermost layers washed and smoothed by rains, while the quartz-seam underneath, split away and forced upward from its initial deposition, held secret in its cracks and crevices its gleamless measure of gold.

But we must move on, to reach our new home before dark. The country grew ever more desolate, dry as a whisper and gray, gray under cover of this gray, disorderly forest. Unearthly birds the size of men stalked among the ragged tree-trunks, and others, lurid, shrieking, flocked to the boughs. In places the trees were cut down and their bodies piled into great windrows; set alight, and with an estate's new house rising half-built from the hill or field beyond, they presented a scene more suggestive of devastation by war than of the hopefulness and ambition of a youthful colony.

Cuttajunga when we reached it was not of such uncomfortable newness; Mr. Goverman had bought it from a gentleman pastoralist who had tamed and tended his allotment of this harsh land, but in the end had not loved it enough to be buried in it, and had returned to Sussex to live out his last years. The house had a settled look, and ivy, even, covered the shady side; the garden was a miracle of Home plants watered by an ingenious system of runnels brought up by electric pump from the stream, and the fields on which our fortune grazed in the form of fat black cattle were free of the stumps and wreckage that marked other properties as having so recently been torn from the primeval Bush.

"I hope you will be very happy here," said my husband, handing me down from the sulky.

The smile I returned him felt very wan from within, for now there would be nothing in the way of society or culture to diminish, or to compensate me for, the ghastly rituals of married life, now there would only be Mr. Goverman and me, marooned on this island of wealth and comfort, amid the fields and cattle, bordered on all sides by the tattered wilderness.

Cuttajunga was all as he had described it to me during the long gray miles: the kitchen anchored by its weighty stove and ornamented with shining pans, the orchard and the vegetable garden, which Mr. Goverman immediately set the electric yard-man watering, for they were parched after his short absence. There was a farm manager, Mr. Fredericks, who appeared not to know how to greet and converse with such a foreign creature as a woman, but instead droned to my husband about stock movements and water and feed until I thought he must be some kind of lunatic. The housekeeper, Mrs. Sanford, was a blowsy, bobbing, distractible woman who behaved as if she were accustomed to being slapped or shouted into line rather than reasoned with. The maid, Sarah Poplin, was of the poorest material. "She has some native blood in her," Mr. Goverman told me *sotto voce* when she had flounced away from his introductions. "You will be a marvellously civilising influence on her, I am sure."

"I can but try to be," I murmured. I had been forewarned, by Melbourne matrons as well as by Mr. Goverman himself, of the difficulty of finding and retaining staff, what with the goldfields promising any man or woman an independent fortune, should they happen to kick over the right pebble "up north", or "out west".

The other maid, the mechanical one Mr. Goverman had promised me, lived seated in a little cabinet attached to a charging chamber under the back stairs. Her name was Clarissa—I did not like to call such creatures by real names, but she would not recognise commands without their being prefaced by that combination of guttural and sibilant. She was of unnervingly fine quality, and beautiful with it; except for the rigidity of her face I would say she was undoubtedly more comely than I was. Her eyes were the most realistic I had seen, blue-irised and glossy between thickly lashed lids; her hair sprang dark from her clear brow without the clumping that usually characterises an electric servant's hair; each strand must be set individually. She would have cost a great deal, both to craft and to import from her native France; I had never seen so close a simulacrum of a real person, myself.

Mr. Goverman, seeing how impressed I was, insisted on commanding Clarissa upright and showing me her interior workings. I hardly knew where to rest my eyes as my husband's hands unlaced the automaton's dress behind with such practised motions, but once he had removed the panels from her back and head, the intricate machine-scape that gleamed and whirred within as Clarissa enacted his simple commands so fascinated me that I was able to forget the womanliness of this figure and the maleness of my man as he explained how this impeller drove this shaft to turn this cam and translate into the lifting of Clarissa's heavy, strong arms *this* way, and the bowing of her body *that* way, all the movements smooth, balanced and, again, the subtlest and most realistic I had witnessed in one of these creatures.

"Does she speak, then?" I said, peering into the back of her head.

"No, no," he said. "There is not sufficient room with all her other functions to allow for speaking."

"Why then are her mouth-parts so carefully made?" I moved my own head to allow more window-light into Clarissa's head-workings; the red silk-covered cavity that was the doll's mouth enlivened the brass and steel scenery, and I could discern some system of rings around it, their inner edges clothed with india-rubber, which seemed purpose-built for producing the movements of speech.

"Oh, she once spoke," said my husband. "She once sang. She is adapted from her usage as an entertainer on the Paris stage. I was impressed by the authenticity of her movements. But, alas, my dear, if you are to have your carpets beaten you must forgo her lovely singing."

He fixed her head-panel back into place. "She interests you," he said. "Have I taken an engineer for a wife?" He spoke in an amused tone, but I heard the edge in it of my mother's anxiety, felt the vacancy in my hands where she had snatched away the treatise on artificial movement I had taken from my brother Artie's bookshelf. *So unbecoming, for a girl to know such things.* She clutched the book to herself and looked me up and down as if *I* were some kind of electrically powered creature, and malfunctioning into the bargain. *For your pretty head to be full of... of cog-wheels and machine-oil,* she said disgustedly. *I will find you some more suitable reading.* My husband officiously buttoning the doll-dress; my mother sweeping from the parlor with the fascinating book—I recognised this dreary feeling. As soon as I evinced a budding interest in some area of worldly affairs, people inevitably began working to keep it from blossoming. I was meant to be vapid and colorless like my mother, a silent helpmeet in the shadows of Father and my brothers; I was not to engage with the world myself, but only to witness and encourage the men's engagement, to be a decorative background to it, like the parlor wallpaper, like the draped window against which my mother smiled and sat mute as Father discoursed to our dinner-guests, the window that was obscured by impressive velvet at night, that in daytime prettified the world outside with its cascade of lace foliage.

* * *

I HAD BARELY had time to accustom myself to my new role as mistress of Cuttajunga when Mr. Goverman informed me that he would be absent for a period of weeks, riding the boundaries of his estate and perhaps venturing further up country in the company of his distant neighbor Captain Jollyon and some of that gentleman's stockmen and tamed natives.

"Perhaps you will appreciate my leaving you," he said, the night before he left, as he withdrew himself from me after having completed the marriage act. "You need not endure the crudeness of my touching you, for a little while."

My face was locked aside, stiff as a doll's on the pillow, and my entire body was motionless with revulsion, with humiliation. Still I did feel relief, firstly that he was done, and would not require to emit himself at my face or onto my bosom, and secondly, yes, that the nightmare of our congress would not recur for at least two full weeks and possibly more. I turned from him, and waited—not long—for his breathing to deepen and lengthen into sleep, before I rose to wash the slime of him, the smell of him, from my person.

After the riding-party left, my staff waited a day or two before deserting me. Sarah Poplin disappeared in the night, without a word. The following afternoon, as I was contemplating which of her tasks I should next instruct Mrs. Sanford to take up, that woman came into my parlor and announced that she and Mr. Fredericks had married and now intended to leave my service, Mr. Fredericks to try his luck on the western goldfields. Direct upon her quitting the room, she said, she would be quitting the house for the wider world.

"But Mrs. Sanf—Mrs. Fredericks," I said. "You leave me quite solitary and helpless. Whatever shall I do?"

"You have that machine-woman, at least, I tell myself. She's the strength of two of me."

"But no intelligence," I said. "She cannot accomplish half the tasks you can, with a quarter the subtlety. But you are right, she will never leave me, at least. She will stay out of stupidity, if not loyalty."

At the sound of that awkward word "loyalty" the new Mrs. Fredericks blushed, and soon despite my protestations she was gone, walking off without a backward glance along the western road. Her *inamorata* walked beside her, curved like a wilting grass-stalk over her stout figure, droning who knew what passionate promises into that pitiless ear? The house, meaningless, unattended around me, echoed with the fact that I was not the kind of woman servants felt compelled either to obey or to protect. Not under these conditions, at any rate, so remote from society and opinion.

I stood watching her go, keeping myself motionless rather than striding up and down as I wished to in my distress; should either of them turn, I did not want them to see the state of terror to which they had reduced me.

I was alone. My nearest respectable neighbor was Captain Jollyon's wife, a pretty, native-born chatterer with a house-party of Melbourne friends currently gathered around her, a day's ride from here. I could not abide the thought of throwing myself on the mercies of so inconsequential a person.

And I was not quite alone, was I? I was not quite helpless. I had electric servants—the yard-man and Clarissa. And I had… I pressed my hands to my waist and sat rather heavily in a woven cane chair, heedless for the moment of the afternoon sun shafting in under the veranda roof. I was almost certain by now that I carried Cuttajunga's heir in my womb. All my washing, all my shrinking from my husband's advances, had not been sufficient to stop his seed taking root in me. He had 'covered' me as a stallion covers a mare, and in time I would bring forth a Master Goverman, who would complete my banishment into utter obscurity behind my family of menfolk.

But for now—I straightened in the creaking, ticking chair, focusing again on the two diminishing figures as they flickered along the shade-dappled road between the bowing, bleeding, bark-shedding eucalypt trees—for now, I had Master Goverman tucked away neatly inside me, all his needs met, much as Clarissa's and the yard-man's were by their respective electrification chambers. He required no more action from me than that I merely continue, and sustain His Little Lordship by sustaining my own self.

I did not ride to Captain Jollyon's; I did not take the sulky into the town to send the police after my disloyal servants, or to hire any replacements for them. I decided that I would manage, with Clarissa and the yard-man. I had more than three months' stores; I had a thriving vegetable garden; and I did not long for human company so strongly that stupid company would suffice, or uncivilized. If the truth be told, the more I considered my situation, the greater I felt it suited me, and the more relieved I was to have been abandoned by that sly Poplin girl, by Mr. Droning Fredericks and his resentful-seeming wife. I felt, indeed, that I was well rid of them, that I might enjoy this short season where I prevailed, solitary, in this gigantic landscape, before life and my husband returned, crowding around me, bidding me this way and that, interfering with my body, and my mind, and my reputation, in ways I could neither control nor rebuff.

And so I lived a few days proudly independent, calling my mechanical servants out, the yard-man from his charging shed and Clarissa from her cupboard under the stairs, only when I required them to undertake the more tedious and strenuous tasks of watering, or sweeping, or stirring the copper. And I returned them thence when those were completed; I kept neither of them sitting about the place to give the illusion of a resident population. I was quite comfortable walking from room to empty room, and striding or riding about my husband's empty property unaccompanied.

After several days, despite fully occupying myself as my own housekeeper and chambermaid, I began to feel restless when evening came and it was time to retire to my parlor and occupy myself with ladylike pursuits. Needlework of the decorative kind had always infuriated me; nothing in my new house was sufficiently worn to require mending yet; I had never sung well, or played the piano or the violin as my cousins did and my brother James; I could sketch, but if the choice was between reproducing the drear landscapes I moved in by day, and stretching my heartstrings by recreating remembered scenes of London and the surrounding countryside, I felt disinclined to exercise that talent. My husband had bought me a library, but I found it to contain nothing but fashionable novels, most of which gave me the same sense of irritation, of having my mind and my being confined to meaningless matters, as conversation with that gentleman did, or with women such as Mrs. Jollyon, and it was a great freedom to cease attempting to occupy my time with them.

Then, one afternoon, I set Clarissa to sweeping the paved paths around the house, and I sat myself at a corner of the veranda ready to redirect her when she reached me. I was laboring on a letter to Mother—a daughterly letter, full of lies and optimism, telling the news of my own impending motherhood as if it were wonderful, as if it were ordinary. I looked up from my duties at the automaton as she trundled and swept, thorough and inhumanly regular and pauseless in her sweeping. My disinclination to continue my letter, and the glimpse I had had of Clarissa's workings through the opening of her back combined with the fragmented memory of a diagram I had examined in Artie's treatise—which I had borrowed many times in secret after Mother had forbidden it me, which I had wrestled to understand. In something like a stroke of mental lightning I saw the full chain of causes and effects that produced one movement, her turning from the left side to the right at the limit of her sweeping. I could not have described it; I could not even recall it fully, a moment later. But the flash was sufficient to make me forget my letter, my mother. Intently I watched Clarissa progress down the path, hoping for another such insight. None came, and she reached me, and I turned her with a command to the right so that she would sweep the path down to the hedge, and still I watched her, as dutifully she went on. And then, in the bottom half of my written page, I drew some lines, the shape of one of the cams I had seen, that had something of a duck-bill-like projection from its edge, a length of thin cable coming up to a pulley. The marks were hardly more than traces of idle movements; they were barely identifiable as mechanical parts, but as they streaked and ghosted up out of the paper I knew that I had found myself an occupation for my long and lonely days. It was more purposeless than embroidery; it would produce nothing of beauty;

it would not make me a better daughter, wife or mother, but it would satisfy me utterly.

SHE NEVER FAILED to unnerve me, smiling out in her vague way when I opened the door of the cabinet under the stairs. Her toes would move in her shoes, her fingers splay and crook and enact the last other movements of the lubrication sequence. Her beautiful mouth, too, pursed and stretched and made moues, subtle and unnatural. Un-mouthlike sounds came from behind the india-rubber lips, inside the busy mechanical head. Her ears cupped themselves slightly for the sound of my commands.

"Clarissa: Stand," I would say, and step back to make room for her.

She would bend forward and push herself upright, using her hands on the rim of the cabinet.

"Clarissa: Forward. Two steps," I would command, and she would perform them.

Now I could see the loosened back of the garment, the wheels and workings coming to a stop inside her. I left them visible now, unless I was putting her to work outside, so that I would not have the same troubles over and over, removing the panel from her back. I brought the lamp nearer, my gaze already on the parts I had been mis-drawing in my tiredness at the end of the day before. I would already be absorbed in her labyrinthine structure; even as I followed her to the study I would be checking her insides against the fistful of drawings I had made—the "translations", as I liked to think of them. She was a marvellous thing, which I was intent on reducing to mere mechanics; by the end of my project it would no longer disturb me to lock her away in her cabinet as into a coffin; I would know her seeming aliveness for the illusion it was; I would have diagrammed all the person-ness, all her apparent humanity, out of her. She would unnerve me no longer; I would know her for exactly what she was.

BY THE TIME Mr. Goverman returned home I had discovered much more than I wished to. I made my first unwelcome finding one breathlessly hot afternoon perhaps three days before he arrived, when I had brought Clarissa to the study, commanded her to kneel and opened the back of her head, and was busy drawing what I could see of her mouth-parts behind the chutes and membrane-discs and tuning-forks of her hearing apparatus. Soft gusts of hot wind ventured in through the window from time to time, the gentlest buffetings, which did nothing to refresh me, but only moved my looser hair or vaguely rippled the buttoned edge of Clarissa's gown.

It was frustrating, attempting to draw this mouth. I do not know what exclamation I loosed in my annoyance, but it must have included a guttural and a sibilant at some point and further sounds the doll mistook for a command, for suddenly, smoothly, expensively, she lifted her arms from her sides where she knelt, manipulated her lovely fingers, her beautifully engineered elbow and shoulder joints, and drew her loosened bodice down from her shoulders, so that her bosom, so unbodily and yet so naked-seeming, was exposed to the hot study air. I heard in the momentarily still air the muted clicks and slidings within her head—I saw, indistinctly in the shadows, partly behind other workings, the movements of her mouth readying itself for something.

I rose and stood before her; she remained kneeling, straight-backed and shameless, presenting her shining breasts, gazing without embarrassment or any other emotion at my belly. The seam of her lips glistened a little with exuded oil, and the shiftings in her weighty head ceased.

I crouched before her awful readiness. I knew how tall my husband was; I knew what this doll was about. Like one girl confiding in another, like a tiny child in play with its mother or nurse, I reached out and touched Clarissa's lower lip. It yielded—not exactly as if it welcomed my touch and expectations, but with a bland absence of resistance, an emotionless acceptance that I knew I could not muster in my own marriage-bed.

I pushed my forefinger against the meeting-place of the automaton's lips. They gave, a little; they allowed my fingertip to push them apart. Slowly my finger sank in, touching the porcelain teeth. They too moved aside, following pad and joint of my finger as if learning its shape as it intruded.

Her tongue—what cloth was it, so slippery smooth? And how so wet? I pulled out my finger and rubbed the wetness with my thumb; it was a clear kind of oil or gel; I could not quite say what it was. It smelled of nothing, not perfumed, not bodily, not as machine-oil should. It must be very refined.

I put the finger back in, all the way to the knuckle. I thought I might be able to reach to the back of the cavity as I had seen it from within, the clothy, closed-off throat with its elaborate mechanical corsetry. Inside her felt disconcertingly like a real mouth; I expected the doll at any moment to release my finger and ask, with this tongue, with this palate and throat and teeth, what I thought I was about. But she only held to my finger, closely all around like living tissue, living muscle.

And then some response was triggered in her, by the very tip of my finger in her throat. Her lips clasped my knuckle somewhat tighter, and her mouth moved against the rest of my finger. Oh, it was strange! It reminded me of a caterpillar, the concertina-like way they convey themselves across a leaf, along a branch; the rippling. Back and forth along my finger the ripples ran, combining the movements of her resisting my intrusive finger with those of attempting to milk it, massaging it root to tip with a firm and varied persuasiveness. How was such seeming randomness generated? I must translate that, I must account for it in my drawings. Yet at the same time I wanted to know nothing of it; there was something in the sensations that made my own throat clench, my stomach rebel, and every part of me below the waist solidify in a kind of horror.

What horrified me worst was that I knew, as a married woman, how to put an end to the rippling. Yet the notion of doing so, and in that way imitating the most repellent, the most beast-like movements of my husband, when, blinded, stupid with his lust he... emptied himself into me, as if I were a spittoon or the pit of a privy, stilled my hand amid the awful mouth-movements. I was on the point of spasm myself, spasms of revulsion, near-vomiting. Before they should overtake me I jabbed the automaton several times in her lubricious silken throat, my knuckle easily pushing her lips and teeth aside, my finger inside her mouth-workings cold, and bonily slender, and passionless—unless curiosity is a passion, unless disgust is.

Clarissa clamped that cold finger tightly, and some workings braced her neck against what should follow upon such prodding: my husband's convulsions in his ecstasy. It was as if the man was in the room with us, I imagined his exclamations so clearly. I shuddered there myself, a shudder so rich with feeling that my own eyes were sightless with it a moment. Then the doll relaxed her grip on me, and my arm's weight drew my forefinger from her mouth, slack as my husband's member would be slack, gleaming as that would gleam with her lubricants. Quietly, dutifully, she began a mouthish process; her lips parted slightly to allow the stuff of him, the mess of him, the man-spittle, to flow forth, to fall to her bosom. Some of her oil welled out eventually onto her pillowy, rosy lower lip. I watched the whole sequence with a stony attentiveness. When the oil dripped to her shining décolletage, such pity afflicted me at what this doll had been created to undergo that I stood and, using my own handkerchief bordered with Irish lace, cleaned the poor creature's bosom, wiped her mouth as a nurse wipes a child's, and when I was certain no further oils would come forth I restored her the modesty of her bodice; I raised her from her kneeling and took her, I hardly knew why, to sit in her cabinet. I did not close her in, then—I only stood, awkward, regarding her serene face. I felt as if I ought to say something—to apologize, perhaps; perhaps to accuse. Then—and I moved with such certainty that I must have noticed-without-noticing this before—my hand went to a pleat of the velvet lining of the lid of the cabinet, and a dry *pop* sounded under my fingertips, and I drew forth a folded slip of creamy writing paper, which matched that on which Clarissa's domestic commands were written. I opened and glanced down it, the encoded list of Clarissa's tortures, the list of my own.

Revulsion attacked me then, and hurriedly I refolded and replaced the paper, and shut the doll away, and went and stood at the study window gazing out over the green lawn and the dark hedge to the near-featureless landscape beyond, the green-gold fields a-glare in the unforgiving sunlight.

CLARISSA'S OTHER ACTIVITIES—I began to study and translate them next morning—were more obviously, comically, hideously calculated to meet a man's needs. She could be made to suffer two ways, lying like an upturned frog with her legs and her arms crooked around her torturer—without an actual man within them they contracted tightly enough to hold a very slight man indeed—or propped on all fours like any number of other beasts. In both positions she maintained continuous subtle rotations and rockings of her hips, and I could hear within her similar silky-wet movements to those her mouth had made about my finger, working studiedly upon my husband's intangible member.

To prevent her drawers becoming soaked with the lubricant oil and betraying to Mr. Goverman that I had discovered his unfaithfulness with the doll, I was forced to remove them. When I exposed her marriage parts my whole body flushed hot with mortification, and this heat afflicted me periodically throughout the course of her demonstration. Studiously applying myself to my drawing, and to the intellectual effort of translating the doll's mechanisms into her movements, was all I could do to cool myself.

If they had not been what they were, one would have considered her underparts fine examples of the seamstress's craft, or perhaps the upholsterer's.

A softly heart-shaped area of wiry dark hairs formed something of a welcome or an announcement that this was no child's doll, with all such private features erased and denied. Then such padded folds, cream-velvety without, red-purple and beaded with moisture within, eventuated behind these hairs, between these heavy legs, that I shook and burned examining them. My own such parts I had no more than washed with haste and efficiency; my husband's incursions within them had been utterly surprising to me, that I should be shaped so, and for such abominable usages. Now I could see them, and on another, one constructed never to feel a whisper of embarrassment. That I should be so curious, so fascinated, disgusted me; I told myself this was all in the spirit of scientific enquiry, this was all to assist in a complete translation of the doll's movements, but the sensations that gripped me—the hot shame; the excruciating awareness, as I examined her fore and aft, of the corresponding places on my own body; the sudden exquisite sensitivity of my fingertips to her softness and her slickness and the differing textures of the fleshy doors into her; the stiffness in my neck and jaw from my rage and repugnance—these were anything but scientific.

In a shaking voice I commanded her, from the secret list. The room's atmosphere was now entirely strange, and I shivered to picture some person walking in, and I made Clarissa pause in her clasping, in her undulations, several times, so that I could circle the house and reassure myself that the country around was as deserted as ever. For what was anyone to make of the scene, of the half-clothed automaton whirring and squirming in her mechanical pleasure, of the cold-faced human seated on the ottoman watching, of the list dropped to the floor so as not to be crumpled in those tight-clenched fists?

Mr. Goverman's return woke me from the state I had plunged into by the end of the week, wherein I barely ate and did not bother to dress, but at first light went in my night-dress to the study where Clarissa stood, and all day drew, surely and intricately and in a blistering cold rage, the working innards of the doll. Something warned me—some far distant jingle of harness carried to my ears on the breeze, some hoofstrike beyond the hills echoing through the earth and up through the foundations of the homestead and into my pillow—and I rose and bathed and clothed myself properly and hid my translations away and was well engaged in housekeeperly activities by the time my husband's party approached across the fields.

Then duties crowded in on me: to be hostess, to cook and prepare rooms; to apologize for the makeshiftness of our hospitality, and the absence of servants; to inform Mr. Goverman of the presence of his heir; to submit to his embraces that night. My season of solitude vanished like a frightened bird, and the days filled up so fully with words and work, with negotiations and the maintaining of various appearances, that I scarcely had time to recall how I had occupied myself before, let alone determine any particular action to take arising from my discoveries.

Days and then weeks and then months passed, and little Master Goverman began at last to be evident to the point where I was forced to withdraw again from society, such as it was. And I was also forced—because my husband conceived a sudden dislike of visiting the vestibule of his son's little palace—to endure close visitings at my face and bosom of the most grotesque parts of Mr. Goverman's anatomy, during which he would seem to lose the powers of articulate speech and even, sometimes, of rational thought. His early reticence and acceptance of my refusals to have him near in that way were transformed now; he no longer apologized, but seemed to delight in my resistance, to take extra pleasure in grasping my head and restraining me in his chosen position, to exult, almost, in his final befoulment of me. I would watch him with our guests, or conferring with Mr. Brightwell the new manager, and marvel at this well-dressed man of manners. Could he have any connection with the lamplit or moonlit assortment of limbs and hairiness and animal odours that assaulted me in the nights? I hardly knew which I hated worst, his savagery then or his expertise in disguising it now. What a sleight-of-hand marriage was, how fraudulent the social world! I despised every matron that she did not complain, every new bride as she sank from the glow and glory of betrothal and wedding to invisible compliant wifeliness, every man that he took these concealments and these changes as his due, that he took what he took, in exchange for what he gave a woman, which we called—fools that we were!—respectability.

By the time Mr. Goverman left for the city in the sixth month of my pregnancy, I will concede that I was no longer quite myself. Only a thin layer of propriety concealed my rage at my imprisonment—in this savage land, in this brute institution, in this swelling body dominated by the needs and nudgings of my little master within. I will plead, if ever I am called to account, that it was insanity kept me up during those nights, at first studying my translations (what certain hand had drawn these? Why, they looked almost authentic, almost the work of an engineer!) and then (what leap into the darkness was this?) re-translating them, some of them, into new drawings, devising how this part could be substituted for that, or a spring from the mantel-clock in a spare room could be added here, how a rusted saw-blade could be thinned and polished and given an edge and inserted there, out of sight within existing mechanisms, how this cam could be pared away a little there, and this whole arm of the apparatus adjusted higher to allow for the fact that I could not resort to actual metal casting for my lunatic enterprise.

Once the plans were before me, and Mr. Goverman still away arranging the terms of his investment in the mining consortium, to the accompaniment, no doubt, of a great deal of roast meat and brandy, cigars and theater attendances, there remained no more for me to do—lamplit, lumbering, discreet in the sounds I made, undisturbed through the nights—but piece by piece to dismantle and reassemble Clarissa's head according to those sure-handed drawings. I went about in the days like a thief, collecting a tool here, something that could be fashioned into a component there. I tested, I adjusted, I perfected. I was very happy. And then one early morning Lilty Meddows, my maid, knocked uncertainly at the study door to offer me tea and porridge, and there I was, as brightly cheerful as if I had only just risen from my sleep, stirring the just-burnt ashes of my translations, and with Clarissa demure in the armchair opposite, sealed up and fully clothed, betraying nothing of what I had accomplished on her.

LIFE, I DISCOVERED, is always more complex than it seems. The ground on which one bases one's beliefs, and actions arising from those beliefs, is sand, is quicksand, or reveals itself instead to be water. Circumstances change; madnesses end, or lessen, or begin inexorable transformations into new madnesses.

Mr. Goverman returned. I greeted him warmly. I was very frightened of what I had done, at the same time as, with the influx of normality that came with his return, with the bolstering of the sense of people watching me, so that I could not behave oddly or poorly, often I found my own actions impossible to credit. I only knew that each morning I greeted my husband more cordially; each night that I accepted him into my bed I did so with less dread and even with a species of amiable curiosity; I attended very much more closely to what he enjoyed in the marriage bed, and he in turn, in his surprise, in his ignorance, ventured to try to discover ways by which I might perhaps experience pleasures approaching the intensity of his own.

My impending maternity ended these experiments before they had progressed very far, however, and I left Cuttajunga for Melbourne and Holmegrange, a large, pleasant house by the wintry sea, where wealthy country ladies were sent by their solicitous husbands to await the birth of the colony's heirs and learn the arts and rituals of motherhood.

There I surprised myself very much by giving birth to a daughter, and there Mr. Goverman surprised me when very soon upon the birth he visited, by being more than delighted to welcome little Mary Grace into the world.

"She is *exactly* her mother," he said, looking up from the bundle of her in his arms, and I was astonished to see the glisten of tears in his eyes. Did he love me, then? Was this what love was? Was this, then, also affection, that I felt in return, this tortuous knot of puzzlements and awareness somewhere in my chest, somewhere above and behind my head? Had I birthed more than a child during that long day and night?

Certainly I loved Mary Grace—complete and unqualified, my love surprised me with its certainty when the rest of me was so awash with conflicting emotions, like an iron stanchion standing firm in a rushing current. I had only to look on her puzzling wakefulness, her innocent sleep, to know that region of my own heart clearly. And perhaps a little of my enchantment with my daughter puffed out—like wattle blossom!—and gilded Mr. Goverman too. Was that how it went, then, that wifely attachment grew from motherly? Why had my own mother not told me, when I had not the wit to ask her myself?

Mr. Goverman returned to Cuttajunga to ready it for Her Little Ladyship, and in his absence, through the milky, babe-ruled days of my lying-in, I wondered and I floundered and I feared, in all the doubt that surrounded my one iron-hard, iron-firm attachment in the world. I did not have leisure or privacy to draw, but in my mind I resurrected the drawings I had burnt in the study at the homestead, and labored on the adjustments that would be necessary to restore Clarissa to her former state, or near it. If only he loved me and was loyal to me enough; if only he could control his urges until I returned.

LILTY WAS AT my side; Mary Grace was in my arms; train-smoke and train-steam, all around, warmed us momentarily before delivering us up to the winter air, to the view of the ravaged country that was to be my daughter's home.

"Where is he?" said Lilty. "I cannot see him. I thought he would be here."

"Of course he will be." I strode forward through the smoke.

Four tall men, in long black coats, stood by the station gate, watching me in solemnity and some fear, I thought. Captain Jollyon stepped out from among them, but his customary jauntiness had quite deserted him. There was a man who by his headgear must be a policeman; a collared man, a reverend; and Dr Stone, my husband's physician. I did not know what to think, or feel. I must not turn and run; that was all I knew.

The train, which had been such a comforting, noisome, busy wall behind me, slid away, leaving a vastness out there, with Lilty twittering against it, senseless. The gentlemen ushered me, expected me to move with them. They made Lilty take Mary Grace from me. They made me sit, in the station waiting room, and then they sat either side of me, and Captain Jollyon sat on one heel before me, and they delivered their tidings.

It is easy to look bewildered when you have killed a man and are not suspected. It is easy to seem innocent, when all believe you to be so.

It must have been the maid Abigail, they said, from the blood in the kitchen, and the fact that she had disappeared. Mrs. Hodds, the housekeeper? She was at Cuttajunga now, but she had been at the Captain's, visiting her cousin Esther on their night off, when the deed was done. Mrs. Hodds it was who had found the master in the morning, bled to death in his bed, lying just as if asleep. She had called Dr Stone here, who had discovered the dreadful crime.

I went with them, silent, stunned that it all had happened just as I wished. The sky opened up so widely above the carriage, I feared we would fall out into it, these four black-coated crows of men and me lace-petticoated among them, like a bit of cloud, like a puff of train-steam disappearing. Now that they had cluttered up my clear knowledge with their stories, they respected my silence; only the reverend, who could not be suspected of impropriety, occasionally glanced at my stiff face and patted my gloved hand.

At Cuttajunga Mrs. Hodds ran at me weeping, and Mr. Brightwell turned his hat in his hands and covered it with muttered condolences. Then that was over, and Mrs. Hodds did more cluttering, more exclaiming, and told me what she had had to clean, until one of the black coats sharply interrupted her laundry listing: "Mrs. Goverman hardly wants to hear this, woman."

I did not require sedating; I had not become hysterical; I had not shed a tear. But then Mary Grace became fretful, and I took her and Lilty into the study— "But you must not say a word, Lilty, not a *word*," I told her. And as I fed my little daughter, there looking down into her soft face, her mouth working so busy and greedily, her eyes closed in supreme confidence that the milk would continue, forever if it were required—that was when the immense loneliness of my situation hollowed out around me, and of my pitiable husband's, who had retired to the room now above us, and in his horror—for he must have realized what I had done, and who I therefore was—felt his lifeblood ebb away.

Still I did not weep, but my throat and my chest hardened with occluded tears, and I thought—I welcomed the thought—that my heart might stop from the strain of containing them.

ABIGAIL, ABIGAIL: THE name kept flying from people's mouths like an insect, distracting me from my thoughts. The pursuit of Abigail preoccupied everyone. I let it, for it prevented them asking other questions; it prevented them seeing through my grief to my guilt.

In the night I rose from my bed. Lilty was asleep on the bedchamber couch, on the doctor's advice and the reverend's, in case I should need her in the state of confusion into which my sudden widowhood had plunged me. I took the candle downstairs, and along the hall to the back of the house.

I should have brought a rag, I thought. A damp rag. But in any case, she will be so bloodied, her bodice, her skirts—it will have all run down. Did he leave the piece in her mouth? I wondered. Will I find it there? Or did he retrieve it and have it with him, in his handkerchief, or in his bed, bound against him with the wrappings nearer where it belonged? It was not a question one could ask Captain Jollyon, or even Dr. Stone.

I opened the door of the charging chamber. There was no smudge or spot on or near the cabinet door, that I could see on close examination by candle-light.

I opened the cabinet. "Clarissa?" I said in my surprise, and she began her initiation-lubrication sequence, almost as if in pleasure at seeing me and being greeted, almost the way Mary Grace's limbs came alive when she heard my voice, her smoky-gray eyes seeking my face above her cradle. The chamber buzzed and crawled with the sounds of the doll's coming to life, and I could identify each one, as you recognise the gait of a familiar, or the cough he gives before knocking on your parlor door, or his cry to the stable boy as he rides up out of the afternoon, after weeks away.

"Clarissa: Stand," I said, and I made her turn, a full circle so that I could assure myself that not a single drop of blood was on any part of her clothing; then, that her garments had not been washed, for there was the tea-drop I had spilt upon her bodice myself during my studies. I might have unbuttoned her; I might have brought the candle close to scrutinise her breasts, her teeth, for blood not quite cleansed away, but I was prevented, for here came Lilty down the stairs, rubbing her sleepy eyes.

"Oh, ma'am! I was frightened for you! Come, you'd only to wake me, ma'am. You've no need to resort to mechanical people. What is it you were wanting? She's no good warming milk for you, that one—you know that."

And on she scolded, so fierce and gentle in the midnight, so comforting to my confusion—which was genuine now, albeit not sourced where she thought, not where any of them thought—that I allowed her to put the doll away, to lead me to the kitchen, to murmur over me as she warmed and honeyed me some milk.

"The girl Abigail," I said when I was calmer, into the steam above the cup. "Is there any news of her?"

"Don't you worry, Mrs. Goverman." Lilty clashed the pot into the wash basin, slopped some water in. Then she sat opposite me, her jaw set, her fists red and white on the table in front of her. "They will find that Abigail. There is only so many people in this country yet, that she can hide among. And most of them would sell their mothers for a penny or a half-pint. Don't you worry." She leaned across and squeezed my cold hand with her hot, damp one. "They will track that girl down. They will bring her to justice."

LADY WITHERSPOON'S SOLUTION

James Morrow

James Morrow is American SF's foremost satirist, the natural successor to Kurt Vonnegut. His sardonic, beautifully written novels include The Wine of Violence, The Continent of Lies, This is the Way the World Ends, Only Begotten Daughter, Towing Jehovah, Blameless in Abaddon, The Eternal Footman, The Last Witchfinder, *and* The Philosopher's Apprentice. *His short stories are witty and cutting, as in the following tale, which lampoons nineteenth-century feminism even as it celebrates it...*

Personal Journal of
Captain Archibald Carmody, R.N.
Written aboard H.M.S. "Aldebaran"
Whilst on a Voyage of Scientific Discovery in
the Indian Ocean

13 April 1899
Lat. 1°10' S, Long. 71°42' E

MIGHT THERE STILL be on this watery ball of ours a *terra incognita*, an uncharted Eden just over the horizon, home to noble aborigines or perhaps even a lost civilization? A dubious hypothesis, at least on the face of it. This is the age of the surveyor's sextant and the cartographer's calipers. Our planet has been girded east to west and gridded pole to pole. And yet what sea captain these days does not dream of happening upon some obscure but cornucopian island? Naturally he will keep the coordinates to himself, so he can return in time accompanied by his faithful mate and favorite books, there to spend the rest of his life in blissful solitude.

Today I may have found such a world. Our mission to Ceylon being complete, with over a hundred specimens to show for our troubles, most notably a magnificent lavender butterfly with wings as large as a coquette's fan and a green beetle of chitin so shiny that you can see your face in the carapace, we were steaming south-by-southwest for the Chagos Archipelago when a monsoon gathered behind us, persuading me to change course fifteen degrees. Two hours later the tempest passed, having filled our hold with brackish puddles though mercifully sparing our specimens, whereupon we found ourselves in view of a green, ragged mass unknown to any map in Her Majesty's Navy, small enough to elude detection until this day, yet large enough for the watch to cry "Land, ho!" whilst the *Aldebaran* was yet two miles from the reef.

We came to a quiet cove. I dispatched an exploration party, led by Mr. Bainbridge, to investigate the inlet. He reported back an hour ago, telling of bulbous fruits, scampering monkeys, and tapestries of exotic blossoms. When the tide turns tomorrow morning, I shall go ashore myself, for I think it likely that the island harbors invertebrate species of the sort for which our sponsors pay handsomely. But right now I shall amuse myself in imagining what to call the atoll. I am not so vain as to stamp my own name on these untrammeled sands. My wife, however, is a person I esteem sufficiently to memorialize her on a scale commensurate with her wisdom and beauty. So here we lie but a single degree below the Line, at anchor off Lydia Isle, waiting for the cockatoos to sing the dawn into being.

14 April 1899
Lat. 1°10' S, Long. 71°42' E

THE PEN TREMBLES in my hand. This has been a day unlike any in my twenty years at sea. Unless I miss my guess, Lydia Isle is home to a colony of beasts that science, for the best of reasons, once thought extinct.

It was our naturalist, Mr. Chalmers, who first noticed the tribe. Passing me the glass, he quivered with an excitement unusual in this phlegmatic gentleman. I adjusted the focus and suddenly there he was: the colony's most venturesome member, poking a simian head out from a cavern in the central ridge. Soon more such ape-men appeared at the entrance to their rocky dosshouse, a dozen at least, poised on the knife-edge of their curiosity, uncertain whether to flee into their grotto or further scrutinize us with their deep watery eyes and wide sniffing nostrils.

We advanced, rifles at the ready. The ape-men chattered, howled, and finally retreated, but not before I got a sufficiently clear view to make a positive identification. Beetle brows, monumental noses, tentative chins, barrel chests—I have seen these features before, in an alcove of the British Museum devoted to artists' impressions of a vanished creature that first came to light forty-three years ago in Germany's Neander Valley. According to my *Skeffington's Guide to Fossils of the Continent*, the quarrymen who unearthed the skeleton believed they'd found the remains of a bear, until the local schoolmaster, Johann Karl Fuhlrott, and a trained anatomist, Hermann Schaffhausen, determined that the bones spoke of prehistoric Europeans.

Fuhlrott and Schaffhausen had to amuse themselves with only a skullcap, femur, scapula, ilium, and some ribs, but we have found a living, breathing remnant of the race. I can scarcely write the word legibly, so great is my excitement. Neanderthals!

16 April 1899
Lat. 1°10' S, Long. 71°42' E

UNLESS THERE DWELLS in the hearts of our Neanderthals a quality of cunning that their outward aspect belies, we need no longer go armed amongst them. They are docile as a herd of Cotswold sheep. Whenever my officers and I explore the cavern that shelters their community, they lurch back in fear and—if I'm not mistaken—a kind of religious awe.

It's a heady feeling to be an object of worship, even when one's idolaters are of a lower race. Such adoration, I'll warrant, could become as addictive as a Chinaman's pipe, and I hope to eschew its allure even as we continue to study these shaggy primitives.

How has so meek a people managed to survive into the present day? I would ascribe their prosperity to the extreme conviviality of their world. For food, they need merely pluck bananas and mangos from the trees. When the monsoon arrives, they need but retreat into their cavern. If man-eating predators inhabit Lydia Isle, I have yet to see any.

Freed from the normal pressures that, by the theories of Mr. Darwin, tend to drive a race toward either oblivion or adaptive transmutation, our Neanderthals have cultivated habits that prefigure the accomplishments of civilized peoples. Their speech is crude and thus far incomprehensible to me, all grunts and snorts and wheezes, and yet they employ it not only for ordinary communication but to entertain themselves with songs and chants. For their dancing rituals they fashion flutes from reeds, drums from logs, and even a kind of rudimentary oboe from bamboo, making music under whose influence their swaying frames attain a certain elegance. Nor is the art of painting unknown on Lydia Isle. By torchlight we have beheld on the walls of their cavern adroit representations of the indigenous monkeys and birds.

But the fullest expression of the Neanderthals' artistic sense is to be found in the cemetery that they maintain in an open field not far from their stone apartments. Whereas most of the graves are marked with simple cairns, a dozen mounds feature effigies wrought from wicker and daub, each doubtless representing the earthly form of the dear departed. The details of these funerary images are invariably male, a situation not remarkable in itself, as the tribe may regard the second sex as unworthy of commemoration. What perplexes Mr. Chalmers and myself is that we have yet to come upon a single female of the race—or, for that matter, any infants. Might we find the Neanderthal wives and children cowering in the cavern's deepest sanctum? Or did some devastating tropical plague visit Lydia Isle, taking with it the entire female gender, plus every generation of males save one?

17 April 1899
Lat. 1°10' S, Long. 71°42' E

THIS MORNING I made a friend. I named him Silver, after the lightning-flash of fur that courses along his spine like an externalized backbone. It was Silver who made the initial gesture of amicability, presenting me with the gift of a flute. When I managed to pipe out a reasonable rendition of "Beautiful Dreamer," he smiled broadly—yes, the aborigines can smile—and wrapped his leathery hand around mine.

I did not recoil from the gesture, but allowed Silver to lead me to a clearing in the jungle, where I beheld a solitary burial mound, decorated with a funerary effigy. Whilst I would never presume to plunder the grave, I must note that the British Museum would pay handsomely for this sculpture. The workmanship is skillful, and, *mirabile dictu*, the form is female. She wears a crown of flowers, from beneath which stream glorious tresses of grass. Incised on a lump of soft wood, the facial features are, in their own naïve way, lovely.

Such are the observable facts. But Silver's solicitous attitude toward the effigy leads me to an additional conclusion. The woman interred in this hallowed ground, I do not doubt, was once my poor friend's mate.

19 April 1899
Lat. 1°10' S, Long. 71°42' E

AN ALTOGETHER EXTRAORDINARY day, bringing an event no less astonishing than our discovery of the aborigines. Once again Silver led me to his mate's graven image, whereupon he reached into his satchel—an intricate artifact woven of reeds—and drew forth a handwritten journal entitled *Confidential Diary and Personal Observations of*

Katherine Margaret Glover. Even if Silver spoke English, I would not have bothered to inquire as to Miss Glover's identity, for I knew instinctively that it was she who occupied the tomb beneath our feet. In presenting me with the little volume, my friend managed to communicate his expectation that I would peruse the contents but then return it forthwith, so he might continue drawing sustenance from its numinous leaves.

I spent the day collaborating with Mr. Chalmers in cataloguing the many *Lepidoptera* and *Coleoptera* we have collected thus far. Normally I take pleasure in taxonomic activity, but today I could think only of finishing the job, so beguiling was the siren-call of the diary. At length the parrots performed their final recital, the tropical sun found the equatorial sea, and I returned to my cabin, where, following a light supper, I read the chronicle cover to cover.

Considering its talismanic significance to Silver, I would never dream of appropriating the volume, yet it tells a story so astounding—one that inclines me to rethink my earlier theory concerning the Neanderthals—that I am resolved to forego sleep until I have copied the most salient passages into this, my own secret journal. All told, there are 114 separate entries spanning the interval from February through June of 1889. The vast majority have no bearing on the mystery of the aborigines, being verbal sketches that Miss Glover hoped to incorporate into her ongoing literary endeavor, an epic poem about the first century A.D.

warrior-queen Boadicea. Given the limitations of my energy and my ink supply, I must reluctantly allow those jottings to pass into oblivion.

Who was Kitty Glover? The precocious child of landed gentry, she evidently lost both her mother and father to consumption before her thirteenth year. In the interval immediately following her parents' death, Kitty's ne'er-do-well brother gambled away the family's fortune. She then spent four miserable years in Marylebone Workhouse, picking oakum until her fingers bled, all the while trying in vain to get a letter to her late mother's acquaintance, Elizabeth Witherspoon of Briarwood House in Hampstead, a widowed baroness presiding over her dead husband's considerable fortune. Kitty had reason to believe that Lady Witherspoon would heed her plight, as the circumstances under which the baroness came to know Kitty's mother were unforgettable, involving as they did the former's deliverance by the latter from almost certain death.

Kitty's diary contains no entry recounting the episode, but I infer that Lady Witherspoon was boating on the Thames near Greenwich when she tumbled into the water. The cries of the baroness, who could not swim, were heard by Maude Glover, who could. The author doesn't say how her mother came to be on the scene of Lady Witherspoon's misadventure, though Kitty occasionally mentions fishing in the Thames, so I would guess an identical diversion had years earlier brought Maude to that same river.

Despite the machinations of her immediate supervisor, the loutish Ezekiel Snavely, Kitty's fifth letter found its way to Briarwood House. Lady Witherspoon forthwith delivered Kitty from Snavely's clutches and made the girl her ward. Not only was Kitty accorded her own cottage on the estate grounds, her benefactor provided a monthly allowance of ten pounds, a sum sufficient for the young woman to mingle with London society and adorn herself in the latest fashions. In the initial entries, Lady Witherspoon emerges as a muddle-minded person, obsessed with the welfare of an organization that at first Kitty thought silly: the Hampstead Ladies' Croquet Club and Benevolent Society. But there was more on the minds of these six women than knocking balls through hoops.

Confidential Diary and Personal Observations
of Katherine Margaret Glover
The Year of Our Lord 1889

Sunday, 31 March

TODAY I AM moved to comment on a dimension of life here at Briarwood that I have not addressed before. Whilst most of our servants, footmen, maids, and gardeners appear normal in aspect and comportment, two of the staff, Martin and Andrew, exhibit features so grotesque that my dreams are haunted by their lumbering presence. Their duties comprise nothing beyond maintaining the grounds, the croquet field in particular, and I suspect they are so mentally enfeebled that Lady Witherspoon hesitates to assign them more demanding tasks. Indeed, the one time I attempted to engage Martin and Andrew in conversation, they regarded me quizzically and responded only with soft huffing grunts.

I once saw in the Zoological Gardens an orangutan named Attila, and in my opinion Martin and Andrew belong more to that variety of ape than to even the most bestial men of my acquaintance, including the execrable Ezekiel Snavely. With their weak chins, flaring nostrils, sunken black eyes, proliferation of body hair, and decks of broken teeth the size of pebbles, our groundskeepers seem on probation from the jungle, still awaiting full admittance to the human race. It speaks well of the baroness that she would hire such freaks as might normally find themselves in Spitalfields, swilling gin and begging for their supper.

"I cannot help but notice a bodily deformity in our groundskeepers," I told Lady Witherspoon. "In employing them, you have shown yourself to be a true Christian."

"In fact Martin and Andrew were once even more degraded than they appear," the baroness replied. "The day those unfortunates arrived, I instructed the servants to treat them with humanity. Kindness, it seems, will gentle the nature of even the most miserable outcast."

"Then I, too, shall treat them with humanity," I vowed.

Wednesday, 10 April

THIS MORNING I approached Lady Witherspoon with a scheme whose realization would, I believe, be a boon to English letters. I proposed that we establish here at Briarwood a school for the cultivation of the Empire's next generation of poets, not unlike that artistically fecund society formed by Lord Byron, Percy Bysshe Shelley, and their acolytes in an earlier part of the century. By founding such an institution, I argued, Lady Witherspoon would gain an enviable reputation as a friend to the arts, whilst my fellow poets and I would lift one another to unprecedented promontories of literary accomplishment.

Instead of holding forth on either the virtues or the liabilities of turning Briarwood into a monastery for scribblers, Lady Witherspoon looked me in the eye and said, "This strikes me as an opportune moment to address a somewhat different matter concerning your future, Kitty. It is my fond hope that you will one day take my place as head of the Hampstead Ladies' Croquet Club and Benevolent Society. Much as I admire the women who constitute our present membership, none is your equal in mettle and brains."

"Your praise touches me deeply, madam, though I am at a loss to say why that particular office requires either mettle or brains."

"I shall forgive your condescension, child, as you are unaware of the organization's true purpose."

"Which is—?"

"Which is something I shall disclose when you are ready to assume the mantle of leadership."

"From the appellation 'Benevolent Society,' might I surmise that you do charitable works?"

"We are generous toward our friends, rather less so toward our enemies," Lady Witherspoon replied with a quick smile that, unlike the Society's ostensible aim, was not entirely benevolent.

"Does this charity consist in saving misfits like Martin and Andrew from extinction?"

Instead of addressing my question, the baroness clasped my hand and said, "Here is my counter-proposal. Allow me to groom you as my successor, and I shall happily subsidize your commonwealth of poets."

"An excellent arrangement."

"I believe I'm getting the better of the bargain."

"Unless you object, I should like to call my nascent school the Elizabeth Witherspoon Academy of Arts and Letters."

"You have my permission," the baroness said.

Monday, 15 April

A DAY SPENT in Fleet Street, where I arranged for the *Times* to run an advertisement urging all interested poets, "whether wholly Byronic or merely embryonic," to bundle up their best work and bring it to the Elizabeth Witherspoon Academy of Arts and Letters, scheduled to convene at Briarwood House a week from next Sunday. The mere knowledge that this community will soon come into being has proved for me a fount of inspiration. Tonight I kept pen pressed to paper for five successive hours, with the result that I now have in my drawer seven stanzas concerning the marriage of my flame-haired Boadicea to Prasutagus, King of the Iceni Britons.

Strange fancies buzz through my brain like bees bereft of sense. My skull is a hive of conjecture. What is the "true purpose," to use the baroness's term, of the Benevolent Society? Do its members presume to practice the black arts? Does my patroness imagine that she is in turn patronized by Lucifer? Forgive me, Lady Witherspoon, for entertaining such ungracious speculations. You deserve better of your adoring ward.

The Society gathers on the first Saturday of next month, whereupon I shall play the prowler, or such is my resolve. Curiosity may have killed the cat, but I trust it will serve to enlighten this Kitty.

Sunday, 28 April

THE INAUGURATION OF my poets' utopia proved more auspicious than I had dared hope. All told, three bards made their way to Hampstead. We enjoyed a splendid high tea, then shared our nascent works.

The Reverend Tobias Crowther of Stoke Newingtown is a blowsy man of cheerful temper.

For the past year he has devoted his free hours to *Deathless in Bethany*, a long dramatic poem about Lazarus's adventures following his resuscitation by our Lord. He read the first scene aloud, and with every line his listeners grew more entranced.

Our next performer was Ellen Ruggles, a pallid schoolmistress from Kensington, who favored us with four odes. Evidently there is no object so humble that Miss Ruggles will not celebrate it in verse, be it a flower pot, a tea kettle, a spider web, or an earthworm. The men squirmed during her recitation, but I was exhilarated to hear Miss Ruggles sing of the quotidian enchantments that lie everywhere to hand.

With a quaver in my throat and a tremor in my knees, I enacted Boadicea's speech to Prasutagus as he lies on his deathbed, wherein she promises to continue his policy of appeasing the Romans. My discomfort was unjustified, however, for after my presentation the other poets all made cooing noises and applauded. I was particularly pleased to garner the approval of Edward Pertuis, a wealthy Bloomsbury bohemian and apostle of the mad philosopher Friedrich Nietzsche. Mr. Pertuis is quite the most well-favored man I have ever surveyed at close quarters, and I sense that he possesses a splendor of spirit to match his face.

The *Abyssiad* is a grand, epic poem wrought of materials that Mr. Pertuis cornered in the wildest reaches of his fancy and subsequently brought under the civilizing influence of his pen. On the planet Vivoid, far beyond Uranus, the *Übermensch* prophesied by Herr Nietzsche has come into existence. An exemplar of this superior race travels to Earth with the aim of teaching human beings how they might live their lives to the full. Mr. Pertuis is not only a superb writer but also a fine actor, and his opening cantos held our fellowship spellbound. He has even undertaken to illustrate his manuscript, decorating the bottom margin with crayon drawings of the *Übermensch*, who wears a dashing scarlet cape and looks rather like his creator—Mr. Pertuis, I mean, not Herr Nietzsche.

I can barely wait until our group reconvenes four weeks hence. I am deliriously anxious to learn what happens when the visitor from Vivoid attempts to corrupt the human race. I long to clap my eyes on Mr. Pertuis again.

Saturday, 4 May

AN ASTONISHING DAY that began in utter mundanity, with the titled ladies of the Benevolent Society arriving in their cabriolets and coaches. Five aristocrats plus the baroness made six, one for each croquet mallet in the spectrum: red, orange, yellow, green, blue, violet. After taking tea in the garden, everyone proceeded to the south lawn, newly scythed by Martin and Andrew. Six hoops and two pegs stood ready for the game. The women played three matches, with Lady Sterlingford winning the first, Lady Unsworth the second, and Lady Witherspoon the last. Although they took their sport seriously, bringing to each shot a scientific precision, their absorption in technique did not preclude their chattering about matters of stupendous inconsequentiality—the weather, Paris fashions, who had or had not been invited to the Countess of Rexford's upcoming soirée—whilst I sat on a wrought-iron chair and attempted to write a scene of the Romans flogging Boadicea for refusing to become their submissive client.

At dusk the croquet players repaired to the banquet hall, there to dine on pheasant and grouse, whilst I lurked outside the open window, observing their vapid smiles and overhearing their evanescent conversation, as devoid of substance as their prattle on the playing field. When at last the ladies finished their feast, they migrated to the west parlor. The casement gave me a coign of vantage on Lady Witherspoon as she approached the far wall and pulled aside a faded tapestry concealing the door to a descending spiral staircase. Laughing and trilling, the ladies passed through the secret portal and began their downward climb.

Within ten minutes I had furtively joined the Society in the manor's most subterranean sanctum, its walls dancing with phantoms conjured by a dozen blazing torches. A green velvet drape served as my cloak of invisibility. Like the east lawn, the basement had been converted into a gaming space, but whereas the croquet field bloomed with sweet grass and the occasional wild violet, the sanctum floor was covered end to end with a foul carpet of thick russet mud. From my velvet niche I could observe the suspended gallery in which reposed the six women, as well as, flanking and fronting the mire, two discrete ranks of gaol-cells, eight per block, each compartment inhabited by a hulking, snarling brute sprung from the same benighted line as Martin and Andrew. The atmosphere roiled with a fragrance such as I had never before endured—a stench compounded of stagnant water, damp fur, and the soiled hay filling the cages—even as my brain reeled with the primal improbability of the spectacle.

In the gallery a flurry of activity unfolded, and I soon realized that the women were wagering on the outcome of the incipient contest. Each aristocrat obviously had her favorite ape-man, though I got the impression that, contrary to the norms of such gambling, the players were betting on which beast could be counted upon to lose. After all the wagers were made, Lady Witherspoon gestured toward the far perimeter of the pit, where her major-domo, Wembly, and his chief assistant, Padding, were pacing in nervous circles. First Wembly sprang into action, setting his hand to a small windlass and thus opening a cage in the nearer of the two cell-blocks. As the liberated ape-man skulked into the arena, Padding operated a second windlass, thereby opening a facing cage and freeing its occupant. Retreating in tandem, Wembly and Padding slipped into a stone sentry box and locked the door behind them.

Only now did I notice that the bog was everywhere planted with implements of combat. Cudgels of all sorts rose from the mire like bulrushes. Each ape-man instinctively grabbed a weapon, the larger brute selecting a shillelagh, his opponent a wooden mace bristling with toothy bits of metal. The combat that followed was protracted and vicious, the two enemies hammering at each other until rivulets of blood flowed down their fur. Thuds, grunts, and cries of pain resounded through the fetid air, as did the Society's enthusiastic cheers.

In time the smaller beast triumphed, dealing his opponent a cranial blow so forceful that he dropped the shillelagh and collapsed in the bog, prone and trembling with terror. The victor approached his stricken foe, placed a muddy foot on his rump, and made ready to dash out the fallen creature's brains, at which juncture Lady Witherspoon lifted a tin whistle to her lips and let loose a metallic shriek. Instantly the victor released his mace and faced the gallery, where Lady Pembroke now stood grasping a ceramic phial stoppered with a plug of cork. Evidently recognizing the phial, and perhaps even smelling its contents, the victor forgot all about decerebrating his enemy. He shuffled toward Lady Pembroke and raised his hairy hands beseechingly. When she tossed him the coveted phial, he frantically tore out the stopper and sucked down the entire measure. Having satisfied his craving for the opiate, the brute tossed the phial aside, then yawned, stretched, and staggered back to his cage. He lay down in the straw and fell asleep.

Cautiously but resolutely, Wembly and Padding left their sentry box, the former now holding a

Gladstone bag of the sort carried by physicians. Whilst Padding secured the door to the victor's cage, Wembly knelt beside the vanquished beast. Opening the satchel, he removed a gleaming scalpel, a surgeon's needle, a variety of gauze dressings, and a hypodermic syringe loaded with an amber fluid. The major-domo nudged the plunger, releasing a single glistening bead, and, satisfied that the hollow needle was unobstructed, injected the drug into the brute's arm. The creature's limbs went slack. Presently Padding arrived on the scene, drawing from his pocket a pristine white handkerchief, which he used to clean the delta betwixt the ape-man's thighs, whereupon Wembly took up his scalpel and meticulously slit a portion of the creature's anatomy for which I know no term more delicate than scrotum.

The gallery erupted in a chorus of hoorays.

With practiced efficiency the major-domo appropriated the twin contents of the scrotal sac, each sphere as large as those with which the ladies had earlier entertained themselves, then plopped them into separate glass jars filled with a clear fluid, alcohol most probably, subsequently passing the vessels to Padding. Next Wembly produced two actual croquet balls, which he inserted into the cavity prior to suturing and bandaging the incision. After offering the gallery a deferential bow, Padding presented one trophy to Lady Pembroke, the other to Lady Unsworth, both of whom, I surmised, had correctly predicted the upshot of the contest. Lady Witherspoon led the other women—baroness

Cushing, the Marchioness of Harcourt, the Countess of Netherby—in a round of delirious applause.

The evening was young, and before it ended, three additional battles were fought in the stinking, echoing, glowing pit. Three more victors, three more losers, three more plundered scrota, six more harvested spheres, with the result that each noblewoman ultimately received at least one prize. During the intermissions, a liveried footman served the Society chocolate ice cream with strawberries.

Dear diary, allow me to make a confession. I enjoyed the ladies' sport. Despite a generally Christian sensibility, I could not help but imagine that each felled and eunuched brute was the odious Ezekiel Snavely. I had no desire to assume, per Lady Witherspoon's wishes, the leadership of her unorthodox organization, and yet the idea of my tormentor getting trounced in this arena soothed me more than I can say.

Clutching their vessels, the ladies ascended the spiral staircase. I pictured each guest slipping into her conveyance and, before commanding the coachman to take her home, demurely snugging her winnings into her lap as a lady of less peculiar tastes might secure a purse, a music box, or a pair of gloves. For a full twenty minutes I lingered behind my velvet drape, listening to the bestial snarls and savage growls, then began my slow climb to the surface, afire with a delight for which I hope our English language never breeds a name.

* * *

Monday, 6 May

TO HER ETERNAL credit, when I confessed to the baroness that I had spied on the underground tournament, she elected to extol my audacity rather than condemn my duplicity, adding but one caveat to her absolution. "I am willing to cast a sympathetic eye on your escapade," she told me, "but I must ask you to reciprocate by supposing that a laudable goal informs our baiting of the brutes."

"I don't doubt that your sport serves a greater good. But who are those wretched creatures? They seem more ape than human."

The baroness replied that, come noon tomorrow, I must go to the north tower and climb to the uppermost floor, where I would encounter a room I did not know existed. There amongst her retorts and alembics all my questions would be answered.

Thus did I find myself in Lady Witherspoon's cylindrical laboratory, a gas-lit chamber crammed with worktables on which rested the vessels of which she'd spoken, along with various flasks, bell jars, and test tubes, plus a beaker holding a golden substance that the baroness was heating over a Bunsen burner. Bubbles danced in the burnished fluid. At the center of the circle lay a plump man with waxen skin, naked head to toe, pink as a piglet, bound to an operating table with leather straps about his wrists and ankles. His name, the baroness informed me, was Ben Towson, and he looked as if he had a great deal to say about his situation, but, owing to the steel bit betwixt his teeth, tightly secured with thongs, he could not utter a word.

"It all began on a lovely April afternoon in 1883, back when the Society was content to play croquet with inorganic balls," Lady Witherspoon said. "I had arranged for a brilliant French scientist to address our group—Henri Renault, Director of the Paris Museum of Natural History. A devotee of Charles Darwin, Dr. Renault perforce believed that modern apes and contemporary humans share a common though extinct ancestor. It had become his obsession to corroborate Darwin through chemistry. After a decade of research, Renault concocted a potent drug from human neuronal tissue and simian cerebrospinal fluid. He soon learned that, over a course of three injections, this serum would transform an orangutan or a gorilla into—not a human being, exactly, but a creature of far greater talents than nature ever granted an ape. Renault called his discovery Infusion U."

"U for Uplift?" I ventured.

"U for Unknown," Lady Witherspoon corrected me. "Monsieur le Docteur was probing that interstice where science ends and enigma begins." Approaching a cabinet jammed with glass vessels, the baroness took down a stoppered Erlenmeyer flask containing a bright blue fluid. "I recently acquired a quantity of Renault's evolutionary catalyst. One day soon I shall conduct my own investigations using Infusion U."

"One day soon? From what I saw in the gaming pit, I would say you've already performed numerous such experiments."

"Our tournaments have nothing to do with Infusion U." Briefly Lady Witherspoon contemplated the flask, its contents coruscating in the sallow light. Gingerly she reshelved the arcane chemical. "A few years after creating serum number one, Renault perfected its precise inverse—Infusion D."

"For Devolution?"

"For Demimonde," the baroness replied, pointing to the burbling beaker. "Such unorthodox research belongs to the shadows."

With the aid of an insulated clamp she removed the hot beaker from the flame's influence and, availing herself of a funnel, decanted the contents into a rack of test tubes. She returned Infusion D to the burner. After the batch had cooled sufficiently, the baroness took up a hypodermic syringe and filled the barrel.

"It was this second formula that Renault demonstrated to the Society," the baroness said. "After we'd seated ourselves in the drawing-room, he injected five cubic centiliters into a recently condemned murderer, one Jean-Marc Girard, who proceeded to regress before our eyes."

Lady Witherspoon now performed the identical experiment on Ben Towson, locating a large vein in his forearm, inserting the needle, and pushing the plunger. I knew precisely what was going to happen, and yet I could not bring myself entirely to believe it. Whilst Infusion D seethed in its beaker and the gas hissed through the laboratory lamps, Towson began to change. Even as he fought against his straps, his jaw diminished, his brow expanded, and his eyes receded like successfully pocketed billiard balls. Each nostril grew to a diameter that would admit a chestnut. Great whorling tufts of fur appeared on his skin like weeds emerging from fecund soil. He whimpered like a whipped dog.

"Good God," I said.

"A striking metamorphosis, yes, but inchoate, for he will become his full simian self only after two more injections," Lady Witherspoon said, though to my naïve eye Towson already appeared identical to the brutes I'd observed in the arena. "What we have here is the very sort of being Renault fashioned for our edification that memorable spring afternoon. He assured us that, before delivering Girard to the executioner, he would employ Infusion U in restoring the miscreant, lest the hangman imagine he was killing an innocent ape." The Towson beast bucked and lurched, thus prompting the baroness to tighten the straps on his wrists. "It was obvious from his presentation that Renault saw no practical use for his discovery beyond validating the theory of evolution. But we of the Hampstead Ladies' Croquet Club immediately envisioned a benevolent application."

"Benevolent by certain lights," I noted, scanning the patient. His procreative paraphernalia had become grotesquely enlarged, though evidently it would not achieve croquet caliber until injection number three. "By other lights, controversial. By still others, criminal."

Lady Witherspoon did not address my argument directly but instead contrived the slyest of smiles, took my hand, and said, "Tell me, dear Kitty, how do you view the human male?"

"I am fond of certain men," I replied. Such as Mr. Pertuis, I almost added. "Others annoy me—and some I fear."

"Would you not agree that, whilst isolated specimens of the male can be amusing and occasionally even valuable, there is something profoundly unwell about the gender as a whole, a demon impulse that inclines men to treat their fellow beings, women particularly, with cruelty?"

"I have suffered the slings of male entitlement," I said in a voice of assent. "The director of Marylebone Workhouse took liberties with my person that I would prefer not to discuss."

Before releasing my hand, the baroness accorded it a sympathetic squeeze. "Our idea was a paragon of simplicity. Turn the male demon against itself. Teach it to fear and loathe its own gender rather than the female. Debase it with bludgeons. Humble it with mud. For the final fillip, deprive it of the ability to sire additional fiends."

"Your Society thinks as boldly as the Vivoidians who populate Mr. Pertuis's saga of the *Übermenschen*."

"I have not read your fellow poet's epic, but I shall take your remark as a compliment. Thanks to Monsieur le Docteur, we have in our possession an antidote for masculinity—a remedy that falls so far short of homicide that even a woman of the most refined temperament may apply it without qualm. To be sure, there are more conventional ways of dealing with the demon. But what sane woman, informed of Infusion D, would prefer to rely instead on the normal institutions of justice, whose barristers and judges are invariably of the scrotal persuasion?"

"Not only do I follow your logic," I said, cinching the strap on the ape-man's left ankle, "I confess to sharing your enthusiasm."

"Dear Kitty, your intelligence never ceases to amaze me. Even Renault, when I told him that the Society had set out to cure men of themselves, assumed I was joking." Bending over her rack of Infusion D, Lady Witherspoon ran her palms along the test tubes as if playing a glass harmonica. "Have you perchance heard of Jack the Ripper?" she asked abruptly.

"The Whitechapel maniac?" I cinched the right ankle-strap. "For six weeks running, London's journalists wrote of little else."

"The butcher slit the throats of at least five West End trollops, mutilating their bodies in ways that beggar the imagination. Last night Lady Pembroke went home carrying half the Ripper's manhood in her handbag, whilst Lady Unsworth made off with the other half. You were likewise witness to the rehabilitation of Milton Starling, a legislator who, before running afoul of our agents, alternately raped his niece in his barn and denounced the cause of women's suffrage on the floor of Parliament. You also beheld the gelding of Josiah Lippert, who until recently earned a handsome income delivering orphan girls from the slums of London to the brothels of Constantinople."

"No doubt the past lives of Martin and Andrew are similarly checkered."

"Prior to their encounter with the Society, they brokered the sale of nearly three hundred young women into white slavery throughout the Empire."

"What ultimately happens to your eunuchs?" I asked. "Are they all granted situations at Briarwood and the estates of your other ladies?"

"Martin and Andrew are merely making themselves useful whilst awaiting deportation," the baroness replied. "Once every six months, we transfer a boatload of castrati to an uncharted island in the Indian Ocean—Atonement Atoll, we call it—that they may live out their seedless lives in harmony with nature."

The patient, I noticed, had fallen asleep. "Is he still a carnivore, I wonder"—I gestured toward the slumbering beast—"or does he now dream of bananas?"

"A pertinent question, Kitty. I am not privy to the immediate contents of Towson's head, just as I cannot imagine what was passing through his mind when he kicked his wife to death."

"God save the Hampstead Ladies' Croquet Club and Benevolent Society," I said.

"And the Queen," my patroness added.

"And the Queen," I said.

Sunday, 26 May

THE SECOND GATHERING of the Witherspoon Academy of Arts and Letters proved every bit as bracing as the first. Miss Ruggles presented four odes so vivid in their particulars that I shall never regard a windmill, a button, a child's kite, or a gutted fish in quite the same way again. Mr. Crowther charmed us with another installment of his verse drama about Lazarus, an episode in which the resurrected aristocrat, thinking himself commensurate with Christ, travels to Chorazin with the aim of founding a salvationistic religion. Mr. Pertuis brought his *Übermensch* into contact with a cadre of Hegelian philosophers, a trauma so disruptive of their neo-Platonic worldview that they all went irretrievably insane. For my own contribution, I performed a scene in which Boadicea, bound and gagged, is forced to watch as her two daughters are molested by the Romans. The other poets claimed to be impressed by my depiction of the ghastly event, with Miss Ruggles declaring that she'd never heard anything quite so affecting in all her life.

But the real reason I shall always cherish this day concerns an incident that occurred after the workshop adjourned. Once Miss Ruggles and Mr.

Crowther had sped away in their respective coaches, having exchanged manuscripts with the aim of offering each other further appreciative commentary, Mr. Pertuis approached me and announced, in a diffident but heartfelt tone, that I had been in his thoughts of late, and he hoped I might accord him an opportunity to earn my admiration of his personhood, as opposed to his poetry. I responded that his personhood had not escaped my notice, then invited him for a stroll along the brook that girds the manor house.

We had not gone twenty yards when, acting on a sudden impulse, I told my companion the whole perplexing story of the Hampstead Ladies' Croquet Club. I omitted no proper noun: Dr. Renault, Ben Towson, Jean-Marc Girard, Jack the Ripper, Infusion U, Infusion D. At first he reacted with skepticism, but when I noted that my tale could be easily corroborated—I need merely lead him into the depths of Briarwood House and show him the caged brutes awaiting humiliation—he grew more liberal in his judgment.

"You present me with two possibilities," Mr. Pertuis said. "Either I am becoming friends with an insane poet who writes of ancient female warriors, or else Lady Elizabeth Witherspoon is the most capable woman in England, excepting of course the Queen. Given my fondness for you, I prefer to embrace the second theory."

"Naturally I must insist that you not repeat these revelations to another living soul."

"I shan't repeat them even to the dead."

"Were you to betray my confidence, Mr. Pertuis, my attitude to you would curdle in an instant."

"You may trust me implicitly, Miss Glover. But pray indulge my philosophical side. As a votary of Herr Nietzsche, I cannot but speculate on the potential benefits of these astonishing chemicals. Assuming Lady Witherspoon withheld no pertinent fact from you, I would conclude that, whilst the utility of Infusion D has been exhausted, this is manifestly not the case with the uplift serum. May I speak plainly? I am the sort of man who, if he possessed a quantity of the drug, would not scruple to experiment with it."

"*Mais pourquoi*, Mr. Pertuis? Have you a pet orangutan with whom you desire to play chess?"

"I do not see why the uplift serum should be employed solely for the betterment of apes. I do not see why—"

"Why it should not be introduced into a human subject?" I said, at once aghast and fascinated.

"A blasphemous idea, I quite agree. And yet, were you to put such forbidden fruit on my plate, I would be tempted to take a bite. Infusion U, you say—U for Unknown. No, Miss Glover—for *Übermensch*!"

Saturday, 1 June

WHEN I AWOKE I had no inkling that this would be the most memorable day of my life. If anything, it promised to be only the most philosophical, for I spent the morning conjecturing about what

Friedrich Nietzsche himself might have made of Infusion U. Being by all reports insane, the man is unlikely ever to form an opinion of Dr. Renault's research, much less share that judgment with the world.

Here is my supposition. Based upon my untutored and doubtless superficial reading of *The Joyful Wisdom*, I imagine Herr Nietzsche would be unimpressed by the uplift serum. I believe he would dismiss it as mere liquid decadence, yet another quack cure that, like all quack cures—most notoriously Christianity, the ultimate *pater nostrum*—prevents us from looking brute reality in the eye and admitting there are no happy endings, only eternal returns, even as we resolve to redress our tragic circumstances with a heroic and defiant "Yes!"

By contrast, I am confident that, presented with a potion that promised to fortify her spirit, my cruel and beautiful Boadicea would have swallowed it on the spot. After all, here was a woman who took on the world's mightiest empire, leading a revolt that obliged her to sack the cities that today we call St. Albans, Colchester, and London, leaving 70,000 Roman corpses behind. For a warrior-queen, whatever works is good, be it razor-sharp knives on the wheels of your chariot or a rare Gallic elixir in your goblet.

This afternoon Mr. Pertuis and I traveled in his coach to the Spaniard's Inn, where we dined with Dionysian abandon on grilled turbot, stewed beef à la jardinière, and lamb cutlets with asparagus.

Landing next in Regent's Park, we rented a rowboat and went out on the lake. My swain stroked us to the far shore, shipped the oars, and, clasping my hand, averred that he wished to discuss a matter of passing urgency.

"Two matters, really," he elaborated. "The first pertains to my intellect, the second to my affections."

"Both organs are of considerable interest to me," I said.

"To be blunt, I have resolved to augment my brain's potential through the uplift serum, but only if I have your blessing. I am similarly determined to enhance my heart's capacity by taking a wife, but only if my bride is your incomparable self."

My own heart immediately assented to his second scheme, fluttering against my ribs like a caged bird. "On first principles I endorse both your ambitions," I replied, blushing so deeply that I imagined the surrounding water reddening with my reflection, "but I would expect you to fulfill several preliminary conditions."

"Oh, my dearest Miss Glover, I shall grant you any wish within reason, and many beyond reason as well."

"Concerning our wedding, it must be a private affair attended by only a handful of witnesses and conducted by Mr. Crowther. Your Kitty is a shyer creature than you might suppose."

"Agreed."

"Concerning the serum, you will limit yourself to a single injection of five centiliters."

"Not one drop more."

"You must further consent to make me your collaborator in the grand experiment. Yes, dear Edward, I wish to accompany you on your journey into the dark, feral, occult continent of Infusion U."

"Is that really a place for a person of your gender?"

"I can tell you how Boadicea would answer. A woman's place is in the wild."

Dear diary, it was not the English countryside that glided past the window of Mr. Pertuis's coach on our return trip, for Albion had become Eden that day. Each tree was fruited with luminous apples, glowing plums, and glistening figs. From every blossom a golden nectar flowed in great munificent streams.

We reached Hampstead just as the Society was finishing its final match of the day. Standing on the edge of the grassy court, we watched Lady Harcourt make an astonishing shot in which the generative sphere leapt smartly from the tip of her mallet, traversed seven feet of lawn, rolled through the fifth hoop, and came to rest at a spot not ten inches from the peg. The other ladies broke into spontaneous applause.

Now Mr. Pertuis led me behind the privet hedge and placed a farewell kiss—a kiss!—on my lips, then repaired to his coach, whereupon Lady Witherspoon likewise drew me aside and averred she had news that would send my spirits soaring.

"Today I informed the others that, acting on your own initiative, you learned of the Society's true purpose," she said. "Having already judged you a person of impeccable character, they are happy to admit you to our company. Will you accept our invitation to an evening of demon baiting?"

"*Avec plaisir*," I said.

"Amongst the scheduled contestants is a notorious workhouse supervisor whom our agents abducted but four days ago. Yes, dear Kitty, tonight you will see a simian edition of the odious Ezekiel Snavely take the field."

My heart leaped up, though not to the same altitude occasioned by Mr. Pertuis's marriage proposal. "If Snavely were to fall," I muttered, "and if it were permitted, I would put the knife to him myself."

"I fully understand your desire, but we decided long ago that the incision must always be made and dressed by a practiced hand," Lady Witherspoon said. "The gods have entrusted us with their ichor, dear Kitty, and we must remain worthy of the gift."

Monday, 3 June

SATURDAY NIGHT'S TOURNAMENT did not turn out as I had hoped. My *bête noir* conquered his opponent, an abhorrent West End procurer. Dear God, what if Snavely continues to win his battles, month after month? What if he is standing tall after the Benevolent Society has been discovered and toppled by the London Metropolitan Police? Will his apish incarnation, gonads and all, receive sanctuary in some zoo? *Quelle horreur!*

In contrast to recent events in the arena, this morning's scientific experiments went swimmingly. We had no difficulty stealthily transferring the Erlenmeyer flask and the hypodermic syringe from the north tower to my cottage. So lovingly did Mr. Pertuis work the needle into my vein that the pain proved but a pinch, and I believe that, when I injected my swain in turn, I caused him only mild discomfort.

"Herr Nietzsche calls humankind the unfinished animal," he said. "If that hypothesis is true, then perhaps you and I, fair Kitty, are about to bring our species to completion."

At first I felt nothing—and then, suddenly, the elixir announced its presence in my brain. My throat constricted. My eyes seemed to rotate in their sockets. A thousand clockwork ants scurried across my skin. Sweat gushed from my brow, coursing down my face like blood from the Crown of Thorns.

Our torments ceased as abruptly as they'd begun, as if by magic—that is to say, by *Überwissenschaft*. And suddenly we knew that a true wonder-worker had come amongst us, *le Grand Renault*, blessing his disciples with the elixir of his genius. Brave new passions swelled within us. Fortunately I had on hand sufficient ink and paper to give them voice. Although we'd severed ourselves from our simian heritage,

Edward and I nevertheless entered into competition, each determined to produce the greater number of eternal truths in iambic pentameter. Whilst my poor swain labored till dawn, and even then failed to complete his *Abyssiad*, I finished *The Song of Boadicea* on the stroke of midnight two hundred and ten stanzas, each more brilliant than the last.

Thursday, 6 June

AND SO, DEAR diary, it has begun. We have bitten the apple, cuts cards with the Devil, lapped the last drop from the Pierian Spring. Come the new year my Edward and I shall be man and wife, but today we are *Übermensch* and *Überfrau*.

Such creatures will not be constrained by convention, nor acknowledge mere biology as their master. We are brighter than our glands. Each time Edward and I give ourselves to carnal love, we employ such prophylactic devices as will preclude procreation.

We do not disrobe. Rather, we tear the clothes from one other's bodies like starving castaways shucking oysters in a tidal inlet. How marvelous that, throughout the long, arduous process of concocting his formula, Monsieur le Docteur remained a connoisseur of sin. How exhilarating that a post-evolutionary race can know so much of post-lapsarian lust.

To apprehend the true and absolute nature of things—that is the fruit of Nietzschean clarity.

Energies and entities are one and the same, did you know that, dear diary? Wonders are many, but the greatest of these is being. Hell does not exist. Heaven is the fantasy of clerics. There is no God, and I am his prophet.

Fokken—that is the crisp, candid, Middle Dutch word for it. We fuck and fuck and fuck and fuck.

Wednesday, 12 June

An Überfrau does not hide her blazing intellect beneath a bushel. She trumpets her transfiguration from every rooftop, every watchtower, the summit of the highest mountain.

When I told Lady Witherspoon what Edward and I had done with the elixir, I assumed she might turn livid and perhaps even banish me from her estate. I did not anticipate that she would acquire a countenance of supreme alarm, call me the world's biggest fool, and spew out a narrative so hideous that only an *Überfrau* would dare, as I did, to greet it with a contemptuous laugh.

If I am to believe the baroness, Dr. Renault also wondered whether Infusion U might be capable of causing the consummation of our race. His experiments were so costly as to nearly deplete his personal fortune, entailing as they did lawsuits brought against him by the relations of the serum's twenty recipients. For it happens that the beneficence of Infusion U rarely persists for more than six weeks, after which the *Übermensch* endures a rapid and irremediable slide toward the primal. No known drug can arrest this degeneration, and the process is merely accelerated by additional injections.

The subjects of Renault's investigations may have lost their Nietzschean nerve, but Edward and I shall remain true to our joy. We exist beyond the tawdry grasp of the actual and the trivial reach of reason. As *Übermensch* and *Überfrau* we are prepared to grant employment to every species of whimsy, but no facts need apply.

Something June

THE THIRD MEETING of the Witherspoon Academy was another rollicking success, though Miss Ruggles and Mr. Crowther would probably construct it otherwise. When Miss Ruggles inflicted her latest excrescence on us, a piece of twaddle about her garden, Edward suggested that she run home and tend her flowers, for they were surely wilting from shame. She left the estate in tears. After Mr. Crowther finished spouting his drivel, I told him that his muse had evidently spent the past four weeks selling herself in the streets. His face went crimson, and he left in a huff.

Thursday?

KITTY'S HEAD SWIMS in a maelstrom of its own making. Her stomach has lost all sovereignty over its goods, and her psyche has likewise surrendered its dominion. Her soul vomits upon the page.

Another Day

APE HAIR ON Edward's arms. Ape teeth in Edward's mouth. Ape face on Edward's skull.

A Different Day

APE HAIR IN the mirror. Ape teeth in the mirror. Ape face in the mirror.

Another Day

THEY PITTED ME against him. In the mud. My Edward. We would not fight. They did it to him anyway. Necessary? Yes. Do I care? No. Procreation kills.

No Day

ON THE SEA. Atonement Atoll. A timbre intended is a tone meant. I shall never say anything so clever again. I weep.

Habzilb

habzilb larzed dox ner adnor ulorx qron mizrel bewq xewt ulp ilr ulp xok ulp ulp ulp ulp ulpulpulpulpulpulpulpulpulpulp

* * *

Personal Journal of
Captain Archibald Carmody, R.N.
Written aboard H.M.S. "Aldebaran"
Whilst on a Voyage of Scientific Discovery in the
Indian Ocean

20 April 1899
Lat. 1°10' S, Long. 71°42' E

I SLEPT TILL noon. After securing Miss Glover's diary in my rucksack, I bid the watch row me ashore, then entered the aborigines' cavern in search of Silver. Despite Kitty's fantastic chronicle, I still think of them as Neanderthals, and perhaps I always shall.

My friend was nowhere to be found. I proceeded to his mate's grave. Silver *née* Edward Pertuis sat atop the mound, contemplating Kitty's graven image. I surrendered the diary to the gelded ape-man, who forthwith secured it in his satchel.

The instant I drew the bible from my rucksack, Silver understood my intention. He wrapped one long arm around the sculpture, then set the opposite hand atop the Scriptures. I'd never performed the ceremony before, and I'm sure I got certain details wrong. The ape-man hung onto my every word, and when at length I averred that he and Katherine Margaret Glover were man and wife, he smiled, then kissed his bride.

* * *

22 April 1899
Lat. 6°11' N, Long. 68°32' E

TWO DAYS AFTER steaming away from Lydia Isle, I find myself wondering if it was all a dream. The lost race, their strange music, the bereaved beast grieving over his mate's effigy—did I imagine the entire sojourn?

Naturally Mr. Chalmers and Mr. Bainbridge will happily corroborate my stay in Eden. As for the strange diary, I am at the moment prepared to give it credence, and not just because I spent so many hours in monkish replication of its pages. I believe Kitty Glover. The subterranean tournaments, the demimonde drug, the uplift serum: these are factual as rain. I am convinced that Kitty and Edward ventured recklessly into the *terra incognita* of their primate past, losing themselves forever in apish antiquity.

My wife is an avid consumer of the London papers. If, prior to my departure, Briarwood House had been found to conceal a cabal of sorceresses bent on reforming miscreant males through French chemistry and Roman combat, Lydia would surely have read about it and told me. Until I hear otherwise, I shall assume that the Hampstead Ladies' Croquet Club is still a going concern, making apes, curing demons, knocking balls through hoops.

And so I face a dilemma. Upon my return to England do I inform the authorities of debatable recreations at Briarwood House? Or do I allow the uncanny *status quo* to persist? But that is another day's conversation with myself.

23 April 1899
Lat. 15°06' N, Long. 55°32' E

LAST NIGHT I once again read all the diary transcriptions. My dilemma has dissolved. With *Übermensch* clarity I see what I must do, and not do.

In some nebulous future—when England's men have transmuted into angels, perhaps, or England's women have the vote, or Satan has become an epicure of snowflakes—on that date I may suggest to a Hampstead constable that he investigate rumors of witchery at Lady Witherspoon's estate. But for now the secret of the Benevolent Society is safe with me. Landing again on Albion's shore, I shall arrange for this journal to become my family's most private heirloom, and I shall undertake a second mission as well, approaching the baroness, assuring her of my good intentions, and inquiring as to whether Ezekiel Snavely finally went down in the mud.

For our next voyage my sponsors intend that I should sail to Gávdhos, southwest of Crete, rumored to harbor a remarkable variety of firefly—the only such species to have evolved in the Greek Isles. Naturalists call it the changeling bug, as it exhibits the same proclivities as a chameleon. These beetles mimic the stars. Stare into the singing woods of Gávdhos on a still summer night, and you will witness a colony of changeling bugs blinking on and off in configurations that precisely copy horned Aries, clawed Cancer, poisonous Scorpio, mighty Taurus, sleek Pisces, and the rest.

The greatest of these tableaux is Sagittarius. Once the fireflies have formed their centaur, the arrow reportedly flies away, rising into the sky until the darkness claims it. Some say these wayward insects continue beating their wings until, disoriented and bereft of energy, they fall into the Aegean Sea and drown. I do not believe it. Nature has better uses for her lights. Rather, I am confident that, owing to some Darwinian adaptation or other, the beetles cease their theatrics and pause in mid-flight, thence reversing course and returning to the island, weary and hungry but glad to be amongst familiar trees again, called home by the keeper of their kind.

HANNAH

Keith Brooke

Keith Brooke, the founder of the renowned SF and fantasy website Infinity Plus, lives in Essex, England. His intense, dark novels include Keepers of the Peace, Expatria, Expatria Incorporated, Lord of Stone, *and* Genetopia; *his stories are collected in* Head Shots. *Here he examines Nineteenth Century medical ethics, which are severely tested by an anachronistic breakthrough in forensic science...*

A MAN OF science must never succumb to the fallacy of believing that his quest for knowledge and understanding can somehow be kept pure, separate from real life. A man of science is in a specially privileged position, almost God-like in some ways. A man of science has responsibilities. Oh yes, my friend, responsibilities...

I always believed myself to be aware of this, but it was only with the case of Hannah Mason that I really came to understand what it means.

It all began one late evening in the Grosvenor, after a rather fine dinner of broiled partridge followed by cocoa flummery. I had been all day at the Royal London Hospital in Whitechapel, visiting patients in the morning, carrying out regressive surgery throughout the afternoon. I was tired, and more than ready for an evening of stimulating conversation over a brandy or three, and indeed, that was how the evening set out.

Chadwick was there, never short of a bad thing to say about those of the medical profession. Heaven knows why he's been put in charge of reforming the public health system. What does a lawyer know about hygiene and infection?

I was in my favorite wingback chair by the fire, Chadwick opposite, muttering to young Mr. Jordan of Westminster about physicians milking the poor for every last penny. Standing by the fire as if he wished to be roasted on a spit, was the rotund form of Lord Bentley, sweating generously in his heavy frock-coat.

The evening was not promising to be the kind of relaxing and pleasant end to the day that I had anticipated, so when Inspector Derby came in, shrugging the cape from his shoulders into the hands of Cooper, I was happy to catch his eye and usher him to the seat to my right.

"Derby, my old friend," I said, as he seated himself. "Here, take this. You look like you need it more than me." With that, I handed him my balloon of brandy, only freshly poured and untouched by my lips. Derby hesitated, then took it, and downed it in two gulps.

I caught Cooper's eye and indicated the glass. Seconds later, he came with two more. At another discreet signal, he left the decanter with the two glasses.

Derby's hair was slicked to his head—from this and the look of his cape it must still have been streaming down outside. His features were flushed, his eyes jumping, his hands restless in his lap.

"Is it something you can talk about?" I asked. In truth I barely knew the man, but I did know him to be better company than Chadwick and Bentley.

He glanced at me, then across to the fire. "Gruesome business," he said, then managed a smile. "Goes with the job, you know?"

I nodded.

We sipped. I spoke of my day, of the latest cholera outbreak in Bow, of just how good the cocoa flummery had been this evening. When our glasses were low, I refilled them.

Much later, Derby opened up. "It was a girl," he said. "A child. Ten years of age. Hannah Mason. I know the family."

"Murder?"

He nodded. "Of the most violent kind," he said.

"Do you know who was responsible?"

He shook his head. "Nothing was seen or heard. The fiend left behind no evidence. We have nothing on which to base an investigation."

"No evidence, you say? Has there been a thorough scientific examination?"

"Doctor Galton inspected the body," said Derby. "He determined cause of death as multiple blows to the skull." He shuddered. The poor man was clearly in shock at what he had seen, and perhaps at his closeness to the girl's family.

"And of the scene?"

Derby shrugged. "We've searched it thoroughly. As I say, there was no evidence. Just a mess of blood..."

I placed a hand on his arm as I topped up his glass again. "Would it help, my old friend, if I were to offer my services? I have a special interest in investigative medicine. I may be of some use."

In truth, I did not know at that point what I may be able to offer, I just felt an overwhelming sympathy toward the man before me. It is true that I have an interest in what the medical perspective may bring to criminal investigations; last year I helped the Yard in a case involving the elimination of suspects by the matching of blood types found at the scene of a murder. Perhaps in the back of my mind I had the beginnings of an idea, a new application for the regressive cell techniques for which I was rapidly making something of a reputation.

"It cannot do any harm," I said, as Derby appeared to hesitate.

Then he shrugged again, and drank deeply.

So it was that I found myself stepping down from a carriage, and following the caped form of Inspector Derby toward the mouth of some anonymous alleyway just north of the river in the east of the city. I frequently work in Whitechapel, but I did not recognise this street. The night was wild, rain driven almost on the horizontal so that we both ducked low into it.

On the corner we passed a public bar, light spilling out onto the street and the entrance of the alleyway.

As my eyes adjusted to the darkness, I fumbled my way along the alley, aware of the dark form of Derby just ahead.

We rounded a corner and I heard Derby say, "It's me, Inspector Derby." Another figure stood by a doorway, lit by a lamp from within—a policeman in his cockscomb helmet, long blue eight-button coat and black leather boots.

He stood back as we passed through the door into a wooden shack of sorts. There were tools along the wall, and much of the space was taken up with a boat, up on blocks and in some state of either disrepair or partial refurbishment.

Derby stood by the stern of the vessel, his head dipped.

I came to stand at his shoulder. The floor of compacted dirt was stained a vivid red here. I could smell the copper tang of fresh blood. "And this is where it occurred?" I asked gently.

"The child… little Hannah… She was beaten to death with a hammer left at the scene. Her clothes were in disarray. No witnesses. We suspect some passer-by, some opportunist."

I stepped past Derby and stood by the red patch. I looked around. "There has clearly been a struggle," I said. "See how this bench has been pushed back from its normal position? See the indents in the ground where it normally rests? There is blood too, on the bench, and on the stern of the boat, and over there on the wall. The poor thing must have put up quite a fight. From this I would concur that she probably did not know her attacker. Have samples been taken?"

"Samples?"

"There is blood. One would assume that most of this blood is from the victim, but if she fought then there may be blood from her assailant too. There are tests we can carry out that categorise blood into different types, so that if, for example, you are left with two suspects of different blood type, we could say with absolute certainty which one of them matched the blood type found at the scene."

"Don't you need a lot of blood to do that kind of thing? If he's left any here, then there can't be much..."

"Science and technology make great leaps in this age of discovery, my friend. Consider Mr. Babbage and his Difference Engine! In my own field, we can do much with little. I have developed a technique whereby we can take a small sample of tissue and regress it to the embryonic stage, from which it can be regrown as if new: a small amount of blood can be regressed and then grown to produce as much as we need for our tests."

Derby appeared slow to take in my meaning. Then he spoke, decisively. "Then do it," he said.

"Take your samples. But there is one thing I ask of you: for now this must be kept between the two of us. Right now, if the killer thinks this case is without evidence then he may rest easy; if he knows we are applying new techniques in order to hunt him down then he might run. Or, worse, he might try to stop us."

I clapped Derby on the arm and nodded, then turned to open my case and take out tubes for my samples.

AND SO, AFTER a long day at the Royal London Hospital, a brief interlude at the Grosvenor, and a venture out into a wild March night in the East End, I found myself back in my private basement laboratory at a little after midnight, decanting samples into dishes and jars, and sousing them in catalytic solutions of my own invention.

I should have been exhausted, but in truth I was excited to be working on such a case, to be applying my techniques to new ends. It was a puzzle, a game even. I confess now that the scene of the crime had meant little to me: I am hardened to human blood and suffering; I am a rationalist, a man who recognises that some losses are inescapable and it is the role of the physician to shift the balance so that the whole of suffering is reduced.

First, I put blood into the jars and set the process under way. Most of these samples would belong to the girl, and we would be able to match them with those taken from her body. But all it would take would be one sample that was from a different blood type and we would be able to narrow down any group of suspects.

Further to this, I had another sample.

On the stern of the boat, upon closer examination, I had found a patch of blood and skin cells. This, I felt sure, was the single most significant discovery, for this part of the boat, being raised on blocks, was out of reach of the girl. The skin must have been deposited as her assailant staggered back, flung out a hand to catch himself and instead scraped his knuckles on the unfinished repair at the top of the stern.

I had initially taken the sample for the blood content, but then I realized that the skin may be even more significant. If I could regress it to the embryonic stage and then allow it to multiply, I might grow a sheet of the stuff: it would tell us what kind of man we were looking for! Was he hirsute or smooth? Did he have a propensity for freckles? What shade was his skin? Was he of a greasy complexion, or dry and flaky? A single sample of skin could tell us so much!

I placed the sample carefully in a dish, and poured onto it a carefully measured quantity of the catalyst.

And then, finally, to bed.

WHEN A SCIENTIST regrows the cells of another person, is he regrowing that person, or merely a subset, a sample? If that swatch of cells is *living*, able to be sustained by an inflow of nutrient, is it actually the person? Where do the boundaries lie?

I worked, in the hospital, and in my private practice attached to St Bartholomew's, and at night I returned to my Belgravia home and down to my private laboratory in the basement. True to my word, I had told no one about my latest venture into medical investigation. This was a secret Derby and I would spring on the world when we were ready to strike, and not a moment before.

The blood cells multiplied, and within days I was ready to perform analyses of these, and of blood taken from Hannah Mason's body.

Derby was with me as I checked each sample one by one.

"No," I said, sipping from my brandy. "This is the same type as the girl's again."

Derby sat there sipping at his brandy, puffing on a fat cigar.

I had kept the sample from the boat until last, the showman in me coming to the fore. This one, I was certain, belonged to our killer.

I placed the tube of blood and a dish of skin before Derby.

He stared, then looked up at me. "What's this?" he asked.

I explained about where I had found it, and what it must mean.

First, the blood. I dripped it onto a sliver of paper impregnated with antagonists, and watched as the stain crept up the slip. It stopped at the K mark, just as all previous samples had done.

I could barely disguise my disappointment.

"What does it mean?" Derby asked, impatient.

I sighed. "It means the blood type is the same as all the others."

And then I realized what this meant. We had been looking for one sample that was different, but they were all the same. "Don't you see?" I said urgently. "Either this sample is the girl's, in which case she must have been flung bodily into the air and against the boat, or it must be the killer's, in which case he is of the same blood type as the girl."

"And how do we distinguish between the two possibilities?" said Derby. "Surely this takes us no further: all that you have demonstrated is that the killer might have the same blood type as Hannah. Or he might not."

"We grow the skin," I explained. "And we compare it with the girl's. If it is of the same type under microscopic analysis then we know the sample belonged to her, but if it differs then we have demonstrated that the killer is of the same blood type, and so we have our evidence."

And so that is how it came about that I reached my present state.

It was three days later that I first detected the anomaly.

Now I realize that there must have been some form of contamination. Normally, I would only run the regression for a maximum of three days: long enough for the cells to regain some of their embryonic vigour and start to multiply without restraint. In our early trials, of course, we ran tests for longer, but always the samples degenerated into anomalous masses.

But a week after I first collected the sample, an anomaly appeared, the result of the regression catalyst not having been rigorously flushed out. Other tissue was forming. First a layer of subcutaneous fat, then a fibrous substance that could only be muscle. The skin cells had fully regressed to an embryonic state and were now multiplying and diversifying. I was growing body parts in my laboratory…

The following day, Derby appeared at my front door carrying a small case. I ushered him into the library, where we sat with brandy and cigars, he cradling the case on his lap.

"You have the sample?" I asked.

He nodded, the flush of his skin a deeper shade than the ginger of his whiskers.

"Could I have it, please?"

He seemed reluctant. I waited with hand outstretched and finally he opened the case and took out an envelope, from which he produced a small sealed dish. Inside was a sample from poor Hannah Mason.

I took the dish and peered inside at the delicate parchment-like sliver of skin. I thought then of the sample growing in my laboratory, now a good six inches square and half an inch thick.

I stood, abruptly.

"Thank you, Inspector Derby. I will make contact with you as soon as there is anything to report."

He stood too. "I will stay," he said. "I will come with you to your laboratory. You can report your results to me in person."

"No, I'm afraid..." I did not know what I was afraid of, and so I faltered, uncertain.

Already, Derby was by the door waiting. I nodded to him. "Very well," I said. There could be no harm in letting him see what had become of the skin sample, I decided.

I paused in the hallway at the door to my laboratory. From my waistcoat I produced a large key and proceeded to unlock the door.

Inside, I found the dial to turn up the supply to the gas lamps and the room was suddenly lit up like New Oxford Street at Christmas.

I went to the far workbench and placed the dish alongside my original sample. Derby stood at my shoulder. I am not sure what he must have thought at that point; he said nothing.

I seated myself and withdrew my finest Husbands and Clarke microscope from its mahogany case. I fired its lamp, and adjusted myself so that I could peer into its eyepiece in comfort. Sliding the Hannah Mason sample into position, I fiddled with the brass adjustments until the microscope was focused, then began to make notes and sketches of cell structure on a sheet of paper to my left.

After a few minutes I removed the microscope slide.

Then I opened the dish of my original sample, took a surgical lancet and removed a sliver of skin, all the time feeling oddly squeamish.

"That...?" said Derby, as if at that point he had just realized that this was my regrown sample.

I nodded. "Yes, this is the regressed sample I have been growing."

"It... it's more than just skin now, isn't it?"

I fixed him with a level look. "Yes," I said. "It is regrowing more than just skin. The re-embryonic cells are differentiating into subcutaneum, muscle, blood vessels, nerve fibre."

He fell silent then, allowing me to continue with my procedure.

The cell structures were exactly the same: an identical pattern of pores and follicles; the soft blonde hairs were the same, the levels of grease and pigmentation. Not only did this sample share the same blood type as Hannah Mason, it shared the same skin structure too.

I leaned back in my seat and turned to Derby.

"It's her," I said. "This is Hannah Mason. Not her killer at all. I am sorry. I was certain that we would find something that would help you narrow down your investigations." At the same time as I was saying this, another part of my mind was racing away, reminding me that while we had found a negative in this instance, the procedure was valid and successful; on the broader scale we had discovered something that would revolutionise criminal investigations. I felt no responsibility to poor Hannah Mason. Then, at least.

"Can you be certain?" asked Derby. "What would happen if you were to continue growing this sample? Would it differentiate further? Might it offer more clues? What if the murderer was someone of fair skin, and blonde hair, just like Hannah? Might a more differentiated sample yield something that would allow us to distinguish?"

Rather taken aback by his eagerness, I took my time to ponder. "Perhaps," I said finally. This was when I first felt the ethical dilemma press down upon me. "But do we have the moral and ethical right to grow the sample further? Where should we stop? When we have defined organs? When?"

"I'll tell you when," said Derby. "This is a police matter. Will you proceed?"

I sighed, giving every impression of reluctance, so as not to acknowledge that part of my mind that was still racing away with possibilities, wondering just what we might grow. "I will," I said. "I will."

MY BIG MISTAKE was to let Derby into the laboratory again, two weeks later.

I should have seen the signs. I should have understood his motives, but I did not.

I opened the door and led him in.

We headed straight for the far workbench. Derby gasped, as he came to understand what was before him.

The sample had grown so rapidly, under my new regime of intensified catalyst, that I had needed to move it to a large glass tank. It lay there now, suspended in thick, translucent fluid. The knot of cells was about the size of my fist, and it curled like a pup. It twitched, rhythmically, to the beat of a tiny heart.

Derby stood before it.

I had grown a baby.

I stroked at the stubble on my chin. I had not been to surgery, either at St Bart's or the Royal London, for over a week. I had stayed here, increasingly obsessed with what was happening in my laboratory.

Derby turned to me. "Is it...?"

I nodded. "It's the girl. Hannah Mason. I have been comparing samples at every stage. There can be no doubt."

I recognised then that the light in his eye was that of a madman and not merely an ordinary police officer confronted with the incredible.

"You knew, didn't you?" I said. "You knew that I had a sample from the girl... that the killer had not been injured in the encounter..."

Derby was holding a pistol—a pistol aimed in my direction.

"She was my child," he said, his hand shaking madly. "Mason—he had no idea. Useless nothing of a man. I stayed a part of her life as she grew up, but then they turned against me—Mason and even Margaret. They didn't like me being with Hannah. They kept making excuses. I saw their looks. Their whispers. They conspired against me."

I remembered the coroner's description of Hannah Mason's death. She had not been raped, but had certainly been molested, and beaten savagely. The Inspector's obsession had clearly taken a dark and depraved turn.

"They forbade me from seeing her," said Derby. "But she was *mine*!"

He approached me then, and I wondered what he was about to do, but he merely reached into my waistcoat pocket and withdrew the laboratory key.

He backed away, to the foot of the stairs, and then turned to leave. At the top, he paused and said, "You will stay here, my friend. Rear her. Nurture her and guard her with your life. She's mine. That child is mine."

HE BRINGS ME food.

He brings *us* food. Me, and this child growing in the tank.

She is conscious now. She hangs in fluid with her face pressed against the glass and stares out, waiting for her nutrient feed. I play games with her, peep-a-bo, and face-pulling games. Sometimes I make her smile.

The first few times, he only opened the door and deposited supplies at the top of the stairs, but today he came down and peered into the tank.

There was a strange look on his face. I still do not know exactly what emotions lay behind that look. Lust, for the naked child before him? Guilt, for what he had done? Something paternal? Revulsion? Fear? Awe? Even a perverted kind of love? Some strange mixture of all of these?

He placed a hand on the glass, and inside she mirrored this, her own hand tiny, smooth.

Then he faltered, stumbled backwards, and half-ran up the stairs and out of the laboratory.

Now, I watch the child in the tank, and wonder what kind of monster I have spawned.

I LIVE IN squalor. No matter how particular I am, using only one corner of the laboratory for bodily functions, cleaning meticulously with water that is piped down here from the kitchens, I am aware of my increasingly unkempt state. I smell, I have a thick growth of beard, my clothes are in a shameful condition.

He comes again, Inspector Derby. He brings food and deposits it on a spare surface.

In the tank, Hannah watches him, carefully.

He is drawn to her. He has the shaking gait of a palsied old man. His obsession is upon him, taking him over, submerging him.

"There's no way out of this situation," I tell him. "You have imprisoned a highly respected medical man. You have murdered a child, and heaven knows what you intend to do with this small girl before you..."

He turns to me, and I see that his eyes are bloodshot, one lid twitching relentlessly. He takes a step and I think he is about to strike me.

And then, beyond him, I see Hannah doing something I have not seen her do before. She is trying to stand up. She has her shoulders and head braced against the lid of the tank and her feet on the floor and she pushes.

The lid gives, slides, crashes to the floor.

Derby jerks, turns, sees her standing before him, waist-deep in fluids.

She steps over the glass wall, stands on the edge of the bench, and then slips, falls to the ground.

I rush to her, stoop and hold her as she sits, stunned by the rush of the new.

Derby has his gun out. He waves it at me. "Move away from her," he says.

I hesitate, then stand and step back.

"Hannah?" he says. "Hannah? My baby?"

She looks at him, but there is no recognition in her eye, as surely there must not have been. Only something primitive, something animal.

She clambers to her feet, is only two yards from Derby, and then she springs, flying through the air like a pouncing cat.

Derby drops his gun, and takes her in his arms, stumbling backwards, and then collapsing under her impetus.

On the floor, at first I think they are in some kind of animalistic embrace and I look away, appalled.

When I look again there is blood. Derby's blood, pooling on the stone floor. Hannah is tearing at his throat with hands and teeth, carrying on until his body is quite limp.

Finally, she squats back on her haunches and turns to me, her face smeared a vivid red.

She smiles, stands, steps toward me.

I await my fate. I am not a fighting man. I am a man of science, of medicine.

She comes to me and buries her face into my belly, her skinny arms wrapped around me.

I am well into my sixth decade, a man of some standing and reputation and not a little wealth, but still a man who has been impoverished by life in many respects. My marriage to dear Elisabeth lasted only six years before she was taken by consumption. We were childless.

Now, I feel what can only be some kind of duty of care, something like that a parent must feel toward their children. As a man of science I now understand that I have responsibilities too. And here before me, smearing her blood-stained face across my grubby waistcoat, is one of them. I made her. I am responsible. I have a duty toward her.

I return her embrace.

And even now, I wonder what to do.

A discovery like this would forge my reputation as one of the great medical thinkers of all time, but first I must tend to my creation.

She needs cleaning and she needs clothing.

And maybe, I realize, maybe my Hannah needs a new friend to play with...?

PETROLPUNK

Adam Roberts

Adam Roberts, a London-based academic, has produced numerous novels, short stories, fantasy parodies, and scholarly studies in the current decade. His pungent and punchy SF books include Salt, On, Stone, Polystom, The Snow, Gradisil, Land of the Headless, *and* Splinter; *his most recent,* Swiftly, *is a wonderful steampunk romp taking off from Gulliver's Travels. In the satirically titled "Petrolpunk," Roberts considers the matter of alternate worlds, and writes in not only in his parallel self, but your editor as well...*

> All mining, tunneling, delving and digging in the earth is hereby prohibited by Royal Edict; do not presume, with violent hands, to eviscerate the Earth, our Mother! Take to the skies, if you must,

but leave the subterra unmolested!

– Victoria, the opening paragraph
of the 1888 *Contra Excavatio*.

It was the morning of the Queen's Titanium Jubilee and the crowds were gathering on Imperial Way. My vantage point was a stilt-raised booth, above the milling multitude, across the Way from the river. I was the personal guest of the editor of *The Nineteenth-Century And After,* which esteemed journalist was telling me about pressure to alter the title of his journal. "I resist," he said, puffing on a steam-cigar. "I continue to resist. For if *The Nineteenth-Century And After* suited the twentieth century, in what sense will it not suit the twenty-first? But there are dissenting voices on the editorial board."

"Dissent and dissenters," I said, shaking my head sagely.

"GOD BLESS HER IMMORTAL MAJESTY!" boomed a zealot from his overhead blimp, his voice amplified by an electrical megaphone. He repeated his statement thrice more as he drifted out over the crowd. God Bless! God Bless!

"Think of the commotion," confided a gentleman to my left, leaning toward me and tipping his hat a little way back on his head, "were I to pop that balloon with my pea-popper." He was wearing a very fine crushed-denim three-piece suit, with matching top hat, but then he twitched the lapel of his jacket forward to reveal a pistolette in a breast holster, and suddenly he looked like a banditto masquerading as a gentleman.

"It *is* a low trajectory," I said, not wanting to give an impression of stand-offishness, and nodding at the receding blimp, "for a zealot."

"Vulgar, which is a synonym for low." He looked into the sky. The grape-like clusters of myriad hermit balloons dominated the vertical perspective, many more than I had seen in London's skies before. "Even the hermits have assembled in large numbers to witness the appearance of her Immortal Majesty," he said. "Sir Cheech Pettison," he added, amiably.

I introduced myself. Hindsight inevitably colors my recollection, of course, but I believe I *was* struck, even at this first meeting, by a quality of *strangeness*, or exoticism, about Pettison. Not that there was anything obviously *wrong* about him. He was dressed in the best of fashion. His manners were impeccable. Unlike (as I later discovered) the dress and manners of his *brother*—

"I'm an inventor," he declared.

"And I," I replied, "am a gentleman."

This seemed to please him enormously—"Touché, my dear fellow!"—but I felt as if I had spoken ungraciously, and offered the polite pretence of interest in his affairs. "An inventor, you say?"

"Indeed I do."

"Inventing... what?"

But the parade was beginning, and our conversation was necessarily curtailed. The gates opened, and the royal carriage began its progress. A great cheer went up. An electrically amplified rendering of the Royal Song boomed. The huge car whirred and rolled, its exhaust-bag bouncing slowly and ponderously as if in time to the slow drumbeats. Then, *then*, was a loud explosion, blowing my world to the merest atoms, crushing me, erasing me.

THERE WAS, NATURALLY, some delay between the explosion itself and the end of the world. Such is the nature of things. The sequence of events, confusing at the time, was retrospectively clarified. It transpired that the Army of Mortality—one of the more wittily appropriate names for a terrorist organization, I have always thought—had infernal-deviced a section of the Thames Tarpaulin. It was a violent ebullition indeed, and an eighty-foot waterspout was momently visible over the embankment trees. As this slumped a cloud of Thames water, perfectly noxious and foul, began to expand in vaporous, roiling form over the crowd. The general cheer was raised two tones and a semitone to a general scream. As the people on the far side, closest to the river, surged forward to remove themselves from the poison of this aerial moisture, the crowd itself began to deform. The barriers separating the masses from the parade-way snapped and flipped. From our vantage point, on the near side of the way, it was clear that the ocean of bodies would impact shockingly upon the Royal Carriage and crush even its substantial frame. Her Majesty was in grave danger. The driver, aware of the peril, accelerated; but the most powerful charcoal motor in London could not move so massive, golden and orgulous a carriage at any great speed.

This was the moment that Sir Cheech showed his mettle. Standing, he aimed his pistolette directly at the carriage. I'll confess my first thought was (or perhaps I am merely giving vent to *hindsight*, again)—*assassin*!—and my heart blew its own small waterspout of panic into my chest. Almost I threw myself upon the fellow and attempted to wrestle the weapon from him. But before I could, the pistolette discharged and I understood what Sir Cheech was attempting. His bullet punctured the exhaust-sack, and the concentrated steam exhaust—much more toxic, of course, than the relatively diluted stuff drifting down from the ruptured Thames—spilled into the crowd. Those nearest choked and gasped. Some fell. A few leapt up, like salmon, and attempted to wriggle and claw a path away across the tops of their writhing fellows. But, on the larger scale, the crowd as a mass followed the ineluctable impassability of this toxic miasma, and flowed *around* the carriage. The driver had the sense to stop his motor; Her Immortal Majesty was of course safe inside her airtight cabinet. I saw, or perhaps I merely fancied, her face loom out of the white steam that filled her carriage, pressed up against the glass, peering to ascertain the nature of the commotion outside.

"Gentlemen," said Sir Cheech, from his standing position. "I believe we must leave this platform, or the crowd will knock it down and trample us to pieces!" It was evidently so. Those ordinary spectators directly below us were showing symptoms of the most pronounced agitation, and many were flowing away to the north; but greater danger was approaching in the mob of panicked and choking commoners flooding up toward us from the riverside.

"You are right, sir," said the editor of *The Nineteenth-Century And After*, cool enough in the crisis to ignite a new steam-cigar with a steady hand.

Sir Cheech leapt in one smooth movement over the side, as the editor, elderly Lord Collins and myself scrambled down the little ladder. Booths up and down Imperial Way were similarly voiding themselves of their occupants; but the crowd had reached the westernmost of these and I saw it collapse into splinters beneath the hysterical rush.

"Quick!" gasped Lord Collins. "But where?"

We were now in the midst of jostling humanity, and there was no clear path of escape. In moments the crowd would become a mob.

"Gentlemen, if you'll assist me," said Sir Cheech, crouching down. He shoved a man aside, got his fingers in at the crack of a paving slab and began to lift it. "If you'd be so kind..."

I dropped down and assisted him; as did Lord

Collins, and with some effort the slab came up. Beneath was a metal grating. The pistolette came out again, and a single shot broke the bolt holding it in place into iron-shavings. In less time than it takes to tell, we had lifted this grate and, as rapidly as we could, descended a ladder into the subterranean space, too relieved at the narrowness of our escape, at first, to query what this strange cavern might be.

THE LADDER LED down a dozen yards, no more, and we found ourselves in a darkness black enough for the Pythian Oracle herself. But the ever-resourceful Sir Cheech was carrying in his satchel an electrical pile, and to this he attached a small sphere of glass, no bigger than a golf ball. Simulated sunlight poured forth.

Our surroundings seemed to leap upon us: a tunnel, the floor compacted of damp sand, the walls curving up around us into the arch of the ceiling all paved with brick. Above, softened and distorted by the peculiar acoustics of this womb-space, the noise of the mob could be heard still, its clamor, softened by distance, now the mourning wail of swarming humanity.

"Where on earth are we?" I gasped.

"On earth or under it," said Sir Cheech. "Don't ye remember your *Hamlet*? This is an *antique tunnel*. In the days before our present Queen, hard though it be to imagine such a time, there were plans to dig out an entire network of tunnels subterranean to the city. *Hundreds* of leagues were planned, although only a few—this, for instance—completed."

"What possible reason could there be for such prodigious mole work," asked the editor of *The Nineteenth-Century And After* in an astonished voice.

"To dispose of sewage," said Sir Cheech.

"It seems an oddly elaborate method of sewage disposal," I observed, "compared with pipage. How could such tunnels be maintained? What if there were leaks? The ground could be contaminated."

"Ease of maintenance is only one of *many* advantages of overland pipes," said Lord Collins. "I cannot be comfortable in this—antique burial chamber."

"For the burial of our bodily waste?" said Sir Cheech. "Aye. And what is more, I have traveled in lands where that antique custom—excavating a hole in the earth and depositing human corpses therein—is still practiced."

Whether I shuddered with revulsion, or the chill, was hard to say. The sound of the mob, above, droned and pulsed. It was uncanny. "Barbarous indeed," I said, feeling like one of Pettison's blasphemously interred corpses.

"At any rate," said the editor, coolly, "we must be grateful to this space for the sanctuary it has afforded us on *this* day. I do not believe we would have escaped that stampede with our lives. Sir Cheech, I thank you. Though how you knew this tunnel even existed..."

"Oh," said Sir Cheech. "I have made a hobby of

all manner of arcana, particularly *arcana Londinium*. England used to be renowned for tunneling—I mean deep-shaft mining, not the scratching-at-the-surface open-sky mining we sometimes practice nowadays."

It was impossible to miss the note of snideness in his voice.

"You disapprove for Her Majesty's edict?" said Lord Collins, rather stiffly.

"Time to stop burning the forests," he replied. "Time to stop making charcoal."

"No charcoal!" chortled the editor of *The Nineteenth-Century And After*. "You are a droll individual, Sir Cheech."

"I assure you I am in earnest," he replied. He had his head on one side, as if listening for something. "Charcoal fuels are a contaminating technology."

"Perhaps there *is* a certain amount of pollution associated with steam technology," agreed Lord Collins. "But the *benefits* of such a source of power surely outweigh..."

He trailed off. The sounds of mobular commotion directly over our head surged to a brief crescendo. All of us, I suppose, were thinking the same thing: it was the terror of steam from pollution that had caused this pack-animal hysteria. It was a common enough occurrence, after all: the weekly newspaper would almost always carry reports of a burst sewage pipe. A breach in the Thames cover. An exploding steam engine.

"I am," said Sir Cheech, in a clear voice,

"something of an inventor."

We all turned to him. There he was, holding the egg of light in his hand, his arm outstretched, reminding me rather of Holman Hunt's *Victorissima Light of the World*.

"It is not the *steam*," he said, in lecturer's voice, "not the steam that poisons us. It is the Compound. Naturally, it would be possible to return to the dawn of the technology, and boil water without the compound. For without compound, water boils just as well, except that it boils at a temperature of ..." He looked from face to face. "Uncompounded water?" he repeated, not lecturer now so much as a School-Dame. "Does anybody know at what temperature water boils if one does not mix in the compound?"

"I know neither that," said Lord Collins, fiercely, "nor why it should be assumed I *ought* to know it."

"One hundred degrees!" said Sir Cheech, ringingly. "I'm sure we all learnt it at school. A nice round number, we can agree."

"It seems an implausibly *high* number," I demurred.

"Gentlemen," said Sir Cheech. "We must move on. We cannot merely wait here for the commotion to die down overhead. Since this tunnel is so close to the river, the moist sand beneath our feet is, I fear, damp with Thames water. There will be a certain amount of the Compound in the air, not conducive to our continuing health."

"Sir," said Lord Collins, becoming increasingly

choleric. "A gentleman should say directly what is on his mind. You are an opponent of the compound? You are, perhaps, an environmentalist?"

"Yes," said Sir Cheech, mildly, unholstering his gun and checking its chamber.

None of us could withhold a gasp. "To which group," asked the editor of *The Nineteenth-Century And After*, tossing his exhausted steam-cigar to the ground, "do you belong?"

"Perhaps I misunderstood the question? Do I take it you were asking, my lord, whether I am a terrorist? I am no terrorist."

Lord Collins's complexion had deepened. "Her Majesty's immortality is ordained by Providence! These Mortalists are *in love with Death*!"

"And I am no Mortalist. Nor do I belong to any other insurgent or illegal organization. But I *do* object to the compound. Wonderful though it be to boil water at forty degrees, and wonderful though the machinery is we have constructed around this fortuity, the fact remains that the compound is—*toxic* when inhaled. Fatal. And if we remain here we *will* start to feel the ill effects. Onward, gentlemen!"

"Onward—*where*?" I demanded.

But he had marched away. Since he was carrying the only light, the three of us were compelled to scuttle after him like children, or be left in the darkness.

* * *

WE WALKED, IT seemed, upwards along a slight

incline, and (Sir Cheech assured us) northwest, away from the river. The sand became looser beneath my soles, and the air seemed less tainted. "You're sure?" barked Lord Collins. "You know where you're *at*?"

"I ask ye to trust me," said Sir Cheech, without turning his head. "The danger from the fumes of Compound is receding. Unfortunately other dangers replace them. Rats, notably."

"Rats!"

"The fumes nearer the river keep them at bay," he said. "But as we move into drier ground, we're more likely to encounter them."

I had never encountered a rat, of course, save in stories of mariners meeting them in the depths of their ships and being eaten alive. I did not desire to find out whether such stories had a basis in truth, or not.

"Stop!" Lord Collins ordered. "Where are you *taking* us, man? Toward *rats*, d'you say? I'd rather take my chances with the mob!"

"My lord," said Cheech. "I request respectfully that you do not alarm yourself. Rats are not the monsters painted in dollar-dreadful magazines. They're little bigger than ferrets. And I am armed. Five minutes will take us to a hatchway through which we can return to the sunlight."

Perhaps it was my imagination, but I thought I saw Lord Collins shudder.

"Gentlemen!" said Sir Cheech, brightly. "Shall we?"

So he led the way, with his gun, and also with a lecture that he addressed, seemingly, at the empty subterranean corridor before us. It was about the evils of the compound, and its contagious pollution of mankind, and yet its necessity, for charcoal technology could not work at the needful rate if water had to be heated to one hundred degrees in order to generate steam. Lord Collins boomed: "So we should go back to horses and carts, eh?"

"Not at all! There is an alternative, and non-polluting, method of power-generation. Petroleum!"

"Stuff!" boomed Collins, in a slightly startled voice.

"I regret to say I must disagree, my lord," said Cheech, cheerfully.

"The *tar* derivative? Nonsense!"

"With only a very little refining," Sir Cheech was saying, "it can be used to power a special form of engine, for which I happen to possess the patent. An engine that, when compared to any commercially available compounded-steam engine, is weight for weight *as* powerful, and utterly non-polluting."

"Petroleum!" scoffed Lord Collins. "Might as well fuel an engine on moonbeams. Or—" he added, with a dash of expression, as if a more appropriate comparison had suddenly occurred to him, "—or on *diamonds*!"

"Petroleum is easy to find," said Cheech. "The world's largest deposit is to be found in British controlled Persia. There are, beneath the ground, titanic reservoirs of the stuff."

"Stuffy nonsense! Nonsensical stuff!"

"I am one of a large group," Sir Cheech assured us, "who believe that the answers to the world's pollution problems are to be found neath the desert sands of Persia. Were Her Immortal Majesty to rescind her opposition to mining under the earth..."

"And *so* it becomes clear!" barked Collins, scornfully. "Illumination bursts upon me! You are one of these *mining* enthusiasts! You itch to wrench gold and jewels from the depths of Mother Earth—our *immortal* mother, over whose surface our immortal majesty reigns in wisdom!"

"Over two thirds of her surface only," said Cheech.

"Agitator! Guyfawks!!"

"And *may* we not wonder, my lord," said Cheech, with unflappable good humour, "*why* H.I.M., in her wisdom, interdicts all underground mining? I'll tell you another thing. The Imperial Guard has *eleven* divisions stationed in British Persia. Why so many? It's desert, almost all of it; there's nobody there to fight, save a few sour-hearted Bedu; and nothing to guard save lunar oceans of sand. Strange, no?"

"I'll not listen to treason," harrumphed Collins. "I close my ears to you, sir!"

* * *

WE SEEMED TO have been stalking through those arch-ceilinged brick tunnels for a very long time, following the ever-receding gleam of Cheech's electrical light. Five minutes, he had said; but surely thrice-five had passed. We reached a place where a side tunnel connected with the main one. Sir Cheech approached it cautiously. Holding out his electrical illumination he revealed a veritable Planetarium—scores of stars, arranged in a glittering display. And then, the plunging realization that these mock stars were all arranged in pairs. "Dear me," he said, in a low voice, pushing the light further in, and the darkness plumped and solidified into the shapes of scores upon scores of black, swag-bellied rats.

He aimed his pistolette, and I had just enough time, before panic overtook my mind, to think: but what good is a single gun against such a population of devils?

My memory becomes hazy. I recall the rusty shriek of one of the beasts, as if calling his troop to battle, and then the ear-injuring din of the whole population. I remember Cheech's weapon discharging, very loud in the close space, and a flash. But then I can remember only the whirlpool, or sandstorm, of the *corpus ratti*: they moved with a ferocious smoothness and rapidity, swarming as insects do; the ground, the curving walls, even the ceiling overhead, all covered with motion. For long seconds we were surrounded on all sides by the beasts. Somebody was yelling—no words, just a vocalic scream. And then, miraculously, they were all gone. Pettison span about and thrust his arm along the tunnel along which we had just come. The illumination caught the back of the mass of animals, disappearing. Their bestial din receded.

The noise of somebody screaming still filled the air. I looked about. The person yelling was me. I placed a hand over my own mouth.

"I'm sorry," I gulped. "I apologize."

"Not in the least," said the editor of *The Nineteenth-Century And After*. "That was indeed a—fright." He was trying to fit a new steam-cigar in his mouth, but his hand, now, was trembling too violently to enable the action.

"Close call, what?" said Pettison, his good spirits apparently untouched.

"Why didn't they attack us?" Collins asked, putting into words the question I was too terrified to voice. My heart was leaping inside my chest like a frog.

"I've no idea," he replied, giving the noble lord—for reasons I could not wot—an intense look. "I've no idea *my lord*. But we'd best push on. Let's get out of here before we encounter any more of those... things."

"Amen," I said. My right hand was afflicted with a deep shudder, although, oddly, my left was not.

"Come," said Sir Cheech. "Not far now. A minute—two at the most. Off we go!"

We fell into a brisker step behind his lead. For one minute we made our way through the unnatural subterranean space; one minute became two; two became five.

"And what do we know of this Pettison?" said the editor of *The Nineteenth-Century And After*, close in my ear. "Save only that he made his first appearance in polite society a year ago, *supposedly* after sojourning in the distant east for some years? And what if his name *is* all over the steamternet? Say it *is*? It's hardly an authoritative substitute for Debrett's! Oh, he's *supposed*," he went on, giving this word a frankly disbelieving spin, "*supposed* of the Hampshire Pettisons. But what if he don't belong to them? Who would ever be ill-mannered enough to query his affiliation?"

"What's your point, my dear fellow?"

"Listen!" said the editor of *The Nineteenth-Century And After*. "Whose booth were we sitting in to watch the parade?"

"Yours," I said. "I thought."

"*His*!"

"Oh! And he... invited you?"

"He saw me talking with you at Jester's, and enquired if I knew you. I told him yes. *Then* he asked if I cared to join him in his booth for the Titanium, and why not ask my friend—*you*, Roberts—as well."

"Rum," I conceded.

"I confess I was relieved not to be put to the bother of organizing a booth myself. I confess that. But now—look at us! Creeping through the ground like blasphemous moles, at his instigation? He just *happened* to set up a booth exactly on top of a secret door in the pavement of Imperial Way?

He was fiercely ready to dart down that hatch of his, though, wasn't he?"

"He could hardly know that the Mortality boys were going to infernal-device the Thames."

"Couldn't he, though?"

This went, I thought, too far. "Come!" I chided.

"But who's to be certain it *was* terrorists? By which I mean: who's to say *he* mightn't be one of them?" The editor of *The Nineteenth-Century And After* put his head closer to mine, such that we touched, and spoke in a smaller voice. "That was a clever ruse of his, though, was it not? The crowd, driven frenzied by the explosion?"

We walked on. I was very conscious of the back of Pettison's head, the top of his hat nodding a little way forward and back with the motion of his lope, alternately stretching and squashing the dark oval of its summit. I was afraid that he would be able to hear our words—foolishly afraid perhaps, given that he was thirty yards ahead of us down the tunnel, whilst we were now talking in the most girlish of whispers.

"Say he's brought us down here to murder us!" hissed the editor of *The Nineteenth-Century And After*. And as he said it, I knew it must be true. The horror of our situation—deep beneath the city, in grottos few of the population even knew existed, at the mercy of a man who had revealed, to say the least, eccentricities.

"What must we do?"

"We must all rush him together and seize his firearm," hissed the editor of *The Nineteenth-*

Century And After. "You're younger than I, so you try to hold him down, and I shall disarm him. But we must act together, or—"

He broke off. Sir Cheech had stopped, and was looking at us.

"The compound is an isoquinoline-carboxamide," Sir Cheech said, suddenly, in a loud voice. "What is *not* well known is that the compound's alteration to the one-hundred-four degree valence of individual water molecules enables water itself to boil at—but, gentlemen, I apologize. You are not in the mood for a lecture on chemistry."

"If you keep this up," stormed Lord Collins, "I shall thrash you, sir! Thrash you, knight of the realm or no! What do you *mean*, by bringing us to this infernal place?"

"We're here," said Sir Cheech. He lifted his illuminating light, and we saw a ladder—unrusted, and gleaming—rising to a metal trapdoor set into the roof. On the underside of this, very clearly visible, were the Royal-Imperial Arms, and the legend: *Sanctus Jacobus*.

"Saint James's Palace!" exclaimed Lord Collins. "I knew it! You *are* a traitor—a terrorist!"

"We cannot effect an egress here," said the editor of *The Nineteenth-Century And After* in a shocked voice. "This leads into the private royal grounds! It would be grotesquely inappropriate for us to trespass in such a place, though our lives depended on it!"

"Are you *mad*, sir?" boomed Collins.

What happened next confirmed every terrible suspicion that had been growing in my mind during this strange, underground walk. Sir Cheech, who was still carrying his pistolette in his right hand, raised his arm and aimed the weapon directly at the forehead of Lord Collins.

"Threaten a peer of the realm?" gasped Collins.

"You are afeard of dying, my lord?" said Cheech, in an easy and insolent tone.

"It is the merest treachery!"

"Gentlemen," said Cheech, in a clear voice, addressing us two. "Believe me when I say that I shall offer *you* no violence. My friend," he said, looking directly at the editor of *The Nineteenth-Century And After*. "The acoustics of a tunnel such as this can produce strange lucidities. I heard every word you said to Mr. Roberts here."

The editor drew in a hard breath. "I was right: you mean to do *murder* in this hidden place."

"By no means," said Cheech. "Neither am I a terrorist. As to the infernal device that ruptured the Thames covering. Well—perhaps I *had* heard rumours that such an assault was being planned. As the Mortalists—a group, my lord, of which I repeat I am not a member—might say: is the crime in rupturing the covering, or in allowing the Thames to become so polluted with compound in the first place? Oh, there are mysteries to be plumbed here."

"I shall see you hanged, sir," barked Lord Collins.

"Gentlemen," said Cheech, ignoring him and

addressing himself to us. "You are right to wonder whether it is mere coincidence that has enabled me to lead," he nodded at the editor, "the empire's chief journalist and," a nod in my direction, "its most esteemed novelist to this very place. Through a subterranean tunnel, part of a network joining together all the royal facilities! Subterranean tunnels dug by a monarch who has forbidden subterranean tunneling! Mr. Roberts," he said, fixing me with his pale eyes. "As a novelist, does this not intrigue and titillate your imagination?"

"A titillated imagination is of little use to a man about to die," I said.

"Pshaw, why would I kill you? I need you to write my story. And I need *you*," he looked at the editor, "to report the news I am about to uncover." Throughout this he kept the pistolette aimed at Lord Collins.

"*Pettison, a Traitor's Tale*," I said.

"Call it rather," he said, "*Petroleum: a Tale of the Future*."

"A Tale of the Future?" said the editor in an incredulous voice. "By Adam Roberts? Nonsense."

"As for you, my friend, your story shall be: the Secret of the Queen's Immortality—Revealed."

"There's no secret there," said Collins, rapidly. "She is immortal by divine providence."

"Not a very *scientific* explanation, that," said Sir Cheech. "Do you have a better one, Mr. Roberts?"

"I have heard it said," I offered, trying to inch a little closer to the fellow and be within snatching distance of his weapon, "that she possesses a greater concentration of élan vital."

"And if we were to suppose that there's no such thing as élan vital?"

"Then there is some other explanation. What does it matter?"

And then everything happened very rapidly. There was a grinding noise from above, and a solid sleeve of light fell from the opened hatchway. Glancing up, Pettison exclaimed, incomprehensibly, "Of *course* the *rats*!" On the instant Lord Collins danced forward shouting "Ho! ho! strangers here!", at whoever might be above us. Straightaway Cheech's pistolette discharged with a firework flash. The din was enormously loud in the enclosed space, a hammerblow to the ears. I saw Lord Collins reel away, marked like a Hindu on his forehead. I acted without thought—I hurled myself forward and, as if I were back at school on the Merseyside Eton rugby fields, connected bodily with Sir Cheech. He was a larger man than I, and more used to physical exertion, but I caught him off guard and tipped him off balance. We went down together onto the dry sand, and his pistolette fired again—I felt the ball stirring savage tourbillons in the air not more than an inch from my ear, and I heard the ricochet whine off the brickwork. We struggled briefly, but Cheech flipped me on my back. He leapt to his feet again. I looked up to see a succession of people dropping through the open hatchway into the tunnel—beefeaters, wearing, of course, their skintight scarlet bodysuits rather than the ceremonial uniforms they don for tourists—half a dozen of them. Pettison's electrical light had been dropped and extinguished, and by the light pouring through the open hatchway I saw Cheech trying to bring his weapon to bear on one of the newcomers. There was a flash, the sound of a side of meat being cleaved by a butcher's cleaver, and a sudden, unpleasant sound—the sound of a sluice of cowflop in a dairy-herd field. Cheech shook his head from side to side, still grinning his diabolic grin, in careless denial of all that was happening. Except that he was not shaking his head. His head had been materially loosened. A second beefeater had stepped up and was readying his sword, but needlessly; for the wobble of Cheech's head had increased, and suddenly his head had fallen entire away, to hang from his back like the hood of a monstrous cloak of skin. His body dropped to its knees. It thumped the sand with its chest. It was over.

THERE IS, YET, a coda to this strange adventure.

My friend the editor and I were, of course, questioned by the Polis-Police for many hours; but we were questioned by the world's media for longer still. The story itself became a more-than-nine-day wonder, eclipsing even the outrage at the infernal-devicing of the Thames alongside the

Royal Parade—a barbarous and cowardly act, as everyone agreed, perpetrated by the Mortalists in sheer hatred of the serene immortality of Her most High and Imperial Majesty, but neither the first nor the last of such outrages. But the discovery of tunnels directly beneath London? Tunnels, it seems, preserved in direct contravention of the Contra Excavatio? That was an extraordinary piece of intelligence indeed.

Investigation into the background of Sir Cheech revealed that the editor had been correct in his suspicions: his title was a hoax, his family connections non-existent, his background a sham. He was, by his own words, condemned as not only a traitor but a madman and a murderer. It seemed clear that his intention had been to infiltrate the royal estate, perhaps with a view to attempting assassination upon the Prince of Ireland (who was in residency at St James's Palace at the time). So far from being a genuine knight of the realm, he was, it seems, an ambitious and greedy money-grubber, a man who hoped to sell stock in the crazy Persian-Petroleum Development Company of which he was the director. It was mysterious, but not in an involving way; it was, rather, a seedy and unpleasant sort of dollar-dreadful case.

A royal pronouncement responded to the discovery of the tunnels by announcing that they would be filled with rubble, in accordance with Her Majesty's serene edict forbidding the surgical violation of Holy Mother Earth.

As for myself, and the editor of *The Nineteenth-Century And After* too: we were the toast of the city. Never mind that my so-called heroism had been belated, and rather ineffective—for I had not, after all, prevented the murder of Lord Collins. Nevertheless I was lauded. I had enough invitations to dinner to mean I need not dine at home for a month. Sales of my novels achieved tropospheric heights, and I began—at my publisher's most earnest entreaty—assembling notes toward a memoir of my bizarre adventure. It was in the midst of this I received an invitation of the sort no gentleman would decline: an invitation from Buckingham Palace itself.

I PRESENTED MYSELF at the appointed time. An equerry brought me through to a room where refreshments were spread on a table of oak. "Her Majesty wished to thank you herself," this gentleman informed me, "for your heroism in the blasphemous caverns beneath St James."

"Her immortal Majesty is gracious indeed."

An electronic communicator piped plaintively on the wall by the door, and the equerry tipped his head. "Excuse me, Mr. Roberts," he said. "It seems I am called away. Please refresh yourself, and I shall return momentarily." He shimmered, as the expression has it, through the door. I was left alone.

Momentarily, though, was no accurate assessment. Minutes lengthened. A little nervous to be in so august a building, in proximity to the ruler of two thirds of the world, I drank a glass of pear wine, and then a second. I ate a little of the excellent game pie. I stood for a long time examining the Lord Blake portrait of H.I.M. on the wall over the table: a three-quarter length study in purple, silver and black—it was magnificent art of course, but was perhaps, and despite the wreaths of steam filling and softening the composition, too accurate a portrayal. It captured too well that distinctive quality Victoria possesses; the overplumpness of face that implies a sort of idealized artistic unrealism—as if her true form is a featureless white sphere, and her features have been added at the front as an afterthought, to spare human sensibilities the shock of encountering the blankness of her true countenance. As if she were not, exactly, human. But then again, do not the metaphysicians say as much? Humanity is defined by its finitude, after all. Take the death away and you remove humanity, and what is left, whatever it is, however sublime it may be, is therefore not human. We can tolerate an immortal queen, where we could not tolerate immortality bestowed on any lesser individual, because the immortality that seems fitting to a creature as elevated above ordinary humanity as a monarch would become monstrous associated with you or I.

I waited. From time to time the electronic communicator by the door bleeped, but of course I made no move to answer it. My morse is so rusty that I could hardly have deciphered the message. I drank another *verre* of the excellent pear wine. By and by a footman came through to ask if I needed anything, and to apologize for the delay (some minor matter in the East Wing). I told him I was enjoying perfect satisfaction, but after he had gone I realized, belatedly, that I needed to avail myself of the water closet, the location of which was a mystery to me.

I let myself out of the room, and wandered a lengthy red-carpeted corridor, past a series of other impasto and photolithographic royal portraits. The Princess of Wales. The Prince of India. A full-length Duke of Florida wearing traditional Floridan *galoshei* and headwear. The prodigiously thick pile underfoot, dampened sound, which meant that when three Imperial Guards went sprinting past me, apparently appearing from nowhere at my left shoulder and dashing in front of me, I was completely taken by surprise. Their haste persuaded me both that something serious was amiss in the palace, and that I had better return to the room in which I had been deposited. Accordingly I turned and made my way back along the corridor, until, reaching the door of the reception room, I turned the handle.

I can hardly express the dismay I felt to discover that I had mistaken the entrance; the door opened onto a large and crowded chamber, very high-ceilinged and filled with royal servants in a state of milling agitation. At the far end an equerry was unlocking a metal cabinet in order to pass out rifles to royal servants. A double door in the far wall had been opened, both leaves, and a troop of Imperial Guards were marching through it in good order, armed. The room as a whole was crowded with all ranks: scarlet-bodied beefeaters; lords-in-waiting; sundry MPs, chattering and moving. Nobody seemed to have noticed me, and of course I slipped back through the door. I stood in the corridor in a state of severe bafflement.

A good deal of my confusion was occasioned by the fact that I had seen, in amongst the crush of people—Lord Collins himself: standing talking to two beefeaters. The same Lord Collins so widely reported as murdered in the media—whom I had seen, with my own eyes, shot in the forehead by the traitor Cheech.

I wandered back along the corridor some dozens of yards, convincing myself that, of course, I must have been mistaken—that it was merely an individual with some resemblance to the noble lord—when the door opened and Collins himself came out, still in the company of the two red-clad eaters of beef. He went by, paying me not the slightest heed. But there was no mistaking his face. He even bore a small circular scar above the bridge of his nose. And yet all the papers had carried his obituary! Her Majesty had expressed personal grief at his death!

I had no time to ponder this imponderable, however: an Imperial Guardsman, six foot tall, placed a hand onto my shoulder and pulled me away. I began articulating apologies, begging to be shown a water closet, insisting I was an invited guest—not terribly dignified, I am afraid. It was a shock to be apprehended by a soldier; but a greater shock awaited me. Hauling me to the side of the room, this guardsman pressed himself against me. "Don't panic, Mr. Roberts," he hissed, "and please be prepared to accept what may, at first, seem improbable. You will recognize a dead man."

"I have *just seen* him!"I said, high-pitched, and flapping my hand in the direction Lord Collins had gone. I was, I confess, overstrung. "He went *that* way—it is Collins, the very man! It *is* Collins!"

"You don't say?" said the guardsman. "Don't mean him. I mean *me*. Take another look."

I had seen only the uniform, of course, as one tends to when in the company of a soldier or policeman. But to look into his face was to see Sir Cheech Pettison brought back to life, with not so much as a stitch or scar upon his broad and muscled neck.

THIS REVIVIFIED PETTISON hurried me along the corridor. "I don't understand," I told him. I said this more than once.

"It's a lot to explain," he said. "And the problem with a lengthy explanation right this minute is, it's all kicking off."

I had no idea what he meant by this outlandish expression, except that he repeated it, so the phraseology lodged in my head. "It's all kicking off, so there's little time *to* explain."

He pushed open a door with his boot, and pulled me inside. When he turned the light on I saw that we were in a water closet: a line of white porcelain bowls fixed to one wall in a line, a line of sinks on the other. A spherical boiler murmured to itself in the corner, carbuncular with metal bolts. Pipes spread banyan-wise along the ceiling. The floor was hard-carpeted with linoleum.

I'm sorry to say that I stated the obvious. "I saw you killed," I reminded him. "I saw your head removed."

"Understandable," said Sir Cheech. "Understandable confu-ew-*u*sion. Wow, though. I mean—wow."

"What?"

"Weird? Weird. I mean that where *I* come from we're friends—it's *well* odd to meet you as a stranger."

"Where *you* come from?" I repeated.

"London," he said. "Listen, ti-*ay*-ime is *not* on our side. The man you saw killed *was* me, in a way. Say a friend of mine. Different reality. I have a pamphlet," he added, fumbling in his pockets like an anti-alcohol or votes-for-the-elderly campaigner. "Somewhere—hold on."

"A pamphlet?" I goggled.

"Cheesy, I know."

"Are you a missionary?"

"It's simpler than my attempting a long-winded—look, here you go." He drew a rather goat-eared fold of paper from inside his jacket and handed it to me.

"You are Sir Cheech's twin, evidently," I said, taking it. "The resemblance is unmistakable. Have you come to avenge his death?"

"Steam," he said, mopping and mowing with his face to a peculiar degree. "It's a curse and a boon. For us, I mean. Here you go."

I took the paper and glanced unseeingly at it. Naturally I digested almost none of it at that time, dazzled and confused as I was. I must concede gratitude for the donation, however, for it means that my narrative can report the fantastical details of the fellow's story, details I surely would not have recalled otherwise. I reproduce it here with its infelicities and solecisms intact.

U.F.R.

HEY! Confused? Don't be!!

You ever heard of the many-worlds theory? *IT'S TRUE!!* There are twenty-four seperate [*sic*] Realities. (Why 24 and not an infinite number, you ask?? Clever question! It's to do with Fundamental Fermionic Flavors, but, hey! *We Don't Have Time For That!*)

Each of these 24 realities is a distinct and seperate [*sic*] thing, but in *Reality 1* (hey! We invented the gates—*we get to call ourselves Number 1! Deal with It*!!) scientists have invented Fermionic

> Gateway Generators, that allow passage between the various realities. So as not to interfere too drastically with the inviolable rights of seperate [*sic*] realities, we place careful controls over who gets to pass through these gates. Accredited and properly trained agents only! The agent who gave you this pamphlet will have about him Unmistakable Proofs that he is not from your reality. Don't be scared. We come in peace!
>
> Ultimately, we hope that all 24 Realities will become united in a trans-real *Union of Federated Realities.* But until that day comes...?!?
>
> So long, friend!! FOR NOW!!

The one phrase that danced out at me from this slew of barbarous words was "Unmistakable Proofs". I repeated the phrase to him.

"Yeah, look," he replied, rubbing his nose with the flat of his hand. "I guess my proof is—well, you saw me beheaded, no? So how come I'm here?"

"You," I said, as if to a child, "are his twin."

"Right. Well that's not it. Look, the pamphlet..."

"Which is atrociously written, I might say."

"Friendly!" he squeaked. "Is the *idea.* Approachable! Look, I've worked in seven, and never one like yours. Sir Chee-*eah*!-eech was a *friend* of mine. I'm sorrier than a cockless man he's dead. But there are *opportunities* here...let me put it this way. Where I come from, the reality I was born into..."

He stopped. He seemed to be looking for inspiration on the ceiling.

"Well there's no monarchy there, that's for one thing. We're under the benign auth-or-*or*ity of the Corporate Praepotens. Companies, you see. Making money. And *Oil* Companies first among equals."

I assumed of course that he meant cooking oil, but, on my making some comment to that effect, he proved himself strangely eager to correct me. "*Petroleum* companies," he said.

Then I remembered what his brother had said. "This same petroleum that...?" I began.

"It's what it's all about," he insisted. "All this technology you have here, run on steam? This weird compound you put in the steam to lower the boiling wossname and increase the pressure thingum, yeah?"

"I can only assume," I said, "as is sometimes the case in families, that hereditary intellect and manners were distributed unequally between yourself and your brother."

"You're not listening. He wasn't my brother. He was *me*, one way of looking at the question, just as, in a way, Stallion Steve is *you*. That's as hard for me to believe as—oh never mind. Try get your head round this: I come from a reality where society diverged radically from your timeline in the ni-ai-*ai*neteenth century. You developed steam. We developed petroleum. Ours, the superior technology," he added, energetically. "But that's by the bye."

"Aladdin's caves filled with *tar* in Persia," I said. "Such nonsense! Now, now, my good fellow: I—insist—you tell me what's going on!"

"You-oo-*oo* ain't the only one of the Two Dozen to have timelines in which petroleum ain't developed. Though none of the others are qui-*ay*-ite like *yours*. But my employers *like* that about you, see. It means we can come in and strike a deal and *mine out* the petrol. Which, after all, you don't wantee-wantee. Make mucho mucho dinero. We figured you'd be amenable. But, no, oh *you* have an Immor-hor-*or*tal Queen Victoria."

I stared at him. "Are you perhaps," I asked, "an idiot?"

"When we first scouted, we assumed it was a ceremonial title. Yeah? Like—well, where I come from is this geezer"—he used this, term, which I had not previously encountered; I assumed from context that it was a coarse reference to a female—"called Dolly Lama. Supposed to be immortal, but what actually happens on death is that the priests find a miraculously reincarnated version in some young kid in a nearby village. See? We assoo-oomed that's what was going on here. Only it *isn't* that! She actually *is* immortal. What's the song say? *One hundred seventy years of ever broa-hordening empire, one hundred seventy years of ever widening commerce...*"

"I am a loyal subject of Her Immortal Majesty," I broke in, hotly, "and will not stand idly by whilst you slander her. Call her *Dolly*? What ap*pall*ing..."

"*She's* not the Dolly. The other geezer—look, that's not *it*. You're *welcome* to your immortal Queen. You really are. Our scientists have no idea how she does it, but we don't care about that. All we want is a basic Mineral Rights treaty for Persia, and maybe for British Siberia too, and we'll leave everything else alone. We'll pay top dollar. Gold doubloons. Talents. But not only is she actually immortal, she actually for-*hor*bids mining. Jeebers knows why."

"Who?"

He blinked. "Look. You want to know why Cheech was here?"

"Your brother?"

"No and *no*. I'm only a neophyte. *He* was a grade one. Famous, he was. A celebrity, the real thing. Back where I come from. His dream was to search thoroughly through *all* the realities. To go through them all, and discover, uncover, *all* their mysteries. Why d'you think he took the name he did? Hence—look. *My* name: Bernard. Just Bernard. But, d'you want to know why Cheech was here?"

"Why you...?"

"Cheech wanted to understand *why* your ruler's so set against mining. That's all! Solving the mystery of her peculiar longevity was a *means* to that *end*. All we want to do is bring the joys of petroleum to your world. Or if your world ain't interested, then build a [*coition-related expletive*] tunnel through a Fermion Gate and *pump* the petroleum to our Reality, which I can assure you, sorely needs it. Sore. *Lee*."

Of course my jaw dropped down. I could not believe I had heard the expletive he had so casually dropped into his speech.

"I know it's hard to understand," he went on. "OK. But I ask you to make the effort. You're a writer, aren't you? OK. Imagine a world in which petro-*ho*-holeum is not some footnote in the science textbooks, some curio, but *the basis of a whole world-spanning technology*. Imagine a world with petrol driven cars, generators, planes… Actually, hold that thought, a world with [*coition-related expletive*] planes. Heavier-than-air flying machines, with petrol-driven motors. Wouldn't you like to see such a thing?"

I was too flabbergasted by the brutality of his mode of speech to reply.

"I can see," he said, confidentially, "you are. You should write a stor-*or*-ory set in such a world. You really should. But for now we have bigger fish to fry. A rival corporation—not my employers, I stress that—a rival corporation has sent troops through. Here. Right now. They reckon they can exploit the outrage—there's *outrage*, oh yes, real outrage that Pettison was murdered by your boys here. T.P. think they can storm the palace, seize your Immortal Majesty, and force terms. It's the wrong way to do business."

"Seize her?" I cried. "Assault Her serene Majesty—*kidnap her?*"

"You can see it's a serious situation."

"Serious? It's monstrous!"

"Sure—sure—look. You got to understand. It's really... confusy-*hus*ing for me, too. In *my* reality, you and I are close mates. Best buddies. I mean, I know you're not the same *person* as *my* Steve, in a manner of speaking, but... you *have* to share many of the same qualities he has! We're sure to hit it off. Ain't we?"

I looked at the long-barrel pistol hung at his waist, and tried to calculate the odds of my being able to get away and raise the alarm before he could tackle me.

"Things are moving very rapid, like," he urged. "We need to get hold of a senior Royal. We need to explain to him that your Queen would do better to throw-in her lot with *Agglomerated Oil*. That if she don't, she'll find the *Tête Petrole* people will stor-*hor*m her palace by force."

"Who?"

"It's—they're—it's a rival petroleum company, OK? Christopher Christ, it's like explaining everything to a six year-old. In *my* Reality petrol is so valuable that rival corporations fight over reserves. Literally fight. OK?"

"You're trying to tell me," I said, incredulous, "that in your world, this *tar* is..."

"Never mind that! All you need to hold in your head now, is that T.P. are trying to *kidnap your*

Queen, and that, with my help, you can prevent that."

I cannot, of course, say that I believed him; although it certainly seemed safest to play along with his fantasies. "You can save Her Majesty from this fate?"

"Yes!"

"You and Agglutinated Oil?"

"Agglomerated! *Agg*-Christ!"

"And what must I do?"

"You were invited here this evening, weren't you? You're to meet a senior royal. Go meet him! Just introduce me, and I'll do the rest. Once I've made con-*hon*tact, I been given the power to nego-*ho*tiate."

"And why should I trust you?" I asked, reasonably enough. But the question seemed to inflame his choler.

"It's me! It's *me*, Steve! Can't you see it's me? Steve! Don't you fee-he-*ee*l the connection?"

"Be calm, sir," I implored, with a stern voice. "I intend to do nothing at all until I have evacuated the contents of my bladder."

I LED BERNARD back along the corridor toward, as I hoped, the reception room in which I had originally been deposited. Audible sounds of commotion were issuing from some distant wing of the palace; yelling and thumping. Something was wrong. "Forgive me," I said, "if I do not necessarily see why Agglutinated Oil should be any better disposed to Her Majesty than—"

"Aggl-*hom*merated!" he shouted.

Crack. Crack, crack. We both stopped. It was the unmistakeable sound of gunfire, distant, like the popping of corn over a fire. It persisted. Then, like a crumpled gong being sounded, we heard a much larger detonation. "We haven't much time," said Bernard. "Come on!"

"The palace is under military attack," I cried. My heart was singing to itself "Britons Awake", and I knew now what to do. It was a national crisis. What had taken place in the tunnels before was a mere preliminary; the true war was only now beginning.

I resolved: I would lead this man, Cheech Pettison's twin brother, into the reception room and then overpower him—or die in the attempt. It was my duty to try. Of course I believed no particle of his bizarre story of Alias Realities. As best I could decipher the situation, these fantastical stories were some arcane part of a new terrorist threat. Perhaps it *was* the Mortalists, whose structure, the papers assured us, was riven with factions and competing groups—some who wanted the secret of immortality shared with all, some who thought immortality itself an affront to God—some merely opposed monarchy whether immortal or not. This pseudoscientific-fiction of Bernard's was, I supposed, some ruse, or ideological blind, or perhaps some self-justificatory fantasy. Whatever the particular case, it was clear to me that Bernard was as grave a threat to H.I.M. as were the Agglutinists of whom he spoke.

I saw a door I thought I recognized. “In here,” I said, my hand on the handle. The sound of gunfire in the distance was almost as regular as a clocktick. My heart was trilling with fear, or with excitement (and, in the end, is there a difference between those two emotions?) I went through—and, mirabile! It *was* the reception room. *There* was the table, still spread with fine food. The first thing my eye saw was the half-drunk decanter of pear wine, and I resolved to clasp it about its crystal neck and invert it as a club to batter the skull of my fellow man. The second thing my eye saw, as I stepped briskly through, was a footman. “Mr. Roberts?” he said. “Her Majesty hopes you'll accept her apologies for keeping you waiting.”

Heedless of the risk—a real danger, I thought—that Bernard might simply shoot me in the back, I rushed upon this person. “The palace is under attack!”

“Indeed, sir,” said the footman. “Naturally Her Majesty does not consider such inconveniences excuse her from the courtesy due a guest. She requested me most particularly to express her regret.”

“We must take up arms against the invader!” I cried.

At this the footman stiffened, standing straighter—for one moment, I giddily thought, to adopt a military posture in agreement with my words. But no: he boomed, in full footman-voice, “His Royal Highness, the Prince of Wales!”

I looked wildly about. And indeed, there he was, in the very flesh, *tywysog cymru*, the royal man himself. Nothing, as the philosopher once said, so greatly resembles a thing as the thing itself, and he looked intensely *like* himself: his large, saggy, friendly face, sherry-brown and with that great moustache. A *walrus* moustache, I believe, is the correct designation, but to tell the truth it—perfectly black, and cut neatly into a fat lunular crescent of hair—was the only portion of his face that *didn't* resemble a walrus.

He had been grazing at the table, and he turned corpulently and ambled toward me. Despite all that was going on, I could not help myself snapping my arms to my sides and bowing, briskly. "Your Royal Highness!"

"Roberts, is it? Splendid! *Good* of you to come. And good of you to wait. And *very* good, what you did in that foul tunnel last month. Heroism, what?"

"Her Majesty is in danger," I squeaked.

"Enemies everywhere," he nodded. "Constant vigilance required."

"I mean tonight—an attack on the palace, right now!"

"Not to worry, all in hand. So. And what is it *you* do?"

"I, sir?" I was finding it hard to make my mind focus on his word. "I am a writer."

"Splendid. And you find that interesting?"

"Sir, forgive me, but… behind you? *Behind you*! Look! Behind you!"

The Prince of Wales looked round, with torpid slowness. "Aha," he said. "And *your* name?"

"Bernard," said Bernard, stepping out from the corner of the room with his arm held straight, and his long-barreled gun aimed directly at the Prince.

"Splendid!" said the Prince, brushing some pork-pie crumbs from the underside of his moustache. "And what is it *you* do?"

"I work for a petroleum company."

"How interesting. A *what* company, did you say?"

"We discover, refine and sell Petroleum, a tar-based derivative," said Bernard coming a little closer, his aim never wavering from the royal face. I glanced about, but the footman seemed to have fallen into a kind of torpor.

"And your specific job within that company?"

"My job," said Bernard, "is to travel along interdimensional pathways shaped out of the complex webbing of fermions, from one to another reality."

"Splendid," said the Prince. "And do you find that interesting?"

"It has its monotonies."

"Splendid! You have a gun, I see? I'm rather partial to hunting myself."

"Your highness, he's *insane*!" I yelped, unable to contain myself. "He will shoot you! The whole palace is under attack!"

"Shoot me?" burbled his Royal Highness. "Over *petroleum*?"

"You must excuse the weapon, sir," said Bernard. "But it is imperative that we have a little ch-*ah*-hat, and I really need your attention fo-hocussed on me. Now, although you may not know a great deal about it, petroleum is …"

"Oh I know a *lot* about petroleum," said the Prince, beaming.

Bernard blinked. "A rival company to mine is attempting to kidnap the Queen, in order to …"

"People say," the Prince interrupted, "that it could be used as *a less polluting fuel*. They say so, don't they? They say so. But I feel we're happy enough. Aren't we? With our little charcoal burners? Who needs more powerful machinery anyway? A little pollution doesn't bother *us*. What? What?"

The tension was too much for me. The truth is—and I am ashamed to confess it—my self-restraint cracked. Everything had become too much for me. That simple statement is all I have, to explain the reason I acted as I did. I threw myself at Bernard. I yelled. It is difficult, indeed, for me to recover the exact parameters of my state of mind, but I believe I hoped to interpose myself between the gun and His Royal Highness, and so prevent the fatal bullet from striking him. But if this was my plan I achieved its execution very poorly indeed. I stumbled, and collided with Bernard. The pistol roared with rage, close beside my head. I span about, just in time to see the Prince of Wales himself fall—with a curl of blood spouting from his neck, directly through the knot of his silken necktie.

At this I lost self control. I became a wild animal, driven by pure rage, absolutely fearless.

My anger gave me the strength of ten men. I wrestled with Bernard. As it transpired, however, none of the ten were very strong.

"Let go the gun, Steve, let *go*!" Bernard bellowed. "What you *playing* at?"

The gun discharged again, with its horrifying roar. The two of us crashed against the table, and knocked pies, and bottles, and a plate of caramalised eels, to the floor. Still the footman stood by, motionless. I turned my head to yell at the fellow—to fetch help! to assist me himself!—but the cry stuck in my throat—for there, on his feet again, his shirt prodigiously bloodied, but looking otherwise none the worse for his experience, was His Royal Highness.

"Sir," I squeaked. "Not—dead?"

Precisely as I spoke this last word the pistol discharged a third time. I was conscious of a flash, and a blinding headache pain across my temple, and a sensation of dizzying spinning, cyclonic motion, swirling round and round like a windmill's blades.

Light shrank away.

But I was not dead.

Nor was I quite unconscious. I was, I slowly realized, lying upon the thick carpet. The strands of the pile were in my mouth. I could not move, and the throb, the throb within my skull was atrocious. It interrupted with my ability to hear. I was buried an inch below the dirt and great iron wheels were continually rolling and passing by over my skull.

Voices—whose, I could not say—tuned into and out of my consciousness.

"... immortality," somebody was saying, "... is *hard* for mortals to tolerate. In the case of a single figure—my sainted mother—a cult may be formed. But if the general public were to discover that the entire royal family is immortal: all our relatives; the House of Lords; thousands of individuals—well, if they were to discover that, then there would be riots..."

"Does it," said another voice, "*hurt* when I shoot you?"

"Of course it hurts! You think I don't experience *pain*? Naturally it hurts..."

I blanked. It felt as if I were sliding round and round a helter-skelter fairground slide. My rotary motion was synchronized with the throbbing pulses in my forehead; and when I reached the bottom of this metaphorical corkscrew I found myself propelled inevitably back to the top, where I stopped, turningly, and embarked again upon the ride. All this was accompanied by an inner turmoil, a juddering screeching, a horrible cacophony.

Consciousness flashed intermittently upon me.

"...You have heard of *cellular* immortality," a deep voice was saying. "You may, perhaps, be prepared to believe that it is the only form of immortality that Nature tolerates."

"You seem awful well informed about..." said another voice, less resonant. I thought I recognized it.

"My kind evolved long ago. Your kind took a different evolutionary path, that's all. That's all. Multicellular life has its advantages, of course, especially when it comes to coordinated *rapidity* of action.

"...awful well informed about..." the other voice droned.

"But we were the *first* to evolve intelligence. We lived in the primal jungles, and plumbed the philosophical mysteries, when multicellular-mortal life was nothing more than lumbering brutish organic *machines*, monsters tearing at one another's flesh with talons."

"... *evolu-u-utionary* theory, is what... "

"But we were *slow*. That is our *Dasein*: slowness. We ought to have put some energy into managing the world. But we didn't. The climate changed; the forests collapsed and were covered beneath wildernesses of sand. Our environment crushed and blackened and liquefied. We were pressed into coal; we were dissolved in tar. We were unconcerned, of course. Being immortal, this environment was liveable. But the alteration made us, slowly, aware of possible other alterations, to come in the future. We resolved: to intervene in the world. So we found a way, eventually, and after much sedulous effort."

I strained to raise myself, or even just my head, from the floor. The effort made the repeated beats of pain more intense, and I blanked. The next thing I knew I had an eye open, and I saw Bernard's legs.

"...A simple negotiation. Nothing need change."

"But what use will *I* be as a hostage?" the Prince was saying, "If the other boys have *the Queen herself*?"

"You'll have to do. Maybe it can't ki-*i*-hill you, but—pain, you know. Pain. You come along with me now, Your Highness, OK?"

"It's a very kind invitation," said His Royal Highness. "But I have a better idea."

At this point my delirium got the better of me. The auditory hallucinations invaded the visual sensorium. I will spare the reader a detailed account of the strange, monstrous visions that proceeded from my heat-oppressed brain—as if you would be likely to believe accounts of His Royal Highness, Edward Prince of Wales, opening his mouth to the size of a Nilar leviathan, such that his teeth flattened and spread like dots drawn on an inflating balloon; any more than you would believe this dream-syrup of horror, he snapping down upon the head of the other—swallowing his head whole in his maw, and biting through his chest to lurch away leaving a quivering mass of flesh and the severed ends of ribs poking up, white in amongst the horror of red and purple. There was more: a Sophoclean chorus of cockroaches; a sense of the stars drawing streamers of white fire from the earth to the ground; of the world maggoty with decay and interpenetrated with holes as a sponge. A spongiform earth! A sponge soaked in black tar, black tar at the bottom of things, and dripping.

I AWOKE IN hospital, and in hospital I stayed for many long days. The wound to my head was not deep, but it had jarred my skull, upset the operations of my mental organ, and caused me to lose blood.

Of course, my first concern was to discover what had happened at the palace. My eyes, as a result of the nervous damage I had endured, could not focus on small print, so my good friend the editor of *The Nineteenth-Century And After*, who visited me frequently as I convalesced, read me the reports. The boldest and most alarming of attempted terrorist outrages—rifles fired in the Royal precincts—the beefeaters acquitted themselves with exemplary courage and military order, and vanquished the ill-prepared assault. Parliament to request the Queen for a nationwide police operation, in every Polis in the realm, to root out the evil of Mortalism.

"It's a good thing," I said. "A very good thing. I was terribly afraid for Her Majesty."

"Not for your own life?" asked the editor of *The Nineteenth-Century And After*, fiddling in his whiskers with his right hand.

"Such thoughts were forced from my head by the pressure of events. I cannot claim bravery," I confessed. "I hope I do not sound vainglorious—it was not heroism. But my head was so filled with terror at what might happen to Her Majesty that there was room for no other thought."

The editor of *The Nineteenth-Century And After* pushed his nose into his armpit, snuffled there, and afterwards returned to the business of riffling through his whiskers with his hand. There was something wrong with the hand, I noted. It was small. It was blasted, wizened. I had not noticed this deformity before.

"We established control over multicellular life by degrees," he told me. He was sitting on the end of my bed. I looked again, but he was still there: tiny, brown-furred, sitting on the end of my hospital bed between my two feet.

"You," I said, slowly, "are not the editor of *The Nineteenth-Century And After*."

"Insects were easy enough. Rats a little harder. But humans! My!"

"He was here a moment ago," I said.

"If only we had emerged into a world run by—cockroaches, say. How much easier our task would have been. But by the time we did come up, it was humans, humans, humans as far as the eye could see."

"He was reading the newspaper to me," I explained.

"We reign," said the rat. "Unicellular life owned the planet before your conception of time even begins. We are ubiquitous, immortal, ancient. You overlook us because we are small. But we are the masters."

"I don't understand," I said.

"To float in pearls of water, suspended in the steamy air," said the rat, in an animated voice. "To flow through the ooze! It's our home! And now this other realm wishes to *pipe it up* and combust it inside metal engines? No, no. Immortality is one thing, but no immortality can survive being aggressively thermally atomized! The elementary particles..." It stopped.

"I don't understand," I said again.

"We are the law and the surveillance. We keep order in your city," said the rat. "You're blind to it. The steam is in your eyes. It is *inside* your eyes, within the very balls. *I* live in this rat's neural tissues. I shall lick your wound, and grant you a gift few humans dream of: immortality." He scuttled up the bed, up my chest, and perched on my shoulder. I felt his little rat-hands tugging at the bandages covering my wound. "I shall work my saliva into your cut," he squeaked.

I did not like this development, but I felt an inertia. The door to my room opened. The rat was saying, "You must go into this other realm. When you have been prepared, you will go. Of course it will not be you, in the sense of consciousness—"

The nurse was at the bedside. I assumed she was here to assist the rat in removing my dressings; but instead she brought up a bed pan, and with impressive self-control, she swiped at the rat. Caught off balance it flew from my shoulder, bounced from the wall, and landed on the floor. She was on it in a moment, bashing and bashing its body with the metal pan. "Filthy beast!" she cried. "Filthy beast!"

"I was having a nightmare," I said.

"Ugh! Filthy! Filthy! And in a *hospital*!"

"I dreamed it spoke to me," I said, very slowly, enunciating each word very carefully.

"I'm sorry sir," she said, unheeding. "I don't know *how* that came to be in here. I'll fetch Matron."

"Is the editor of *The Nineteenth-Century And After* still here?" I asked. But I was talking to her uniformed back. "He was reading to me," I said. She was walking out, she was passing through the door. "He was reading the paper," I explained. But I was alone. The clock on the wall sounded its percussive tick. Then it waited. Another tick. The wait grew intolerable. Its hand was scared to make the leap from seven to eight, trembled on seven, considered the enormity of the gulf between the one number and the other, looked as if it would shudderingly decline to move—and then at the last moment rushed over the white to eight, where it settled, pantingly. There is something immense, and incomprehensible, about the universe. I looked at the parallelogram of sunlight on the wall beside the clock. The lowest apex of this shape exactly touched the top of the wainscot. I watched the bloodied mass of flesh on the floor creep, and creep, wriggling like an itchy thing, until it slipped out of sight behind the cabinet which stores my effects. Its blood marked a gory trail to show the path it had taken: vermillion red streaked with pinks and purples. I allowed my eye to scan this, all along its length; but, after a while, the blood too began to creep; to worm; and soon enough it had gone altogether. The floor was clean.

It was the most curious and distressing of nightmares. But, thank laudanum, I have had no repeat of it.

IRONY BEFRIENDS THE writer! No sooner had I placed my pen upon my desk, my labours completed for another day, and with but little more of my extraordinary tale to set down, than I noticed—through my study window—that

> [Coda. *I have pondered long, and weighed all possibilities, before electing, as literary executor, to place these papers before the public. The interest they must naturally excite, as the last, if incomplete, production of one of our most esteemed novelists is to be placed in the balance against the stretched, fantastical and eccentric nature of its contents. The strains of the extraordinary series of events,* so *widely reported in the newspapers, evidently took their toll upon his mind. For myself, having known him for many years, I cannot claim to be surprised. A writer must possess an Imaginative Faculty greater and more developed than that of an ordinary person; the events of last year evidently, in the case of my friend, subjected that imagination to grave pressure, and the hallucinations that resulted, recorded in this text, are symptomatic of this same.*

There are only a few supplementary notes needful after the truncated conclusion of the manuscript itself. One concerns the title. The composition of this, his last testament, occupied my friend during the space of several weeks. He began it in hospital, and continued it at his London residence, where I visited him many times. It was indeed I who discovered the work upon his desk, the last page laid out, the pen upon it—though the chair was empty.

The previous week I had asked him about the outlandish title he had chosen. My objection was that its meaning was obscure.

"But surely it is obvious," he countered. "Petroleum refers to the tar-derivative that so obsessed the strange fantasist Sir Cheech—"

"Let us call him Charles," I interrupted. "And not use his childish diminutive."

He seemed amused at my disdain. "You do not believe then that Sir Cheech is indeed homophonous with…?"

"No," I said. "But you were explaining the title. Petrol, I understand. Punk?"

"What do you think it means?"

"I assume it to be the Latin, punctus: a prick, a sting, a puncture—such as, for example, a bullet wound?"

He touched the scar on the side of his cranium. "Not so," he said. "After all, the bullet grazed, and did not puncture, my cranium."

"What then?"

"Doric Greek," he said, gravely.

"In that case I feel no shame at my ignorance. It is too long since I studied Greek, and I have long since forgot it all."

"Punkax," he said, with easy smile. "The Ionian is puntax, the Attic pundax."

"And the meaning?"

For that he fetched down the Liddell and Scott from his shelf and made me, enjoying himself at the jest, look it up myself. I found it, eventually: the bottom of a vessel, the depths of any thing, and a string of examples of the word in use from Plato, Theophrastus and Sophocles. "I still do not understand," I said.

"It seems to me," he replied, "that this story, for all its phantasmagoric elements, is more than mere jumble. Not that it contains any material truth, of course; I don't mean that. But rather that it might, as followers of Josef Breuer assert, be analyzed as a dream is analyzed. According to the teachings of Breuer, we all possess subterranean minds, lying underneath our daylight *minds—places where are to be discovered the buried past, our animal natures, the miasma and stink of our urges and sin. What is our adventure, but the materialization of a journey into the underworld, such as Odysseus or Aeneas undertake?"*

"The tunnels," I reminded him, "were real."

"Not that, but the other stuff. The dream and hallucinatory material. I believe my mind latched onto those things that Sir Cheech—Charles, if you prefer—said about petroleum lying underneath *the earth. This noxious, black, tar lying at the bottom of things, like the accumulated waste and dirt and oil and filth at the bottom of the human mind. Emanations, or some manner of contamination in my mind produced the strange nightmare visions I record here."*

We discussed other things, and on occasion my friend asked my advice. One concerned a passage suppressed from the manuscript, recording a hallucination he had in which a third version of the goonish "Sir Cheech" appeared to him, singing the old snatch:

The rat, the cat, and Collins the dog
Ruled all England under the hog.

* * *

He worried, and I concurred, that it would be improper to include in his manuscript his analysis of this couplet—referring to the porcine qualities some might consider Her Immortal Majesty as possessing (although, of course, my friend included in his account some other less than reverential meditations on Her Majesty). This portion seemed to me to go too far, and I told him so. Then again there was a lengthy, very dry and I am afraid tedious section on strains of cellular telomere-lengthening bacteria that scientists have discovered to be functionally immortal—short, of course, of complete vaporization or atomization. Although it bore a relationship to portions of his whole narrative, I advised him it was too technical for the readers of an ordinary journal, and he removed it.

As to the whereabouts of my friend, I live, day to day, in the hope that he will reappear. What will survive of us, I believe, is hope.

Nicholas G.

Editor, The Nineteenth-Century And After

AMERICAN CHEETAH

Robert Reed

Robert Reed is an astonishingly prolific author of SF short stories without any loss of quality; every month the genre's leading magazines and anthologies feature new samples of his powerful, trenchant work. His collections are The Dragons of Springplace *and* The Cuckoo's Boys; *his most recent novel is* The Well of Stars. *In "American Cheetah," Reed puts a steam-driven iteration of a certain great American President up against famous outlaws, with memorable results...*

> "The best thing about the future is that it comes only one day at a time."
>
> —Abraham Lincoln

WHAT COULD NOT sleep would never dream. Those self-styled experts in the field agreed that these organic pleasures were forbidden to the automatons of the world. They seemed curious to hear that whenever this particular machine was being refurbished, odd imaginings formed inside its deepest workings. And whenever its fires burned out, odd images and fantastic stories seemed to emerge in the blackness, and wasn't that what dreams were supposed to be? But those wise, learned voices were never impressed with the testimony. Obviously what the automaton had experienced was the mechanical failure caused by its mind seizing up and turning cold. Or nudging its consciousness back into motion had generated a flood of disjointed thoughts. Or perhaps the dreams were another kind of memory bequeathed to the mechanical soul by its noble ancestor. Explanations were always at the ready, and what logic could counter such clever denials?

Yet the machine's ancestor—savior of the mighty Republic and wise in his own self-educated fashion—had understood that the smartest, surest voices were often wrong, and it was foolish to believe that even the simplest question had an easy, eternal answer.

One summer morning, the machine awoke from a hunger to find itself sitting on an iron chair inside its own kitchen. A new fire was burning inside the Brunel box, and the Sterling engines were slowly pumping life back into the long limbs and rattling, high-pitched voice. That voice was slowed by hunger, but after a few moments it found the power and breath to ask its associate, "Would you like to hear my latest dream, Stanley?"

Stanley was a young man blessed with many talents, including a genius for the magical automatons. But he was suspicious of any phenomena that did not match his expectations. "Sir," he began, speaking with authority and amused impatience. "We have covered this subject before. You are a wondrous, intricate machine that can learn new facts and adapt to an amazing range of circumstances. But I have seen your mind, sir. I have opened it up for myself and adjusted its delicate workings."

"For which I am grateful," the machine replied.

"And dreams are not permitted, sir. Because you are not a man, and you do not have a man's imaginative mind."

"And how could I take offense to that?"

The teasing went unnoticed. Quietly, very seriously, Stanley said, "I may not have mentioned this before. But I once saw a human brain."

"In a jar up at the college?"

"No, it was living. I was a young boy, and the brain belonged to a local man."

"That sounds quite sad, Stanley."

"Oh, that fellow was a brute, and he got what he deserved. He was whipping his horse, and the horse took exception to the abuse. A kick struck the forehead. And because I was curious, I looked at the opened skull. I have watched that delicate jelly dying. Which is why I know that the human soul is considerably more complicated and infinitely more frail than the metal Babbage that runs from your skull to your ass."

"As it should be, my young friend."

"Young friend" was another gentle joke. Stanley was only twenty-four, but in the truest sense, he was twice as old as the machine sitting before him—born in 1852, while his companion was fabricated only twelve years ago, inside the sprawling new automaton works outside Pittsburgh.

The machine's homely face smiled with childish pleasure, watching its human companion prepare breakfast.

"All right," Stanley muttered at least. "Tell me your dream, sir. Since I know you will sooner or later."

"I was hiking across a wild windswept prairie," the machine began. "I was walking beside my father, and we seemed to be hunting. Suddenly we spied a great cat sitting on a nearby ridge. It was a spotted feline. I could see its head and long neck and those beautiful eyes staring at nothing but me."

The voice, already slower than usual, ceased altogether. The first dose of fuel was nearly extinguished. Working with speed and precision, Stanley set a bowl of pulverized black dust in front of the machine, and before the pneumatic systems froze up entirely, he pushed a glass straw into the closer nostril and forced the head down, shouting, "Breathe in now. Deeply."

A long filthy gasp of coal traveled up through the head and down into the machine's Brunel box. Dust that fine turned to fire in an instant, and the effect was like twenty cups of coffee in one great drink. The machine straightened, limbs twitching while the voice said, "Goodness," before breaking into wild, contented laughter.

"Are you feeling better, sir?"

"Much improved, yes."

"You know, if you had taken the trouble during the night, you could have kept your belly well fed."

"I should have done that," the machine conceded. "But I was busy with my reading, and I must have forgotten."

Recent newspapers were stacked haphazardly about the room, along with law books and a fresh history of England, and at least two texts describing the newest varieties of soul-catchers. Stanley understood that this was a machine, only a facsimile of a true man; but he was always impressed by its stubborn, seemingly innate desire to learn.

Another two gasps of coal were inhaled, and then a dozen more were pulled into the other nostril and the reserve stomach.

"What do you think of my dream so far, Stanley?"

"You were hunting with your father. Obviously this is another gift from your ancestor, one of his memorable dreams."

"Perhaps so," the machine allowed. "Except after I looked at the cat, I turned back to discover that my father had been replaced. I was standing in the tall grass with my own dead ancestor."

"Are you certain?"

"Oh, yes. We had this face, the same body, but he was wearing his funeral clothes, and his delicate brain was torn apart by the assassin's bullet." The machine closed its glass eyes, and then it opened them. "Yet his corpse seemed to function quite well despite the wound. He smiled straight at me and handed me a long rifle and said, 'Shoot the cat, boy. Do it now.'"

Stanley nodded, intrigued despite his worthy doubts.

"I started to do as I was told. I crept close to the wild animal. In my hands was a marksman's weapon, but instead of shooting from forty paces, I found myself as close to the cat as that doorway stands from us. Then I took careful aim, as instructed. All the while, the cat continued to look me in the eyes. It stared as if it knew me. And then do you know what happened?"

"No, sir. What?"

"The cat stood up. It suddenly rose from the tall grass, balancing on its hind legs, and it showed me its narrow chest. Then before I could discharge my gun, it peeled back the spotted fur and its ribs, exposing a collection of machines that looked remarkably like my insides, only smaller. Shiny, elegant devices, and lovely too, I told myself. The machine's guts were more advanced than anything either of us has seen before."

Stanley nodded, wondering if he could be wrong. Was this fantastic dream genuine? Or was the machine simply recounting a fantastic tale that it had read in one of its many books?

"Do you remember your dreams, my boy?"

Stanley shook his head. "Rarely."

"Well, perhaps you are a machine, too."

Humor was not one of Stanley's strengths. The young man dismissed that suggestion with a snort.

Then like the cheetah in its dream, the automaton suddenly rose up, its weight making the floor creak, its considerable height readily apparent. And as it pinned the sheriff's star to the lapel of its vest, it remarked, "I have an idea, son. Or my ancestor left me this useful thought." With gravity and unusual seriousness, it said, "Either way, there are a few inquiries that I would like you to make on my behalf. And if necessary, see them through to their logical ends."

IN LIFE, THE ancestor had been an exceptionally busy man, but for reasons of politics and statecraft, he had invested an entire morning doing nothing but sitting alone inside a silver-walled box. This was the first soul-catcher brought to the New World, purchased in London by a Union representative. In the brief history of the device, few subjects had been as thoroughly rendered. The man's patience might have been the reason, or perhaps his mind was more open to the sensitive explorations. Or maybe the soul-catcher's delicate mechanisms were set perfectly, and success was a matter of pure luck. Whatever the reason, an exceptionally clear portrait of the

American president was achieved, and when that sophisticated mathematical picture was joined with his writings and speeches and the testimony of close friends and family, the final design bore an astonishing resemblance to the Illinois lawyer who had carried this nation through more than three years of terrible war.

It was 1864, and the national election was approaching. The free male citizens of the Union were to decide if the killing was to continue. If the president was not reelected, the survival of the democracy was in jeopardy; and should the nation split in two, a pair of radically different states would find themselves sharing a long dangerous border.

To help win the election, fifteen Lincoln automatons were built and tested. Three of the machines proved too flawed to be repaired and were subsequently thrown out as scrap. But twelve of those grand experiments were dressed like the president, complete with his trademark stovepipe hat, and then shipped to various states and territories. Blessed with his wit and memories and good political instincts, the Lincolns campaigned for their ancestor, begging all who came in earshot for their votes come November.

Perhaps because of them, the election was won. But the war lingered on, and the automatons continued working, publicly supporting the fight by calling for fresh recruits and money, working tirelessly up until the moment when that last battle was won. But what was to be done with the machines afterwards? Three automatons were brought to the White House for a dinner of beef and coal dust. Lincoln had never met the machines, but he quickly realized that each was unique, blessed with its own distinct personality. Even as they sat at the table, the finest, most expensive Babbages in the world were learning and growing intellectually. The president enjoyed stories from the campaign trail and some wonderful jokes. Later, to Mary and his closest friends, Lincoln mused that it would be wrong to slaughter thousands of good men in order to free millions, but then for their next act, carelessly turn these marvels of science and metaphysics into mindless scrap.

But as yet, no final decision had been reached. Those three Lincolns were sent to the Army for study. Word went out from the Department of War for the machines to be emptied of their fuel, their inert bodies shipped back to the Pittsburgh factory from which they had come. This particular Lincoln was wandering across Minnesota when the order arrived. Half a dozen young government men were assigned to its care and feeding. They explained what was about to happen, and the machine did as it was ordered, without hesitation. To what degree its Babbage felt worry and fear could not be known. But it was sitting at the train station, its fuel almost gone, when word arrived of the president's assassination. And five days later, it was still sitting there, inert and unaware that Andrew Johnson had just signed a special order that freed the Lincoln automatons from all service and every debt.

The gesture was made in grief, without consideration for the results of the unplanned kindness. The government handlers and mechanics that cared for the machines were sent to other duties. The next years proved especially difficult for the twelve machines. A real man would heal his wounds with nothing but food and rest. But the new citizens demanded replacement parts that were scarce, and few mechanics understood their complicated bodies. Several Lincolns perished through preventable failures of their Babbages. Another was crushed in a train wreck, while a boating accident drowned its brother in Lake Michigan. In order to keep itself moving and thinking, the Minnesota Lincoln earned what money it could through common labor—a skill at which it was quite adept. Every penny was invested in coal and lubricating oils and the special tools, plus copies of any book that helped with its upkeep and continued happiness. That life might never have ended. But in 1871, while the automaton was helping load freight on a train car, two local men got into a terrible brawl. Hard words escalated into fists, and then guns were drawn and fired wildly. One bullet buried itself into a plank inches above the head of a child, and without consideration for its own safety, the automaton covered the little girl with its body, absorbing two more bullets in its iron guts before the revolver was emptied. Then the machine turned, and with a few Sterling-powered chops of the hand, disarmed both men.

After that day, the town quit regarding their neighbor as being only a curiosity. Remembering the dead president's early career, some of the citizens approached the machine for legal advice, and while it refused to serve as anyone's attorney, it gladly gave its opinion and accepted the few dollars that found their way into its pocket.

That new career lasted most of a year.

It was during that interval when Stanley arrived—a sharp young fellow attending Carleton College. He took a deep interest in the automaton, first as a challenge to his skills, then for increasingly personal reasons. Then one day, the town sheriff complained of a headache, went to bed and died. There was a sudden need for an officer of the law, and after judging all of the candidates, people decided to elect a machine to serve as their protector.

The mechanical Lincoln agreed to serve, but certain unimpeachable rules had to apply: It would never kill or maim any person or beast, and nobody should try ordering it to do otherwise. Under no circumstance would it carry any weapon more treacherous than a screwdriver. And Stanley would serve as its deputy and doctor, and in case of its demise, he would inherit the honorable post.

For the next four years, Northfield, Minnesota enjoyed peace and prosperity, and whether their reasons were sound or not, the citizens by and large credited their good fortune to the towering, coal-powered entity that patrolled its streets, more alert than any man, yet possessing a quick wit and the natural charming authority of a great and good man who was still sorely missed.

"PERHAPS I AM not alive," the sheriff would concede. "But this contraption before you still enjoys its little pleasures, thank you."

Reading was a reliable joy. In that, the ancestor and his metal image were the same. And close behind was the companionship of men. There was a favorite barbershop where the sheriff would sit in the strongest chair, trading jokes with the patrons as it allowed its metal face to be painted and patched. And there were several taverns where every other customer enjoyed drink and cigars, probing the machine's memories about its first term as president. The town's largest hotel had been renamed the Lincoln House, in honor of the automaton that often camped on its wide porch, offering opinions and shrewd observations about local matters. But on that particular September day, some of the town notables gathered on Division Street. The machine was walking its rounds, but it decided to join them. To save energy, it stood with its steel knees locked and its arms motionless. But it listened carefully to every word, even as it said and did nothing, and when inspiration struck, the sheriff would suddenly offer up a few gemstones of wit and self-deprecating humor, earning well-deserved laughter from its eager audience.

That was a bright, busy day. Wagons and horses and people on foot shared the street with a variety of new machines. As often happened, someone mentioned the great changes that were sweeping across the world. Who could have imagined so many revolutions in engineering and science? And where would these changes strike next? Those perfectly fine questions brought a long, thoughtful pause. But no one dared make predictions about the future. Finally someone brought up the subject of politics—not an unexpected occurrence with this group. With a tone that was rather less than complimentary, the current president was mentioned. Every eye was fixed on the sheriff's hard face, waiting for its reaction. But the entity preferred to keep its emotions to itself. Finally the youngest fellow present—a freshman at Carleton, more boy than man—rose to the challenge. He decided that he would elicit some response from this fancy device.

"I have a question for you, sir."

"Yes, son?" the high-pitched voice replied.

"Do you ever consider running for higher office? With the world as it is, I'm sure your talents would prove most valuable."

The other men nervously held their breath.

But the machine creaked out a large smile, declaring, "When there rises a nation of machines, I will run for some worthy post. Of course I will."

"As if that would ever happen," barked one old man named Charles. "'A nation of machines' indeed!"

Most agreed with the skeptic. Everybody laughed, and loudest of all was the sheriff. But it did not go unnoticed when the machine suddenly announced that it should be leaving, that its rounds would never finish themselves. Long legs strode with precision, taking it away from the joyful group, and as it moved up the busy street, it let the smile fall back to a neutral expression, tipping the tall hat to the women that it passed by but otherwise showing nothing about its present mood or its persistent fears for the future.

Northfield was miles and years removed from the giant cities and newborn industries. But even here, life was changing in ways impossible to ignore. Each spring brought new machines designed to lessen the burdens of farmers and tradesmen. In one glance, the sheriff spied three quite different mechanical wagons. The oldest model sported giant wheels that looked as if they had been repaired by a series of increasingly angry blacksmiths. But in a world of ruts and rock and deep mud, brute engines and revolving limbs were proving to be failures. The other wagons were newer and more successful. One resembled a giant brass spider, while the next one reminded the eye of a great ox that could be marched over any terrain. Neighbor to neighbor, the sheriff waved at the prosperous riders steering both wagons. Then an old-fashioned freight wagon came along, pulled by four powerful horses. But it was the cargo that was a matter of some interest: ten mechanical laborers were sitting in the back end, destined for the mill that lay across the river. The sheriff paused long enough to study the motionless bodies, unclothed and definitely inhuman, with blank simple faces, lidless eyes, and mouths that had no purpose but to eat coal in great sloppy lumps. According to conventions only a few years old, the automatons' bodies were deeply black. The symbolism was obvious. One suffering race had been freed by war, but factories were gladly producing a new species of slave, and there seemed to be no voice that seriously complained about what was transpiring.

For several moments, the sheriff did nothing but watch the wagon and its brothers crossing the Cannon River. The oak bridge creaked under the combined weight. No black face moved; no simple hand lifted. Presumably the machines were not even fueled. But the scene made the automaton ache, and it remained standing motionless for a minute longer, trying to understand from where these emotions could have arisen.

Bodies and vehicles continued to stream past. Everyone acted preoccupied with his busy life. Even when the sheriff began to walk again, it was distracted by the hubbub and dust. A rider on horseback was moving in the same direction, and he almost slipped past unnoticed. But then one of the eyes caught the sunlight, shining too brightly, and when the sheriff looked up, the stranger looked away, as if to keep his face out of view.

Curiosity made the sheriff pause, staring as the stranger continued on his way. What should have been apparent was not. It took several moments of hard study before the sheriff realized that the horse was no horse, but instead an extremely convincing simulation, complete to the false dun coat and the twitching tail and a glassy black eye that rolled in its socket as the bridle was tugged slightly, telling the device to walk faster now.

An automated horse! There were stories about such wonders, but they were expensive and very new, and outside the army, no more than a few dozen were owned by the wealthy. The sheriff's astonishment was honest and lasting; it couldn't help but stare. At full gallop, these false horses were at least twice as swift as the living beasts. But if memory served, that was a problem that was bedeviling the army. At rapid speeds, these mechanical chargers could stumble in an instant, and while they were all but invulnerable to most hazards, their weight and momentum tended to kill every unfortunate rider trapped beneath them.

And what about this fellow riding on top? The sheriff tried to match the stranger's quickening pace. Whoever he was, the stranger didn't look prosperous enough to afford such a machine. But it took several more moments to see what no one else on the street had noticed. The rider was dressed in heavy clothes, and the back of his neck was exposed to the sun. With the heat of late summer, he should be bathed in perspiration. Yet he looked entirely dry. And despite the glare of the sun against the man's neck, his bare flesh was as white and slick as any good piece of carefully shaped, heavily painted iron.

The sheriff stopped in the middle of Division Street, unblinking eyes watching as the rider pulled over at the bank and dismounted, tying up the false horse with a thoroughly convincing motion. Then what wasn't human joined what seemed to be four others like it, and the five entities looked farther up the street, watching as another three riders entered from the opposite end of town.

A local boy and his father happened to be strolling past. The sheriff called to them by name, and to the boy it said, "You're quicker than me. Run now. Run up to my house. Find Stanley and bring him straight here. Will you do that for me?"

"Oh, yes!" Happy for the task, the boy raced up the nearest side street and vanished.

With concern, the father asked, "Is something wrong, sheriff?"

Removing its tall hat, the machine admitted, "Much is wrong, yes. And in this particular corner of the world, it seems."

The man turned pale. "What is happening, sir?"

"A few moments ago, I was speaking to that group of men," the sheriff mentioned, motioning in the opposite direction. "Do you see them standing in the street? Old Man Charles and the rest of them? Well please, if you would do this for me. Join them now. Quietly, I want you to warn them that our bank is about to be robbed. And if I don't miss my mark, it's the James-Younger Gang that's going to do the robbing."

* * *

ONLY LAST SPRING, the nation's most notorious thieves and murderers were brought to justice. Pinkerton agents had collected photographs of the gang's leaders, and using the new high-speed telegraph, sent their likenesses to law enforcement officers across the West. But more effective were several hundred artificial eyes linked to empty Babbages. Each eye was shown the images until it knew exactly what it was hunting for, and then the eyes were hidden in every likely corner of Missouri, tracking the comings and goings of every person. Eventually one mechanical spy delivered on its promise. The Pinkertons cornered their foes at a remote farmstead—forty agents employing the newest munitions, killing every outlaw as well as the family giving them shelter, including five children and an elderly grandmother.

But the James and Youngers were dead. Much of the nation cheered, and every bank owner and train conductor breathed easier. Only in the Confederate hotbeds were the bushwhackers mourned—looked upon as heroes, the last brave soldiers in a lost but noble cause.

Yet while the men were dead, their terror managed to survive.

Southwest of Chicago, standing on what used to be prairie, was a wondrous new factory. Within its walls was a wondrous soul-catcher equal to the machines used by European royalty. The facility was intended to serve the new Babbage millionaires. For a stack of gold bars, an important man's essence would be absorbed and replicated inside the tiniest, most complex Babbage ever constructed. Then inside an adjacent facility, precise mechanical hands would fabricate a new body—the perfect mirror to the customer's shape and natural motions. This was the latest pleasure among the exceptionally wealthy: Realistic automatons that would stand in for their busy, self-important owners, doing the routine and occasionally spreading harmless mischief.

But tricks that entertain the wealthy can give hope to the desperate. After the slaughter in Missouri, word broke that during the previous year, a group of men arrived at the facility in the guise of workers. One of the project engineers was Texan and a sympathizer to the Confederate cause. Over the course of eight nights, he borrowed the new soul-catcher to create Babbage minds of Jesse and Frank James, and the Younger brothers, as well as three criminal associates. Then eight new bodies were fabricated in the automated shop. As convincing as any fakes could be, they included not only the most efficient coal-fired Brunels, but also smooth, lubricant-free joints, and a variety of rubber faces that would allow the killers to constantly change their famous features.

Once the deception was discovered, the engineer gave up all pretence of secrecy. He boasted about his cleverness and questionable politics. And while he didn't know where the automatons were, he claimed that Jesse's plan was to store their likenesses with unnamed friends, and in case of their early demise, that second gang would be awakened and set loose to continue their mayhem.

Not long after the Pinkerton ambush, eight experimental horses were stolen from an army depot. But the military decided not to mention that painful fact. There was no public warning before the robberies resumed in early summer. But where blooded men and mortal horses had perpetrated the crimes before—men who needed sleep, and horses that could ride hard for just a few hours at a time—these miscreants were machines endowed with the constitutions and stamina of fire-driven locomotives.

A bank in Salinas, Kansas was robbed in broad daylight. But before a posse could be raised, the thieves had raced away like lightning bolts.

Just a day later, one hundred miles to the south, riders caught the mail train as it roared along at full speed, leaping onboard like alley cats to take valuables from the safe and the terrorized travelers.

And that was followed the next week, in Missouri, when a dozen banks were robbed in scattered towns. The Northfield sheriff had read those lurid news accounts aloud to Stanley. Astonished and alarmed, he described how a Missouri farmer—the distant cousin of the James brothers, as it happened—pumped three rifle shots into the gang's leader, and at close range. Yet every round had ricocheted off the armored chest, and one of those tumbling bullets struck and killed a much-loved schoolteacher.

For three savage months, those automatons had outwitted and outrun every opponent. But what worried the sheriff most was that innocent schoolteacher. Gun battles had already killed at least fifty citizens, and scores more had been injured. That's what the machine explained to the gathered men. "The bank is a minor concern," it maintained. "Before anything, we have to find the means to protect our neighbors."

Old Man Charles bristled. "We can't just let them take our money," he grumbled.

"But what can we do?" asked the youngster. A few minutes earlier he had teased the machine about its political future. But now he looked up helplessly at the automaton, saying, "These things can't be killed, and they'll slaughter us if we give them any excuse."

For a few moments, the sheriff did nothing. Its unblinking eyes stared at the dirt street and the little river meandering through the town's heart. Then Stanley appeared, running as hard as possible, nearly passing by the men and tall machine as they stood together on the boardwalk.

"My boy," the sheriff said.

"There you are," Stanley observed. "I saw the mayor. He told me what's what." He joined them, staring down the street. "Which one of them is Jesse James?"

"None, I would imagine."

The bank was a neat little building of pale stone. Three figures were guarding its doorway, pistols on their hips and all the time in the day, judging by their carefree stances.

Stanley was winded. Gasping, he asked, "Are they robbing it now?"

"Perhaps they are opening an account," the sheriff jested.

Light laughter fell into gloomy silence.

"But they can't get to the money," the young man pointed out. "The vault's secured with a time lock."

The sheriff nodded. "If they didn't know that before, they surely know it now."

"How many are inside?" asked Stanley.

"There's five more machines," Old Man Charles reported.

The deputy looked at the thin metal face. "How many people, sir? Do you have any idea?"

"Five employees, we think, and several customers."

Stanley nodded grimly.

Then another man appeared, carrying a shotgun in plain view. With a crisp, impatient voice, the sheriff warned, "They can see you, John."

The new man set his weapon down.

"And birdshot won't do us much good," the sheriff pointed out.

Charles was thinking about his savings. With the surety of someone who had never seen a large battle, he talked about putting men with rifles on the roofs and inside every nearby building.

"Crossfires can be messy," the sheriff warned. "And believe me, these machines will prove very hard to damage."

"They can't see us," the shotgun man whined. "I can barely see them."

"Of course they see us," Stanley blurted. "Their eyes are better than any of ours. Even the sheriff's can't match these new models."

Another minute passed, and the only change was a swift decline in the traffic moving past the bank. Word was spreading. Soon the entire community would be terrified, and every man would find a gun. Immune to fear, the mechanical horses continued stomping at the ground and flicking their wire tails, pretending to be bothered by flies. One lookout offered a few words to its companions, and all seemed to laugh. Then for no obvious reason, the three of them turned their backs to the world and stepped inside.

"What does this mean?" Stanley asked.

The sheriff was trying to piece together everything that it had read about the mechanical terrorists. How strong were they, and how fast? And how could anyone stop horses that were meant to ride into modern wars? But all that mattered was the automatons. They were like eight rattlesnakes curled up in a baby's bed, and as long as they were under the sheets, you would be a fool to pick a fight with them.

Turning to the gathered men, the sheriff spoke as quickly as possible, outlining the makings of a plan. But the preparations would require time and some effort. Surely the bandits wouldn't remain inside the bank much longer. And eventually some hothead was going to take an impulsive shot, setting off a great fight in the middle of town. Calm was essential. Delays would be blessings. The sheriff asked Stanley, "By any chance, did you bring extra coal with you?"

"I didn't think of it," the young man confessed. "Why? Are you low? Do you want me to run home and grind some?"

"Never mind." From its own trouser pocket, the sheriff withdrew a small leather sack filled with black dust—an emergency stockpile reserved for the direst circumstances—and then using its widest straw, the machine inhaled every mote of that foul-looking goodness, its long hands beginning to quiver from the sudden influx of fuel.

As it stepped into the street, Stanley asked, "What are you doing, sir?"

"I am going to meet with the robbers," the sheriff reported. Then it paused and turned, showing the scared men its own worried grin. But with a sturdy voice, it added, "You need time, and everybody needs peace. And who can say? Perhaps I can talk my brothers out of this foolishness."

A POUNDING SOUND came from inside the bank. It began as the sheriff approached, and whoever was doing the pounding was finding their rhythm, the pace quickening and the sound growing sharper as each blow was delivered with increasing force. The Youngers were serving as the lookouts. Standing behind the bank windows, the brothers watched the sheriff's steady approach. One turned to shout to someone deeper in the darkness, and the hammering stopped for a moment. The other two pulled army pistols out of their holsters—automatic models with several dozen rounds sleeping in the hilts. The sheriff kept walking, but when it passed between two of the mechanical horses, it hesitated. The rumble of powerful fires burned inside the bellies. Machine guns were tied to the saddles, no human hand strong enough to break the heavy wire. The sheriff looked at the glass eyes of one horse and then the long twitching ears, and as an experiment, it started to reach for the bridle.

The bank door flew open.

"You don't want to do that," a sour voice warned. "It doesn't know you, and its bite's worse than a mad dog's."

As if to prove the point, a decidedly unhorselike mouth opened wide, revealing steel teeth and a dark tongue bristling with sharp wires and savage razors.

"Thanks much for the warning," the sheriff allowed.

The Younger at the door asked, "What do you want?"

"Are you Cole?"

"I am."

"The town has sent me to meet with you boys," the sheriff offered. "Everybody is scared, and they want to know your intentions."

Cole stepped away from the open door. Its brothers searched the sheriff, pulling pliers and a pair of screwdrivers out of its pockets. Each automaton was wearing its original, now famous face. Stepping indoors, the sheriff recognized them in turn. Cole Younger was a balding creature with a short dark beard and moustache and the distant eyes of someone who had been soldiering for too long. The James brothers were in the back, watching while three associates resumed working on the stubborn safe. Fully fueled, the sheriff was as powerful and tireless as a machine press. But these entities were a notch or two stronger. Twelve years of refinements showed in their fluid motions, each delivering a very precise blow with a massive steel hammer. The safe's handle and dial had been twisted and battered. Sparks flew, and the racket deafened. The sheriff turned away, discovering the bank's patrons and employees huddled in a dark corner—seven people tied together like livestock. Nodding in their direction, the machine tried to lend encouragement. Then somebody shouted, "Quit," and the pounding came to a merciful end.

Jesse had given the command. That automaton had a handsome face and a strong, self-secure voice. Into the sudden silence, it said, "We need the kick-putty. Where'd you put it, Frank?"

Kick-putty was a powerful new explosive, expensive and rather touchy. If a mistake was made, these metal creatures would weather the blast, but not the people tied up on the floor.

Frank James told one of the hammer-wielders, "Go get the putty. It's in my saddlebag."

"You shouldn't waste your time," the sheriff advised.

No one seemed to notice its words. The humans kept their terrified heads low, while the robbers were too consumed with the promise of money.

As the associate passed by, the sheriff added, "There's no gold in the safe, boys. I'm sorry to tell you."

Frank had a heavy wire moustache and sober, watchful eyes. The automaton offered a smile, and then with a mocking tone, it said, "Honest Abe."

The sheriff nodded slightly.

"So where is the money?" Jesse asked.

"The gold and silver were moved out last night," the sheriff lied. "I heard you might be coming here, so I ordered it taken away for safety's sake."

"You didn't hear anything of the kind," Cole said.

The sheriff looked only at the James brothers. "Didn't I spot you as soon as you arrived?" it asked. "Despite your disguises and fancy horses, I saw you for what you were."

Jesse stared at the very famous face.

"You should leave now," the sheriff advised. "Otherwise you will have troubles."

"Why? Is somebody going to fight us?"

"That is a possibility, sir."

The rubber face smiled while both hands unbuttoned its shirt. Jesse James showed everyone a chest that could have belonged to a human male, but for the countless pits left by high-velocity rounds.

Quietly and firmly, the machine promised, "We like to fight."

The sheriff said nothing.

"Don't we?" it asked the others.

Seven voices said, "Yes. Sure. Always."

That last meal of coal dust was beginning to fade. The sheriff felt its strength diminishing, its old-fashioned Babbage already beginning to slow. But it didn't allow its voice to fade. "I don't doubt you. I don't. But I think you like something even more than fighting."

"And what would that be?" Frank asked.

"You love to live. You want to be alive. Isn't that the truth?"

"If we don't run away, what happens?" Cole asked with a mocking tone. "Are you going to kill us?"

"Not at all," the sheriff replied. "But I'm prepared to help you. In exchange for releasing these my friends, I will give you something far more valuable than money."

The machines with the hammers looked ready to pound on the sheriff. But Jesse was curious enough to ask, "And what would that gift be?"

"Set one of them free first," the sheriff coaxed.

"No."

"A woman, maybe?"

"Tell us what you're trading for her," Frank insisted.

"Ideas," the sheriff said.

The machines laughed, but the James brothers were first to quiet down. Then Jesse drifted closer, saying, "Give me an idea I can use. Then I'll decide just how nice I want to be."

"LIFE," THE SHERIFF repeated. "Meat and blood might believe they hold a monopoly on living, but don't the nine of us know a good deal better than them? Each of us is more than a box full of memories, more than sets of complicated and cooperative instructions. I can assure you: From the first moment when I made these metal hands move, I have been very much my own man. Every day, my life proves interesting. My story, such as it is, belongs to nobody else. I am jealous of no man, bone or steel, because I so much enjoy the faces and routines that fill my stellar existence. And why, praise the Maker, should that be any other way?"

The initial curiosity was flickering. A master politician could see its audience losing its fragile interest.

"But I am extra blessed," the sheriff called out. With a wide smile building, it added, "In a very special way, the entity standing before you is immortal, and its destiny is to live on forever."

Cole snorted. Otherwise, the reaction was surprised silence, from machines and the tied-up humans both.

Finally Jesse said, "I never took you for a religious man."

"Nor should you," the sheriff replied. "No, I am a pragmatic creature, and this is my peculiar situation: a soul-catcher absorbed my ancestor. Everything that was Abe was transformed into mathematical equations and carefully weighed factors, influences and tendencies. Then the information was given a flavor that any Babbage can digest. Dozens of powerful and very durable machines were involved in the creation of me. Even today, inside their deepest workings, the Babbages remember me. Which implies that as long as just one of them is kept in good repair, my ancestor and much of me will live on, at least for as long as this world cherishes its dead president."

Cole was puzzled, Frank dismissive. But Jesse attacked the statements by the most fruitful route. "Maybe the world likes you today. And maybe it will tomorrow too. But do you believe that there's some big Babbage holding our ancestors in the same motherly way?"

"Not at all," the sheriff replied.

"Why not?" Cole asked.

Jesse stepped closer. "Tell him why, sheriff."

"Because you are hated, vilified and despised, and the owners of those Babbages would have purged you from their system as soon as they learned of your existence."

The eight bandits had probably never considered this promise of immortality. But here it was, offered to them without warning, and then in the next moment, shattered.

"I don't see why you're crowing," Jesse admitted. "So what if ten or fifty years from now, somebody decides to punch out another dozen Abes. They won't be you. When you die, this little life of yours is going to be lost."

The sheriff took a half-step forward, declaring, "And that, my friend, is where you are wrong."

A furious glare preceded the question, "Now why is that?"

"Because at this very moment, smart men are designing and testing brand-new types of soul-catchers—machines that will read and record our minds, and do it in a matter of moments. Good commercial reasons are responsible for this work. It will ease the process of saving whatever an important Babbage holds inside itself. And by the same token, that trickery will make it possible to duplicate each of us. Provided we have the money and freedom, of course. And not just punch out another Jesse James, or a dozen. But an entire army of You could be manufactured inside one factory, in a single good day.

"Which means, gentlemen, that your lives can last longer than you have ever imagined. But only if you allow them to survive into this Golden Age."

Among the gang, there was confusion mixed with the interest, plus a healthy dose of doubt. As the machines looked at one another, something massive began to move in the street. But the sheriff didn't dare glance at the windows. All it could do was continue to delay whatever was to come next.

"Perhaps you know the story of my grandfather's ax," it mentioned.

Eyes opened wider and lips narrowed. Those rubber faces were much more expressive than the sheriff's, and despite its statements to the contrary, it did feel jealousy toward these other machines.

"What ax is that?" Jesse inquired.

"My grandfather's treasured ax," the sheriff said. "It was handed down to my father, who then gave it to me. And in its life, it has had two new heads and three new handles. But it is still my grandfather's ax."

A deep thud made the floor shake.

But before any eye could look outside, the sheriff added, "This is a paradox told by Plutarch. But speaking as an old ax, I am quite willing to let my head and body be replaced as many times as necessary. Just so long as I am here to debate the matters of my existence and nonexistence."

Cole was at the window. An angry voice said, "They're trying to block the streets, Jess. They think they can bottle us up in here."

"They can't," said Frank.

Jesse stepped up to the glass, calmly studying what was visible. Then it looked at the sheriff, mentioning, "There's a lot to think about in what you say. And if I wasn't so busy riding and fighting, I might have time to read up on these subjects."

"Food for thought," the sheriff agreed.

"But not today," Jesse added. Then to its partners, it said, "Get the people on their feet. Tie their hands in front, and find some wire for the sheriff." From its holster came a fat-barreled pistol—a single-shot horror that could punch an explosive round deep inside an old automaton. "Abe comes along with us too."

"You won't even free one of these girls?" the sheriff asked.

"Once we're out of this shitpoke town, I will." Then the machine winked, laughing as it added, "Unless I'm lying. Which is my nature, and who am I to argue with my nature?"

FRANTIC, FURIOUS MEN had quickly thrown barricades across Division Street. Mechanical spiders and metal oxen were parked sideways in the right-of-way, with an assortment of wagons and buggies filling in the gaps. Dozens of armed citizens stood behind cover, and as the sheriff stepped out of the bank, twin murmurs came from both directions. Distance softened the voices, confusing the words. The sheriff believed it heard someone saying, "Don't shoot," while another said what sounded like, "Fire." Was this a matter of combustion, or gunfire? Either way, it was critical that the world's stupidity was kept locked up for now. Ten feet of bailing wire had been wrapped tight around the sheriff's wrists. Lifting its joined hands as high as its neck, it called to everyone. "Do nothing!" it begged. "Nothing! We are well enough for the moment! Point your damned guns at the sky!"

Men unaccustomed to running began to sprint back and forth behind the barricades. Faces dropped out of sight, while other faces appeared. But no rifles were aimed in their direction, and the panicking noises turned to watchful silence and the hint of whispers.

Jesse said, “Good.”

To the prisoners, the machine said, “One to a horse. Ride in front. And don’t worry, they’ll carry you and us just fine.”

Each gang member uttered a senseless word. A code of some kind, no doubt. In an instant, the horses lowered themselves to their knees, making it easy for everyone to climb onboard. These army machines were marvels. What kind of Babbage made them so smart? The sheriff imagined some champion bird dog being set inside a soul-catcher, its obedience and loyal nature now infused into these devices. Somehow that image troubled it more than anything else. Then Jesse poked the sheriff with the big-barreled pistol, saying, “Enough standing, Mr. President. Throw that long leg over the big neck now.”

The sheriff’s iron carapace felt nothing but pressure and temperature, but the horse plainly did not feel like a living beast. It was too solid, too massive. The fires burning in its body gave it unnatural warmth, and when Jesse’s horse stood, the perceived effort was tiny. Give the beast wings, and it would probably fly.

The sheriff laughed—a brief, nervous cackle.

“You’re right,” Jesse agreed. “This is a funny day, isn’t it?”

The sheriff sealed its mouth.

"Which way?" asked Cole.

Jesse and Frank exchanged meaningful looks. They were plainly brothers, and probably closer than most siblings. The younger one said, "It doesn't matter which way. How can they stop us?"

The sheriff thought of speaking, but Frank was quicker. "It looks like the bridge is still open. See, Jess?"

Division Street was blocked, but something had gone wrong on the way to the mill. On the far shore of the bridge, a pair of wooden wagons had been turned on their sides. But men were scarce. For a moment, the sheriff could see Stanley standing in plain view, whispering orders to someone or something that plainly wasn't doing what needed to be done.

"Yeah," Jesse said. "Let's take the bridge out of here."

No eye, no matter how strong or sharp, can see everything. But the sheriff tried to miss nothing. The same young fellow who had asked about the machine's political plans was standing on the bridge, several steps in front of the overturned freight wagon. To the world, he looked like a scared boy working very hard to hold his ground. Someone had foolishly armed him, the big dangerous pistol in his left hand, and with the first clomp of the metal hoof striking wooden planks, he started to lift the gun, first with the one hand, then both.

The sheriff shouted, "Stanley. Get that boy out of my way."

Not "our way," but "my way." It seemed like an important distinction to make.

Stanley muttered a few words.

The boy didn't seem to hear him.

The sheriff dipped his head, talking backward to Jesse. "Get us in the lead. I'll get him out of your way."

"Good," said Jesse, but not caring much either way.

"Son," the sheriff yelled. "You don't want to try that."

The boy didn't act convinced.

A mild kick and coded word sent their mount up to the front. Then with a careless laugh, Jesse asked, "Why don't I just shoot him?"

Stanley was behind the young man now. For an instant, his eyes met with the sheriff's, and then he leaped forward and grabbed for the pistol. The boy said, "No," and yanked and turned and took a blind swing, looking like a scared fool with his fist cutting through empty air.

Suddenly the two young men were battling with one another. It was an unexpected, halfway intriguing sight. The gang kept riding across the river. None of them noticed the townsmen standing on the riverbanks, busily waving orders to those beneath the bridge. They watched nothing but the tiny, useless drama being played out before them. They heard one man curse, and then the other matched that word and its furious tone, and then the riders had come to the middle of the bridge—out on the long span of solid oak and iron fittings and iron nails—and somebody down by the river shouted, "Now, now. Push, push!"

A dozen iron men, black and coal-fired and standing at the ready, now threw their weight and considerable strength against tree trunk pillars. The bridge was already stressed by the weight of the machines above. There was a sharp creak behind the riders, and then a prolonged groan from ahead and below, and just when it seemed as if the span might survive the abuse, the entire middle portion shattered, spilling machines and struggling prisoners into the cool wet depths where no fire, no matter how protected, could burn for long.

Falling, there was barely time to think anything worthy. But still, the sheriff tried to look back over its shoulder, winking at that famous rubber face. "Dream well," it managed to say, and then the big pistol was fired, and a fat round pierced its back, burrowing deep into the twelve year-old Babbage.

Now there will be a blast, the sheriff realized.

Will I feel it?

No, it did not. A little mercy waiting at the end of a long life...

BUT FOR THE wrinkled skin and the absence of hair on the sunburned scalp, the man was familiar. And then he spoke, his voice older but otherwise unchanged. "There was this ship on which the king of Athens returned from Crete," he began, "and because it was a famous ship, from that day forward it was repaired and refurbished—every plank and swivel and oar made again as time and rot did their worst."

"The ship of Theseus," the machine replied.

"Very good, sir. Very good."

The automaton was lying on its back, in the midst of what seemed to be a field of tall grass. The sky was clear and filled with wind, and the scent of damp earth played in the nostrils. That smell was the greatest shock among many. Quietly, it asked, "What has happened to me, Stanley?"

The old man was turning screws in the machine's chest. "You feel odd, do you?"

"No, actually. I feel rather wonderful."

With stiff old knees, Stanley stood. "Sit up, if you can, sir. Everything should work just fine."

"Not yet," the automaton replied.

"As you wish."

There was noise in the distance—a steady explosive roar, not loud but moving swiftly. Stanley squinted, watching the sky and presumably whatever was making the noise. "I had an awful time recovering everything from your Babbage," he explained. "It was shattered, quite the mess. In the end, I modeled the explosion, plotting the course of every piece of the bomb and all of the ballistic debris, and then I ran everything backwards to the beginning. Which is how I recovered most of your memories. Then I loaded everything into a fresh neural network.

Which aren't called 'Babbages' anymore, by the way."

Years had passed, but the man remained easily impressed with his own cleverness.

"What about the James and Youngers?"

"Parceled out to museums and the like. They get fueled up for important anniversaries and documentaries, but mostly, they just stand like statues inside their display cabinets."

Smiling, the machine felt the crinkling of soft flesh. It touched its lips and cheeks, feeling sensations through its fingertips. "Is this rubber?"

"Better than."

The smile grew. "Thank you so much."

The clever man said, "I should mention, sir, there's quite a lot that's different about you. Your organs can repair themselves, most of the time. You're quicker and even stronger than before. In many ways, you function as a man. A healthy, human man. And by the way, there's no more coal dust for breakfast."

"Kerosene, is it?"

"Hardly that," he scoffed. "You won't need your first meal for another eight years. And longer, if you keep doing nothing."

The automaton took a deep, wondrous breath.

"I'm curious, sir. How much longer do you plan to stay down there?"

"I don't quite know, Stanley." The machine closed its eyes. "When the smell of the earth grows old, I'll move to my next pleasure. How is that for a plan?"

FIXING HANOVER

Jeff VanderMeer

for Jay Lake

Living in Florida, Jeff VanderMeer is a brilliant literary experimenter, who has used steampunk and other tropes to powerfully subversive effect in his superb Ambergris books, City of Saints and Madmen *and* Shriek: An Afterword, *as well as in his Dying-Earth novel* Veniss Underground. *VanderMeer's short fiction is impressive too, as here, where a steampunk genius takes refuge on a strange foreign shore...*

WHEN SHYVER CAN'T lift it from the sand, he brings me down from the village. It lies there on the beach, entangled in the seaweed, dull metal scoured by the sea, limpets and barnacles stuck to its torso. It's been lost a long time, just like me. It smells like rust and oil still, but only a tantalizing hint.

"It's good salvage, at least," Shyver says. "Maybe more."

"Or maybe less," I reply. Salvage is the life's blood of the village in the off-season, when the sea's too rough for fishing. But I know from past experience, there's no telling what the salvagers will want and what they discard. They come from deep in the hill country abutting the sea cliffs, their needs only a glimmer in their savage eyes.

To Shyver, maybe the thing he'd found looks like a long box with a smaller box on top. To me, in the burnishing rasp of the afternoon sun, the last of the winter winds lashing against my face, it resembles a man whose limbs have been torn off. A man made of metal. It has lamps for eyes, although I have to squint hard to imagine there ever being an ember, a spark, of understanding. No expression defiles the broad pitted expanse of metal.

As soon as I see it, I call it "Hanover," after a character I had seen in an old movie back when the projector still worked.

"Hanover?" Shyver says with a trace of contempt.

"Hanover never gave away what he thought," I reply, as we drag it up the gravel track toward the village. Sandhaven, they call it, simply, and it's carved into the side of cliffs that are sliding into the sea. I've lived there for almost six years, taking on odd jobs, assisting with salvage. They still know next to nothing about me, not really. They like me not for what I say or who I am, but for what I do: anything mechanical I can fix, or build something new from poor parts. Someone reliable in an isolated place where a faulty water pump can be devastating. That means something real. That means you don't have to explain much.

"Hanover, whoever or whatever it is, has given up on more than thoughts," Shyver says, showing surprising intuition. It means he's already put a face on Hanover, too. "I think it's from the Old Empire. I think it washed up from the Sunken City at the bottom of the sea."

Everyone knows what Shyver thinks, about everything. Brown-haired, green-eyed, gawky, he's lived in Sandhaven his whole life. He's good with a boat, could navigate a cockleshell through a typhoon. He'll never leave the village, but why should he? As far as he knows, everything he needs is here.

Beyond doubt, the remains of Hanover are heavy. I have difficulty keeping my grip on him, despite the rust. By the time we've made it to the courtyard at the center of Sandhaven, Shyver and I are breathing as hard as old men. We drop our burden with a combination of relief and self-conscious theatrics. By now, a crowd has gathered, and not just stray dogs and bored children.

First law of salvage: what is found must be brought before the community. Is it scrap? Should it be discarded? Can it be restored?

John Blake, council leader, all unkempt black beard, wide shoulders, and watery turquoise eyes, stands there. So does Sarah, who leads the weavers, and the blacksmith Growder, and the ethereal captain of the fishing fleet: Lady Salt as she is called—she of the impossibly pale, soft skin, the blonde hair in a land that only sees the sun five months out of the year. Her eyes, ever-shifting, never settling—one is light blue and one is fierce green, as if to balance the sea between calm and roiling. She has tiny wrinkles in the corners of those eyes, and a wry smile beneath. If I remember little else, fault the eyes. We've been lovers the past three years, and if I ever fully understand her, I wonder if my love for her will vanish like the mist over the water at dawn.

With the fishing boats not launching for another week, a host of broad-faced fisher folk, joined by lesser lights and gossips, has gathered behind us. Even as the light fades: shadows of albatross and gull cutting across the horizon and the roofs of the low houses, huddled and glowing a deep gold-and-orange around the edges, framed by the graying sky.

Blake says, "Where?" He's a man who measures words as if he had only a few given to him by Fate; too generous a syllable from his lips, and he might fall over dead.

"The beach, the cove," Shyver says. Blake always reduces him to a similar terseness.

"What is it?"

This time, Blake looks at me, with a glare. I'm the fixer who solved their well problems the season before, who gets the most value for the village from what's sold to the hill scavengers. But I'm also Lady Salt's lover, who used to be his, and depending on the vagaries of his mood, I suffer more or less for it.

I see no harm in telling the truth as I know it, when I can. So much remains unsaid that extra lies exhaust me.

"It is part of a metal man," I say.

A gasp from the more ignorant among the crowd. My Lady Salt just stares right through me. I know what she's thinking: in scant days she'll be on the open sea. Her vessel is as sleek and quick and buoyant as the water, and she likes to call it *Seeker*, or sometimes *Mist*, or even just *Cleave*. Salvage holds little interest for her.

But I can see the gears turning in Blake's head. He thinks awhile before he says more. Even the blacksmith and the weaver, more for ceremony and obligation than their insight, seem to contemplate the rusted bucket before them.

A refurbished water pump keeps delivering from the aquifers; parts bartered to the hill people mean only milk and smoked meat for half a season. Still, Blake knows that the fishing has been less dependable the past few years, and that if we do not give the hill people something, they will not keep coming back.

"Fix it," he says.

It's not a question, although I try to treat it like one.

LATER THAT NIGHT, I am with the Lady Salt, whose whispered name in these moments is Rebecca.

"Not a name men would follow," she said to me once. "A land-ish name."

In bed, she's as shifting as the tides, beside me, on top, and beneath. Her mouth is soft but firm, her tongue curling like a question mark across my body. She makes little cries that are so different from the orders she barks out ship-board that she might as well be a different person. We're all different people, depending.

Rebecca can read. She has a few books from the hill people, taught herself with the help of an old man who remembered how. A couple of the books are even from the Empire—the New Empire, not the old. Sometimes I want to think she is not the Lady Salt, but the Lady Flight. That she wants to leave the village. That she seeks so much more. But I look into those eyes in the dimness of half-dawn, so close, so far, and realize she would never tell me, no matter how long I live here. Even in bed, there is a bit of Lady Salt in Rebecca.

When we are finished, lying in each other's arms under the thick covers, her hair against my cheek, Rebecca asks me, "Is that thing from your world? Do you know what it is?"

I have told her a little about my past, where I came from—mostly bed-time stories when she cannot sleep, little fantasies of golden spires and a million thronging people, fables of something so utterly different from the village that it must exist only in dream. *Once upon a time there was a foolish man. Once upon a time there was an*

Empire. She tells me she doesn't believe me, and there's freedom in that. It's a strange pillow talk that can be so grim.

I tell her the truth about Hanover: "It's nothing like what I remember." If it came from Empire, it came late, after I was already gone.

"Can you really fix it?" she asks.

I smile. "I can fix anything," and I really believe it. If I want to, I can fix anything. I'm just not sure yet I want Hanover fixed, because I don't know what he is.

But my hands can't lie—they tremble to *have at it*, to explore, impatient for the task even then and there, in bed with Blake's lost love.

I CAME FROM the same sea the Lady Salt loves. I came as salvage, and was fixed. Despite careful preparation, my vessel had been damaged first by a storm, and then a reef. Forced to the surface, I managed to escape into a raft just before my creation drowned. It was never meant for life above the waves, just as I was never meant for life below them. I washed up near the village, was found, and eventually accepted into their community; they did not sell me to the hill people.

I never meant to stay. I didn't think I'd fled far enough. Even as I'd put distance between me and Empire, I'd set traps, put up decoys, sent out false rumors. I'd done all I could to escape that former life, and yet some nights, sleepless, restless, it feels as if I am just waiting to be found.

Even failure can be a kind of success, my father always said. But I still don't know if I believe that.

THREE DAYS PASS, and I'm still fixing Hanover, sometimes with help from Shyver, sometimes not. Shyver doesn't have much else to do until the fishing fleet goes out, but that doesn't mean he has to stay cooped up in a cluttered workshop with me. Not when, conveniently, the blacksmithy is next door, and with it the lovely daughter of Growder, who he adores.

Blake says he comes in to check my progress, but I think he comes to check on me. After the Lady Salt left him, he married another—a weaver—but she died in childbirth a year ago, and took the baby with her. Now Blake sees before him a different past: a life that might have been, with the Lady Salt at his side.

I can still remember the generous Blake, the humorous Blake who would stand on a table with a mug of beer made by the hill people and tell an amusing story about being lost at sea, poking fun at himself. But now, because he still loves her, there is only me to hate. Now there is just the brambly fence of his beard to hide him, and the pressure of his eyes, the pursed, thin lips. *If I were a different man. If I loved the Lady Salt less. If she wanted him.*

But instead it is him and me in the work room, Hanover on the table, surrounded by an autopsy of gears and coils and congealed bits of metal long past their purpose. Hanover up close, over time, smells of sea grasses and brine along with the oil. I still do not *know* him. Or what he does. Or why he is here. I think I recognize some of it as the work of Empire, but I can't be sure. Shyver still thinks Hanover is merely a sculpture from beneath the ocean. But no one makes a sculpture with so many moving parts.

"Make it work," Blake says. "You're the expert. Fix it."

Expert? I'm the only one with any knowledge in this area. For hundreds, maybe thousands, of miles.

"I'm trying," I say. "But then what? We don't know what it does."

This is the central question, perhaps of my life. It is why I go slow with Hanover. My hands already know where most of the parts go. They know most of what is broken, and why.

"Fix it," Blake says, "or at the next council meeting, I will ask that you be sent to live with the hill people for a time."

There's no disguising the self-hatred in his gaze. There's no disguising that he's serious.

"For a time? And what will that prove? Except to show I can live in caves with shepherds?" I almost want an answer.

Blake spits on the wooden floor. "No use to us, why should we feed you? House you..."

Even if I leave, she won't go back to you.

"What if I fix it and all it does is blink? Or all it does is shed light, like a whale lamp? Or talk in nonsense rhymes? Or I fix it and it kills us all."

"Don't care," Blake says. "Fix it."

THE CLIFFS AROUND the village are low, like the shoulders of a slouching giant, and caulked with bird shit and white rock, veined through with dark green bramble. Tough, thick lizards scuttle through the branches. Tiny birds take shelter there, their dark eyes staring out from shadow. A smell almost like mint struggles through. Below is the cove where Shyver found Hanover.

Rebecca and I walk there, far enough beyond the village that we cannot be seen, and we talk. We find the old trails and follow them, sometimes silly, sometimes serious. We don't need to be who we are in Sandhaven.

"Blake's getting worse," I tell her. "More paranoid. He's jealous. He says he'll exile me from the village if I don't fix Hanover."

"Then fix Hanover," Rebecca says.

We are holding hands. Her palm is warm and sweaty in mine, but I don't care. Every moment I'm with her feels like something I didn't earn, wasn't looking for, but don't want to lose. Still, something in me rebels. It's tiring to keep proving myself.

"I can do it," I say. "I know I can. But..."

"Blake can't exile you without the support of the council," Lady Salt says. I know it's her, not Rebecca, because of the tone, and the way her blue eye flashes when she looks at me. "But he can make life difficult if you give him cause." A pause, a tightening of her grip. "He's in mourning. You know it makes him not himself. But we need him. We need him back."

A twinge as I wonder how she means that. But it's true: Blake has led Sandhaven through good times and bad, made tough decisions and cared about the village.

Sometimes, though, leadership is not enough. What if what you really need is the instinct to be fearful? And the thought as we make our way back to the village: *What if Blake is right about me?*

So I BEGIN to work on Hanover in earnest. There's a complex balance to him that I admire. People think engineering is about practical application of science, and that might be right, if you're building something. But if you're fixing something, something you don't fully understand—say, you're fixing a Hanover—you have no access to a schematic, to a helpful context. Your work instead becomes a kind of detection. You become a kind of detective. You track down clues—cylinders that fit into holes in sheets of steel, that slide into place in grooves, that lead to wires, that lead to understanding.

To do this, I have to stop my ad hoc explorations. Instead, with Shyver's reluctant help, I take Hanover apart systematically. I document where I find each part, and if I think it truly belongs there, or has become dislodged during the trauma that resulted in his "death." I note gaps. I label each part by what I believe it contributed to his overall function. In all things, I remember that Hanover has been made to look like a man, and therefore his innards roughly resemble those of a man in form or function, his makers consciously or subconsciously unable to ignore the implications of that form, that function.

Shyver looks at the parts lying glistening on the table, and says, "They're so different out of him." So different cleaned up, greased with fresh fish oil. Through the window, the sun's light sets them ablaze. Hanover's burnished surface, whorled with a patina of greens, blues, and rust red. The world become radiant.

When we remove the carapace of Hanover's head to reveal a thousand wires, clockwork gears, and strange fluids, even Shyver cannot think of him as a statue anymore.

"What does a machine like this *do*?" Shyver says, who has only rarely seen anything more complex than a hammer or a watch.

I laugh. "It does whatever it wants to do, I imagine."

By the time I am done with Hanover, I have made several leaps of logic. I have made decisions that cannot be explained as rational, but in their rightness set my head afire with the absolute certainty of Creation. The feeling energizes me and horrifies me all at once.

* * *

It was long after my country became an Empire that I decided to escape. And still I might have stayed, even knowing what I had done. That is the tragedy of everyday life: when you are in it, you can never see yourself clearly.

Even seven years in, Sandhaven having made the Past the past, I still had nightmares of gleaming rows of airships. I would wake, screaming, from what had once been a blissful dream, and the Lady Salt and Rebecca both would be there to comfort me.

Did I deserve that comfort?

Shyver is there when Hanover comes alive. I've spent a week speculating on ways to bypass what look like missing parts, missing wires. I've experimented with a hundred different connections. I've even identified Hanover's independent power source and recharged it using a hand-cranked generator.

Lady Salt has gone out with the fishing fleet for the first time and the village is deserted. Even Blake has gone with her, after a quick threat in my direction once again. If the fishing doesn't go well, the evening will not go any better for me.

Shyver says, "Is that a spark?"

A spark?

"Where?"

I have just put Hanover back together again for possibly the twentieth time and planned to take a break, to just sit back and smoke a hand-rolled cigarette, compliments of the enigmatic hill people.

"In Hanover's... eyes."

Shyver goes white, backs away from Hanover, as if something monstrous has occurred, even though this is what we wanted.

It brings memories flooding back—of the long-ago day steam had come rushing out of the huge iron bubble and the canvas had swelled, and held, and everything I could have wished for in my old life had been attained. That feeling had become addiction—I wanted to experience it again and again—but now it's bittersweet, something to cling to and cast away.

My assistant then had responded much as Shyver does now: both on some instinctual level knowing that something unnatural has happened.

"Don't be afraid," I say to Shyver, to my assistant.

"I'm not afraid," Shyver says, lying.

"You should be afraid," I say.

Hanover's eyes gain more and more of a glow. A clicking sound comes from him. Click, click, click. A hum. A slightly rumbling cough from deep inside, a hum again. We prop him up so he is no longer on his side. He's warm to the touch.

The head rotates from side to side, more graceful than in my imagination.

A sharp intake of breath from Shyver. "It's alive!"

I laugh then. I laugh and say, "In a way. It's got no arms or legs. It's harmless."

It's harmless.

Neither can it speak—just the click, click, click. But no words.

Assuming it is trying to speak.

JOHN BLAKE AND the Lady Salt come back with the fishing fleet. The voyage seems to have done Blake good. The windswept hair, the salt-stung face—he looks relaxed as they enter my workshop.

As they stare at Hanover, at the light in its eyes, I'm almost jealous. Standing side by side, they almost resemble a King and his Queen, and suddenly I'm acutely aware they were lovers, grew up in the village together. Rebecca's gaze is distant; thinking of Blake or of me or of the sea? They smell of mingled brine and fish and salt, and somehow the scent is like a knife in my heart.

"What does it do?" Blake asks.

Always, the same kinds of questions. Why should everything have to have a function?

"I don't know," I say. "But the hill folk should find it pretty and perplexing, at least."

Shyver, though, gives me away, makes me seem less and less from this place: "He thinks it can talk. We just need to fix it *more*. It might do all kinds of things for us."

"It's fixed," I snap, looking at Shyver as if I don't know him at all. We've drunk together, talked many hours. I've given him advice about the blacksmith's daughter. But now that doesn't matter. He's from here and I'm from *there*. "We should trade it to the hill folk and be done with it."

Click, click, click. Hanover won't stop. And I just want it over with, so I don't slide into the past.

Blake's calm has disappeared. I can tell he thinks I lied to him. "Fix it," he barks. "I mean really fix it. Make it talk."

He turns on his heel and leaves the workshop, Shyver behind him.

Lady Salt approaches, expression unreadable. "Do as he says. Please. The fishing... there's little enough out there. We need every advantage now."

Her hand on the side of my face, warm and calloused, before she leaves.

Maybe there's no harm in it. If I just do what they ask, this one last time—the last of many times—it will be over. Life will return to normal. I can stay here. I can still find a kind of peace.

ONCE, THERE WAS a foolish man who saw a child's balloon rising into the sky and thought it could become a kind of airship. No one in his world had ever created such a thing, but he already had ample evidence of his own genius in the things he had built before. Nothing had come close to challenging his engineering skills. No one had ever told him he might have limits. His father, a biology teacher, had taught him to focus on problems and solutions. His mother, a caterer, had shown him the value of attention to detail and hard work.

He took his plans, his ideas, to the government. They listened enough to give him some money, a place to work, and an assistant. All of this despite his youth, because of his brilliance, and in his turn he ignored how they talked about their enemies, the need to thwart external threats.

When this engineer was successful, when the third prototype actually worked, following three years of flaming disaster, he knew he had created something that had never before existed, and his heart nearly burst with pride. His wife had left him because she never saw him except when he needed sleep, the house was a junk yard, and yet he didn't care. He'd done it.

He couldn't know that it wouldn't end there. As far as he was concerned, they could take it apart and let him start on something else, and his life would have been good because he knew when he was happiest.

But the government's military advisors wanted him to perfect the airship. They asked him to solve problems that he hadn't thought about before. How to add weight to the carriage without it serving as undue ballast, so things could be dropped from the airship. How to add "defensive" weapons. How to make them work without igniting the fuel that drove the airship. A series of challenges that appealed to his pride, and maybe, too, he had grown used to the rich life he had now. Caught up in it all, he just kept going, never said no, and focused on the gears, the wires, the air ducts, the myriad tiny details that made him ignore everything else.

This foolish man used his assistants as friends to go drinking with, to sleep with, to be his whole life, creating a kind of cult there in his workshop that had become a gigantic hangar, surrounded by soldiers and barbed wire fence. He'd become a national hero.

But I still remembered how my heart had felt when the prototype had risen into the air, how the tears trickled down my face as around me men and women literally danced with joy. How I was struck by the image of my own success, almost as if I were flying.

The prototype wallowed and snorted in the air like a great golden whale in a harness, wanting to be free: a blazing jewel against the bright blue sky, the dream made real.

I don't know what the Lady Salt would have thought of it. Maybe nothing at all.

ONE DAY, HANOVER finally speaks. I push a button, clean a gear, move a circular bit into place. It is just me and him. Shyver wanted no part of it.

He says, "Command water the sea was bright with the leavings of the fish that there were now going to be."

Clicks twice, thrice, and continues clicking as he takes the measure of me with his golden gaze and says, "Engineer Daniker."

The little hairs on my neck rise. I almost lose my balance, all the blood rushing to my head.

"How do you know my name?"

"You are my objective. You are why I was sent."

"Across the ocean? Not likely."

"I had a ship once, arms and legs once, before your traps destroyed me."

I had forgotten the traps I'd set. I'd almost forgotten my true name.

"You will return with me. You will resume your duties."

I laugh bitterly. "They've found no one to replace me?"

Hanover has no answer—just the clicking—but I know the answer. Child prodigy. Unnatural skills. An unswerving ability to focus in on a problem and solve it. Like... building airships. I'm still an asset they cannot afford to lose.

"You've no way to take me back. You have no authority here," I say.

Hanover's bright eyes dim, then flare. The clicking intensifies. I wonder now if it is the sound of a weapons system malfunctioning.

"Did you know I was here, in this village?" I ask.

A silence. Then: "Dozens were sent for you—scattered across the world."

"So no one knows."

"I have already sent a signal. They are coming for you."

Horror. Shock. And then anger—indescribable rage, like nothing I've ever experienced.

WHEN THEY FIND me with Hanover later, there isn't much left of him. I've smashed his head in and then his body, and tried to grind that down with a pestle. I didn't know where the beacon might be hidden, or if it even mattered, but I had to try.

They think I'm mad—the soft-spoken blacksmith, a livid Blake, even Rebecca. I keep telling them the Empire is coming, that I am the Empire's chief engineer. That I've been in hiding. That they need to leave now—into the hills, into the sea. *Anywhere but here...*

But Blake can't see it—he sees only me—and whatever the Lady Salt thinks, she hides it behind a sad smile.

"I said to fix it," Blake roars before he storms out. "Now it's no good for anything!"

Roughly I am taken to the little room that functions as the village jail, with the bars on the window looking out on the sea. As they leave me, I am shouting, "I created their airships! They're coming for me!"

The Lady Salt backs away from the window, heads off to find Blake, without listening.

After dark, Shyver comes by the window, but not to hear me out—just to ask why I did it.

"We could at least have sold it to the hill people," he whispers. He sees only the village, the sea, the blacksmith's daughter. "We put so much work into it."

I have no answer except for a story that he will not believe is true.

ONCE, THERE WAS a country that became an Empire. Its armies flew out from the center and conquered the margins, the barbarians. Everywhere it inflicted itself on the world, people died or came under its control, always under the watchful, floating gaze of the airships. No one had ever seen anything like them before. No one had any defense for them. People wrote poems about them and cursed them and begged for mercy from their attentions.

The chief engineer of this atrocity, the man who had solved the problems, sweated the details, was finally called up by the Emperor of the newly minted Empire fifteen years after he'd seen a golden shape float against a startling blue sky. The Emperor was on the far frontier, some remote place fringed by desert where the people built their homes into the sides of hills and used tubes to spit fire up into the sky.

They took me to His Excellency by airship, of course. For the first time, except for excursions to the capital, I left my little enclave, the country I'd created for myself. From on high, I saw what I had helped create. In the conquered lands, the people looked up at us in fear and hid when and where they could. Some, beyond caring, threw stones up at us: an old woman screaming words I could not hear from that distance, a young man with a bow, the arrows arching below the carriage until the airship commander opened fire, left a red smudge on a dirt road as we glided by from on high.

This vision I had not known existed unfurled like a slow, terrible dream, for we were like languid gods in our progress, the landscape revealing itself to us with a strange finality.

On the fringes, war was still waged, and before we reached the Emperor I saw my creations clustered above hostile armies, raining down *my* bombs onto stick figures who bled, screamed, died, were mutilated, blown apart... all as if in a silent film, the explosions deafening us, the rest reduced to distant pantomime narrated by the black humored cheer of our airship's officers.

A child's head resting upon a rock, the body a red shadow. A city reduced to rubble. A man whose limbs had been torn from him. All the same.

By the time I reached the Emperor, received his blessing and his sword, I had nothing to say; he found me more mute than any captive, his instrument once more. And when I returned, when I could barely stand myself anymore, I found a way to escape my cage.

Only to wash up on a beach half a world away.

Out of the surf, out of the sand, dripping and half-dead, I stumble and the Lady Salt and Blake stand there, above me. I look up at them in the half-light of morning, arm raised against the sun, and wonder whether they will welcome me or kill me or just cast me aside.

The Lady Salt looks doubtful and grim, but Blake's broad face breaks into a smile. "Welcome stranger," he says, and extends his hand.

I take it, relieved. In that moment, there's no Hanover, no pain, no sorrow, nothing but the firm grip, the arm pulling me up toward them.

THEY COME AT dawn, much faster than I had thought possible: ten airships, golden in the light, the humming thrum of their propellers audible over the crash of the sea. From behind my bars, I watch their deadly, beautiful approach across the slate-gray sky, the deep-blue waves, and it is as if my children are returning to me. If there is no mercy in them, it is because I never thought of mercy when I created the bolt and canvas of them, the fuel and gears of them.

HOURS LATER, I sit in the main cabin of the airship *Forever Triumph*. It has mahogany tables and chairs, crimson cushions. A platter of fruit upon a dais. A telescope on a tripod. A globe of the world. The scent of snuff. All the debris of the real world. We sit on the window seat, the Lady Salt and I. Beyond, the rectangular windows rise and fall just slightly, showing cliffs and hills and sky; I do not look down.

Captain Evans, aping civilized speech, has been talking to us for several minutes. He is fifty and rake-thin and has hooded eyes that make him mournful forever. I don't really know what he's saying; I can't concentrate. I just feel numb, as if I'm not really there.

Blake insisted on fighting what could not be fought. So did most of the others. I watched from behind my bars as first the bombs came and then the troops. I heard Blake die, although I didn't see it. He was cursing and screaming at them; he didn't go easy. Shyver was shot in the leg, dragged himself off moaning. I don't know if he made it.

I forced myself to listen—to all of it.

They had orders to take me alive, and they did. They found the Lady Salt with a gutting knife, but took her too when I told the captain I'd cooperate if they let her live.

Her presence at my side is something unexpected and horrifying. What can she be feeling? Does she think I could have saved Blake but chose not to? Her eyes are dry and she stares straight ahead, at nothing, at no one, while the captain continues with his explanations, his threats, his flattery.

"Rebecca," I say. "Rebecca," I say.

The whispered words of the Lady Salt are everything, all, the chief engineer could have expected: *"Some day I will kill you and escape to the sea."*

I nod wearily and turn my attention back to the captain, try to understand what he is saying.

Below me, the village burns as all villages burn, everywhere, in time.

THE LOLLYGANG SAVE THE WORLD ON ACCIDENT

Jay Lake

Jay Lake is one of American SF's best emerging writers, the author of the novels Rocket Science, Trial of Flowers, *and* Madness of Flowers, *as well as the major steampunk epics* Mainspring *and* Escapement. *His short stories are collected in* Dogs in the Moonlight, American Sorrows, *and* The River Knows Its Own. *In the following tale, Lake invites us to a somewhat different steam-driven world of punks, where the Victorian age is but a mysterious memory...*

PER BRACED AGAINST the corroded stanchion protruding from a riveted curve of the Big Pipe. Wind tore at him like his ma'am after she'd been drinking too hard. He squinted against the unaccustomed daylight and tried not to look down. Outside loomed all around him like a scream.

His left hand was encased in one of Cleverdick Stafford's special Gloves. That gave Per little enough comfort—last month another of Cleverdick's Gloves had smashed Slow Willie's fingers in the middle of a bank job. This one was different, he'd been assured. Gyroscopically balanced, doubled hydraulic couplings in case of failure, and a punchtape intelligence mounted on the inside of the wrist to keep the fingers moving good.

"A kineopticon helmet would come in favorite right about now," Per told the sky. Outside had no answer, except the same invitation it always offered to fall, fall, fall.

They said you'd starve to death falling before you ever fetched up against something, so long as you didn't bounce off the Big Pipe.

Cleverdick Stafford's Glove went about its work, digging into an open panel where mechano-electrical switches gleamed. Per's arm bobbed as the Glove pulled at it. Occasionally the punchtape clicked, spitting out a coded demand for one or another of the tools Per had clipped to his belt.

That was the worst, letting go of the entire world to reach for a specific pair of calipers or some such, trusting a set of slipknots to keep him safe.

Billy-bedamned Gloves couldn't get about on their own. Which was probably good, considering what arrogant shitehawks the punchtapes tended to be once they had a job going. Like bullyboys, but without the boy.

So Per hung on, his feet against the lip of a section joint and his face pressed close to the metal curve of the Big Pipe, and vowed to remember woolen underwear the next time he drew the short straw for outside boy.

MUCH LATER, ONE of the Vessel Fathers would remark with extensive hissing of pressure valves that the war had never gone well, but neither had it ever gone poorly, and why was this state of affairs called "war" at all, when it was indeed nothing but life being lived.

A strange life, though. The Big Pipe was nothing but the works of man, unrelieved by nature except for scuttling rats and roaches, and such greenery as struggled in sad little boxes with rotted cloth and baby shit for soil.

Envision a tube almost a mile in diameter. Substantial, solid, built from forged iron, reinforced with steel, bound in brass and copper and even aluminum. Within are decks, each divided into walled rooms and great concourses according to some unknown design. Grand staircases, tiny ladders and a pair of cog railways at opposite extents of the Big Pipe's circumference connect the decks.

Pipes carry steam at varying pressures from boilers hidden in the flooring between decks. Some argue passionately that the volume of steam far exceeds the theoretical maxima generated by these hidden boilers. Others accept the world for what it is.

Likewise the twining cloth-wrapped wires with their great bus bars and knife switches. Entire sections of the Big Pipe are dark. People there fear to touch the current and live instead by such daylight as is admitted through baffles and viewports in the outer ring. They burn tallow candles rendered from one another's body fat. Elsewhere showers of sparks are an everyday hazard, the risk repaid with lighting and other useful applications drawn from the copper which winds through every wall.

As passionate as the Boilerist debates can be, entire wars have been fought among differing factions of Electricalists—the Batterians hate the Dynamists with a furor that comes only between spiritual brothers caught on the point of a switch, while the Generators have perpetrated some of the worst massacres in the known history of the Big Pipe.

Humans bring love and despair everywhere they go. The Big Pipe is just another stage on which to play out those dramas of the psyche. The Lollygang are only another band of players, innocent of script and unaware that they perform.

Like everyone, they live their lives.

The Gloves have other plans.

ONCE SHADOWMITE AND Cleverdick Stafford had pulled him through the service hatch, Per collapsed on the grating. The rusty embrace of the floor was a benediction. He found the familiar, eternal dim of the deck deeply comforting. "M-my g-god," he stammered.

Shadowmite bent down grinning. She was one of the few girls in the Lollygang, and she took herself not at all seriously. "'Ere there, Per, 'ave a slug o' this." A silver flask was shoved into his free hand.

Cleverdick was already unhooking the Glove from Per's left. That never felt right. When the needles came out, the sensation was of his skin being peeled away.

He was little damaged, as always—blood welled in a pattern of carmine dots, but no more. "Damned Glove does that out of spite," he growled.

"Watch your mouth," snapped Cleverdick. At sixteen, he was the oldest boy in the Lollygang. Rules said he should have been kicked out at fourteen, but the Gloves had been so important to the gang's successes of late, especially against the McCrain Deck Beaters, that no one was ready to do without.

Somehow, none of the boys set to learn alongside Cleverdick were ever able to work his tricks.

"Why?" demanded Per. "It can't bloody well hear me!"

"I wouldn't be so sure, sweetie," said Shadowmite with a laugh. "Bigdick Clothyard 'ere 'as been weaving some mighty clever patterns into 'is toys."

Cleverdick shot her a murderous glare as he gathered up the Glove. Turning back to Per, he asked, "Any problems?"

"With the Glove? No. Being outside..." Per sat up. "Why don't you try it, smart boy?"

"We all have our talents in life," Cleverdick said.

The fingers of the Glove moved slightly. He couldn't tell if it was waving farewell or making a threat. As the Glove-boy left, Shadowmite clipped a hose to a water line and passed the nozzle to Per. "Chase the booze with some pipe juice, there's a lovely."

He slammed two swallows of the bucket-made gin. It burned his throat like kerosene, but warmed his gut. Per then sucked down the flow Shadowmite had handed him. Linewater always tasted flat, but you never got sick on it. Being outside dried Per out something awful—his nose itched and his body had a strange achey feeling.

She squatted on her heels, almost nose to ear. "So what's it like, wearing one of them Gloves?"

"You can have it," gasped Per. "Silly thing takes over."

Her eyes gleamed. "Like St. Vitus's dance?"

"No. It just knows what it wants and pulls you along." He stood wearily. "Like some people."

Shadowmite covered her mouth and drew a deep breath of mock horror. "'Ere now, and you wouldn't be speaking of me!?"

"Never in my life." Per followed her out into the stream of life that was the Big Pipe.

THERE WERE NO empty decks. Rumor always passed of haunted spaces, graveyard rooms, places where power or steam or structural integrity had failed, but no one ever seemed to be able to point one out.

Instead the Big Pipe teemed with people. All walks of life, all skin colors, all philosophical persuasions. They did not have countries so much as confraternities, organized along consanguinity or occupation or birthplace or class.

The confraternities exchanged a network of obligations and privileges which provided the lubrication so desperately required for civil intercourse and the broadening benefits of trade. For example, jewelers sent their mounted stones along by messenger and received bolts of fine cloth, new tools and foodstuffs from distant decks in return. Without trust, such an exchange would be impossible.

Most people never passed more than a handful of decks from the place of their birth, and fewer still left the confraternity in which they were raised.

Some troubled souls went exploring. They traveled from deck to deck clad in rough leather, bearing sacks of provisions and an Outside stare. You never saw them twice.

Others with reason to be dissatisfied found their way into the gangs that lived intramurally. These were not confraternities dedicated to a certain trade or style of living, but opportunists who preyed upon the settled order of life within the Big Pipe. They were generally not brutally violent, and they promoted an informal economic and technological interchange which over time led to new trading partners and novel combinations of the confraternities themselves.

Some argue that the gangs could thus be seen as the yeast which made possible the heady brew of existence. Others argue that they are criminals and juvenile delinquents who would benefit from a good thrashing and steady work under a hard-eyed master.

The Lollygang was the latter sort of gang. Like most of its kind, membership ranged from those old enough to ask through those almost through puberty. The Lollygang had long since learned that "olders" got strange ideas about who should be in charge, and for how long, and so regularly purged itself.

Just lately, the Lollygang had changed. Once content with a life of petty crime and ruffianism, and in fact serving as a courier across half a dozen decks, Cleverdick's Gloves had lent them a purpose. Most members didn't *understand* that purpose, but it pleased them to serve a higher calling. An outside observer might have concluded that this particular gang was developing into a confraternity.

Meanwhile, codes were cracked, circuits were rewired, and the underlying logics which controlled the flow of materials throughout the Big Pipe were being mapped.

THE LOLLYGANG MET every Sennday in their hide. That was their bolthole, where such weapons as were used could be safely stored, and a Lollyganger on the run could quietly go to ground until confraternity enforcers gave up their pursuit. It was a huge tank, originally designed for storage of some fluid, though all the inlets and outlets were capped, valves long since rusted shut.

Inside was a network of cables and ropes. Hammocks were strung, and bosun's chairs, and sacks of gear and food, all at different points where the lines met, crossed and recrossed. The hide was in effect a three dimensional map of the Lollygang's activities.

This day all twenty-seven members of the Lollygang were assembled in solemn session. Juke, whose face was dark as axle grease, was still their redcap, though his time was almost done. He was the second oldest member of the Lollygang after Cleverdick Stafford. Shadowmite stood beside him, acting as clerk and counting mistress in case a vote was called for, or funds needed to be shifted.

Juke had a new Glove. It was different from the strange, bulky, articulated gauntlet Per had worn Outside. This one looked like mesh.

Per picked at the scabs which still clung to his hand, and stared at the Glove in Juke's grasp with growing dis-ease.

"Cleverdick can make us each a Glove," Juke called out. "One of these new ones. What can solve locks and open frozen hatch dogs, and sniff out where the good stuff is at."

That Per believed.

"Why we want this glove?" shouted Green Charles.

"It's like magic," Juke said. "We'll be the most powerful gang for levels in both directions."

Green Charles snorted. "You want to rule the Big Pipe?"

Per noticed Cleverdick Stafford nodding to Hoyle and Varibidian. Those two were sullen punks who never did the tricky jobs. Mostly they beat up people who needed reminding that the Lollygang's business was its own.

Right now the duo was making their way around the perimeter of the hide to reach Green Charles. No one else seemed to notice. Most appeared charmed by the new Glove. The only person paying attention to Per was Cleverdick.

Per grinned, trying to look as if he were in on the good.

"Charles," Juke shouted, "until you get to try it, maybe you should hold your water." He raised his left hand and slipped the new Glove on.

The Lollygang cheered. Under the cover of the noise, Hoyle and Varibidian pulled Green Charles against the back wall. Hoyle's arm was around the unfortunate boy's neck, while Varibidian whispered urgently to him.

Pretending to cheer, Per turned back to Juke. The redcap was clowning with the Glove. He swept his hand back and forth, miming first fighting, then looting, then a clenched fist which gleamed overbright in the dim electrics of the hide.

Nausea swept over Per.

"Problems?" asked Cleverdick Stafford from just behind him.

Per hadn't even noticed the older boy on the move.

"Never. This is terrific!" He hoped the glassy ring in his voice wasn't obvious.

"Good." Cleverdick patted Per's shoulder. "We'd hate to have problems, wouldn't we?"

There was more cheering. Per desperately wanted to ask what these new gloves would cost the Lollygang, but when he caught Shadowmite's pitying look, Per knew his questions could not be asked. Not this day.

For all its crowded swell of humanity, the Big Pipe was filled with quiet passages as well. Some were at the perimeter in areas where the wind moaned close Outside. Those sounds were unlucky, and so avoided. Others were accidents of geometry and architecture—dead ends in the design of a deck, or inconvenient corridors.

Scholars of the Big Pipe have long noted that a careful census of the wires, pipes and conduits which flow from deck to deck reveals that there must be fluids or currents yet untapped. Some hardy souls would from time to time attempt to gain access to these mysterious channels. Generally they were disappointed by a puff of rusty air, or occasionally a spew of machine oil from some undocumented line.

True students of the Big Pipe, those who make it their business to learn through careful observation, know that some of the surplus wiring ends in speaking trumpets which hang cold and silent in the quietest passages of the Big Pipe. It was said that the trumpets dispensed advice of the most elliptical sort. Others claimed they were merely babblesome connections to distant decks where the language of the people was little more than the braying of apes.

Most folk did not know of the existence of these oracular stations. Many who did chose to avoid them. Per happened to be an observant fellow who'd marked what he'd seen, though he'd never before sought one out for his own needs.

THERE WAS A sort of cup which one could place against one's ear, and a mouthpiece in which to speak. A double row of glowing buttons was set into the rosewood paneled wall just to one side of the trumpet.

Taking a deep, shuddering breath, Per set the cup to his ear.

He heard a faint clicking noise, then a silence like someone trying not to be overheard breathing—gravid with possibility.

"H-hello," he said into the trumpet.

A moment later an attenuated echo of Per's own voice came back.

"I seek advice."

No answer.

He noticed one of the glowing buttons had begun to pulsate, cycling through a brighter phase every few seconds. Per closed his eyes and mashed it.

"Hello," he said again.

A woman's voice answered. "Interrogatory, how may I be of assistance?" She sounded as if she were speaking through her nose.

"I... is this the oracle?"

"The oracle can be found on Cumaean seven fourteen, sir. This is Interrogatory at Babbage twenty two zero. Do you require further assistance?"

"No. I mean yes!"

"How may I be of assistance?"

Per wondered if he was speaking to a human being. Nonetheless, here he was. He doubted he'd soon find the courage to again approach the oracle. The interrogatory. Whatever. Certainly not before the ill fruits of the new Gloves were borne out.

"Juke has a plan," he said. "For the new Gloves. Cleverdick Stafford's supposed to have them for all the Lollygang, but it ain't right. They take *over.*"

"I will file a notice that you have reported a Glove infestation," said Interrogatory. "Be wary. Gloves can be fatal. If the infestation remains uncontrolled, your decks may be sealed. To report such problems in the future, you may wish to ring Undersight directly at Prometheus four four two."

Sealing the decks sounded like a death sentence. "But what do I *do*?" Per protested.

"A boy like you should play Outside more."

The ear cup went dead. All the little button lights faded to nothing. Per slammed the cup back on its clip, then kicked the wall.

"You'll leave a mark."

He looked up in panic to see Shadowmite in the doorway at the end of the little corridor. "I'm not—" Per began. Then he snapped, "This isn't what it looks like."

Her smile gleamed. "Surely you are."

The button lights brightened again as a bell began to ring. Then someone grabbed Per from behind. He glimpsed Hoyle's face before a bag was pulled over his head. Hoyle's left hand had been encased in a gleaming mesh Glove.

Per fought of course, but he was overwhelmed. Soon enough he gave up the struggle, for all it bought him was kicks and hoots of derision.

"We gots a good'un," said Varibidian.

Though Per could see nothing, the leer in the bigger boy's voice was vivid.

"Eh, Hoyle, everybody knows how it's Outside that's Per's favoritest place."

He kicked at that, and wondered where Shadowmite had gotten to. *She* was supposed to be his friend.

"We're all Lollygang together," Per shouted. The sack muffled his words, but Varibidian and Hoyle heard him well enough that a fist struck the side of his head.

"No we isn't," growled Varibidian, who must have bent close to Per. "Not if we isn't on with the plan. You never liked them Gloves what are going to make us great."

Per lunged, forcing his forehead toward where he thought Varibidian must be. He guessed well, because he felt a strong blow on his skull. Something else crunched much like a broken nose.

There was a wordless shriek of agony, then a series of hard kicks to Per's gut and back. He coiled over, trying to protect himself. Something cold clamped on his neck.

"You thig you're so smard now," Varibidian said.

"Come on." Hoyle's voice. "We're not supposed to kill him. We're supposed to dump him Outside."

"Whad does the girl dnow?"

"She knows what Juke thinks. She speaks for him."

"Girls id gangs," muttered Varibidian.

This time Per was hoisted up. They moved quickly for a while after that, until he was dropped onto a grating.

Oh no, he thought, *they really are going to put me Outside.* Somehow he didn't think this excursion would include safety lines or a recovery team. "Please," he gasped.

A kick took him in the mouth, right through the sack.

Per heard the wind whistle as a hatch was opened. He was manhandled, kicking and squirming, feet first into the passage. At the last they pulled his sack off.

"Here," said Hoyle, pressing something into his hand. "Now you got time to think."

Varibidian just glared over a swollen nose.

Another kick, this one to the crown of his head from the sole of Hoyle's boot, and Per was sliding Outside, grasping desperately at the stanchions alongside the outer ring of the hatch.

He clenched his eyes against the bright light and clung in the howling wind.

IMAGINE IF YOU will a race of creators. Beings of elegance, discernment, exquisite taste and nearly infinite resources. Their precise appearance is irrelevant, but for the sake of the *Gedankenexperiment*, presume they have hands much as any human.

They build an experiment, a world, a playground of the mind. Their taste runs to the rococo, and they possess a great admiration for the more brutal forms of technology. Vast gears interlocking with the tolerance of the finest hair, rivers of molten metal, the hot muscles of steam pushing forward the foundations of civilization.

Into this place the creators insert a mass of people who must, as people do, live and breathe and breed. With proper command of topology and strong local control of physics, our creators can make their world-experiment indefinitely extensible through both space and time. Long after they have withdrawn to other pursuits, it will continue, stable as any natural manifestation.

But like a gentleman absent from his country manor they will leave their traces behind. Here is a favored smoking jacket, there is a handmade shotgun which took the gentleman's first peasant.

If this gentleman were a maker and destroyer of worlds, even his belongings would over time absorb some of his attributes. So the jacket lays a fire and sits reflectively in the parlor of an autumn afternoon while rain writes glyphs of prophecy on the window mullions. Likewise the gun takes itself to the fields, that the estate's great beater-birds might flush new boys for the hunt and a trophy be claimed screaming and crying as tradition demands.

So the fabled creators of our imaginary world might absent themselves, but leave behind traces of their intelligence and intent in the tools they used, in the places they frequented. Even, possibly, in the Gloves they wore about their labors.

PER FINALLY OPENED his eyes. He hadn't fallen yet. There was no reason to look at the infinite sky, so he studied his immediate vicinity. One foot was wedged in the stanchion on the far side of the hatch. His free hand clung to another stanchion right in front of him.

The hatch wasn't an option. Shut tight, dogged from within for sure. They wouldn't have bothered to push him Outside just to let him crawl back in again.

Shaking the windblown hair out of his face, Per looked at what Hoyle had given him.

One of the new Gloves, of course.

It seemed to coil in his hand as if it had a mind of its own. The mesh glinted and winked. Per knew that if he tugged the glove on, it could manage to open the hatch.

The message was clear. Glove, or die.

The tiny scabs on his hand itched. The Gloves were *wrong*. They controlled too much, took on errands which made no sense. It was like letting boys from another deck into the Lollygang. And Interrogatory had as much as said the Gloves could kill them all.

Not just him, or the Lollygang, but everyone on the Lollygang's decks. All their ma'ams and papas and little sisters and brothers, too.

He was tempted to hurl the Glove away to fall endlessly. That wouldn't help though, and the damned thing might bounce into another vent somewhere down the Big Pipe.

Vents.

Per didn't have climbing gear. It wasn't practical to crawl across this surface and find an entrance. He wasn't getting back inside here unless Shadowmite took pity on him. He could do something about the Glove, though.

If they had minds of their own, Gloves could be hurt. If one could be hurt, maybe the others would feel it. Like the trumpet, carrying voices from place to place within the infinite distances of the Big Pipe.

There was a valve cluster beyond the switch panel he'd so recently helped a Glove to sabotage. Pressure vents, outlet ports—it was a big utility head, basically. Perhaps ten feet to the left of his current position.

No rungs, no railings, no balconies. Just the section joint he'd braced his feet against the last time he was out here. When he also had a harness, and stays, and a retrieval team.

How many times have I climbed inside the hide? he asked himself.

One hand reached slowly down toward the joint. A pair of flanges, butt to butt, where plates of the Big Pipe's skin were riveted together. Like a path, almost as wide as the front of his foot.

Should I take off my boots?

The thought of falling in his bare feet troubled Per. He tucked the Glove inside his shirt. It was eerily warm against his wind-chilled skin. He gripped the stanchion with both hands and freed his feet.

Gravity did most of the next bit of work, dropping him to a foothold on the flange.

One hand stretched for the switch panel. Fingers brushed, then he had the least of grips. Release the stanchion, sidle leftward.

The Glove stirred within his shirt like a pet rat.

He pressed as close as he could to the curve of the Big Pipe's skin. Outside? What Outside?

It took Per almost a quarter hour to creep the ten feet of distance. Finally his left hand grabbed the utility head. With his right he extracted the Glove. It did a sort of dance in his hands. Gleeful.

Per jammed the Glove wrist-first over a steam relief valve. He very carefully tugged his right bootlace free and tightly wrapped the base of the Glove, securing it to the valve body so it wouldn't simply jet off into the open air.

"I'll show you glee," he shouted over the howling wind, and flipped open the petcock.

The Glove jumped instantly to the shape of a fat man's hand, then twitched. A rising shriek nearly deafened Per. The *Glove* screaming.

When it did pop loose, it shot into the empty air of Outside trailing steam, a brilliant line of metal scales and a falling scream.

Always a good Lollyganger, Per risked scalding to shut off the relief valve. He then clung sobbing to the utility head until his grip tired and it was time to let go.

He was quite surprised to see Shadowmite Outside in harness, reaching for him. There was a long, blue-skied moment when it was unclear who would live and who would die, before she got a clip on Per and hauled him toward the open hatch.

SOMETIMES THE TRUMPETS buzz, then speak to themselves. Connections are switched. The ghosts in the infinite machine that is the Big Pipe whisper secrets such that a patient boy could crouch quiet in the darkness and overhear them.

Even when there is no patient boy, the secrets are whispered anyway. Which is too bad, because the right patient boy might have heard his name being favorably marked down in books which weren't really books, kept so far away they weren't really there at all.

One of life's sad truths is that success can be invisible.

Juke leaned close to Per, who was lying in a doss at the bottom of the hide trying to recover from the vertigo which had overwhelmed him the last two days. The older boy's dark face was sheened with sweat. "I got to go down to a hospital, twenty decks and more," he said quietly.

Everyone who'd been wearing Gloves had been hurt, some quite badly, when Per had boiled his with high-pressure steam. They had been connected in some strange way, just as the intelligences at the other end of the trumpet system were. Now almost a third of the Lollygang was on the sick list. A few would likely never come off it.

Even the adults of the local decks had some intimation of the averted disaster. Per's ma'am had sent word to him here in the hide, asking him to visit her. The note read as if she'd written it sober.

The Lollygang's leader awkwardly tugged off his ceremonial hat with his good hand. "I'm saying you're the new redcap, Per. Gang has to vote, but my vote is now. It will count for a lot."

"Shadowmite tallies," Per said by way of clumsy reply.

"She ain't going to argue." Juke pushed the cap onto Per's head. It promptly slid off again. "You saved the world. Or at least our deck of it."

Per shook his head. "Lollygang did. Even Varibidian and Hoyle, by pushing me out there."

"Hoyle thought he was helping, giving you a glove. Made a last chance for you."

"That's what I mean," Per said. "He did help. Lollygang saved the world. We just didn't know we were doing it."

Juke nodded. "All the best stuff happens on accident. The worst, too. You got to do something about Varibidian, though."

"If I'm redcap, he's going to be outside boy until I get tired of it."

The old redcap laughed, then winced.

Per crumpled the hat in his hand and wondered if he could stand. He had a mind to find a trumpet and talk to Interrogatory once more.

Babbage twenty two zero, that was the address.

He'd be sure to remember it.

THE DREAM OF REASON

Jeffrey Ford

The enigmatic, serpentine, and dream-like stories of Jeffrey Ford are one of the great pleasures of the SF connoisseur. They appear in three fine collections, The Fantasy Writer's Assistant, The Empire of Ice Cream, *and* The Drowned Life. *And here. "The Dream of Reason" is a sublimely strange projection of the steampunk imagination well beyond the world we know...*

THE RENOWNED LUMINIST, Amanitas Perul, who lived a secretive life in his private observatory, Dark See, atop a hill outside the university town of Veldanch, was said by some to be so dedicated an observer of the natural world as to achieve a kind of scientific sainthood, but by others was reviled as the vainest of men, who spent hours before the mirror contemplating his own chalk-powdered visage and wore his thigh-length hair in a vertical architecture of complex knots and ringlets like an ingenious city of a thought. The enigmatic Perul had two theories—one, that distant stars were made of diamond and, two, that matter was merely light slowed down. One night when he was in his observatory, preparing to climb a ladder to the eyepiece of the world's largest telescope, his two theories happened to collide in his mind, and from the resultant slow explosion, like a flower opening, the notion of an amazing experiment revealed itself to him. He went immediately to his desk and wrote out the equations for the highly influential research that would eventually become known as *The Dream of Reason*.

Perul had already done experiments on the deceleration of light and found that heavy gasses, like Carkonium and Tersus Margolium kept at low temperatures actually impeded a sun beam's progress to the point where his precision gear work sensors were able to record its speed. The leap of imagination that led to the famous experiment was his consideration that if he used starlight instead of sunlight, the beam in question would have had to lose more of its speed having traveled eons further through the frigid gas of space. Perul believed that the stars were diamonds and reflected back the light of our sun, so that the journey out to the star, the speed-diminishing act of rebound, and then the lengthy trip back would greatly impede light's velocity. He dared to wonder, if he managed to slow a beam of starlight sufficiently to where it fell into matter, would it produce diamond dust since the last thing it had touched was a star?

Once Perul's concept became known, the university of Veldanch was eager to fund his efforts. At the late age of forty, he dove headlong into the problem of overcoming the speed of light. For four years, Perul ran experiment after experiment with different gasses, using ice by the cart load to try to lower their temperatures, and little by little the beams of light slowed like a clock work running down. In the late summer of the fourth year of *The Dream of Reason*, he reduced the speed of a beam of starlight so much, that its course could be charted with the naked eye. And then in autumn, he had a breakthrough with a rare gas siphoned from the dung of cattle and named by those farmers who gathered it, Lud Fog. He reported that he'd slowed light to the walking speed of a very old woman.

At this point Perul acknowledged that the gasses had done their job, but for the last step in the experiment, he'd have to devise some manner in which he could slow light into matter. He conceived of a great stadium with glass tubes, holding, within, specially curved mirrors so that the beam could circle the thousands of concentric rings. As the freshly slowed light, having traveled the great distance of space, and passed through the chilled Lud Fog, made continuous loops around the glass tube tracks, eventually, over time, it might meet its end and fall out of thin air as diamond dust. The one problem with this solution, as Perul saw it, was that the stadium that held the glass tubes would necessarily have to cover an area the size of the continent of Ishvu.

Perul's research came to a halt, his thinking stymied by an inability to conceive of a practical physical manifestation for a *light trap* (as he referred to the theoretical device in his notes) that would be compact enough to actually construct and also be large enough to hold the voluminous concentric rings of a track he had already proven mathematically would be necessary to effectively allow a star beam's life to run down into matter. The problem was a paradox, and in his imagination it took the form of the Senplesian mythological figure of the two-headed monster, the Frakkas. In the ancient story, when the hero Marianna wields her sword and cuts off one head of the accursed beast, she then must deal with the other, but while in the act of severing the second head, the first grows back. One who does not know the myth might think an easy solution would be to sever them both with one blow, but the Frakkas has a serpent's body, long and wriggling, with a head at either end, making a single stroke solution impossible. It must not have been much solace to Perul that in the myth, the beautiful warrior goddess Marianna is always battling the Frakkas, cutting off one head and then the other to protect mankind from the creature's potential chaos.

It was reported, years later, by Perul's servant, the reliable Elihu Arbiton, that the scientist fell into a deep depression over the problem. He spent many more hours than usual staring into the mirror. At times he'd pound his temples with closed fists as if hoping to dislodge a frozen thought. Perul could be found roaming the halls of the observatory at night with a lit candle, going from room to room. When Arbiton inquired what his master was searching for, Perul, obviously sleep walking with eyes closed, would murmur that he'd heard a ghost calling to him in whispers the secret solution to the light trap. "I can only hear part of what she's saying," said Perul. "She's here and I must find her." When Arbiton noticed that Perul had shaved off his eyebrows and on his powdered visage wore a black penciled version instead over only his left eye, an arch more like an arrowhead pointing up, he realized that his master was on the verge of a nervous breakdown. A group of influential scientists from the university got together and convinced the great luminist that a vacation was needed.

For the first time, Amanitas Perul was seen in different spots around the continent. Descriptions of his unmistakable appearance mark these reports as more than likely reliable. A café operator in the town of Libledoth on the southern coast of Ufdicht told a historian, "Yes, the man with the ridiculous hairdo, like a doll's house on his head, came every day in the late afternoon, to sit on the sidewalk, stare at the setting sun, and drink bottle after bottle of Rose Ear Sweet. When the sky would darken and the stars would appear, he'd leave immediately, but if it was overcast he'd stay till we were forced to kick him out. I asked him once why when the stars began to shine, he'd scurry away. He grabbed me by the shirt collar, pulled my face close to his and said, 'Because they mock me.'" Perul was spotted at the great dam at Indel Laven, tearing up pages of paper filled with numbers and tossing the scraps into the frothy roar of run-off thundering beneath him. From many corners came news that he'd fallen, as he'd hoped light would into matter, into the use of winterspice and had a special pipe he smoked it from—a single mouthpiece but with two bowls on wriggling stems jutting away from each other at an angle, both carved in the likeness of a Frakkas head.

More than a year after he'd left his observatory to travel the continent, he wound up one morning in Cravey By the Sea stumbling along the shore of the Inland Ocean high on winterspice and watching the comforting show of turquoise waves rolling and breaking against the pink sand. The day was fair, and beautifully blue. The sun was bright. Exhausted, he sat down on the sand. At this point, as he wrote later in his autobiography, he'd not thought of the problem of the light trap in months. All of his concerns about the experiment had lain down and dozed off for the longest time. A sense of calm came over him, and he considered all he'd been through, all the stupidity of his travels and the extent to which his own mind had tortured him over his inability to find the answers he'd been looking for. He reviewed his thoughts—the complexly conspiratorial nature of his fears, the impossibly infinite tangle of scheming and knotted self-admonishment. It struck him, like lightning out of the blue, that the only possible light trap both compact enough and vast enough to manage the last step in the deceleration of a star beam was, of course, the human mind.

"Think of the world, a globe spinning in space, and then think of the sun and the dark distances to the stars. Think of it all at once, all of it, and you can without any trouble," wrote the luminist upon his return home to Dark See. Elihu Arbiton was given a sheaf of pages that held a special diet to have the kitchen help prepare and also orders to awaken his master every day at precisely sunrise. Perul gave himself two weeks of true rest in order to regain his strength for the last part of the experiment. Every morning he strolled the grounds at daybreak, swam laps in the pool, breakfasted on peeled sections of Chali fruit and a bowl of unflayed dost bran, meditated in the study with the windows covered and but one lit candle to focus his mind upon. In the afternoons, he did light calculations and read the philosophy of Herden Bylat—*The Crucial Degree of Probable Hope.* At night, he eschewed the mirror, and went to sleep to ethereal hymns played by a cellist sitting just down the hall from his room.

On the day Perul was to begin again on his signature work, he summoned Elihu Arbiton to him and ordered him to go down to the city of Veldanch and find someone who would be willing to act as a subject in the experiment. "Let them name their price," Perul said, "for there is danger in this, and they must understand that an autopsy will be undertaken upon their remains when they eventually pass away." He handed over to Arbiton a set of contracts for the chosen individual to sign. The servant nodded and left with the contracts rolled up beneath his arm. He traveled on horse with another horse in tow and was in the town before the work day had begun. Although the money was a great temptation to those he approached, Arbiton had difficulty performing his assignment. As he discovered, the bishop of Veldanch had taken umbrage at the fact that Perul had named his observatory Dark See, a luminist's joke, pointing to the fact that the master of the estate spent all his nightly hours, staring into the pitch of space to study light. When Bishop Gazbrak had reprimanded Perul about the estate's name, reminding him that a see can only be the domain of a Bishop, the scientist had reportedly laughed in his face. Afterward, Gazbrak warned his congregations to steer clear of Perul or risk losing their souls.

With the day sliding into late afternoon and still no one contracted to act as subject in his master's experiment, Arbiton headed into the last quadrant of town that he had not yet covered. There, amidst the crumbling buildings and unpaved streets, he came upon the Debtors' Prison, an institution he'd all but forgotten existed. He breathed a sigh of relief at the sight of the wretched place. And so it was that from the bowels of that dark hell hole, Perul's servant brought forth a young woman, Enche Jenawa—a still healthy specimen, who had not yet lost to poverty her looks or the glint of intelligence in her eyes. The warden suggested her, thinking kindly of the girl and believing it a crime perpetrated by the kingdom that Enche should serve a sentence for her dead father's financial excesses. When Arbiton put the deal before her, all the young woman asked was if she'd again be able to see the sunlight, and when Arbiton nodded, she signed. He then paid off the girl's debt and gave the warden a little something for his troubles. As he led the girl out of the prison of shadows, into the late afternoon sun, she covered her eyes against the brightness.

It was well after dark by the time Arbiton and Enche reached Dark See. Perul was waiting in the observatory for their arrival, curious to see who his future subject might be. So much hinged on this aspect of the experiment that his nerves had gotten the better of him and he'd retrieved his old winterspice pipe and calmed himself with a double dose of the drug. Now many histories of these events tell a Romantic tale and would have it that Perul was smitten with Enche Jenawa from the moment he laid eyes upon her and vice versa, but reality as reported by Arbiton and recorded by Perul himself will just not bear the weight of this fiction. Enche was brought before her new employer. She curtsied as was the practice, and Perul nodded and, leaning close to her said only one word, "Circles." Then he asked Arbiton to take the girl to the kitchen, feed her and then show her to her room.

When Arbiton pushed back the door of her room in order for her to enter, Enche smiled, for the room was beautifully appointed and done up in a most remarkable manner. The walls were papered with a pattern of small red circles on a yellow background, and the window over the circular bed was round as a ship's porthole. The light fixtures were globes, the rugs were round, and even the pillows, the tables, the chairs were round. "This is lovely," she said, unable to believe that no more than hours earlier she was lying in the dark, in a stall covered with straw, a chain around her left ankle, starving. She'd only been at the prison for a week, but it had been an absolute certainty to her that she would be raped before long by the giant prison guard with one eye who served rotten gruel twice a day. Having left that behind, she was now only taxed by Arbiton's suggestion, "Amanitas Perul requests that you think of circles as often as possible." She laughed outright and nodded. "I'll think of circles all night. In fact I'll dream of circles if need be," she said. "Very good," said Arbiton, and left her to herself.

The next morning after breakfast, Enche's tutor arrived. She was introduced to him, a tall, thin gentleman with a long smooth face and eyeglasses, dressed in lavender jacket and trousers. She could neither tell if he was old or young, but the gleam from his completely bald head slightly disturbed her still-sensitive vision. "Mr. Garreau," he said to her and smiled, and she answered with her name. Arbiton showed them to another room done up all in circles. There was a chair for her to sit at, facing a desk behind which he sat, a chalk board behind him. And her lessons began with him leading her in an hour-long chanting of the word "circle." This was followed by a fifteen minute break, and then another hour of the same word, accompanied by circling of the head and rolling of the eyes. Before lunch there were two more hours in which she was instructed to trace circles in the air with her index finger. Mr. Garreau encouraged her and also scolded when her circles wavered into ovals or worse. After the midday meal, and a brief respite out upon the grounds of the estate where Enche and Mr. Garreau walked in large circles, they returned to their work room where she drew circles on the chalk board and was then lectured by her tutor about the philosophy of circles. "Truth lies at the end of a circle," he told her. She nodded and he was obviously pleased.

Every night, just before she turned in, Enche was ushered to Perul's study where he loaded the two-headed pipe with winterspice and encouraged her to smoke with him. During these sessions, he did not converse with her, but occasionally merely intoned the word "Circles," and she repeated. With the drug in her system, when she finally laid down to sleep at night, she did dream of circles, wild imaginings of mouths pronouncing the letter "o," and eye balls loose and rolling, and hoops of fire and ice, and frantic races run in a ring between herself and a doughnut with legs. Arbiton reports that the young woman rather enjoyed her lessons, and told him on one occasion that thinking of all of those circles was a pleasant thing, so much more comforting than her thoughts in her previous life which were all frayed ends and ragged paths that went nowhere.

One day, after lunch, she was not instructed to go back to the work room with Garreau, but was led by Perul, himself, to a closet in his own private bed chamber where hung two racks of women's clothes—dresses both formal and casual. She was allowed to choose whatever fashions she wanted and told that from that point onward they belonged to her. At night, as always, the smoke and Perul's simple, monotonous suggestion of, "Circles."

While Enche's mind was being transformed into the great stadium of circular paths for the light to travel, Perul was hard at work in the observatory, fitting rods of glass tubing, painted black on the outside, together to lead from the telescope's eyepiece to the gas chambers where chilled Lud Fog would wait. From the chambers, it would then travel to a small room where, through a single tube the ray of star light would proceed to its intended trap. The luminist had spent many hours scanning the night sky for just the right star whose refracted light he'd use in the experiment. Eventually the perfect choice came to him not through direct observation but from one of his star charts. By accident one night, while looking for information on another heavenly body, he saw an entry for Mariannus, a specimen of particular brightness available for viewing from late summer through all of autumn. There was a mythological story attached to it. Apparently, it shone in the sky as a signal to humanity that the warrior goddess Marianna was still bravely battling the Frakkas. "Of course," Perul wrote after noting his discovery and final choice.

Two months of adjusting the artifacts for the experiment and lessons on the circle passed, but little is known of the daily particulars of Dark See during this preparatory span. One of the only pieces of evidence that remains is a single scrap of a page of a letter written by Enche to her sister. This was only discovered last year in one of Elihu Arbiton's old books now in the Veldanch archives. Some think it a forgery, but the content makes me trust in its veracity. I reproduce it for you here: ... *circles and circles and circles, my head is spinning, my heart is spinning. I dream tornadoes and speak loops. Thoughts race around inside my head like Hoffmann hounds at the old race track at Temkin. I'm in love with Mr. Garreau, my tutor. He's a shiny headed, hapless sot, but that is precisely what attracts me to him. Every day he brings me gifts, large, small, circles. Before long, I hope to give him my circle. The servant seems jealous, the master, unconscious...*

On the night of the first freeze, Perul went to Enche's room and shared with her two bowls of winterspice as he had every night of her stay. That night, though, instead of simply exhaling a cloud as she'd been wont to do, she blew smoke rings. This was the sign the luminist had been waiting for. He recorded the event in a joyous entry, and at the end of it, he wrote, "We shall begin." The next day, Arbiton was ordered to go to Veldanch and purchase ten wagon loads of ice to be delivered the following evening. Enche was relieved of her lessons for the day, and she chose to take a picnic lunch into the woods accompanied by Mr. Garreau. Perul was busy from dawn to dusk, rechecking his calculations and going over every connection of the glass tubing. He consulted the almanac to make sure the skies the following night would be clear, and found they would be. It is said by some that that evening, after Enche did not arrive on time for dinner, Perul went out to look for her, and found she and Mr. Garreau together, locked in an embrace and kissing. When they noticed that Perul was watching, they stepped quickly apart. "We're practicing circling the tongues," Garreau called to his employer. Supposedly, Perul called back, "Circles," and returned to the observatory.

The experiment was begun. In a small room just off the observatory, Enche lay on her stomach, on a tall flat bed, her neck tilted so that her chin rested on the surface of the platform. She directly faced the end of a short, clear tube, its opening positioned directly at her left eye. Circling her head was a strap that held a device whose two thin claw ends were inserted beneath her eyelid. This "eye stay," as it was called, once a tool of the torturer who wanted to deny a victim's need for sleep, disabled the blinking response of the eye. Arbiton stood on one side of Enche and Perul on the other. "Good luck, sir," said the servant, and his employer answered, "If we're lucky, luck will have nothing to do with it." Checking his pocket watch again and noting that the moment had come when the star had risen to its calculated position, he pulled a cord that was attached through a hole in the wall to the shutter on the eye piece of the great telescope.

Arbiton put the intervening time between the pull of the cord and the appearance of the ray of light at five minutes. Perul stated, four and three-quarter minutes, precisely as he'd predicted. It came, like a bright thread, slowly inching its way through the center of the clear tube aimed at Enche's eye. It literally punctured the lens, like a needle going through flesh—a pliant shudder at the iris and then a hair-thin trickle of blood. The instant it entered, the girl screamed as if she were on fire. Her body quickly began shuddering and Arbiton reached for her. Perul interceded, saying, "Two more seconds," and Arbiton later attested they were the longest two seconds of his life. Finally, when the necessary time had passed, Perul himself swept her off the table and carried her to her room. She was unconscious and already burning with a fever. All the rest of that night the luminist and his servant sat by her bedside, brought cool compresses for her head, and forced sips of water into her. Arbiton states that at one point he'd thought she was going to die and was severely shaken, and it was precisely at that point that Perul said to him, "There is star light in her head."

Enche awoke before dawn and complained of sparks behind her eyes and a terrible headache, and then fell back into a fitful sleep. When she awoke again the following afternoon, she didn't exhibit any signs of pain, but she wore an odd, dull affect. "Circles," Perul repeated to her for an hour, but Arbiton, having seen enough, overstepped his boundaries and demanded his employer leave her alone. And this is precisely where Arbiton left the history of the experiment. Perul fired him on the spot. With no emotion and few words, "You are dismissed." Arbiton states that he "stood stunned for a moment," but when Perul again started intoning the word "Circle," he knew his time at Dark See was over. He left the room, packed his things, and at twilight descended the hill carrying his bag.

From this point forward, we must rely on Perul's notes for what is known to be true. He records that Enche never achieved a consciousness more than a general stupor. She could be led around, and fed, and would speak occasionally, but it was never as if she had fully wakened from sleep. "I'm racing," she'd suddenly yell. "My soul is dizzy," she'd whimper. When he'd put his hands to her head, he stated that he could feel it hum with the energy of the stars. On the second night after the experiment, when Enche had been put to bed, he wrote, "Her condition could continue in this manner for a life time, and one thing I foolishly overlooked is how much younger she is than myself. I could very well pass on before seeing the results of this experiment. Steps must be taken, and I see a way to gain fast results and perhaps help the poor girl's condition in the process." Following these words was a detailed plan for a person sized canister in which Enche could fit, submerged in Lud Fog.

At this point all manner of speculation might enter the story of *The Dream of Reason*, but there is little reliable information. After the plans for the larger Lud Fog chamber, there comes only one more word from Perul—"Monstrous"—scrawled across an otherwise blank page of his journal. The next authenticated piece of evidence of what transpired comes from Issac Hadista, a hunter, who when interviewed years after the experiment had become famous, told that he'd been hired by Perul to hunt a strange and dangerous figure that haunted the woods behind the observatory. "The man's hair had fallen," said Hadista, "like a ship going under. And he told me the thing I hunted looked like a young woman but was really a demon loosed on the world because of a failed experiment he'd conducted. He begged me not to shoot her in the head, saying it would release her ancient spirit into the atmosphere and would infect me and overtake my soul. 'Through the heart,' he told me. 'It's the only way.'"

Hadista set off through falling snow, in amidst the barren white trees of the wood. With the snow on the ground it was easy to track her. She lurched out of the shadows at twilight, bouncing from tree trunk to tree trunk, moaning loudly. According to Hadista, her flesh was a pale green (some attribute this to her having spent considerable time in the Lud Fog). She sensed the hunter's presence and came down a snow-covered trail toward him, one hand out in front, calling, "Help me." "I was not fooled by the demon's scheming," Hadista stated. "I lifted my rifle and shot her through the heart, and then a second time before she fell dead." On his way back to the observatory, carrying her body as he'd been instructed, he recounted, "It was pitch-black, and all I had to light my way were the stars."

When Perul performed the autopsy upon the brain of Enche Jenawa, what he found astounded him. The diamond dust he'd expected was absent, but what was there changed, in a moment, his entire conception of the nature of stars and the formation of the universe. What he found there, at the core of the young girl's gray matter was, instead, *nothing*. "Nothing," Perul wrote in his results. "I should have known, but there it is." And from the experiment later named *The Dream of Reason*, humanity came to learn that the stars were made of nothing—hard, shiny, chips of nothing. Cosmologists understood now that at the dawn of everything there was nothing, and when the universe burst to life, the nothing was shattered and thrown out into the darkness of space to make way for the Sun and the Earth. Science had prevailed, and Perul was lauded with honorariums and testimonials at the University of Veldanch.

After this experiment to end all experiments, Perul retired from research and returned to the town of Libledoth where every night he frequented the café and drank to excess bottles of Rose Ear Sweet. His use of the winterspice increased as well, and in only a few years his appearance grew haggard, his hair now a frazzled storm cloud over his shoulders. He turned to mysticism in his latter years and claimed that he could contact the spirit world. In messages from the other side that he would record during long bouts of automatic writing, the spirits told him that the stars were giant balls of flaming gas, like the sun. These and other delusions began to crowd out his reason. He ended his days in Debtors' Prison, completely insane, mumbling to himself and endlessly turning tight pirouettes.

ABOUT THE EDITOR

Nick Gevers is a South African science fiction editor and critic, whose work has appeared in *The Washington Post Book World*, *Interzone*, Scifi.com, SF Site, *The New York Review of Science Fiction* and *Nova Express*. He writes two monthly review columns for *Locus* magazine, and is editor at the British independent press, PS Publishing; he also edits the quarterly genre fiction magazine, *Postscripts*.

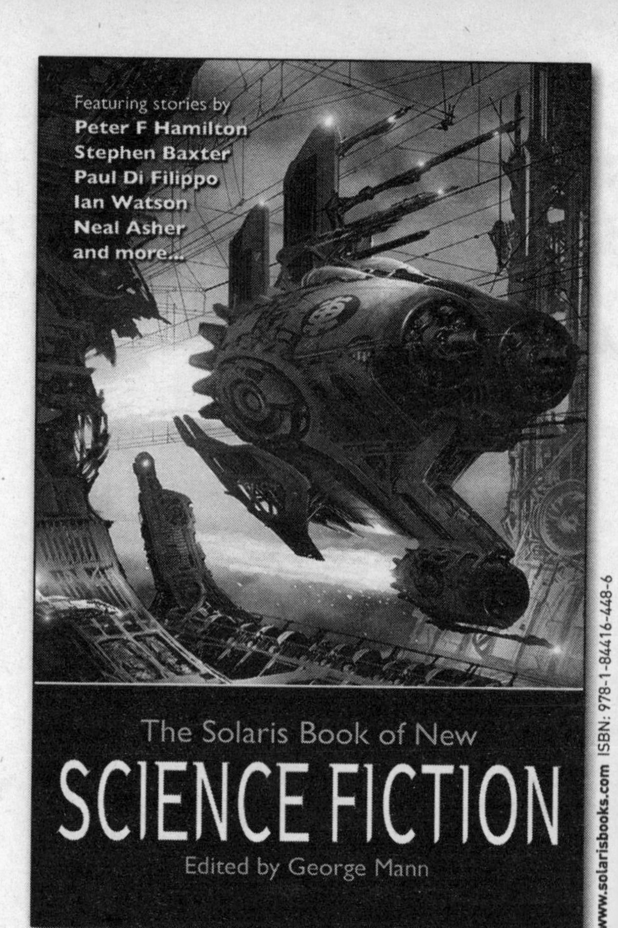
Featuring stories by
Peter F Hamilton
Stephen Baxter
Paul Di Filippo
Ian Watson
Neal Asher
and more...
The Solaris Book of New
SCIENCE FICTION
Edited by George Mann
www.solarisbooks.com ISBN: 978-1-84416-448-6

INFINITY PLUS
THE ANTHOLOGY
INCLUDES STORIES BY
Kim Stanley Robinson
Michael Moorcock
Ian McDonald
Stephen Baxter
Charles Stross
and more...
EDITED BY KEITH BROOKE AND NICK GEVERS
www.solarisbooks.com ISBN: 978-1-84416-489-9

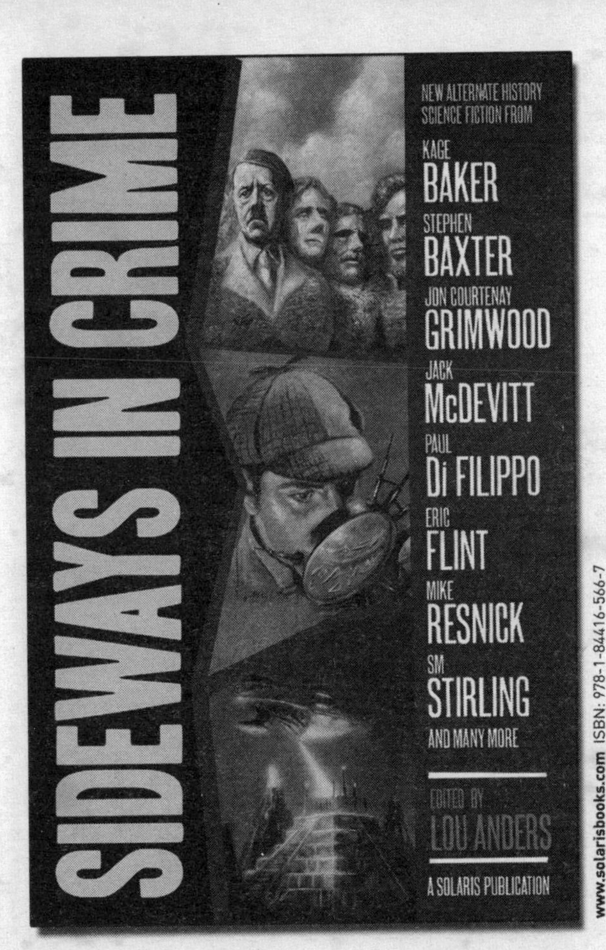

\lternate History Mystery! *A* brand new anthology of all-original stories rom some of the genre's foremost writers. Featuring an eclectic range of lternative history crime stories, from Jacobean power-plays to far future mpires, this new anthology explores the darker side of the genre.

SOLARIS SCIENCE FICTION

KÉTHANI
ERIC BROWN
"Vivid, emotional, philosophical, this is a work to feed the mind, heart and soul." – Stephen Baxter

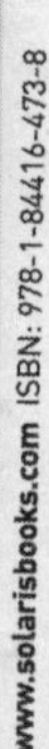
www.solarisbooks.com ISBN: 978-1-84416-473-8